If Only You Knew

Claire Allan

POOLBEG

Published 2011
by Poolbeg Press Ltd
123 Grange Hill, Baldoyle
Dublin 13, Ireland
E-mail: poolbeg@poolbeg.com
www.poolbeg.com

1

A catalogue record for this book is available from the British Library.

ISBN 978-1-84223-448-8

Typeset by Patricia Hope in Sabon 11/14.5
Printed and bound by CPI Group (UK) Ltd, Croydon, CR0 4YY

www.poolbeg.com

About the author

Claire Allan lives in Derry with her husband Neil and her children Joseph and Cara. By day she maintains her mild-mannered reporter persona at the offices of the *Derry Journal* and by night she loves writing, reading, trying to bake the perfect cupcakes and singing her heart out with Encore Contemporary Choir. She recently had a premature mid-life crisis and bought a pair of skinny jeans and got a tattoo. It's very subtle, though. Honest.

If Only You Knew is Claire's fifth novel. You can find out more about Claire at **www.claireallan.com** or you can follow her on Facebook and Twitter.

Also by Claire Allan

Rainy Days and Tuesdays
Feels Like Maybe
Jumping in Puddles
It's Got to be Perfect

Acknowledgements

This is always the tricky part, because I'm always afraid I'll forget someone or offend someone or make an eejit of myself but nonetheless there are people out there who have helped me make this book what it is and they need thanking.

First of all, my family – my husband and most especially my children who didn't mind (too much) when they gave me up for a few months of intense rewrites. I love you so very much, and I promise to make it up to you all. Thanks for being loving, entertaining, supportive and inspiring.

My parents and my siblings – thank you for cheering me on – especially Mammy and Daddy who picked me up on more than one occasion and helped me stay focused.

To those friends who read, supported, laughed, raged and cried – or just said "You can do it" – thank you. As always love to Vicki, Fionnuala, my Auntie Raine, Erin and Catherine who held my hand, dried my tears and made me laugh. For those of you who poured me drinks, a special thanks.

Thanks to my colleagues at the *Derry Journal* and Johnston Press NI.

As always my fellow writers have helped me more than they probably know. To those special people who offered their support and advice without hesitation – thank you. To my fellow Northern Girls – thank you. Especially thanks to Fionnuala (aka Fiona Cassidy) who was always on the end of the phone and, despite being exceptionally busy in her own life, took the time to gee me on. She deserves a medal. Also very special thanks to Shirley Benton who just cheered me on – which meant a lot.

Thanks go to all my Facebook and Twitter friends – and all the fans who have got in touch and shared this journey with me. Thanks to Francesca Norris for helping me find the perfect name for the book – it really suits it so well.

This year I've also had the added support and friendship of my fellow singers from Encóre Contemporary Choir. Yes, I know . . . me, who can't sing . . . in a choir! The laugh of it! But, as it turns out, all I needed was someone to help me find my voice and my new friends have helped me find that, on and off the stage. To my wee Sop 2 crew and to all the men and women who make it brilliant – not to mention our committee (Marie-Louise, Bernie, Lisa and Emmet) – thank you all. "Lean On Me" will happen sometime . . .

At this stage I usually thank my agent – but a simple thank-you this time is not enough. Ger, thank you sincerely from the bottom of my heart. You know we have been on quite a journey with this one – and you have been my cheerleader and my friend and you always had faith in me and my writing. Let's indeed get this show on the road. Thank you, thank you, thank you.

And to all at Poolbeg – thank you again for guiding me on this journey. Special thanks go to Paula Campbell whose never-ending faith, guidance and support have made this book what it is. Yes, we will laugh about it one day. As always thanks also to Gaye Shortland – who has the keenest eye and the sharpest wit in the business.

Finally thanks to all booksellers, book buyers, book borrowers, librarians (especially all at Libraries NI) for your support, friendship and feedback. None of it is taken for granted.

For Neil, Joseph and Cara
Love you so pretty
xxx

Chapter 1

Ava

Standing in the middle of the fresh-produce aisle in Tesco, Ava took a deep breath and hoped that God would grant her the strength to get all the way around to the tinned-goods aisle – and eventually through the check-out and on her way home – without losing her mind entirely.

Maisie had insisted she was much too big a girl for the trolley and was currently running rings round the carrots, flapping her wings behind her and declaring that she was a butterfly. A few people had smiled indulgently at the child as she twirled while a perfectly preened thirty-something had tutted loudly and muttered that children should be left at home if they couldn't behave well in public.

Ava wanted to bite back with something witty and cutting but she was too busy trying to remember whether or not they needed onions, what it was Connor had asked her to pick up for him and whether or not she had locked up her classroom before leaving work for the day.

Instead, even though she knew it was childish, she pulled a face at Ms Perfect and took Maisie by the arm and tried to persuade her to help by selecting a few apples for their trolley. It was all going so well until Maisie belted off at lightning speed, reaching out one

1

chubby little hand to the most precarious apple on the bottom of the pile and set off an avalanche of Pink Ladies which gave Ms Perfect the chance to do the very loudest tut in her repertoire before stepping over the apples and heading on her way. Ava felt like crying as she wrestled an indignant Maisie back into the trolley and set about picking the apples up and stocking them back in the display before anyone suggested she pay for the lot of them.

She would need a drink when she got home. A big, cold, alcoholic drink. In a big glass. Maybe one of those feckers which held an entire bottle.

Putting the last apple in place, she took a deep breath just as she heard Maisie squeal a momentous "*Mammmeeeeee!*" before toppling head first out of the trolley and landing with a scream on the floor.

A&E hadn't been very busy, thankfully, and they had been whisked through triage and onto X-ray relatively quickly. Ava had been tempted to ask the doctors if there was any chance of some mildly mind-altering painkillers to help her escape from the headache which was building in her head and the coronary she had no doubt was building somewhere around her heart.

She had phoned Connor, while Maisie screamed blue murder in the background, and had tried to assure him it was okay and it was only a mild trolley-jumping accident and she was pretty sure no bones were broken in the process. She didn't tell him that Maisie had saved herself from splitting her head open by breaking the fall with her hand. He had sighed deeply, and said he would meet her at the hospital. The staff at Tesco had been more than lovely, bringing an icepack and telling her not to worry about abandoning her half-filled trolley but she had been mortified anyway. And worried, of course. Maisie's wrist was starting to swell and bruise and she couldn't be consoled. The dream of a glass of wine slipped further and further away. When the doctor returned to their cubicle and said the injury was no more than a bad sprain, which would require strapping and some pain relief, Ava felt herself finally sag with relief and tears sprang to her eyes.

Maisie looked up, now doped up on Calpol with her eyes

drooping, and Ava felt like the worst mother in the world for feeling frustrated and angry at how the whole situation had developed. Maisie had just been overexcited after a day at nursery. She had been excited to see her mammy and had gone into hyper mode. She hadn't been naughty – she was just being a typical almost-three-year-old, but Ava hadn't been in the form for it – not after a long week at work. Maybe if she had paid more attention this wouldn't have happened. She would have to try harder. Guiltily, she tearfully kissed her daughter on the head and assured her she loved her all the way to the moon and back.

Eventually Connor popped his head around the curtain, looking equally as frazzled, tired and fecked-off as she felt.

"I drove as fast as I could," he said, "but you know what it's like trying to get out of Belfast at this time of the evening. Is she okay?"

"A bad sprain," Ava said looking down at a now sleeping Maisie. "She'll be fine. They've given her painkillers and are going to strap her wrist up."

"Thank God," he said, sitting down on the plastic chair beside his wife and sagging with relief.

Both of them eyed a trolley-bed opposite them and Ava wondered what it would be like to just climb under the harsh, starchy sheets and fall asleep. She could tell by the look in Connor's eyes that he felt exactly the same.

"I'd fight you to the death for it," she said, smiling at him and at the bed. And she was only half joking.

A few hours had passed and Maisie was sleeping in her mammy and daddy's bed, her poor bandaged arm cradling her favourite stuffed bunny rabbit. She had thrown a minor fit at the very notion of sleeping in her own big-girl bed and, too tired to argue with her after all that the day had thrown at them, Ava and Connor had agreed and had tucked her in before returning to the living room to sit, nursing cups of tea and staring into space.

"It could have been worse," Connor said. "At least it wasn't serious."

Ava nodded. "I know." She sat back, closed her eyes and was just about to drift off into a blissful exhaustion-induced coma when it struck her that she still didn't have her shopping done and she would need to face the supermarket again. "Fuck!" she swore. "Fuck. Fuck. Fuck."

Saturday mornings were reserved for that special kind of hell that was a Soft Play centre. Even with a bandaged and swollen arm, Maisie could not be dissuaded from her weekly trip to the ball pools and slides of Cheeky Monkeys. Ava couldn't argue – not after the act of wilful neglect which had seen her daughter tumble headfirst out of a trolley the day before. So she had packed a bag, filled with cartons of juice, boxes of raisins, a couple of favourite dollies and a change of clothes and had strapped her strong-willed daughter into the back of the car. Connor had padded out to see them, still exhausted from his week of commuting to and from Belfast for work. "I'll take her if you want," he offered and Ava had wanted more than anything to let him but instead she settled for hugging him and thanking him for the offer – even though she knew he had made it knowing full well she would never take him up on it.

Saturday mornings were when she met her mummy friends who would arrive with their charges and regale her with stories about their wonderfulness. It wasn't that Ava didn't find Maisie wonderful – she was constantly amazed by her daughter's flighty wee personality as it developed – but she wasn't one of those who felt the need to boast about her either.

Saturdays were the days she also met Karen – known as 'Hell-mum' to Ava and Connor in their private conversations. Karen had taken to motherhood like a layabout takes to work. She did it because she had to but she took no joy in it. She also very much enjoyed sharing her horror stories, time and time again, with anyone who wanted to (or in many cases didn't want to) listen. Ava felt sorry for her to an extent – she clearly had issues by the bucket-load. Ava looked at Karen's five-year-old sometimes and felt her heart sink to her boots. She wondered if, in quieter moments, Karen was actually more maternal than she appeared in public.

Sighing, Ava pulled into the car park of the centre and tried to contain Maisie from running in front of the wheels of the 4x4s hunting for a prime parent-and-child parking space. She saw Karen's Land Rover among them and she braced herself for the latest chapter in 'How Hard My Life Is Compared to Yours' from her once dear friend.

"C'mon, Maisie Moo!" she called, injecting a fake sense of cheer into her voice. "It's time to play and meet all your friends!"

Karen sat sipping from a latte while Ava cradled Maisie – suddenly overcome with nervousness thanks to her sore arm.

"Oh God, you poor thing. Still it could have been worse. I remember when Sophie was the same age – took a tumble in the park and needed three stitches. Still, I only thought things were tough then. God, Ava, you've no idea. Now that's she five – and at school and learning the badness from the other ones – it's even tougher. You can't watch her these days. Into everything."

Ava nodded sympathetically, all the while thinking that Karen hadn't given a single glance to where her daughter was since she'd sauntered into the café attached to the play centre half an hour before.

"I'm sure her being five has its good points," she offered, hoping that her friend would assure her that of course she was just having a bad day and living with a five-year-old was a joy day in and day out.

"Hmmm," Karen said with a sly smile, "I'm sure it has – I just can't think of any of them at the moment. It's all just work, work, work with some worry thrown in for good measure." She laughed as she said it and Ava had to fight the urge to pick up the cream bun she was just about to tuck into and ram it right into Karen's face to stop her from talking any more. She didn't want to hear that it got worse. She wanted to hear that it got better – and easier and altogether more pleasant. She wanted her friend to tell her that she was only a couple of months away from an altogether easier existence when she would not feel so tired, and worried and overworked 99% of the time.

Deciding that ramming a cream bun in the face of one of her oldest friends was probably not the best way to relieve the knot of tension which seemed to exist on a permanent basis between her shoulder blades, she smiled sweetly and took a large bite from it instead, allowing the sugary softness of the confectionery to give her a momentary saccharine-induced high. If they had served ice-cold Pinot Grigio in the Soft Play, she would have knocked a couple of those back too.

Karen was just about to launch into her latest rant on the perils of motherhood (this time – Play-Doh and why it was the work of the Devil) when Ava's phone burst into life. Gratefully, she pawed in her bag to find it. She didn't care who was phoning. It could have been a heavily accented salesperson trying to persuade her to part with her life savings for a timeshare but she would have spoken to him.

Glancing down she saw that it was her mother. This was definitely strange. Sure, she was due to see her mother later that day anyway. Saturday afternoons were always spent at Granny's house, where Maisie had the run of the place and her very own playroom to wreak havoc in.

"Mum?" Ava answered as Maisie glanced up at her.

"Ava, thank goodness I got you," her mother said, her voice choking with emotion.

"Is everything okay, Mum? Mum, what's wrong?"

Suddenly, even though she knew this made her a very bad person indeed, the thought crossed her mind that if something was wrong she would have the perfect excuse to get up and leave the play centre without any hesitation whatsoever. She glanced at Karen who was staring into the bottom of her coffee cup, disgusted to be cut off from her rant before she got into full flow, and she felt guilty. She was a bad friend and a bad daughter.

"It's Betty," her mum said, her voice cracking.

The memory came to Ava of a well-spoken woman in delicious

purple satin shoes with a delicate floral detail who had held her
hand as she sobbed through her beloved granny's funeral. They had
gone to sink the better part of two bottles of wine at a restaurant
afterwards – talking into the wee small hours. Ava had been very
taken with this bohemian creature with wild curly hair and a gentle
smile, who looked years younger than her age.

"I love your shoes," Ava had told her, admiring the large
sequinned flower, and the flared heels. Betty was a woman who
knew good shoes. Ava had eyed her own sensible flats, which she'd
bought off a hanging stand in Primark, with a sense of disgust.

"They're vintage," Betty had said, "I picked them up for ten
euro in a market in Paris."

"They're amazing," Ava had slurred.

"Tell you what, I'll leave them to you in my will. When I pop my
clogs, you can slip them on your feet and keep them warm for me,"
Betty had said and the pair of them laughed uproariously.

"Oh Ava, pet, can you come over?" Ava's mother sobbed,
cutting through her thoughts. "Betty's dead. My baby sister is
dead!"

When she arrived at her mother's house, having deposited Maisie
back with her still-sleepy father, Ava was shocked at just how bereft
Cora was. It wasn't that she thought her mother to be a heartless
cow or devoid of feeling, just that she had never really spoken of
Betty and when she had it had been in hushed tones. Betty was most
definitely the black sheep of the Scott family, having left Derry for
a bohemian lifestyle in the South of France. Ava couldn't say she
had blamed her one bit for leaving Derry behind – Derry wasn't
exactly a fun place to be by all accounts. Ava would have left too –
especially if she had found a very handsome man to marry who
wanted to take her away from it all. South of France versus the
Bogside and tear gas? Who could have blamed her? But it seemed
there were elements in her family who had felt betrayed in some way
by Betty's departure. Sure they were all meant to be in this together,
weren't they? Whatever the reason, Betty was not someone who was

spoken about very often. There weren't even family holidays en masse to Provence even though at family gatherings it was agreed it must be lovely out there.

Looking at her mother now, bent double in grief in her armchair, her sobs racking her body, Ava wondered if maybe she just hadn't wanted to let her sister go, knowing perhaps she would never come home?

"Oh Mum," she said, kneeling down beside Cora and pulling her into a hug. "I'm so sorry!"

"I just thought I would see her again . . . there was so much we needed to say –" Cora broke off, sniffing loudly right in Ava's ear which made her shudder – she never liked getting too close to a clatter of snotters.

Pulling back, she looked at her mother. "I'm sure she knew how you felt about her," she soothed, not quite knowing why she was saying that. She didn't, in honesty, know if Betty knew a damn about her mother and how she felt about her. Ava didn't know how her mother felt about Betty. She just didn't come up in conversation that often.

"How could she not tell us she was sick? She must have known for a long time – it was cancer. Were we so bad she would rather die out there without a being belonging to her close by? And then to be told by letter . . . she had written it in advance to be sent to me . . ." Cora gestured to a letter on the side table and broke into a fresh dose of sobbing. "I would have gone. I would have been there. I know we all have our lives and we're all busy but we would have gone, or we would have brought her home . . ."

Ava hugged her mother again. "She's been in France a long time. Longer than she was ever here. Maybe she just considered that home?"

Cora sniffed. "Home is always home," she said. "She should have let us say goodbye."

"I'm so sorry, Mum," Ava repeated. "I'll make you a cup of tea. You've had a shock. Have you spoken to the rest of the family yet?"

Cora shook her head. "I just called you. I just wanted you."

Ava felt her heart swell at her mother's honest emotion. An only child, her widowed mother leant on her heavily at times. Of course she would have called her in the circumstances.

Ava kissed her and stood up.

"She's left you something," Cora said as Ava turned on her heel to go to the kitchen.

"What?" Ava stopped and turned, sure she must have misheard. How could, why would, Betty leave her anything?

"It says so in the letter. You have to go to a solicitor's in Belfast on Wednesday to hear more." Cora spoke softly, her head downwards.

Ava felt absolutely and totally confused. Sure they had spoken for a long time at her granny's funeral – laughing like old friends – but to leave her something?

"Really?" she asked. "Why would she do that?"

"You must have meant a lot to her," Cora said, looking up, her eyes filling with tears again. "Sure don't you mean a lot to us all?"

Chapter 2

Hope

Dylan McKenzie was six foot four inches tall and was what could only be described as a sexy fecker. Hope could spend hours just staring at him – at his piercing blue eyes, his chiselled jaw, the bulge in his designer jeans and that perfect smile. When he held her – wrapped her in his arms – she felt as though she belonged. She could stay there forever. If only life didn't have to get in the way.

He knew her better than anyone did. He teased her mercilessly about what he described as her internet addiction. "You're a nosy fecker, Ms Scott," he would tease. "The FBI doesn't know what it's missing not hiring you."

She would laugh back and tell him not to knock it. There wasn't much going on with her friends that she wasn't privy to and with him out working most weeknights and her exiled in Belfast – a full hour and half away from her home city – it was the closest to a social life she came to these days. Dylan was always only too happy to listen to her updates from home. If she was awake when he rolled in from his night shift she would make him a cup of tea and a bacon sandwich and tell him all the latest news.

"Who needs *Coronation Street* when I've got you?" he said on this particular morning, supping his tea and kicking off those Size

11 shoes. "But for once, Ms Scott, you are not the only one with some gossip."

She smiled back, topping up his mug of tea, and leaned over. "Do tell," she said, her face as close to his as decency would allow.

"Cyndi has agreed, finally, to let me take her out. Isn't that brilliant?"

Cyndi. With a Y and an I, in that order. Hope had heard a lot about Cyndi with a Y and an I over the last few months. She had listened to Dylan rave about his passion for her, how he wanted her and yearned for her. She knew Cyndi had blonde hair, was "about the same size" as her and had a very contagious laugh. Dylan had tried to replicate it, without success, on many occasions when they had been sharing a cup of tea over breakfast. His attempts had just resulted in sending Hope into fits of almost uncontrollable giggles until she had looked over and caught sight of his puppy-dog eyes looking wounded at her response.

"Cop yourself on!" she would tease. "You'd laugh at me if I did the same."

Hope also knew that Cyndi was twenty-eight and from "up the country" – so she had an accent thicker than cement. Dylan was quite good at impersonating that.

"I never thought I'd find a countrywoman so damn appealing," Dylan had said after one of his impersonations, "but she just gets under my skin."

Yes, Hope thought, like ringworm, or impetigo or cellulitis . . .

She tried her best not to show the absolute gut-wrenching pain she felt right in the pit of her stomach. He really was crazy about Cyndi, in a way that he had never been crazy about anyone else in the course of their friendship, and in that moment Hope felt her dreams of him ever realising that true love can indeed be just under your nose fall away from her.

The bacon sandwich stuck in her throat as she tried to smile. She ended up gagging, choking and wheezing in a most undignified manner while Dylan looked on, at first incredulous and then – once the gravity of the situation kicked in – with a great deal of concern.

It was ironic, she thought as he stepped behind her, took her in his arms and thrust towards her that not only could she feel the bacon dislodge itself from her oesophagus but also the warmth of his crotch. There was, she realised, as she sipped tea and tried to regain her breath, little chance of her ever feeling the warmth of his crotch again. Not now that Cyndi had finally agreed to go out with him.

"Jesus, Hope, talk about giving a man a heart attack. Are you okay?"

"Something just went down the wrong way," she stuttered, her breath ragged and her throat aching. She pushed the remainder of her bacon sandwich away.

"Well, if you won't have it . . ." Dylan said with a wry grin as he took the top slice of bread off and loaded it with brown sauce. He took a bite – a huge big manly bite – and sat back with his hands behind his head.

"No one makes bacon sarnies like you, babe," he said with a smile.

Hope gave a half-smile, got up and walked to the sink so he couldn't see the pain etched across her face, and resisted the urge to tell him that he'd best remember that when Cyndi was serving him some cheap bacon in some cheap slice of bread and pretending she was the be-all and end-all.

She turned around and watched him sip the last of his tea before standing and stretching and declaring he was off to bed.

"Have a good day, H," he said, smiling at her affectionately and she forced herself to smile back.

There really was feck-all chance her day was going to be good now.

Flopping onto the sofa, pulling her naturally fair hair back from her face and switching on her laptop, she decided the absolute best course of action would be to spend a good half hour reading internet forums where people had problems much worse than hers. She wouldn't work this morning. The freelance journalism world would survive without her. She would feel sorry for herself instead – heart-wrenchingly, gut-churningly sorry for herself.

"Fuckitfuckitfuckit!" she swore, and then, to make herself feel better about her life, she switched on *The Jeremy Kyle Show.*

Half an hour had passed and she was lying prone on the sofa, her head on a cushion, listening to an unholy row develop between two sisters who had been bonking each other's husbands, when the phone rang.

She glared at it where it lay out of reach on the floor. She didn't want to move. She wanted to see if Ugly Sister One would lamp Ugly Sister Two and she desperately needed to know which of the two gormless husband efforts was the father of Baby Beyoncé.

The shrill tone was hard to ignore, as was her inbuilt nosiness (a valuable quality when scrabbling for freelance work) so she rolled off the sofa with a thump and, still lying face down, reached for her phone.

Without looking at it, she said "Hello?" as she glanced to one side to see the earring she had long thought lost nestling under the sofa amid the dustbunnies.

"Hope, it's Mum. I have bad news, darling."

Hope felt her heart sink from her stomach, where it had been resting since Dylan's announcement earlier, to her boots.

"Hang on, Mum," she said, pulling herself to a sitting position and switching off the TV and the roars of the audience baying for a DNA test. She took longer than she should have for this – just seconds but they were seconds she wanted to hold close to her. Bad news was going to change things. She wanted things as they were for a moment longer.

"Right, Mum. Sorry about that," she said, hearing the tremble in her own voice. She pulled her knees close to her.

"It's Aunt Betty, darling. She's gone."

"Oh," was all Hope could manage before the tears which had been pricking in her eyes all morning finally fell. "Oh, poor Betty! Oh Mum, what happened?"

He mother sniffled. "Cancer. It seems. But it was peaceful in the end. It seems. A week ago."

"A week ago? What about the funeral? Are they bringing her home?"

"She left instructions, love. No fuss. They buried her near the vineyards – her friends from the village. Sure they were as much of a family to her as we were. She was in France for a long time. I'm sure they gave her a good send-off."

"Is Dad okay?"

Her mum sniffled again. "You know Dad. He's gone out for a walk. He's trying to understand it all. But I told him, you know, he should have stopped trying to understand Betty a long time ago. She was her own woman. She always was."

"I would have loved to have been there," Hope said sadly.

Betty, her father's sister, had been so kind. She had allowed Dylan and Hope to stay with her for a month while they had their year-long adventure around the world. Betty was mad as a box of frogs – individual to the core – and Hope was sure she had probably been a real troublemaker in her time. Hope would have loved to have said her last goodbyes to her – it seemed so sad that none of her family had been with her.

"She's with Claude now, sweetheart," her mother soothed.

Hope brushed the tears from her eyes and sniffed loudly. "I suppose. She is probably creating merry havoc up in heaven. Oh Mum, she was just a dote! An absolute dote."

"Well, darling, she obviously thought highly of you too. I've a letter here and you've been invited to the reading of her will."

"Fuck off!" Hope breathed, instantly shamed that she had cursed in front of her own mother.

"Hope!" her mother tutted.

"Sorry. She's left me something?" The tears were back, this time thicker and faster than ever.

"Well, according this letter from the law firm of Brady and Semple she has."

"Oh, bless her," Hope breathed through her tears. "Oh, bless her heart! She didn't need to do that."

"Well, she did, and you have to be in the law office on Wednesday at half past four to find out more."

"Are you coming?"

"No!" her mother said, with mock indignation. "Clearly Betty thought more highly of you than she did of me! No, it's just you from our crowd. And your cousin Ava."

"The schoolteacher?"

"Yes, that's what she does."

If it was possible for your heart to sink lower than your boots and through the very ground to the very core of the earth, this would have been that moment for Hope.

Hope had nothing against Ava, per se. On the few occasions they had met – at family weddings and funerals – she had seemed absolutely lovely. And perfect. Sickeningly got-it-all-together perfect. Ava was the family member everyone spoke of. Sure hadn't she a lovely wedding? Didn't she marry that hunky big accountant who, by all accounts, was raking it in? And her house? Feck me! You should see her house. Looks like it belongs in the Next Directory, sure it does. And she has that wee girl – with the impossibly cute curls. Not to mention every child she ever taught has gone on to win fecking *Mastermind* or something and all because of Mrs Campbell and her superb Primary One skills.

Compared with Hope – who was only three months younger – Ava was always going to come out on top. Hope was the flighty one – who travelled the world and lives with a boy. But no, not in "that way". They are "only friends". Nope. She doesn't have a boyfriend. Aye, and she has no job either – not a proper full-time one anyway. And her house is rented.

So, she would see Ava again and the whole family would be waiting to hear the craic about Aunt Betty and her will and Hope would no doubt come away feeling mildly shite about herself and how her life was failing to go anywhere. Oh God, now the people on *Jeremy Kyle* seemed relatively normal and nice even. She would prefer meeting with them for a couple of strong drinks than running into Ava and answering all that small-talk bullshit about what she was doing and who she was seeing. Pah!

Aware that her mother was still talking, she tried to tune back in, just to hear her mother read the address of the solicitor's firm and say she would email the details to her just to be sure.

"She must have cared for you," she said as she finished the conversation.

"Not as much as I cared for her," Hope sniffed, feeling her resolve weaken again.

She ended the call and sat on the floor and cried until her eyes were swollen and her throat was raw. She cried for Aunt Betty and her passing with none of her family around her in France. She had been a young woman. She wouldn't even have been sixty. It just didn't seem right. Not right or fair at all. She cried that Betty would now be reunited with her beloved Claude who she spoke so tenderly of during Hope's stay. She cried that Betty had thought of her enough to leave her some token of their friendship. And she cried for herself and her feelings for Dylan who was so utterly, completely and totally unaware that his best friend of fifteen years had fallen head over heels in love with him.

Chapter 3

The offices of Brady and Semple, Solicitors at Law, were grand and imposing. The receptionist had been not so grand, but imposing nonetheless. Hope had been the first to arrive and she sat tapping her foot nervously and humming to herself in the reception while she waited for Ava. The reading would be a one-off affair, it seemed, carried out by Mr Semple – who might or might not have had a first name but, regardless, definitely preferred the formality of being called mister.

"Mr Semple will see you when Mrs Campbell has arrived," the receptionist had said, glancing at the clock on the wall and back to her appointment book.

"That's fine, I'll just . . . erm . . . take a seat, will I?" Hope asked but the receptionist had already turned her attention back to her work, leaving her standing like a cold snotter.

Hope didn't know why but she was nervous, and the snootiness of the receptionist hadn't calmed her. Surely the woman behind the desk – who was at least in her late thirties so most definitely old enough to know good manners – could have tried to put her at her ease. This was a will reading after all – Hope was a bereaved woman. Hope threw the back of the receptionist's head a half-hearted bad look and went and sat down on the very squeaky leather sofa across the office.

Dylan had offered to come with her. He had been upset when he heard about Betty's death which had only made Hope want to hug him and allow him to comfort her, and then her to comfort him and then maybe there could be some joint (naked) comforting – but she had imposed a no-hug zone on her best friend for the moment for all the reasons just listed.

"She was a lovely woman," he had said as they toasted her with a clink of two bottles of beer.

"She was," Hope agreed.

"I'll never forget that month in France. It was something else," Dylan added.

Hope nodded, and gulped back her beer. Yes, it had been something else indeed.

Hope and Dylan had been intimate on just two occasions in the fifteen years of their friendship – from the day they had met as freshers at university to the right here and right now where they lived in each other's pockets. Both of the 'intimate occasions' were things that happened and were never spoken of again. The first time had been on the last day of their first semester at university together and drink had been taken in the Students' Union. They had walked home, arm in arm, to the halls where they had carried on drinking cheap wine while singing Christmas songs and hanging tatty decorations around the room.

At around ten thirty they had curled up side by side to watch TV and sleepily she had nuzzled her head into his chest. He had kissed the top of her head – the tenderest of kisses – and she had been struck by just how good he smelled (if you ignored the stench of cheap booze and stale cigarettes). She looked up at him to find his piercing eyes looking back at her and something in her shifted. Tilting her head towards his, she felt her breath catch as he leaned towards her for a kiss.

When their lips had touched she braced herself for an explosion of passion but *nada*. Nothing. It was, she realised with a slightly nauseous feeling, like kissing her brother or her uncle or something else entirely inappropriate. Breaking free, she looked up at him and he was looking at her with a strange look on his face.

"Not good," he said. "Not that I mean you are not good. You're a lovely kisser but that was not good."

"Not in the least," she said.

"Friends?" he said.

The second time, well, it had been more than a kiss and it had been certainly not like kissing (or doing other things) with her brother – and it had been on a certain moonlit beach near a certain French villa owned by a certain eccentric auntie.

As Hope and Dylan clinked their beer bottles again and toasted their month in France, she couldn't help but think of that night, twelve years before, and she wondered if he was thinking of it too.

"Oh," he said, smiling at her, "did I tell you? The big date has been set. Friday night at the Merchant. I'm going to buy a new suit. Hope, could you come shopping with me and help me because I have a feeling that an off-the-peg number from Burton's isn't going to cut it."

Hope, feeling the beer turn in her stomach, plastered on a smile and said of course she would but only if he took her to Victoria Square for eats and drinks after.

"Of course, mate," he had said with a smile. "Only the best for my girl."

If only, Hope thought, that were true.

In the increasingly stuffy office of Brady and Semple, Hope wondered if Ava was ever going to arrive. It had gone four thirty-seven and there wasn't a whisper of her cousin.

The grumpy-arsed receptionist was making a point of sighing very loudly and looking in an exaggerated, almost comedic fashion at the clock on the wall. At one point she lifted the phone, which hadn't even rung and said loudly in a broad Belfast accent: "No, Mr Semple, she's not here yet. I know . . . I know." She then looked Hope square in the face as if it were her fault Ava was running late.

Hope felt herself blush. She shrugged in an 'I'm very sorry' way before rummaging in her bag just in case there was a missed call from her cousin to say she was on her way, or was just around the corner or maybe not coming at all. There was nothing, except a text message from Dylan who was just getting ready for work, asking her if she could pick him up a new bottle of his favourite aftershave for his big date while she was in town. She texted back that of course she would – but if things carried on the way they were going she wouldn't get near the shops before they closed.

She glanced at the time again. It was four forty-four. She steadfastly refused to look at the receptionist again for fear of what glare she might be met with. She was just digging through her bag for something, anything, to read to pass the time when the door swung open and her cousin, flustered and not at all like the perfectly controlled and calm person everyone portrayed her to be, stumbled in.

"I'm sorry," she blustered, pushing her blonde bobbed hair behind her ears. "I had to come straight from work. And the bus was late. And then there was a fecking tractor on the road and we just couldn't get past it. And then I couldn't get a taxi and then the taxi man couldn't find the offices and, Jesus, he probably shouldn't be a taxi man at all because my two-and-a-half-year-old can drive better. So anyway, he left me off down the road and I've been wandering up and down trying to find this place and anyway, I'm here now and sorry."

Hope watched as her cousin blew her hair from her face and held onto her sides to try and catch her breath.

The receptionist, not a bit interested in why she was late, just lifted the phone to call the mysterious Mr Semple and tell him that both parties in the Boutin matter were now there and ready to proceed.

"G'wan in," she said, with a smile so fake it almost cracked her face.

Hope looked at Ava and Ava looked back at her. Hope wasn't

sure what to say – what was the etiquette in these matters when seeing a cousin you barely had any contact with?

"This is very strange, isn't it?" Ava said, straightening down her skirt.

"Very," Hope conceded. "Did you know Betty well then?"

"Not really. We got tipsy together at Granny's funeral – you weren't there, you were travelling at the time – and I admired her shoes . . . she said she would leave them to me in her will."

Hope laughed. That would be just like Betty – leaving a coveted pair of shoes to someone. "Oh, she will be missed," she said, walking towards the door of Mr Semple's office.

"She sure will," Ava said, with a genuine warmth which put Hope at her ease.

"I suppose we should get this over and done with then," said Hope. "To be honest, I didn't think they actually did this kind of thing. I thought it was all for the movies – reading of wills in stuffy offices."

The grumpy-arsed receptionist bristled at the word *stuffy* and as she opened the door to let the two cousins in, she sniffed. "They don't normally do this, you know. Most people just get a letter in the post – but Mrs Boutin left very specific instructions. She said she wanted a bit of drama to see her out." She softened a little as she spoke, clearly impressed at the notion of a little drama.

Mr Semple was every inch what Hope had expected him to be. An older gentleman, more than likely in his late fifties, he wore a full suit complete with waistcoat. Hope would have put money on him having a fob watch in one of his pockets and she kind of hoped he would take one out, glance at it and say something posh. He wore round glasses on the end of his very long and very pointy nose and he stood up solemnly as the two ladies entered the room, extending his hand first to Hope and then to Ava.

"I'm very sorry for your loss," he said to each of them individually before gesturing to two leather seats in front of his austere dark-mahogany desk.

Momentarily Hope didn't know how to respond. Her brain froze and the words 'thank you' just wouldn't come. She wondered what Mr Semple with his years in the business made of this whole thing – an aunt who wanted some drama, two cousins together not really sure what to expect. *I bet he thinks I'm a money-grabbing bitch*, she thought irrationally as she felt her palms begin to perspire. As she sat down she felt the urge to tell him she didn't really care about an inheritance – even though a part of her did. Maybe that did make her a money-grabbing bitch, she thought, feeling like a complete cow as she sat down. To her surprise she realised she was shaking and she felt a tear pool in the corner of her eye and fall. She took a deep breath to steady herself and felt the warmth of her cousin's hand on hers, assuring her it was okay.

"Well, ladies," Mr Semple began, "your aunt left instructions that upon her death you were both to be summoned here and I was to inform you of her last wishes. As you know Mrs Boutin had no surviving family in France to execute her last will and testament so that task has fallen to me."

He opened the drawer on his desk and glanced down while Hope felt Ava squeeze her hand again. She glanced over at her cousin who was staring squarely at Mr Semple's bald patch as he continued to look for whatever document he needed.

"Ah," he said, extracting two envelopes, "here we are, ladies. I am to give these to you with the instructions that you are to, and I quote, 'Go somewhere, open a bottle of something, chat a little, open the letters and read their contents together'."

He handed them over and Hope looked down to see Betty's cursive scrawl spell out her name before looking to Ava who was doing the same.

"Now," Mr Semple said, lifting a pen and pushing a document first at Ava, "if you could just sign here to confirm receipt of the letters we can all get away for the day."

"That's it?" Ava asked, her words echoing Hope's thoughts.

Hope hadn't really known what she was expecting except that she was expecting a little more than this.

"That's it," Mr Semple said, pushing the document to Hope for her signature.

She signed without thinking and clutched her envelope to her chest and stood.

"Thank you for your time, ladies. Once again I am sorry for your loss and I wish you both well."

Ava found herself standing on a street in Belfast staring at her cousin who was staring back at her as if neither could quite believe what had just happened. Ava had been expecting something different – a long reading of legal jargon perhaps and the handing over of a pair of purple shoes – not the handing over of an envelope with the instructions she was to go for a drink with Hope, get half-scuttered and read their letters together. She had to get back to Derry. She was supposed to be meeting Connor at six and getting a lift back with him. Cora was minding Maisie and had been tetchy all day about the will-reading and said she could feel a headache coming on and would appreciate it if Ava could get home as quickly as possible once the formalities were done and dusted. Ava sighed and looked at her watch. It had just gone five and she was already feeling under pressure. She couldn't just clear off home and ignore Betty's last wishes no matter how much she needed to be somewhere else. No. That would bring a lifetime of bad karma. Sighing again she looked at Hope who was also looking at her watch. No doubt she had somewhere to be too, Ava thought. From what she knew of her cousin, she was always dashing off to some press launch, or opening night or socialite's party or other. She wasn't tied to a bedtime routine and the fecking *CBeebies* bedtime hour.

"This was unexpected," Ava offered.

"You're telling me. I thought it would be longer, and more detailed and not involving letters."

"Or instructions to go and share a bottle together?"

"Exactly."

"We should do it though, shouldn't we?" Ava said.

"Oh Christ yes, or she'll haunt us or the like. I've no doubt if anyone could come back from the grave to make you pay for your misdemeanours it would be Betty."

"Sounds like you knew her better than I did," Ava said.

"I spent a month with her, in France. I did a gap year after uni

– me and my friend Dylan. She let us stay with her towards the end of our around-the-world trip."

Ava smiled but part of her felt envious. The furthest she had ever travelled was a fortnight all-inclusive in Cancun on honeymoon – and, while it had been lovely, they had barely left the resort and she wouldn't have dared to ever refer to herself as a traveller. That much wasn't likely to change now that she had a toddler. The furthest she had been since in the last five years was a weekend in London and even that had been before Maisie was born.

"She was mad as a hatter – a real livewire. I should have kept in touch with her more when we got back – but you know – life has a way of getting away from you."

Ava knew, she knew exactly. It was only down to her mildly obsessive-compulsive system of organising their day-to-day schedule that she ever got anything done or kept in touch with anyone at all. There wasn't a birthday, anniversary or other special occasion that she didn't know about. She had a box of cards fit for every occasion in a leather-bound box on top of her wardrobe and a host of diaries and calendars marked with different-coloured stickers to remind her, a week in advance, of when she needed to send the cards out. Blue stickers were for children's birthdays. Pink were for friends. Yellow stickers were for anniversaries and purple stickers were for the cards you had to send to people you had to send cards to out of a sense of duty. She realised with a sudden extra heaping dose of guilt that Aunt Betty, who had left her the letter she was now holding in her hand, hadn't featured on any of those lists, pink or purple.

"Life can be tough sometimes," she said, glancing again at her watch. "Speaking of which, and I hate to sound like I'm rushing this, but can we go and get a drink and do what Betty wants because my lift home is leaving in just under an hour?"

Hope smiled. "Of course, I'll just get us a taxi."

Ava watched as Hope stepped forward, raised her arm and a taxi stopped beside her within seconds.

"We'll go to the Merchant," she called over her shoulder. "I want to check it out for a friend anyway."

"Okay," Ava said, not having a blue baldy notion what the

Merchant was, and followed her cousin into the taxi where they sat side by side, clutching their envelopes as the taxi weaved its way through the streets of Belfast until it arrived at the grand hotel that Ava could see was the Merchant.

It didn't look like the kind of place she would venture these days. It didn't look as if it sold anything with chicken nuggets or a free colouring-in book to amuse the younger guests. And while she felt a little out of her depth, a part of her – for the first time that day – felt a little frisson of excitement. Just imagine: this was her, Ava 'reliable' Campbell, about to open a bottle of wine with her cousin while reading a mysterious letter from an eccentric relative. This was not her normal life. This was like someone else's life – someone who was clearly much more glamorous. She'd have to watch herself. She didn't want to drink too much and end up giddy and making an eejit of herself. She followed Hope through the bar and sat down on a cool cream-leather sofa and reached for the wine list.

"What do you think, a glass each?" she said.

"Betty did say a bottle," Hope said. "So I say a bottle. Surely your lift won't mind if you are a little eeny bit late?"

Ava thought of Connor who had been seconded to the Belfast office thanks to a spectacular downturn in his firm's business and who had left their home at six that morning and would be exhausted, and shook her head.

"He – Connor – my husband – he won't mind because he is lovely but he'll also be exhausted. Still, you are right. If the woman said a bottle then we should drink a bottle. White or red? Are you okay with white? And I think we should definitely go for something French?"

"I think," Hope said with a wicked grin, "that maybe we should toast Betty properly. Champagne, my dear, champagne!"

Ava gulped, tried not to think of the cost and tried to fight back the feeling that these purple shoes were proving to be far more expensive than they were worth, and said, weakly, "Of course, champagne."

She had to admit the bubbles felt nice. The only bubbles she was used to these days were the kind she put in Maisie's bath which she poured out of a bottle with a smiling sailor cartoon on the front.

As she looked up she saw Hope sip from her glass, closing her eyes as the bubbles hit. She watched her sigh and sag with relief and wondered if this seemingly exceptionally confident woman in front of her wasn't feeling as uptight as she was.

"This is a nice place," Ava said. "Very fancy. I don't get out much any more."

"Here, neither do I!" Hope exclaimed. "Most nights I'm home living out my social life on Facebook!"

Hope laughed and Ava felt herself relax further – helped by a second and third sip from her glass. She could definitely get used to this.

Their second glasses were filled and Ava had noticed her words were starting to slur just slightly when it was decided they would open the letters.

"You go first," she said to Hope.

"Maybe we should go together?"

Ava looked at the letter and again at her cousin and shrugged her shoulders. "Why not?"

So, as anal about envelope-opening as she was about everything else in her life, Ava slowly started to tear at the corners of the envelope, while she watched Hope rip hers open with the enthusiasm a four-year-old reserved for a birthday present.

Each envelope contained several sheets of paper, all held together with coloured paper clips in the shape of flowers.

"Well, then, I suppose we should start reading," Hope said, lifting her glass to her mouth and taking a long drink before stopping, gesturing with her glass towards Ava's and saying, "Cheers, then. Let's do it!"

Ava clinked her glass against her cousin's, took a similarly large gulp which tickled the back of her throat, set her glass down on the table and glanced at the letter in front of her.

"We'll start after three," Hope said and Ava nodded because she couldn't think of anything else to say.

"1 . . . 2 . . . 3!" Hope said, and the girls began to read in unison.

My dear girls,

I've always wanted to write the following line so please indulge me. It sounds so dramatic – and you both know I liked a bit of drama. "Flair" should have been my middle name. I would have liked that much more than Majella.

Anyway . . . the line:

My dear girls, by the time you read this, I shall be dead . . .

Hope and Ava looked at each other and Ava found herself stifling a giggle. She wished in that moment she had known Aunt Betty that bit better – she knew she would have loved her very much.

"They're duplicate letters then?" Hope said. "Addressed to both of us together?" A glance at Ava's letter confirmed this.

Ava nodded. "Seems so."

The girls bent their heads over their letters again.

First of all I want you to know that you have both, perhaps without even realising it, touched my life in a positive way.

Hope, when you came to stay with me for that month twelve years ago, you lived up to your name and you indeed gave me hope. I know that sounds awfully over the top and cheesy but you know, Hope, how you helped.

I was stuck in a godawful rut with myself – feeling completely lost without Claude – and you came with your young man and you injected such fun into my life. How I loved watching the two of you together and how I loved our little chats on the terrace under the stars.

You have a gift for listening, Hope. Please don't ever forget that.

Ava, sometimes the smallest things can mean the most. When I returned home for my mother's funeral, it was you who held my hand and chatted to me even though you barely knew me. Returning on my own was hard – especially as my brothers and sisters all had families of their own they had to tend to. But you, you were there for me. You let me cry and you made me laugh. That was more than I could possibly have hoped for from you.

I am proud to say I know you both. Proud of such bright, intelligent young women and proud that they are part of my family.

When I thought of the task ahead – of who I could trust to take care of it for me – I couldn't think of anyone but you both.

I have no family in France. I do, of course, have dear friends but, girls, can I be straight? There are only certain people you would trust with sorting through your knicker drawer.

And that is what it comes down to, girls. This letter is to ask you a favour. It is my final request that you visit my house in France and say goodbye to it from me one last time.

I have tried to put my affairs in order as much as possible in these last few months but there are some things which I could not. Could you do them for me? Pack away my last few belongings. Sell them if you wish. Keep what you want. Everything can go. I've no need for any of it any more.

I have made arrangements that money is put aside to pay for your flights and to cover your expenses while you are here. My dear friend Jean-Luc Gilard will be on hand to offer whatever support he can while you are here.

I hope you do not find this an imposition.

Much love,
Betty
x

"She wants us to clean out her knicker drawer?" Hope said incredulously, wiping a tear from her eyes. "God bless her, she was mad as a box of frogs and she wants us to clean out her knicker drawer!"

"It would appear so."

Ava glanced over the letter again, turning the page to find contact details for the mysterious Jean-Luc, and a cheque for £500 which was to cover the cost of her travel. She looked at Hope who was just discovering that she had been sent the same.

Ava didn't know how to react. She was deeply touched by her late aunt's very kind words. She couldn't believe those few hours spent together had meant so much. If the truth were told she felt kind of sorry for Betty. She hadn't had the first notion that Betty had felt so excluded at the funeral. She seemed, well, the life and soul of the party if such things were appropriate at funerals. The obsessive compulsive in her was twitching at the prospect of sorting out a house in France, but the busy working mother in her was screeching that there was no bloody way she could up sticks and go to France to tidy up after some dead woman she barely knew when she had a job, and a daughter, and a husband, and a hundred and one things to do.

"This day just gets weirder and weirder," Hope said, sipping from her glass.

Ava thought that if there was a prize for understatements, that one would probably be a winner. She was about to tell her cousin just that when her phone beeped to life, signalling that Connor was outside and waiting for her. She grabbed a pen from her bag and scribbled her contact details before handing them to Hope.

"I'm sorry to have to rush off," she said, lifting her bag and stuffing the letter into it. "Especially when we have so much to talk about. But, you know, I need to go. But I'll definitely be in touch and we'll definitely talk about this."

She took the business card Hope offered her and they both stood up and hugged – a hug that was mildly less awkward than the one they had shared in the solicitor's office earlier. That could have been down to their possible shared destiny shuffling through their mad aunt's knickers or it could have been down to the champagne, but for a second Ava allowed herself to breathe in the hug and return it without her usual awkwardness.

"It's been nice," she said.

"It's been bloody weird, but nice," Hope replied. "And yes, I will definitely be in touch."

Chapter 4

The bottle of champagne had to be finished and Hope was most definitely not leaving it with a single drop in it. Especially not at the prices charged by the Merchant. It had gone six and the shops would be closed. There was no chance Dylan was getting his fancy cologne. Sipping her champagne and looking at the young, trendy, and exceptionally cool types wander in for their post-work drinkies she had an urge to do something spontaneous and reminiscent of when she actually had a life.

Picking up her phone, she tapped out a message to Dylan: Fancy taking a sickie? In a pub? With me? I have champagne and a story to share about my auntie's knickers.

She hit send and sat back and re-read Betty's letter. Ava's face had been a picture, she thought. Then again she was glad she hadn't been looking at her own reflection when she had read it. She didn't know what she had been expecting of Betty. Maybe a necklace or some other jewellery. She remembered admiring Betty's stunning sapphire engagement ring when she had been in France – at her best guess she had wondered if Betty would leave that to her. But a request to go there and put her affairs in order? She was slightly amazed that Betty had trusted her – notoriously flighty and disorganised in almost every aspect of her life – to sort things out. That was obviously why Ava had been included in the equation too. Ava could organise anything, Hope bet. She struck her as the kind who had her CDs all arranged alphabetically, her books all the right way out and organised in order of height in her bookshelf and an impressive collection of days-of-the-week knickers. Hope and Betty were more cut from the same cloth. Neither could organise a piss-up in a brewery.

Ava seemed nice though – less anal and less bookish than she remembered. But did she want a trip to France with her, just her, for company? Once again her mind sprang back to her trip to France twelve years before, when she had Betty for company . . . and Dylan, of course.

Her phone beeped, pulling her out of her daydream and back to reality.

I'll take a leave day. I could do with chatting to you about the big date. I need you, H, you're my only Hope. Where r u?

She laughed at his message. "You're my only Hope." He used that when he was very nervous. Texting him back that she was in the very fancy Merchant, she said if he met her they could at least do a recce for his big date. He replied that he would be there in half an hour and she topped up her glass and took the small compact mirror from her bag to check her reflection. Her make-up was holding up okay, but her eyes had a slightly glassy look about them from the champagne. Maybe she should order some water to bring her round a bit before Dylan arrived.

She loved watching Dylan walk into a room. He was one of those men who emitted some sort of magnetic attraction to all the single ladies (and most of the married ones) when he walked. He was, generally speaking, mostly unaware of this – but Hope, she wasn't. And she was also aware that the other people in the bar didn't know they were just good friends so she could make a big show of hugging him and kissing him and everyone would be insanely jealous. She knew that made her a little bit of a bunny-boiler but, she reminded herself, there was no harm in it either. Not really. Let's face facts – the only person getting hurt by the situation was Hope and Hope alone.

She had downed two glasses of water and was feeling safe enough to pour out more champagne when he arrived. She stood up to hug him and caught a deep inhalation of his cologne – which made her feel a little dizzy. Closing her eyes, she breathed him in and sat down before pushing his glass of champagne towards him and glancing round the room to catch those telltale jealous expressions on the faces of the trendy young drinkers.

"Cheers!" he said, sipping from his glass.

"Was work okay with you taking the night off?"

He nodded. "My team are well ahead with the current project so they were fine. I'm a bit worried Cyndi might think I'm snubbing her so I've sent a text message. Was that too much?"

His brow was furrowed and he looked worried so, even though Hope had felt herself bristle at the very mention of Cyndi's name, she assured him that no, that was not too much and that if Cyndi was like any other woman on the planet she would probably now be circulating said text message to all her friends, telling them what a catch he was.

He smiled – a broad grin – and, while she was disgusted at how clearly infatuated he was with another woman, she allowed herself to bask in that smile for just a moment and wondered how she had ever seen him as anything other than absolutely perfect for her.

"I can't believe how nervous I am about Friday night," Dylan confided. "I don't think I have ever been this nervous before and you know me, I don't get nervous. Without sounding like a complete prick, I'm not exactly inexperienced when it comes to women."

"Steady there, Joey Tribbiani," Hope said, referencing one their favourite programmes from their student days. "I've seen you nervous before."

"But not this nervous," he said, sitting back and drinking from his glass again.

Hope lifted her glass to note it was almost empty. She was clearly agitated and drinking much faster than was sensible for her. She sat her glass back down and looked at Dylan who had his best tortured-soul expression on him. He would have given Morrissey a big old fat run for his miserable money.

She knew as his best friend she should start listing his attributes

– all positive and glowing of course – and with a few glasses of wine in her there was every chance she would start telling him how sexy he was. No, it was best she just cut this as quickly and cleanly as she could.

"Look, Dylan. You've nothing to be worried about. She'll love you. She'd be mad not to. You're a ride. You know it. Now, my glass is almost empty so could you go and get us both a top-up and see if they have some crisps or the like or are they too posh?"

He smiled again – another blinder – and leaned over the table to kiss her on the cheek. "I do love you, Hope," he said. "I'll be right back."

She watched him walk away and had to bite back the urge to call him back because she was starting to realise that he really was walking away from her and things were changing. For so many years she had wanted him to meet someone special and now that he seemed so convinced that Cyndi was, potentially, that someone very special indeed she didn't like it.

Her eyes suddenly damp, she reached her hand into her bag to find a tissue and brushed against the letter from Aunt Betty instead. Perhaps a break away to France for a bit wouldn't be such a bad thing. Some distance from the situation could be exactly what the doctor ordered.

The post-champagne headache had hit full on and Ava rubbed at her temples while Connor drove over the Glenshane Pass on the final leg of their journey back home to Derry.

"You have to go," Connor said, eyes fixed straight ahead.

"It's not that simple," Ava said.

"Of course it is," her husband said. "The money is there. School holidays are in a few weeks."

"But . . ." Ava tried to think of more excuses but her brain seemed to have stopped working.

"But nothing. Ava, this is your aunt's last request. It might be strange but it's what she wanted and I know you, Ava Campbell. I know you well enough to know that you will only crucify yourself with guilt if you don't."

He had a point. Guilt seemed to be one of Ava's specialist

subjects these days. "But what about Maisie?" she asked, pulling her Ace card. He couldn't argue about Maisie. She was the apple of his eye – fair and square.

"We can survive without you," he said, turning to look at her with a wry smile. "We wouldn't want to do it for a long time – you know, I'd need you every now and again to wash my socks – but we could survive without you."

"Hmmm," she responded, thinking she would no doubt be coming back to one big giant heap of a messy house if she left them to their own devices for anything more than an hour.

"You're thinking that will leave the house a kip, aren't you?" Connor asked.

"No!" The fecker! He always could tell what she was thinking. She glanced at him and he burst out laughing – a loud peal of a laugh that made her feel a little weak at the knees – and she laughed back. "Okay then, so I was."

"Well, you shouldn't. I'll sort the house out. It will be perfect. Absolutely gleaming."

Raising one eyebrow, she looked at him and was surprised he was keeping a straight face while he stared ahead at the road in front of him. "Really?"

"Really. Sure I'll get your mum to come round the day before you come back," he said with a wink.

"You have to go," Cora said, looking at the letter.

"That's what Connor said," Ava laughed, putting on the kettle to make a cup of tea for her mother before she went home. "But it's a big ask," she went on. "And I don't get it."

Cora shook her head and sat down at the kitchen table. She looked tired and Ava felt guilty for keeping her later than planned.

"Is your headache bothering you, Mum?"

"No . . . no," Cora said. "It's just a shock. It's all been a shock. I just wish she had given us the chance to make amends."

"What amends? She didn't talk of many regrets in this letter. Just wanting her knickers sorted." Ava tried to keep the mood light.

"There were just some things I would have liked to say. Things I would have liked to have done."

Ava poured the boiling water from the kettle into the teapot which she placed on the ring of the cooker. "Why not come with us? I'm sure Betty wouldn't mind? Sure it won't bring her back, but you might feel a little closer to her."

She watched as her mother sucked in her cheeks and shook her head. "No. I couldn't do that."

Ava should have known her mother would say no. She was a complete stick in the mud. The furthest she had ever travelled from Derry had been to Dublin for a weekend and even then she had complained as if she were in a foreign country.

"You could do it, Mum, and sure I would be there to translate the menus – well, try to anyway – and do all your running around for you. It would be fine."

"No," Cora said, shaking her head decisively. "No, love. Betty wanted you there . . . and Hope too. If she had wanted me there she would have asked me. This one is just for you and you need to do it." Her voice was choked again as she stood up. "If you don't mind love, I'll skip the tea. Can Connor just take me over home now?"

"Okay," Ava said, hugging her mother tightly.

Maisie had gone to bed – thankfully peacefully and without a mini-riot – and Ava had a shower which cleared her champagne-induced headache. Now she was sitting on their bed, fluffy dressing-gown pulled around her, reading Aunt Betty's letter again. She traced her finger along the words and tried to understand why Betty had chosen her for this task. She had expected to come from Belfast with a pair of amazing purple shoes – not a guilt complex and the funding for a trip to France with a cousin she barely knew. It was strange that she didn't really know Hope at all, despite there only being a few months between them. They had attended the same school but Hope was one of the cool kids while Ava always found herself comfortably ensconced among the smarty-pants swots. In fact she was pretty sure she remembered Hope calling her that once at a family party when they were about fifteen. Hope had sauntered in in her coloured leggings and hyper-colour T-shirt with her up-to-the-minute trainers while Ava had sat, head in a book, glancing in disapproval at the group of rowdies singing 'Sweet Caroline' at the top of their lungs.

Cringing at the memory, Ava thought about how cool Hope still looked – even if she said her life wasn't exactly the high non-stop party train Ava had imagined it to be. She glanced down at her fluffy slippers and kicked them off, deciding there and then to paint her toenails. Okay, so it wasn't full-on glamour. She wasn't going for a pedicure, or getting her legs waxed or going for a vajazzle or anything. But painting her nails would be a nice start.

She was on the third toe of her left foot when Connor pushed the door open and walked in carrying two glasses of red wine.

"I thought you could do with a treat?" he said, handing her one.

She gazed at him, dressed now in his civvies of a pair of stonewashed jeans and a white V-neck T-shirt and he looked irresistible. Yes, she thought to herself, she really could do with a treat. The kind of treat that most certainly did not come out of a bottle and was very certainly not the kind of treat you would expect a rather unremarkable schoolteacher to indulge in on a work night.

"Cheers," she said, taking rather too big a sip which caused her to splutter and choke.

Instantly Connor reached out to pat her back and asked if she was okay and she sat for a moment and realised just how unsexy she must look to him. There she was in her biggest, most comfy dressing-gown – a large and definitely unflattering towelling effort which made her look like she belonged in an ad for fabric softener. Her hair was still wet and tousled from her shower – but unlike those supermodels who could totally rock that look, she looked more wet-look-greasy-chip-pan-head than just-out-of-bed sex kitten. Her toes were half-painted and, while she had been mocking herself only minutes earlier about not having a leg wax or a pedicure, she was suddenly aware that it wasn't only her legs that were in dire need of waxing. She felt a little awkward, nervous even, as he sat down beside her on the bed and she gulped from her glass again.

"Go easy," he soothed her. "You seem really rattled or something."

"I'm not rattled," Ava heard herself snap, pulling her dressing-gown closer around her, looking at him.

He smiled – a warm smile which said he knew she was, of course, very rattled indeed by the day's events – and he took her wineglass from her and kissed her gently on the lips. She was surprised at how easily she felt herself melt into his kiss. Her head felt deliciously swimmy and, even though she knew that the champagne had more than likely left her system by now, she still felt a little drunk.

"I'm a little rattled now," she murmured.

"In a good way?" Connor answered, brushing his lips on her neck, just below her ear – just where he knew she found him completely and utterly irresistible.

"In a good way," she affirmed, pushing all thoughts of France, purple shoes, waxing appointments and being sensible to back of her head. "Definitely in a good way."

Chapter 5

Friday evening could not have come soon enough. Thursday had been a train-wreck – an absolute disaster of a day which had started with a hangover and continued with a hangover and ended with a dirty big hangover. Ava could barely remember the days when she could go out, drink until three in the morning and manage to get through the course of the next day without actually wanting to shoot herself in the head to put her out of her misery.

Then again, she had realised, those days had been few and far between. Ava's wild years had been more a wild few months – and by wild she meant occasionally a bit drunken. But the part of her which regretted missing out on a wilder younger life was being resoundingly drowned out by the part of her which was deeply regretting sharing a bottle of wine with Connor and staying up into the wee small hours doing very naughty things. She had found it hard to look her charges in the face when they arrived in the classroom the following morning and she kept her distance from their parents in case there was whiff of alcohol from her – but she was sure her pallor and the dark circles under her eyes gave away that something was definitely up. Surreptitiously, she had sipped from a bottle of Lucozade hidden in her desk drawer and had tried not to boke when one of her more lively five-year-old pupils had stuck his finger so far up his own nose he had brought on a mega, snotty nosebleed.

With no chance of the hangover abating, she had come home and cooked Maisie her dinner before disappearing into the bath as soon as Connor appeared home – looking equally worn out but with a sly grin on his face which showed her he had very much enjoyed her abandoning her inhibitions the previous night.

"Go," he said. "Have a while to yourself."

She had nodded gratefully and disappeared upstairs where she lit her favourite Jo Malone candle, topped up her bath with a Lush bath-bomb and poured herself a nice, fresh glass of cranberry juice to try and soothe her dehydrated body. Sinking into the bubbles and feeling her muscles start to relax, she was just about reaching her comfy zone when the bathroom door flew open and in ran Maisie, dressed in her pyjamas, some fairy wings, two necklaces and, it seemed, the entire contents of Ava's make-up bag. Needless to say Ava's muscles instantly seized back up into instant lockjaw mode.

"Hi, Mammy," Maisie said, dropping her pyjama trousers and knickers and clambering onto the toilet. There were two other toilets in the house, Ava thought – but no, her daughter needed to use this one. For a poo. A very, smelly poo – which came with the most interesting of toddler running commentaries.

"Oh, Mammy, the water splashed my bum-bum!" Maisie laughed.

As much as she loved the very bones of her daughter, Ava really did not have the energy for this – especially when the call of "Wipe my bum!" rang out.

"Connor!" Ava yelled and listened for her husband's footsteps on the stairs.

He walked in, saw the painted clown sitting on the toilet and smiled apologetically at his wife before embarking on Operation Bum Wipe. Ava closed her eyes and tried to stay in her happy place, hoping against hope the scented candle would soon work its magic and make the room her fragrant sanctuary again.

"Come on now, toots," Connor had urged.

"But I want to stay with Mammy. I just want to talk."

There was more than a distinct whinge to her daughter's voice and Ava felt her temper start to fray – which she knew was unfair. It wasn't Maisie's fault she had a hangover.

It was a lost battle. Mammy Guilt 1, Ava 0.

"Okay, love, you nip on downstairs and I'll be out now," she said, pulling the plug out with her toes.

Grabbing a towel, Ava pulled herself from the bath and roughly dried her skin before slipping on her dressing-gown and slippers. Padding to the living room, she found Maisie now sitting perfectly engrossed in one of her books and not a bit bothered by her mother's arrival. Ava let out a deep sigh.

"What's up?" Connor asking, raising his gaze from the TV and giving her a half-smile.

"Nothing," she replied, a petulant, defeatist tone slipping from her lips before she turned and went back to her room to pull on some pyjamas and dry her hair.

She fought the urge to cry, and decided she was never drinking again.

The hangover had continued through until Friday which had proved no less easy on the stomach than Thursday. One of her charges had been sick everywhere, which prompted three more of her charges to also throw up while one other wee lad – who was never good with drama – had gone into floods of hysterical tears. She had just about made it out of the classroom with her sanity and decided that there was no way in hell she was facing the supermarket for her traditional Friday-night shopping extravaganza. She would order a takeaway instead and, given that the weather was nice, they would sit in the garden and eat it. In fact she would put Maisie to bed nice and early and make the meal just for her and Connor. Perfect. A hangover cure. A sleeping baby. And some sunshine.

She might even get an early night – a proper early night – not the kind of early night she had with Connor on Wednesday which had turned into a very late night indeed. She felt almost giddy at the very notion of it.

Maisie was just watching the Tombliboos say goodnight when Connor arrived. Glad to see him home, Ava greeted him with a kiss and a cold beer. Even more glad to see him home, Maisie greeted him with a full-on bear hug. Watching them together while finally coming out of the fug of her hangover, Ava realised that they probably would be just fine if she did go to France and leave them for a bit. She just wondered if she would be fine without them.

She promised herself she would text Hope later that evening to start on making some plans.

Hope loved her Friday-night routine – well, as much as she could love a routine which was essentially that of a rather dull middle-aged woman and not that of a young, hip and happening thirty-something.

Dylan would go to work and she would momentarily feel a little bereft and then she would brush herself off and remind herself of the pleasures that awaited her. There was no need for keeping up appearances when Dylan wasn't around. She could take her make-up off, slip out of her high heels and into her softest, squishiest slippers and baggiest, comfiest pyjamas. She would pour a glass of wine – just the one – and switch on her computer and catch up with friends old and new and the very latest in celebrity gossip. And then she would discuss the very same gossip at length on Twitter or Facebook or whatever other social-networking site she chose to visit. She would never be lonely.

Tonight was little different though because Dylan was not at work and she wasn't so easily distracted. Instead she had the urge to stick Spotify on her computer and download the very best in 80s soft rock ballads to croon along to while getting rat-arsed and trying not to think about exactly what he was up to that night.

He had been like the proverbial cat on the proverbial hot tin roof before he went out. And the cat he was like was also a cat on heat. He had left in a fug of deodorant, cologne and hair gel. When she had hugged him she had felt the crisp starchiness of his new shirt.

"Do I look okay?" he asked, looking over her shoulder to try and catch his reflection in the mirror over the fire.

"*Dylando, you look wunnnnerful tonight!*" she sang in a broad Belfast accent and he had laughed and kissed her on the top of her head.

"Thanks, Hopeless," he said and she had laughed even though she wanted to kick him square in the nuts. Of all the nicknames he had for her 'Hopeless' was her absolute least favourite – especially that night when it wasn't even one tiny bit remotely funny.

He glanced at himself again and declared it was beer o'clock and he needed some Dutch courage. Opening a bottle from the fridge and sitting down opposite Hope, he looked at his watch and sipped from his bottle.

"Taxi's booked for twenty minutes' time," he said. "Not like me to be ready early."

"No," Hope had replied. "It certainly isn't."

He looked at his watch again and she watched as he loosened his tie and ran his fingers through his hair. It was kind of cute seeing him this nervous – or it would have been if it wasn't killing her.

"Have you decided about France yet?" he asked.

She had told him about Betty's letter as they sat in the Merchant. He had returned from the bar with their drinks and she had shown him the letter and he had immediately urged her to go.

"You have to. Betty was so good to us. You owe it to her and, besides, it's not going to cost you anything. You won't have to up your overdraft or beg, borrow and steal from anyone and this could be just what you need."

"What I need?" she had asked, thinking that what she needed was really just a few feet from her.

"Well, you know I love you, but . . ."

No sentence in the world that started with 'You know I love you, but' ever ended well and Hope braced herself for the onslaught.

". . . you're stuck in a rut these days. You've been working hard and not necessarily getting far and you seem, well, a bit fecked-off some of the time . . . and you've lost a bit of *you*. Does that sound awful?"

She had shaken her head but she had wanted to nod. And cry. But she was not going to cry in the Merchant when there were people all around her who were thinking she was with this hunky man in front of her and being jealous of her. Crying would kind of fuck that up. And, even though Dylan was her best friend in the entire world, she could not get into this type of deep and meaningful conversation with him . . . not there, not then.

And now, watching him sit nervously waiting on his taxi, she was glad that she had not got into that particular hot and heavy conversation. The atmosphere between them would have been really fecking awkward if she had gone down that particular excruciatingly embarrassing route.

"Yes," she said. "I've decided about France. You were right. I kind of knew that before you said it, but yes, I'm going to go. I'm just waiting to hear from Ava to see if she is up for it and if not I guess I'll go it alone. At least I kind of know the area – it may have been a while but Saint Jeannet doesn't strike me as the kind of place which changes much."

She was talking but he was just persistently looking at his watch and gulping at his beer while occasionally looking at his phone, presumably to see if *she* had texted or called. Hope could have told him she was changing her name by deed poll to Nellie the Elephant and running off to join the circus and she was sure he would have responded with the same nervous nod and quiet affirmation that she was doing the right thing.

It was almost a relief when he had gone and she hadn't felt as if she might combust with the tension of the whole damn thing. But that was before she realised she was alone. And it was Friday night. And all she had was her computer for company and some very dodgy 80s rock music.

She would get drunk – so very, very drunk – and try not to think about whether or not he was kissing *her* just there and then.

Lying on the sofa, a square of Galaxy chocolate melting on her tongue while some big-haired man sang about wanting to know what love is, Hope heard her phone beep to life and she reached her hand to the floor to find it.

Three words. Not, admittedly the three words she wanted to hear most of all in the world, but they would do . . . three words: "Let's do it."

She hit reply and tapped a message back to Ava. "You're on. I'll call you tomorrow and we can set the ball rolling proper."

Yes, she was a sad sack lying at home listening to questionable music on a Friday night all on her own but things were going to change.

Chapter 6

Karen's face was a picture – not unlike 'The Scream' by Edvard Munch.

"You lucky, lucky bitch!" she said, probably a little too loudly for a play centre which was mostly populated by very impressionable under-ten-year-olds. "I mean, it's terribly sad that your aunt died of course, and you have my sympathy, but a holiday, in France, without kids – what I wouldn't give –"

"Technically it's not a holiday as such," Ava said, looking over to where Maisie – clearly over her sore-arm injury – was swinging from a rope and doing her very best monkey impressions. "We have to put her affairs in order." She figured 'putting affairs in order' sounded better than sorting through her clothes and personal belongings and giving an old house a good clean.

"Ah, but still, it's France and it's summer and I'm sure there will be at least some time for lounging about," said Karen. "We did France last year but it was Euro-frigging-Disney and a complete pain in the arse. All that all-day happiness and princess nonsense. You know what I wanted? A sun-lounger, a margarita and a trashy book. I tell you, we won't ever be going anywhere again that doesn't have a kids' club."

Ava thought that actually it would have been lovely to take Maisie to Disneyland and she couldn't think of anything worse than going on holiday and handing her daughter over to baby-sitters the whole time she was there. Sure, she craved some time to herself – to be *her* again but the one big fat sticking point in her plans to go to France was Maisie.

She nodded at Karen and sipped from her coffee cup. "I've to make all the plans yet. My cousin is going with me and I suppose I'll have to see when it suits her to go. It will be the school holidays at least."

"Bitch," Karen muttered. "You lucky, lucky bitch."

"You need to maybe stop spending so much time with Karen," Connor said as they walked hand in hand along the beach while Maisie walked on ahead, picking up stones and shells and screaming with laughter as the waves rushed in towards her bare feet. "She gives you the rage."

"I don't know that I would say she gives me the rage. She scares me a bit, I suppose, because I worry I'll end up like her."

Connor laughed. "Never in a million years could you end up like Karen."

"I don't know. Sometimes I find this whole motherhood thing a little overwhelming."

"Everyone finds it a little overwhelming," he said. "You know that. Jesus, it's scarier than I ever imagined being a parent could be but, you know, the good outweighs the bad, doesn't it?"

She looked at Maisie who was closely examining a large string of seaweed. "Of course," she said, "but there are times . . ."

"Of course there are times," Connor interrupted. "But they are just that – times. Not everything."

She took a deep breath and walked on, suddenly grateful that she was wearing sunglasses because tears were smarting in her eyes. She couldn't tell him how she really felt – that she loved her daughter so much it hurt and that she felt crippled with guilt whenever they were apart for more than twenty minutes but how sometimes, when they were together, she didn't remember who she really was any more. She was Maisie's mammy – she knew that. And she was Connor's wife. And she was damn good teacher with a lovely classroom. She had a lovely house filled with lovely things and on paper she had it all but sometimes it didn't feel enough. She knew, she knew deep down she was a godawful ungrateful baggage for even thinking that way. For a while she had thought maybe it was just a phase but when she met with Karen and heard her wax lyrical on her favourite chosen topic of "why life as a mother is so unrewarding" she wondered was the fug ever going to lift.

She squeezed Connor's hand – to reassure herself as much as anything and he squeezed back. "France will be good for you, you know. I know you're worried about Maisie but there is no need. You go – and have fun and a great big adventure and then come back and we'll work this out. Whatever isn't right with you, we'll work it out."

She squeezed his hand again, because she couldn't talk, and then she ran to help Maisie fish a sea urchin out of a rock pool.

Sitting at the kitchen table, laptop on and her glasses perched on the end of her nose, Ava set about googling everything there was to know about the South of France and everything there was to know about getting there as painlessly as possible. This was her comfort zone – organising things. She had a brand-new, crisp and clean manila folder waiting for clean crisp printouts detailing interesting details about flights and rental-car pick-ups and things which most people found interminably boring but which she found mildly thrilling. Shaking her head and smiling to herself, she wondered if this was just another sign that she needed to get out more. Ah well, on a trip to France, whatever the reason, maybe she would find a little of her old self again.

Picking up her phone, she dialled Hope's number and smiled cheerfully when she heard her cousin answer.

"Are you ready to do this?" Ava asked.

"I was born ready," Hope replied cheerfully. "And you have no idea how much I mean that!"

"Bad day?"

"Something like that. It's a long story and one I will no doubt tell you when we are in France and we are drinking some very fine wine and sorting through Betty's things."

"Eeek! Sounds intriguing."

"Perhaps *intriguing* is not the word I would use," Hope said, but her tone was light. "I promise I will fill you in when we are face to face in France."

"Which would be when?" Ava asked. "I'm free to go any time from the first week in July – as soon as the school term is done, so it's really down to you."

"There is something you should know about me . . . and that is I'm pretty much free to go wherever I want, whenever I want."

"Sounds blissful," Ava sighed.

"Well, in theory yes, but at the moment there isn't much work about so it's not as glam as it sounds but I'm very good at making it sound glam. In fact, I'm pitching an article just now about being single in the city. Lucky me – the pick of all the Belfast men!"

Ava laughed. "Well, you never know, you might meet a hunky Frenchman."

"*Oooh la la!*"

"Right, so if we say the first week in July? I'll get on to Mr Gilard about making the arrangements his end and I've flights in front of me here. They're quite reasonable for school holidays."

"Great, sounds good. Are you happy enough making the arrangements? Is there anything I can do?"

"Hope, believe me, if there is something you should know about me it's that I love making plans. It's one of my special skills. Right up there with not wanting to shoot myself in the head when I read *The Gruffalo* for the two-thousandth time and being able to do French plaits in the hair of a very wriggly two-and-a-half-year-old."

"Impressive. I can't even do French plaits in the hair of a non-wriggling thirty-four-year-old," Hope responded.

"I'll do yours for you if you're really desperate!" Ava laughed.

"Grand. We'll do that with the wine and the tale of my sorry life."

"It's a deal. Right, this Mr Gilard. Did you meet him when you were in France – what was he like?"

"Hmmm, I don't think we met him. But I'm sure he's fine. Betty's friends were all lovely – very French and arty and a bit mad, but lovely. They made us feel welcome. I'm sure if Betty had Mr Gilard in her company he'll be lovely too."

"Oooh, do you think they might have been lovers?" Ava said, her gossip radar tingling.

"No," Hope replied. "No, I don't think she could ever have loved anyone but Claude. He was her best friend."

Hanging up the phone, with Ava in raptures at making the necessary arrangements, Hope sat back and looked around her at her living room which looked like the entire contents of the Castlecourt Shopping Centre had exploded all over it.

It was clear Cyndi with a Y and an I was having a very positive effect on Dylan and his personal grooming. He had been up first thing that morning, even though it was a Saturday and he had even presented her with a bacon sandwich – cooked by his very own hands – before declaring he'd had a brilliant night with Cyndi. The smile on his face was so wide, she had been mildly concerned he would launch into a verse of 'I Could Have Danced All Night'.

"It went well then?" she asked as he climbed into bed beside her and offered her a mug of milky tea.

"It went very well. Very well indeed. She's something else, Hope. Something else indeed."

Hope smiled and washed down the sandwich which was sticking in her throat with some tea.

"Do you fancy coming shopping with me today?" he said. "I want a few new things."

Jesus. This was serious. He was up early *and* he wanted to go shopping – a mere two days after he had dragged her round the shops for a new suit. Cyndi must be some girl.

"Yes," she had nodded. "Of course I will."

"I'll treat you to a coffee in Starbucks."

"You are just too kind," she had mocked.

"Yes, I know. I spoil you," he said, kissing her lightly on the cheek and jumping out of bed. "I'm going to get a quick shower. Do you think we could be ready to go in, say, half an hour?"

Inwardly, Hope groaned. Her head was still thumping from the over-indulgence of red wine and bad 80s rock music from the night before – but she would get up anyway and go and be a saddo and let people think they were a couple for a while as they traipsed the shops together.

It had been a long day and now, looking at all he had bought, she was exhausted.

Amongst his haul had been at least four different brands of Lynx deodorant and he had swapped his manky tub of Brylcreem for a host of waxes, gels, foams and sprays. A bulging carrier bag from NEXT spilled a host of new pairs of boxers and socks onto the sofa, which would ensure he had a fresh pair every day of the week without having to go anywhere near the washing machine.

"Hey there, Mr Fancy Pants," she said as he walked back in and sat down, handing her a mug of tea.

Blushing slightly, he sipped from his mug and laughed. "You're one to talk. Don't think I haven't noticed your collection of fancy knickers hanging on the radiators in the bathroom."

Hope felt herself blush at the very thought that he had been looking at her knickers even though they hadn't been on her body at that time and it was very obvious that at some stage in their years of living together he would have encountered them drying on the heaters.

"Yes, but I always wear fancy pants," she countered, "not just when I'm trying to get my end away with a blondey from work."

"Nothing wrong with a man making a bit of an effort, Hope. Don't deny you would feel much more inclined to get rough and ready with a man if his socks and jocks were fresh as a daisy."

"I tend not to sniff either of those areas much, but I get your point," she said, with a smile, trying not to think about his socks and even less about his jocks. "So when will you see her again anyway?"

"Well, I'm on day shift this week, so, basically tomorrow night. We're going out for dinner."

"I'm surprised you have any money left for dinner!" Hope teased, looking at the Debenham's bag bulging with another designer suit, not to mention the new shoes and the new glasses he had absolutely insisted on getting. "Will your budget be more Pizza Hut this time then?"

"Ha ha, very funny. I was thinking more along the lines of the McDonald's Drive-Thru or bringing her back here for one of your bacon sandwiches."

"You'd be lucky, McKenzie. My bacon sandwiches are not for general consumption and if you do bring her back here in the hope of getting one in the morning then you'd better make sure you keep the noise down. There are things I don't need to hear and you doing the horizontal hokey-cokey with Cyndi is one of them." She said it light-heartedly and she maintained the smile on her face but inside she felt her stomach twist at the very notion of hearing him in bed with anyone but her.

"We'll keep it down, Mammy," he teased, sitting back and sipping from his tea. "Thanks for today anyway, Hopeful," he said. "It was nice to get some time with you."

"Yes," she nodded, thinking just how much she had enjoyed it.

"What are your plans for the week ahead anyway? Apart from plotting your big getaway to France? Have you much work on? Any pitches in? Any plots to write a mega-selling bestseller?"

"Not much," she said, "Just pitching a few articles and, yes, I might start writing that bestseller. I'm thinking of something about a sarcastic and narcissistic housemate who is found stabbed to death in his bed with a frozen bacon sandwich or something . . ."

"I'll be locking my bedroom door then," he said.

"Sleep with one eye open, McKenzie," she teased before they sat down to watch a movie together – which was only interrupted twenty-six times by text messages pinging on his phone which, by the smile on his face, she assumed were from Cyndi.

Jean-Luc Gilard sounded like a very lovely man indeed. He had sounded delighted to hear from Ava and even happier to hear that she and Hope would be travelling over to France to put Betty's affairs finally in order.

"She was a lovely woman," he said. "A great friend to so many of us."

He had such a genuine affection for Betty that Ava immediately felt comfortable talking to him. At the same time she felt embarrassed that she hadn't really known this woman he thought so much of.

"Did she have a good send-off?" she asked. "Were you there?"

"It was a very fitting goodbye," he said. "And yes, we were there. Her friends. It was just as she wanted it. We wore bright colours. We sang Beatles songs. It was all very Betty."

"That's nice to know," Ava said. "We feel bad for not being there. If we had known . . ."

"Your aunt was a very determined lady. She wanted no fuss – but I will take you to say your final goodbyes when you come over, if that helps?"

"It helps," Ava said. "It definitely helps."

"So," he said, "when are you coming over?"

"We thought the first week in July. I am just about to book flights now. Betty said you would be there to help us."

"I will," Jean-Luc said. "Anything you need while you are here, you just call me. You will be staying at your aunt's house? There is ample accommodation."

"Yes, yes, I think so."

"I will make sure everything is in order. Would you like me to pick you up from the airport?"

"Actually, I think we will be getting a rental car. That way we won't have to trouble you too much."

"It is no trouble," he said. "Let me know if you change your mind."

"I will."

Ava hung up after agreeing to forward their arrival details by email and he promised to stay in touch. She lifted two cold beers from the fridge and walked to the decking where Connor was soaking up the last of the evening sun while Maisie played in her sandpit.

"So when are you leaving me then?" he asked.

"First week in July, we think. I just spoke to Mr Gilard and he is going help us out."

"Oh," Connor said in mock offence, "you've not even left and you've got yourself a fancy man already!"

"Who is probably pushing sixty and sporting a fine line in sensible shoes and dentures," Ava laughed before reaching out to kiss her husband. "I think you'll still be my first preference."

"Thanks," he smiled, kissing her back and pulling her onto his knees where they kissed again.

"Mammy, Daddy! Stop kissing!" Maisie shouted before clambering up on her parents and hugging them. "Let me in!" she shouted, burrowing her face in her mother's chest.

Ava hugged her close, before turning to Connor and telling him, clearly and with conviction: "I'll definitely be coming back. You can rely on that."

She loved him. She loved everything about him – the smoothness of his hands, the soft touch of his lips, the strength in his arms and as soon as Maisie was in bed she walked back to the kitchen where he was now making a light supper, locking the door behind her.

"I want to pick up where we left off," she said, kissing him gently and then kissing him harder. She pulled him closer to her, not wanting to let go until she felt dizzy with it all. And now there was no chance an almost-three-year-old girl could walk in to catch them, she decided there was no better time than the present to just go for it there and then on the kitchen tiles.

He was just as breathless when they pulled apart. "What did I do to deserve that?" he said with a dazed smile.

"You were just you," she said, cringing at the cheesiness of the line while aware that she was speaking the God's honest truth.

Chapter 7

The second letter from Betty arrived, by registered post, more than a week after Ava and Hope had sat side by side in Mr Semple's office.

It hadn't been the best of days for Hope. She had been out and about, pounding the streets and trying to come up with some story ideas without any luck. In fact, the day had been pretty shite. The heel of one of her more expensive pair of Office shoes had snapped off outside City Hall and when she had gone to the ATM to get some money out for a coffee and a new pair of pumps it had almost laughed at her.

She had hobbled away, red-faced, and made it round to Primark where she picked up a pair of flip-flops which so didn't suit her besuited appearance but were within her limited budget, and made her way to the bus stop to queue for a bone-rattler of a bus back home.

Dylan was on night shift again so she consoled herself with the notion that she could at least go home and be gloriously miserable all on her own. Sighing, she realised she didn't even have enough spare change on her for a king-size bar of Galaxy and a bottle of plonk. Sure, she had money coming into her account the next day but the next day might as well have been next year as far she was concerned.

She could have asked her parents for money, she supposed – her mum worked in Derry City Centre and could have popped out to deposit money into her bank account, no problem – but she was a grown woman and surely to God she should be standing on her own two feet by now?

She was feeling very sorry for herself – and the feet were rubbed off her by the cheap flip-flops – by the time she pushed open the door to her terraced house, collapsed onto the sofa and switched on the TV.

She looked at her laptop and swore. There was no point in switching it on. She wasn't in the mood. She would likely only go on Facebook or Twitter and moan about her life and she was pretty sure everyone was sick of her moaning by now.

Slipping her feet out of the offensive flip-flops and kicking them across the room, she stood up and stalked to the kitchen where she raided the cupboards for chocolate. Dylan always kept a secret stash and she prayed he wouldn't let her down now.

Her heart soared as she found a Wispa in the back of his cupboard and she had inhaled half of it without really tasting it. She stood back, blew her fringe from her face and kicked the cupboard in frustration – of course, having forgotten that she had taken her shoes off.

"Oh for the love of the Wee Baby Jesus!" she swore, grabbing her toes and fighting back tears. "*Ow, ow, ow, ow!*" Could this day actually get any worse?

She had hobbled to the counter to grab a square of kitchen roll to mop her tears when she turned to find Dylan, his eyes still heavy with sleep, staring at her.

"Are you okay?" he asked.

"Shit. Did I wake you? I'm sorry."

"Not to worry. I should have been getting up for work anyway. Anyway, as I said, are you okay?"

She felt a bit childish crying over it, but she knew of all the people in her life Dylan was the one she could be childish in front of and not worry he would use it against her in the future.

"My shoe broke. The bank machine wouldn't give me any money. There are no freelance jobs in this shitey city and I stubbed my fecking toe!" She just managed to get the word 'toe' out before dissolving into body-shaking sobs.

Dylan just looked at her, tilting his head to one side and smiling slightly before pulling her into a bear hug. She buried her head into his chest and revelled in having his warm, downy chest-hair rest against her cheek. Oh, she couldn't tell him – there was no way she could finish her list of woes by adding 'And I love you' to it. It would be completely inappropriate and given that he was quickly falling madly in love with someone else it was unlikely to improve the way her day was going.

He kissed the top of her head and pulled her a little closer before speaking.

"Hope," he said and she looked up at his dark eyes. "Have you eaten my Wispa?"

Dylan had forgiven her indiscretions. He had even gone out and bought her a bottle of wine and the aforementioned Galaxy King Size. Before he had gone to work he had poured her a glass and put a blanket over her legs as she lay on the sofa, her toe still throbbing from the impact with the cupboard door. He had placed her laptop within her reach and switched it on – on strict orders she wasn't even to think about work – and he had kissed her gently on the forehead before picking up his coat, phone and wallet and heading for the door.

"Chin up. It's going to get better. Your toe and your work. Until then, we have chocolate!"

Hope nodded gratefully and blew him a kiss as he winked at her and left the room.

Once again the thought crossed her mind: "I must not think about Dylan McKenzie in that way."

She was just closing her eyes to try and embed that particular affirmation in her head when Dylan walked back in.

"Oh," he said. "I almost forgot. This came for you earlier."

He handed her a slim white envelope and she looked down and was surprised to see Betty's handwriting staring up at her. Ripping it open, she began to read and she could almost hear her aunt's lilting tones – with the tiniest twang of a French accent – as she scanned the page.

My dear girls,

I bet you weren't expecting this – but as you know I liked to be different. I liked to surprise people.

If you are receiving this letter then you have decided to come over to France to fulfil my last wishes. I can't tell you how happy that makes me (actually I don't know how happy it makes me because I'm dead . . . but as an alive person writing this, it makes me happy to think you will come here).

I wanted to let you know that even though I won't be there with you in body, I will be there with you in spirit. But not in a scary ghost kind of way. I'll just, well, I hope, I'll be watching over you.

I have very special reasons for asking you to go to France – which will become clear in time. You will get a few more letters and these will help make it clearer when you are there.

I hope I haven't left the house in too much of a mess. It has been a while since I was there – there came a time when I just had to go into the Hospice where they would look after me. I have missed it – so when you go there can you stand on the terrace and raise a glass to me? Jean-Luc has left you a choice bottle of wine for just this purpose. Feel free to raise as many glasses as it takes to empty it.

Raise a glass to Claude too. You would have liked him. He was the love of my life. I know some people thought I was mad to up sticks and move away from all I knew at home to be with him . . . but I had no choice. It was a tough decision. The toughest decision I have ever had to make – and not without complications. Leaving home, leaving my family . . . it was hard. Walking away when things were how they were. Knowing what I was leaving behind. It was so hard. But I had to make a life for myself.

Anyway, tell everyone back home I said hello. Tell them I was happy, that I have regretted very little about my life – that what I have regretted, I still know was for the best. Tell them that I trust you both implicitly to take care of my affairs. Ava, tell your mum I love her. Hope, tell your father, stubborn and all as he is, that it's all okay.

And when you raise your glass to me on my terrace, remember that sometimes you have to take risks to find yourself. Sometimes, the unthinkable becomes the right answer. I hope that doesn't sound too pretentious.

With much love to you, my darling girls,
Betty
xx

She held the letter to her and found, surprisingly, that her eyes were wet and that the predominant thought in her mind was that somewhere she had lost herself and maybe she needed to be brave. And in that moment that hurt more than whatever Dylan was getting up to.

Ava had not been expecting to hear from her aunt again and when she had come in from work with a tired and over-emotional child in tow, she had been shocked to see the familiar handwriting on the front of the letter sitting on her hall table. She sat Maisie in front of the TV with her favourite programme and her favourite teddy while she walked to the kitchen and sat at the island with a cup of tea, to read.

There was no doubt Betty was a character – that was evident. Ava wondered what her very special reason was for inviting them to France – and she looked forward, with a certain trepidation, to finding out. The letter had left her feeling warm and fuzzy. The love that Betty had for Claude was evident. The confidence she had in her decision was even more so – but most of all Ava took comfort from the fact that at one stage Betty too felt as if she had lost herself. Suddenly she felt less alone.

With the letter in her hand she lifted the phone to call Hope, sure that she would have received the same note.

As soon as Hope answered Ava could tell something wasn't quite right. She sounded subdued – and, from what little Ava knew of her cousin, she knew this was not how things normally played out.

"Are you okay?" she asked and she heard Hope sniff.

"It's part of that long sad story I said I would tell you about in France because, to be honest, your phone bill would be astronomical if I started wittering on about it just now. And, anyway, as previously discussed, wine will make it better."

Ava felt herself warm a little bit more to her cousin – and to the notion of a girly chat in France. She sensed she would be able to confide a little in Hope – in a way that she couldn't confide in Karen or even Connor.

Naturally when it came to Connor, there were times when she wanted to vent about him – which he generally didn't appreciate listening to. And when it came to Karen, she had that magical ability that some women have of turning each and every topic of conversation back to herself and her own experiences.

It was one of those things which disappointed her most about her life. She had always thought that once she became a mum herself she would easily make some brand-new friends for life. She was one of the first of her friends – such as they were – to become a mum and she had desperately wanted a mummy friend to pal around with. So she had padded out to every parent-and-toddler group going in the hope of meeting a kindred spirit. Instead she had met Karen who had been sipping tea while a two-year-old Sophie held court in the play kitchen. At first she had found Karen, with her acerbic wit, a breath of fresh air – but as time passed she realised Karen was a deeply flawed and deeply unhappy person and the absolute last person she could confide in when she needed a listening ear.

"How are you, anyway?" Hope said, cutting through her thoughts. "Never mind me and my Very Sad Story. I guess you got the letter from Betty? Jeez, I wasn't expecting that!"

"Nor was I," Ava said, glancing down again. "Although I'm very much looking forward to the prospect of toasting on the terrace."

"Ah! The terrace! I could die happy on that terrace. I mean, you know, hopefully I won't because that would make for a pretty shite break for you but, Ava, it's amazing. So beautiful that the whole world could just disappear there and then and you wouldn't care. It's a wee piece of heaven on earth."

Ava was relieved to hear that Hope's voice had been transformed from sounding slightly anxious and edgy to having a gorgeous, dream-like quality.

Then a fizzle of excitement shot through Ava. It was delicious and felt a little naughty but she didn't want to try and batten it down – not one bit – and, looking at the calendar on the wall, she suddenly wished the next two weeks would whizz past and the end of term would have been and gone and she could be there feeling the warm sun of the Provence sunshine beating down on her face.

"Oh, you make it sound so nice."

"Believe me," Hope replied, "I'm not doing it justice."

Chapter 8

"We're going to go shopping today, Maisie Moo," Ava declared happily as she struggled to get the wriggling octopus her child was doing a very good impression of into her jacket.

"I don't wanna go shoppin'," Maisie huffed. "I wanna play with my fwiends." Her lisp was cute and the protruding bottom lip verging on adorable but Ava knew she had to play this carefully. The cute and the adorable could very easily turn into a full-on screaming tantrum quite easily.

"She can stay with me if you want," Connor offered, his eyes drooping with sleep and his face begging her silently not to say yes. He needed his Saturday morning lie-in more than anything, what with the commute he had been putting in every weekday for the last six months.

Occasionally Ava had thoughts that maybe, just maybe, she was exhausted too and needed a break herself. After all, when Connor was away from the wee small hours it was she who had to get up, get Maisie sorted and get the house in order before they hit the rush-hour traffic.

Evenings were a blur of being a mammy while trying to prepare for another day in the classroom and yet when Connor practically fell through the door with exhaustion each evening she still found herself fussing round him like a mother hen.

She was worried, so worried, that he would end up so exhausted he would drive himself off the side of the road on the Glenshane Pass one evening coming home, and she put to the back of her mind the times when she wished she could just close her eyes for ten wee seconds as she drove over the Foyle Bridge each night on her way home.

"No. We'll be grand," she said, kissing Connor on the cheek. "Sure isn't this what mammies and their daughters do? Go for shopping trips? Besides, I really do need to get some new things before my trip to France."

He nodded gratefully and she knew that before her car had reached the bottom of the drive his head would be on his pillow and an unattractive puddle of drool would be starting to form.

Maisie was fidgety by the time they reached Dunnes Stores and stood, hopping impatiently from foot to foot, while Ava riffled through a rail of linen trousers looking for something light, airy and South-of-France-y-looking.

"Can we go to McDonald's, Mammy?" Maisie chirped.

"It's only ten in the morning, sweetie, but maybe if you are good girl we can go for lunch."

"Okay," she sing-songed. "Can we go to the shoe shop, Mammy?"

"In a wee bit, darling. Let's just finish here."

"Okay," she sing-songed a little less cheerfully. She reached her chubby hand to a display of folded T-shirts and pulled one towards her which started an avalanche of coloured cotton. "Ooops, Mammy," she muttered, her bottom lip wavering.

"It's okay, darling," Ava soothed her while feeling her own cheeks start to burn. "Let's just fold them up and it will be fine."

"I wanna go the bookshop," Maisie replied, turning on her heel and heading for the exit.

"Maisie!" Ava called, trying to maintain her composure. It was amazing. She could be cool as a cucumber in a classroom of two dozen four and five-year-olds, but one half hour in the city centre with her own child had her wishing Prozac was sold over the counter.

Hastily folding the T-shirts and running after Maisie, she caught up with her just in time for her daughter to declare she had to go to the toilet as she jigged up and down and grabbed at her crotch.

Having raced her to the toilets before the day was lost entirely, Ava stood over her daughter as she declared she didn't have to go after all and tried to remember what life was like before she was a mother. Christ, how she would have loved to have just one of those days again! Waking up after a lazy lie-in beside Connor. Having a bit of morning sex before enjoying a cooked breakfast together. Showering at her leisure. Driving to town without a soundtrack of nursery rhymes blasting in her ears before mooching around the shops. And she could go to the good shops – the shops where she didn't go any more for fear of a sticky hand leaving a mark on a rich wool blend. Shops which sold nice lingerie and expensive bags, not functional mammy knickers which hid her stretch-marks and Peppa Pig rucksacks for storing tiny plastic tiaras and dressing-up shoes.

It was best she gave up on the idea of a nice wander around the shops. She would call and see her mother instead. In fact if God was good to her, her mother might just offer to mind Maisie for a couple of hours and she could come back to the shopping centre all alone. Oh, it would be bliss!

"C'mon, Moo Moo!" she called to Maisie who was fascinated with the automatic taps in the washroom. "Let's go and see Granny."

"And get a McDonald's!" her daughter cheeped as if that was the natural end to any sentence.

Ava's mammy was one of those naturally maternal kind of women who children swarm to. If she had wanted to, she could have got a cracking job as the Pied Piper of Derry. When Ava and Maisie arrived at her house, Cora appeared in a haze of home-baking smells and Miss Dior perfume, smiling beatifically as her granddaughter ran into her arms.

"Granny!" Maisie squealed as Cora swept her through to the kitchen and handed her a toddler-sized apron.

"We have buns to ice and I might just have some Rice Krispies which need covering in chocolate."

Ava watched as her daughter's eyes lit up like headlamps at the promise of icing and chocolate and no doubt Smarties. All thoughts of McDonald's were gone. Ava kind of wished she was a child again and could slip on an apron and join in the fun herself. Her mother always had been mad for the home baking. She was the quintessentially wonderful stay-at-home uber-mum who had a fresh cooked meal on the table each night and who kept a perfect house. Needless to say, Ava's skills didn't stretch quite as far and after a long day at work a couple of fishfingers served with a side order of potato waffles were about as much as she could manage.

"Well, darling," Cora said, as she emptied her baking cupboard of icing sugar and cooking chocolate, "how are you? Is France a goer?"

"Yes," Ava said excitedly, taking a seat by the kitchen window and watching her mother deftly set to work without needing to measure anything or even look down. "Ten days' time. I was just trying to do a bit of shopping there when madam threw one of her hissy fits."

"Well," Cora said, gently ruffling her granddaughter's hair, "the town isn't very exciting for a wee one, is it?"

Maisie shook her head diligently. "S'not, Granny. S'not."

"Well, I have to get my messages done some time," Ava sniffed. "And it's hard, you know."

Cora smiled at her daughter and at Maisie who was gazing wide-eyed into a bowl of melted chocolate. "You modern mammies. You want it all."

"I don't," Ava found herself saying. "I don't want it all. I just want my job and my wee girl and some sense of who I am and not to feel torn in half between all of those."

"There's many a woman who would be grateful for all you have. A great job and a gorgeous wee woman here. I don't know why you tie yourself up in knots over it."

Ava nodded but she wished her mother understood. Then again, how could she? She never worked when Ava was little. She never knew the pressures. She wasn't one of the generation who had been promised they could have it all.

Ava felt the guilt of not being happy with what she had crush down on her again.

"I know, Mum," she said and resisted the urge to follow that with 'but sometimes'. She knew there were times when 'but sometimes' didn't cut it.

Cora looked at her again, and then walked towards her. Ava let her mother envelop her in a big hug, closing her eyes and breathing in her familiar scent.

"My darling, you work too hard and you try too hard. I worry about you. I know I said you should go to France – but do you feel up for it?" She pulled back and studied her daughter. "No, of course you feel up for it. It will do you good. Why don't you head back into town and get what you need and I'll mind this little one. And then when you are done you'll be in better form to look after her again."

Ava nodded before kissing her daughter on the top of her head and heading back into town, feeling deliciously free. She would even stop at Starbucks first and drink a big old latte without having to splash out on some chocolatey creation for Maisie who would inevitably throw it all over herself before she was halfway through it. She would worry about her brownie points as a mummy later. And she would worry about whether or not her mother thought she was cutting it in the parenthood stakes later too.

She was just allowing the warm milky coffee to warm her from the inside out when her phone rang and she lifted it.

"Ava, where were you this morning? We missed you!" Karen breathed.

"I'm in town," Ava answered. "I have to get a few things for my trip to France."

"You booked it then? You lucky thing!" Karen squealed. "What are you buying? Please tell me you are buying lovely pretty things and not boring things like suncream and mosquito repellent."

"I'm shopping for pretty things. And even better, I'm on my own."

She heard Karen take a deep breath and she braced herself for a squeal.

"You lucky, lucky thing! Actually why don't you just wait there and I'll foist Sophie off on her daddy and we can shop together. Oh Jesus, the thought of it! Proper grown-up shopping that doesn't involve Toys 'R' Us or the Early Learning Centre!"

Ava looked at her watch. "I'm kind of on the clock here. My mum has Maisie."

"Sure your mum loves the bones of Maisie. How about we meet in thirty minutes at Clarins' counter in Debenhams. See you then, bye!"

Ava wasn't sure which was more difficult: shopping with Maisie or shopping with Karen. While Maisie could put on that droning whine to go somewhere more exciting like the toy shop or the food court, Karen was a like a magpie drawn towards shiny objects which she would *ooh* and *aah* over while Ava tried to direct her towards the swimwear section or the sunhat section.

"Oh my God, look at this!" Karen declared, trying on a glittering bangle. "Oh, this is lovely! I could go for something like this. Shall I?"

Ava glanced at her watch and back at the bangle, vaguely aware she might well be coming across as rude but counting down in her head to when she needed to be back to get her daughter and get home to her husband so they could at least give this quality time thing a go.

"Would you calm down!" Karen chided, catching Ava's glance. "Your family will be fine without you. You really need to learn to relax more. Let yourself go a bit. Jesus, you can't spend your whole life walking around like you have a stick up your arse. You are out – on your own – enjoy it!"

It shocked Ava to the core to feel tears spring to her eyes. I must not cry, she whispered internally before readjusting her features to plaster on a big fake smile. "You're right," she lied, because in truth she was too scared to argue with Karen. Karen looked like the kind of person who could take on anyone in a fight – and wouldn't need much persuasion to do so.

So Ava stood, while Karen added a shiny ring and a necklace to her haul and waited patiently until they finally headed towards the swimsuit section.

Karen was like a whirlwind when it came to shopping. As Ava contemplated a very sensible one-piece, Karen pushed her aside. "Ava, pet, live a little!"

All Ava could think of was the map of stretch-marks curving up her stomach and she had no desire to live a little – not when it came to swimwear anyway.

Karen handed her a piece of dental floss masquerading as a bikini and grinned. "How about this little number?"

"Erm, no. Not with my stomach," Ava said, feeling herself blush as if she was letting Karen down in some way by concerning herself with matters as trivial as stomach scars.

"Oh God, don't talk to me," Karen said, hanging the bikini back on the rack. "Mine are awful. Not to mention that Caesarean scar I was left with. I tell you, never again! Not for anyone!" She lifted the all-in-one swimsuit and handed it back to Ava." Maybe this *would* be better."

Ava nodded dutifully and went and paid for her purchase, feeling like a big, fat, mammy frump.

She really needed to cut Karen out of her life – and fast. Then again she felt sorry for her. Beneath all that bravado and utter bitchiness, there was clearly a woman who was desperately unhappy with how her life had turned out.

"Drinks!" Karen declared loudly, causing a few fellow shoppers to spin round in surprise. "We should go for drinks. No kids. No husbands. No worries. Drinky poos!"

Yes, shopping with Maisie was infinitely easier.

Karen seemed more palatable after three glasses of wine. In fact, she even seemed fun. Maybe Ava had been walking around with "a stick up her arse" this whole time as her friend had claimed.

After three glasses of wine Ava even found herself feeling a pang of affection for her friend who was swirling the wine around in the bottom of her glass and declaring that this was the best damn Saturday afternoon she'd had in years.

"God, this is great. And you know what, Charlie can just look after Sophie all evening. I might even stay out. Should we stay out? I mean, c'mon, we don't often get the chance. You have work. I have the joys of being a stay-at-home mammy and domestic slave – we deserve it."

Ava thought of just how much of a domestic slave Karen was. Sure she didn't work – because she hadn't much wanted to and Charlie very much wanted to have her at home caring for Sophie. But he didn't expect her to be a slave. She had a cleaner three times a week. Ava would kill to have a cleaner in three times a year. But still, Karen was clearly unhappy.

Yet, there was no way Ava could stay out later. The three glasses of wine had knocked her three sheets to the wind. Any more and she would be in danger of reaching the ungainly stage of drunk where she would start to sing loudly, dance in public and tell taxi-drivers she loved them.

"I'm sorry," she said, shrugging her shoulders. "I'm a lightweight."

"You're a boring lightweight!" Karen snapped back with a strange smile on her face which made Ava really confused about whether or not she was being insulted or whether Karen was just being *funny*. She tried to shrug it off, and even changed the topic of conversation to Lady Gaga, who in all honesty she knew very little about but figured was a trendy conversation topic, but her mind kept screaming "boring" over and over again.

"Am I really very, very boring?" she asked eventually, staring into the bottom of her glass which she had decided absolutely and categorically she was not refilling. Her car would have to sit abandoned in the multi-storey car-park at this rate which would cost a fortune and her mother and Connor would be less than impressed with her sailing home three sheets to the wind. So no, even though the wine tasted very, very nice indeed, she would not have any more.

"No, darling," Karen purred, as she topped up her own glass – clearly without the same reservations Ava had. "But you do need to loosen up a bit."

Ava looked at her wineglass and tried, and failed, to block out the voice that was telling her that she really didn't want to loosen up all that much – not as much as Karen had anyway – and drained the last drops.

"I need to go home," she said, gathering her one bag with the very sensible probably-designed-for-pensioners swimming suit in it.

"Come on, stay!" Karen chimed, waving the open bottle of wine at her.

"No. I need to go home. Maisie will be wondering where I am."

"Maisie will be fine with *CBeebies* and a colouring book. You let her run your life!" Karen said, her eyes tightening.

Something in that second snapped inside Ava – which she realised was more than likely down to the glasses of wine loosening her tongue.

"She's two. She *should* run my life. At least I care about her – which is much more than can be said of you and wee Sophie. Do you even realise you have a daughter half the time, Karen? You act like she's the biggest inconvenience in the world to you when she should be your everything!"

"At least I'm fucking honest!" Karen spat back. "I don't wander around like a big martyr being Supermammy and moaning about it after. Don't think you're any better than me, Ava. You are so *not*."

With that Karen picked up her bags and stormed passed Ava, leaving her red-faced and humiliated, and feeling utterly ashamed as she made her way through the gawping afternoon drinkers to the taxi stand.

Well, that was fucking disaster of a day, she thought to herself as she climbed into the back of a taxi and got ready to face her mother, Connor, Maisie and her own conscience.

Chapter 9

Cyndi with a Y and an I was actually quite nice. Hope had finally come face to face, or more accurately face to shoulder with her arch nemesis just after ten thirty on Saturday night.

As she was packing away her laptop and disposing of the empty (family) bag of Maltesers, the door opened and she was startled by a loud, shrieking laugh followed by Dylan's chuckle.

Hope had frozen in the kitchen, aware that she was wearing her fluffiest, least attractive pyjamas and that her hair was scraped into a high ponytail on top of her head and in desperate need of a wash. Oh fuck it, she cursed under her breath, stashing the empty Maltesers bag at the bottom of the bin and hauling the scrunchie out of her hair in a desperate attempt to look at least half-human.

With the only route upstairs being through the living room, she had no choice but to plaster on her best smile and pretend to be absolutely delighted to finally meet Cyndi.

As she walked into the living room they were standing looking like the oddest couple – her tiny compared to Dylan's large frame. Her head barely reached his chest and he looked awkward – but disgustingly, deliriously happy – as he bent down to kiss her. Hope thought of how she and Dylan fitted together, her head resting on the top of his chest, his hands caressing the small of her back. They didn't look ridiculous together. They looked perfect. No, she reminded herself as she felt her smile slip. She must not come across as the psycho, bunny-boiling housemate. She must play this straight. Absolutely straight.

"You must be Cyndi," she said, extending her arm for a handshake.

"Jesus! Are you Hope? Am I meeting the famous Hope?" Cyndi squealed in excitement. "I'm not shaking your hand, girl. C'mere for a hug!"

As Cyndi's face came into direct contact with Hope's chest, Hope thought no. Definitely no. Cyndi does not fit at all. But she was nice, and friendly and complimented Hope's hair (even though it was a state) and told she had done a great job of keeping Dylan in check. They had laughed together at that and Hope had felt herself warm to her a teeny bit. Not enough not to want her to disappear off the planet, mind – but a little bit.

Hope had to admit she could see a bit of what appealed to Dylan. But later, as she tried to ignore the fact that she screamed like a banshee when she orgasmed, she felt her heart sink. Hope had tried not to listen. She had tried not to hear. She had stuffed her pillow over her head and put her iPod speakers in her ears but she could still hear Cyndi reach her glorious climax calling Dylan McKenzie's name in a strong Ballymena accent.

Hope's cheeks burned and her stomach flipped. She felt embarrassed, flustered and jealous. She'd been intimate with Dylan herself – just the once – a very long time ago, but she could still remember just how good it had been. And just to remind her, she'd had to listen to a chorus of women call out his name in pleasure over the years. Fourteen years of friendship had brought a lot of relationships in and out of their lives and he had undergone a minor tart phase when they were on their travels. It never bothered her before – in fact, she used to rib him mercilessly about it, asking him to "stop murderin' them poor women" and threatening to tell his mother about his wicked ways.

It bothered her now though – and not just because Cyndi had

the audacity to be both really quite good-looking and rather nice to boot. She didn't need to hear Dylan do the deed because it did absolutely nothing – nothing at all – for her bid not to think about him in that way.

When the moaning and groaning subsided, Hope breathed a sigh of relief, praying that there would not be a round two to contend with and she started to drift off to sleep.

It was the slamming of the front door which woke her and as she sat up, wiping the drool from her cheek and trying to get her bearings in the dark, she felt her heart thump as her bedroom door opened.

Feck. Not only had she had the shitest night ever – listening to Dylan hump his way into the loudest orgasm in history record books – now she was about to be murdered in her bed by a complete stranger. She opened her mouth to scream, and lifted the lamp by her bed to use as a weapon but stopped mid-yell when she saw a bleary-eyed Dylan walk into her room and climb into the bed beside her.

"Cyndi had to go home," he said, "so you can be my post-bonk snuggle if you don't mind."

Hope suddenly realised that being murdered in her bed was perhaps not the worst thing that could have happened to her that night.

The good news was that she wasn't needed for a post-bonk snuggle the following night. The bad news was that was because the shagging went on all night.

"Well, we needed to take advantage of our last night before we went back on night shift," Dylan had smiled and winked at Hope when he emerged from his bedroom the following day with the glow of a wee, shagged man about him.

"But, Dylan, there are some things that I just don't need to hear."

"Ah, you don't mind," he teased. "But tell me this – did she sound like she was enjoying herself?"

Hope felt herself cringe, right from the bottom of her stomach through the tips of her hair. "Jesus, Dylan. There is a line in our friendship and you have just crossed it. In fact, you are so far over it, I don't think you could still see it if you tried."

"I was just asking," Dylan said, as he made two mugs of tea – neither of which was for Hope, "because I'm feeling this is something different."

"Yes, yes . . . I gathered that from, you know, the fact that you talk about her non-stop and want to spend every waking moment with her." Hope hoped that she hadn't sounded bitter and twisted when she said that, but she had a notion there was more than a hint of the "feck you, then" about her statement.

"She might be the one," he said, staring dreamily out of the window.

Hope nodded, sitting down at the table and trying to pretend this conversation wasn't happening.

"Do you like her?" he asked, leaving the mugs on the worktop and turning to face his friend. She couldn't help but stare at him, dressed in just jeans, her eyes immediately drawn to the fine line of hair which ran from his bellybutton to his . . .

"Well, do you?" Dylan asked, jolting her from the hot flush which was threatening to surge through her body.

"She seems lovely," Hope said. "Loud – but lovely." She decided to spare him her thoughts on whether or not their bodies moulded together the way bodies should, in her mind, mould together. She didn't think he would get that whole 'not part of the jigsaw puzzle' thing – and, besides, she would have to tell him who she thought was the perfect fit.

Dylan sat down across the table from her and lifted the flier for the local Chinese which she had picked up from the doormat earlier.

"Your tea will go cold," she offered.

"It will be grand," he said, putting the flier down and staring ahead of him before picking it up again.

She couldn't quite put her finger on it, but something was definitely up.

He was fidgeting and unsettled and showing an unhealthy obsession with chicken curry specials. He sighed, putting the flier back on the table again and looked at her. "I need to talk to you, Hope, and the thing is I don't know what way you might react."

She plastered on her best sympathetic face, ready to be there for him.

"The thing is, Cyndi and I, well . . . we want to spend more time together."

"Well, of course you do," she said. "Sure you're in that first flush where you want to spend every moment together. You know, that blissful stage where you don't realise just how much you rag the holy shite out of each other?"

He laughed and she smiled. And then he smiled and she laughed. Then he stopped laughing and smiling and reached out to take her hand. She stopped laughing and smiling too.

"And I was wondering, if you would mind if she, well, moved in. We don't want you to move out or anything but, you know, we work strange hours and living together would make this workable. And it would help with the rent – Lord knows we could do with the help. She works shifts too so she shouldn't get under your feet –"

"But you've only been together five minutes!" she blurted out before she could stop herself.

"We've known each other much longer," he said. "And sometimes when you know, you know . . ."

"Two weeks," Hope muttered.

"We've known each other for months."

She wanted to shout "But *we've* known each other for years. *Years*!" But once again she thought this might just be crossing into bunny-boiling, psycho-housemate territory.

Dylan prattled on but Hope could not hear what he was saying any more. She was too busy imagining the creak of the bed while she tried to work, and the screaming orgasms as she tried to interview her latest source. She was already imagining Cyndi making him his bacon sarnies in the morning while her services became surplus to requirements. She was already imagining Cyndi going back to the McKenzies' Lisburn home each Sunday for dinner while she was left eating a Pot Noodle all by herself in her cold and loveless room. (Okay, so she was getting a little overdramatic, but she couldn't help how she felt.)

She glanced up and saw his face, now animated with love or lust or something for Cyndi and she couldn't rain on his parade. So she plastered on a smile and she nodded while inside she was thinking if she could just move that week in France forward ten days, and maybe extend it indefinitely, life could be so much easier.

The travel insurance was booked, printed out, filed in a Poly Pocket and stored in the spanking-new manila folder. The hire car – a Ford Focus, sensible and economic, complete with Sat Nav – had been booked and the booking details had been printed out, put in a different Poly Pocket and also stored in the manila folder. A travel guide to Saint Jeannet had been printed out and stored. And Ava had made sure they had priority boarding for their flight, were seated together and had extra baggage allowance for the return journey. She still had those stunning purple shoes on her mind.

The planning had taken her mind off the fact that she still hadn't been in touch with Karen and Karen hadn't been in touch with her. Connor had tried to reassure her that it was all fine and it would all blow over. He had even asked her if it was such a bad thing anyway – Karen clearly riled and annoyed her. But Ava couldn't shake Karen's words, or indeed what she had said in return, from her head. She felt weighed down by the guilt of it. Sick to the stomach, boke-on-standby guilty about it. And when she wasn't lost in holiday planning, and packing her suitcase with the precision of an army technical officer, she felt really quite weepy about it. When she had said goodbye to her class that day, wishing them well for their summer holidays and their big progression into Primary Two, she'd had to lock herself in her storeroom for ten minutes afterwards while sobs racked her body. Sure, she was usually a bit emotional to see her charges move on but this was excessive even by her overemotional standards.

She had left work, weighed down by cards and boxes of chocolates, feeling exhausted, and had surprised herself by falling asleep on the sofa – taking full advantage of Maisie being on a playdate with one of her friends from nursery – and remaining unconscious until Connor had arrived in from work.

"Pull yourself together," she muttered as she lifted the phone to call Hope and finalise where they would meet before their flight in just three days.

"Hey, cos!" Hope answered cheerfully. "Are you excited yet?"

"Truthfully," Ava replied, "I can't wait. I usually feel a little nervous about travelling and I thought at this stage I would be going through the horrors at leaving Maisie but I think I need this."

"You're preaching to the converted."

"More developments in the Long Sad Story?" Ava asked, imagining at least that Hope's Long Sad Story would be more exciting than her own.

"One or two."

"Ah grand, well, more to talk about on the famous terrace!"

"Believe me," Hope said, "you will love the terrace."

They chatted on for a while, easily, and made arrangements to meet in Departures after check-in at Belfast International Airport. Ava would drive the hire car because Hope hadn't driven in years. Hope would do the mapreading and ask for directions if needed as she spoke French. It would all be lovely and uncomplicated.

When Hope ended the call a good half hour later she had a smile on her face. The conversation had been a lovely distraction from the impending permanent arrival of Cyndi into her personal space.

The plans had been set in motion very quickly. Dylan had left Hope sitting open-mouthed at the kitchen table that day, picking up his two mugs of tea and sauntering upstairs.

Hope had listened to the murmured muffle of their conversation. The murmur had quickly turned into high-pitched squealing and shortly after Cyndi had appeared in the kitchen, eyes glistening, extra-white teeth grinning, and she had sat down beside Hope and said she hoped they became really good friends as well as housemates.

That had been just under a week ago, and Hope was now watching as Dylan worked himself into an absolute frenzy preparing the house for moving-in day.

He was lost in a frenzy of sheet-washing and dodgy-magazine-clearing-out and he had even made sure all his laundry was done and his boxers and socks were folded and paired and neatly stashed in his drawer.

Hope had emerged from her office after her phone call with Ava to find him choking on the fumes from the oven-cleaner and looking slightly pale.

"It doesn't have to be perfect, you know," she said and he smiled.

"Well, it does and it doesn't. As you well know, my mother would have a shit fit if she knew I was moving a woman in here with a dirty oven!"

"Christ, please don't tell her our oven is dirty! She'll think I'm an awful slattern and never invite me back for a lovely roast dinner again."

Dylan laughed. "I've had a hard enough time telling her I'm moving a woman in without mentioning the state of our oven. She's a bit concerned."

"I can imagine so. She loves you, you know."

"And she's fecked off that I've not fallen madly in love with you."

As he laughed, Hope felt the need to laugh along but she wanted to scream Or indeed cry. Instead she lifted the can of oven-cleaner, sprayed it liberally in the oven and waited for the choking fumes to overcome her.

"Jesus, Hope would you calm down with that? It's frigging toxic."

She rushed to the back door to breathe in some fresh air, then turned and looked at him, tears pricking in her eyes – which she could at least attribute to the fumes. "Sorry," she muttered, and to be honest she was sorry about a lot of things. Not least that he hadn't fallen in love with her and made his mother's dreams come true.

"Things are about to change," she said softly.

"But we'll always be friends," he said, peeling off his rubber gloves and walking over to hug her. Even with the whiff of oven-cleaner off him, she found herself leaning her head towards him and breathing him in as deeply as she could.

"Drink," she muttered – then repeated loudly, "Drink!"

"Drink?"

"We should have a drink? Last night – just us two."

"That sounds like a perfectly wonderful idea, Ms Scott," he declared. "The oven can wait."

Ten minutes later Dylan had headed to the off-licence and Hope was sitting on their sofa, staring at their very clean and tidy living room. She had found the dregs of an already open bottle of wine and had poured it into her glass, downing it a little too fast while switching on her laptop and logging into Spotify. A little music would calm her down, she thought, immediately being transported back to her student days when she would drag a reluctant Dylan onto the dance floor to accompany whatever song was their current favourite.

When he walked back in, two bottles of wine clinking together in a white plastic bag, she looked up and smiled at him as N-Trance's 'Set You Free' played in the background.

"Do you remember this one?" she asked, raising her glass and waving it towards him. "The Students' Union and the M Club?"

"I've tried to block that out," he laughed, walking into the kitchen.

He reappeared with two liberal glasses of dark-red liquid and put one down in front of her.

"We didn't drink this in those days," he said, sitting down opposite her.

"A pint of Harp and a vodka and Coke!" Hope chimed.

"Diet Coke. You were always fussy about that. And then you would have a kebab on the way home."

"Medicinal. Had to prevent the hangover so I would be fit for lectures the next day."

"Of course," he laughed.

She sat entranced by the crinkle around his eyes which hadn't been there, of course, when they first met. He had been so young then. She bit back a swell of emotion and clicked on another song from their student days.

Dylan glugged back his wine and looked at her – a wicked smile on his face.

"C'mon, Ms Scott – time to dance."

Standing up, feeling brave thanks to the wine she had downed, she started to dance, throwing her arms in the air as the strong bass beat of the dance tune hit full force.

She felt free. She felt set free.

The bottles of wine were emptied and the vodka bottle which had sat on the worktop had been demolished. They were dancing still, and laughing, to Lisa Loeb singing 'Stay' in her sweet melodic tones when she looked at him and those wrinkles, well, they were irresistible now. Despite her better judgement, she found herself drunkenly reaching to touch them, to feel his skin on hers. As her fingertips touched his skin, as Lisa Loeb sang about longing, he looked at her, directly into her eyes, as if he had never seen her before. And before she knew it his lips were on hers. She breathed him in, feeling his lips kiss her harder and with a longing she hadn't experienced in a long time.

She knew it was wrong. She knew, even amid the fug of wine and vodka, that she shouldn't be doing it – but God, she had wanted this so much and when he kissed her she couldn't help but kiss him back and feel him move close to her, his body eager to be as close to hers as possible. When she heard him groan, she felt herself gasp and she was lost in him, in his body, in pulling off his T-shirt, in unbuttoning his jean, in allowing him to undress her there and then in the middle of their living room and almost before she knew it, before she had time to really enjoy it, he was there inside her and it was over. And she wanted more. She needed more. But she knew, she just knew, she wasn't going to get any more.

"Fuck," he said. "Fuck."

And he got up and left her lying there feeling the very exact opposite of set free.

Chapter 10

In times of stress Ava's mild OCD tendencies came squarely to the fore. By Friday, when she still hadn't heard from Karen despite sending a grovelling apology on Monday, she was in Control Freak Heaven or should that be Hell?

Her suitcase was packed – her tiny travel-sized bottles of toiletries filled and stashed away. Her manila folders were full of Poly Pockets with every aspect of her trip to France planned. She had been chatting to Jean-Luc via email and had pulled together a list of charity shops and auctioneers to donate Betty's unwanted things to. Jean-Luc had offered to take both Ava and Hope to lunch while they were in Saint Jeannet and had promised to leave a welcome-pack in Betty's house with some provisions to get them through their first day. He did seem a lovely man. Ava wondered again if Betty and he had, at any time, been in a relationship. She liked to think that Betty had her end away at least once after Claude died. She patted her case and mentally worked her way through a list of travel must-haves to make sure she hadn't forgotten anything vital.

"You can buy stuff in France," Connor had laughed. "They have shops. They sell toothpaste and shampoo and all sorts of items related to personal hygiene."

She had stuck her tongue out at him and laughed. She was a sucker for her own brands and always resistant to change. She preferred to know she had her favourite brand of toothpaste rather than panicking about what would be on offer in a French supermarket. Not all minty freshes were the same, she thought as she added '*Listerine Mouthwash*' to her list of things still to buy.

"I just like things the way I like things," she said, sitting down on the bed beside him, "and good for you that I'm not the kind of girl mad into trying a new thing every couple of weeks and being all adventurous."

He gave her a nudge and a wink and replied: "Oh, I don't know. Being a little more adventurous wouldn't necessarily be a bad thing."

Ava felt herself bristle even though she knew he was just making a not-very-funny, semi-rude joke. But right then and there those words "stick up your arse" came right back into her head. Boring, she chided herself. She was boring. Connor reached over to kiss her and she found herself pushing him away – trying to make it look like a bit of carry-on but really being dangerously close to lashing out.

"You'd be lucky," she mocked, trying to keep her voice light but getting up and walking into the ensuite where she closed and locked the door, and stared at her face in the mirror. Her roots needed doing, she noticed. There were a few greys at her temples which were poking through, despite her recent highlighting job. Her hair was cut in a sensible bob. Sensible. Yuck. She suddenly hated that word. Her eyes looked tired. There were wrinkles – definite wrinkles. Shaking her head, she wondered when she had become the kind of woman who worried about wrinkles. She smiled and saw a grimacing woman look back at her.

"Are you okay?" Connor called.

"I'm just going to take a shower," she replied, switching on the hot water full pelt and watching the swirls of stream rise and fill the room. Yes, she would have a shower. Stripping off, she tried not to look at her body, mapped with stretch-marks, in the mirror. She'd need to buy some more Bio Oil, she thought, mentally adding it to her list.

She should have been out that night – with the teaching staff from school. Come the end of the school year, a group of them would always go out on the lash – the older ones staying only for dinner, the younger ones hitting Sandinos or one of the trendier in-places where they would drink into the wee small hours before going on to someone's house and continuing the night out a bit longer. Ava hadn't gone out on any of those nights – not even to the old farts' dinner – since Maisie was born. They had asked the first year and then they didn't any more and Ava had felt relieved in a way. She didn't enjoy going out the way she used to. She felt out of the place with the older crowd and completely out of touch with the younger teachers. At times she felt as if they were speaking a different language – as if the entire world had moved on without her when she was on maternity leave. She had left any ounce of coolness she had in the maternity unit. They got excited about who was playing at Oxegen that summer. She got excited about what was on offer in Dunelm Mill that week. Just recently she had gone in a fit of rapture at buying an enamel home-keeper's box where she could store all her cleaning products. She was even more excited when she discovered there was a matching clothes-peg bucket.

She looked at herself again – feeling stuck somewhere between being old and young and feeling like she was just nothing. Maybe Connor was right. Maybe Karen was right. Maybe she should just get under that damn shower and then get dressed and go out and meet her colleagues anyway. She could fake cool. She could fit in.

Feeling a sense of bravado, she stepped under the shower and scrubbed herself with Flying Fox Shower Gel and conditioned her boring, sensible haircut to within an inch of its life before climbing out and roughly drying herself off. If the world wanted her to show a more adventurous side, she would. She would slip on the skinny jeans she had bought in the January sales and had never had the nerve to wear. She was sure she had a pair of death-defying stilettos in the bottom of her wardrobe and she had a billowing lace top which she had worn at Christmas and never again. She would do her make-up – full make-up, not just a slick of foundation and a dab of blusher. She'd do her eyes, and straighten her hair and spray perfume right between her boobs and everything.

Walking out of the bathroom, towel pulled around her, she saw

Connor still lying on the bed watching TV. Feeling devilish and determined to prove she was far from boring and far from a stick in the mud, she turned to face him, dropped her towel and even though she was cringing from the inside out she shimmied in front of him.

"Adventurous enough for you?" she winked and she could clearly see by the expression on his face and the rise in his trousers that it was.

"C'mere," he whispered hoarsely.

"Later," she said, bending to lift the towel. "I'm going out. For the first time in three years I'm going to go to the staff party. The funky one. In a proper bar."

"Can you not go later?" he said gruffly.

"I have to get ready. I want to look amazing."

"You do look amazing!" he said.

"*Connor, douze points!*" Ava grinned, speaking in a faux French accent.

"So stay . . ." he said, getting up and walking towards her.

She didn't know why but she felt nervous and she held the towel up to her body, covering herself. "I need to go."

He put his finger to her lips and looked deep into her eyes. "I need you to stay . . ."

She looked back at him, torn in that second between wanting him and wanting to be herself – the old unencumbered self who sang and danced till four in the morning and who could never, ever be described as having a stick up her arse or being a martyr to her own cause. Connor kissed her – a kiss that made her feel dizzy and not boring at all – but she still wanted more. But when he kissed her again, deeper this time, she thought about how nice it felt. And safe. And this was a place where there was no chance of her being left alone, nursing a glass of wine and wondering what on earth everyone else was talking about. This was a place where she knew she was welcome – and wanted – and where she didn't have to pretend. Her plans to dress up faded as each kiss grew deeper and more urgent. She wasn't being a bore. She was being a desired wife. She was being wild, here in her own bedroom, doing things which young, wild things did. Sure it was within the safe boundaries but that was okay. That was all just perfectly okay.

Slipping between the sheets and allowing Connor to show her just how much he wanted her, she pushed out every negative thought in her head and allowed herself to believe that this was what she wanted more than anything. And that she hadn't just spent half an hour feeling like an outsider in the life she once knew and loved.

Sitting at her kitchen island and sipping from her coffee, she watched Maisie at her feet. Her daughter was sitting on the floor, face frozen in deep concentration, little tongue poking out the side of her mouth, drawing a picture which would have sat well in any modern art collection.

She had decided not to go to Soft Play – partly because she still wanted to get a few things together for her trip but also because she was kind of scared of bumping into Karen.

"I don't understand you," Connor had said when she tried to explain how Karen intimidated her. "She isn't any better than you."

"But she's loud – and not afraid to speak her mind."

"Except when it comes to telling that husband of hers how utterly miserable she is."

Ava had smiled. For a bloke, Connor could be quite in touch with his feelings and the feelings of others at times.

"You don't understand," Ava said. "Now that we've fallen out she will have badmouthed me to every other mammy on the block. I'll be the wicked witch."

"You need to learn to stand up for yourself," he had said, sitting down beside Maisie and helping her with her drawing.

Ava tried to defend herself, but she couldn't. He was absolutely right. "I will, one of these days."

"You used to be more feisty," he said.

And once again she felt her world shift just that wee bit beneath her feet. It seemed, at the moment, no matter what she did, she never quite hit the mark.

"I'm still feisty," she replied meekly and watched as he laughed. She knew he wasn't being cruel. He was being absolutely spot-on. There she was, in her slippers with her hair tied back in a ponytail, looking like the least feisty person in the entire universe. She picked up the tea towel from beside her and threw it at him.

"If you say so," he laughed. "Now away with you, wife, and get everything ready for your big trip and then you can help me pack for our trip down to Dublin. So far I've only a pair of pyjamas and some stripy tights packed."

She winked and said: "So you're okay for tights . . . what about Maisie?"

"Ha ha."

"Well, I said I could still be feisty," she laughed, but inside she felt a little shaky and a little unsure of herself. She felt ready for an escape. She needed an escape.

Chapter 11

The rhythmic slapping of naked flesh from the room beside hers distracted Hope from her checklist. She lifted the earplugs she had bought for just such a purpose and popped them in her ears before the fever-pitched moaning started. Dylan and Cyndi were very much in the honeymoon period. Just that morning she had walked into the kitchen to find them going at it like rabbits on the kitchen table. When they had – red-faced and white-arsed – retired to their room, Hope had sprayed almost an entire bottle of antibacterial kitchen cleaner on the table and scrubbed it vigorously. She had also vowed to always, always use a plate from now on. No eating anything straight off the table, not even a piece of fruit.

Yes, Cyndi had moved in. Nothing had changed. Nothing had even been mentioned, if the truth was told. Hope shouldn't have expected any different. It wasn't as if he didn't have form for this kind of thing. She shook her head. She had been stupid, bloody stupid, to think it could have been any different.

Dylan had come downstairs the following morning, while she had been hanging over a cup of coffee trying not to vomit, and had said nothing. He had smiled, opened the fridge, commented that there was no bacon and sat down opposite her, lifted her coffee cup and sipped from it.

"Mad night last night. Totally mad. Too much to drink."

"Indeed," she said, looking up at him, her face red with embarrassment. She expected him to say something, anything, about what had happened.

But he didn't. He just pushed her coffee cup back at her. "I'd better tidy up before Cyndi gets here."

She had wanted to call him back as he left the room. She had wanted to shout, from the top of her lungs "*What. The. Fuck?*" She had wanted to ask him why she wasn't good enough. Why hadn't the night before meant anything? Why hadn't the night they spent together in Betty's house meant anything? None of this made sense. She wanted to shout and throw her coffee cup at the door but all that would achieve would be another mess to clean up. Another great big stinking mess of her own making to clean up. And she had enough of those to deal with already.

That was that then, she realised, as she rinsed her (not broken) cup under the sink. Cyndi was still coming. She would still be here. Hope would have to file another experience under W for "What Might Have Been".

There would be no further mention of what had happened. There was no mention of it later that day. No mention of it when Cyndi had gone upstairs to girlify his bedroom and scatter it with pink cushions and cute lamps. There had been no mention of it when Cyndi went for a long soak in the bath and he faffed around the kitchen trying to cook her a welcome-dinner to which Hope was not invited. She had disappeared up to her own room like the stupid gooseberry she was and had eaten a Chinese takeaway while watching *When Harry Met Sally* which she cried the entire way through. No, it was very clear that it was all done and dusted – for him anyway – and she was now living in her own very special kind of hell where she listened to bonking at all hours of the day and night interspersed with increasingly random conversations with Cyndi about whatever topic of the day took her fancy.

Just earlier – prior to the bonkfest that was now assaulting Hope's ears – they had discussed all previous *Big Brother* winners. Although it wasn't so much of a discussion as a full-on monologue on what was clearly Cyndi's "favouritist programme ever".

She was starting to seriously wonder if she should stay on in France, indefinitely. Anything – *anything* – to escape this living hell.

She had written an advance draft of her new 'Single in the City' feature and had set some timed blog posts to go live while she was away. She had packed just about every item of clothing in her wardrobe and had bought a few new things. She had left her bedroom tidy as she suspected Cyndi was the nosey kind. She would be taking her laptop with her – for no other reason than she would only have a complete panic attack if she didn't. Some people had a drink or drug addiction – hers was to WiFi broadband, which – she hoped Betty had. Then again with her aunt's reliance on old-fashioned letters, she doubted it.

Dylan had handed her fifty euro in a pristine white envelope that morning and told her to have a few drinks on him. She had hugged him because it felt like the proper thing to do even though she kind of wanted to slap him, very hard, around the back of the head. Fifty quid, to make up for everything. To make up for him messing with her head. Jesus, she was a cheap date. But since they were playing make-believe that everything was just as it always had been, she said nothing more and focused on the trip ahead of her.

She lifted her bag and closed the door of the house which didn't really feel like home any more.

The girls had agreed to meet in the airport bar, through security. It saved anyone standing around like a spare wheel, Ava had said. She had been grateful for her own forethought when she was the first to arrive at the airport feeling a little shaky after a rather traumatic departure from Maisie and a strange departure from Cora.

It had all been going very well. Maisie had been uber-excited to be heading off to Dublin to see her granny and grandpa and delighted to be seeing Granny Cora beforehand who was going to mind her while Connor cleared up the last of his work.

Maisie had bounded up the front path to her granny's house and had declared loudly, "My am going on my holidays!" in her "best most loudest voice" as Cora answered the door.

"Well, so you are, Miss Maisie. Off to Dublin, you fancy pants. And your mammy is off too. Isn't it all exciting?"

Cora sounded a little put out and Ava wondered should she have pushed her a little harder to come along on the trip. Of course Betty had meant more to Cora than she ever had to Ava. It was still strange that it was Ava who was tasked with sorting through her things. Cora had insisted, loudly, that she was okay with it all but she looked a little on edge.

"Are you sure you're okay, Mum?" Ava asked while she tried to sneak one last cuddle from a very wriggly Maisie who was determined to get the box of toys Granny Cora kept in the corner of the kitchen.

"I'm fine," Cora said, but Ava knew from the tone of her voice and the way she was wringing the life out of the tea towel she was holding that she was far from fine.

"Mum?"

Cora turned her back and started washing the dishes with such ferocity that Ava was sure she would break them to smithereens.

"Ava," she said, between the clatters of cups and saucers and silver spoons, "you'd better be off or you'll miss your flight and we couldn't have that."

Ava walked up behind her mother and wrapped her arms around her, hugging her in the way she had done as a child and she felt her mother's soapy hands on hers and the shake of her crying.

"Mum! I'm worried about you," Ava said. "I don't like leaving you like this."

"Look, Ava," Cora said, turning to face her. "It's just strange, you going off to sort through Betty's things. It just . . . well . . . it's just strange." She seemed to be struggling to find the right words to express what she wanted to say.

"It's okay, Mum. It is strange for sure, but I'll raise a glass to her from you while I'm there. I promise." She felt herself choke up and her mother pulled her into a hug.

"I love you so very much," Cora said softly. "I love you so, so much."

"Mum, I'm only going to France for a week. I'll be back, you know."

Cora sniffed. "I know," she said, plastering a smile on her face which didn't convince Ava one bit.

The trauma of the whole departure had continued half an hour later when she made to leave.

Somewhere in Maisie's almost-three-year-old brain, despite having been told, this hadn't translated into "Mammy is going away for a wee bit" but once Ava had lifted her suitcase to head to the door there had been a toddler catastrophe. Pudgy limbs flailed. High-pitched screams echoed in her ears – and in the ears of everyone within a three-mile radius. Cora had had to literally peel her granddaughter from Ava to allow her to run to the car, lock herself in and drive to the bottom of the road before pulling over and bursting into tears. She had pulled herself together and had driven, probably a little too fast, until she'd arrived early, perhaps too early, at the airport.

At least this meant she was able to walk straight to the top of the queue at check-ins. She didn't have much patience for queues at the best of times but today she was feeling light-headed and more than a little queasy. She put it down to being too nervous to eat breakfast and her crying fit which had left her feeling wrung out. If she could just get through check-in and security she would grab a coffee and Danish – although the very thought of this made her stomach turn and she wondered if this not-so-perfect morning would end up with an even less perfect boking incident just as the security guard patted her up and down.

She was angry with herself – for leaving her mother's in a bad mood and for arriving in the airport feeling flustered and sick. She just wanted to go and do what she needed to do for Betty and maybe, just maybe, enjoy herself a teeny tiny bit – and here she was, slightly grey in colour, fighting with a blasted manila folder to find the right bloody documents to check in.

The woman at the desk tapped her fingers impatiently on the desk as if there was a queue a mile long waiting and, as Ava found herself glancing behind and then back at the desk, she felt the last of her patience slip.

"Can you just check me in and can you just be pleasant about it?" she said. "It won't kill you."

The tapping of the fingers stopped and the perma-tanned woman behind the desk looked at her, slack-jawed, and Ava swore she could almost hear the cogs turning as she tried to come up with a smart retort.

"No need to give me lip, love," she stuttered.

Ava felt herself blush. She never was good with confrontation, as her run-in with Karen had so wonderfully shown, and she felt her heart start to race a little.

"I wasn't . . . I didn't mean . . . I just . . ." she stuttered back, feeling her palms start to sweat. There was no way she was getting anything out of a Poly Pocket the way her hands were sliding all over the place.

"Ticket and passport, love," Perma-tan growled.

"I'm trying!" she bit back.

"And watch your tone."

"My tone is fine," she said, feeling her stomach start to turn even more. Please God, just let me get the damn ticket out of the damn envelope and let me get the hell out of here. She felt tears prick in her eyes and felt herself sag with relief when she found the right form and handed it to the assistant who by now seemed to be enjoying watching Ava disintegrate before her eyes.

Sloping off from the desk, she made it through security and found herself a quiet corner in the café. Sipping from a bottle of water, she tried to settle herself. Hope would be arriving soon and the last thing she wanted was for her cousin to see her as a quivering, pale-faced wreck who was clearly out of her comfort zone doing anything out of the ordinary. No. She would put her best foot forward. She would show Hope that she wasn't some fuddy-duddy stick-in-the-mud who came over weak at leaving her family and who burst into tears if someone so much as looked at her the wrong way.

Hope arrived ten minutes later, smiling brightly and wearing a pair of oversized sunglasses on the top of her head. She waved at Ava, walked over and put her carry-on case down.

"Oh, it's so nice to see you!" she said, grabbing her cousin into a hug.

Ava let herself be hugged and once again felt herself start to well up. Jesus H Christ, she thought. This was getting ridiculous. She was welling up at seeing someone she barely knew in an airport. If it wouldn't have made her look like such a fecking mentalist she would have slapped herself square around the face and told herself, loudly, to wise up.

"You got away okay then?" Hope asked, sitting down and reaching for the drinks menu in front of her.

"It was a bit hairy in places, but I'm here. No problems for you?"

"Apart from the Long Sad Story stepping up a notch, no. It was grand. But you know what, even though it is only half eleven in the morning I'm going to have a very large glass of red wine."

Feeling a little more settled in herself, Ava decided that a glass of wine would be exactly what the doctor – or she herself – ordered.

She watched her cousin head to the bar and smiled. There was nothing to worry about. Nothing at all – this would be grand. Absolutely grand.

Ava breathed out and glanced at the time on her Blackberry – in just forty minutes they would be boarding for Nice.

Chapter 12

"I'm never, ever going to be able to feel even an ounce of fondness for my own house again," Ava said as she stepped out of the car onto the crunchy gravel at Betty's house, nestled on a hill, on the outskirts of what was perhaps the quaintest village in the world ever. Hope's descriptions just hadn't done it justice. It looked as if the French Tourist Board had ticked off a giant big checklist of everything you could ever want to give you a cracking impression of their country and put it all right there on this gorgeous hill in the brightest sunshine she had ever seen. Yes, the house could be described as rustic, but not rustic in a tatty way, she thought, as she lifted her case from the boot of the car and waited for Hope to follow. This was as far from tatty as it came – rustic and stunningly gorgeous, yes, but no one could describe it as tatty.

"It's gorgeous, isn't it?" Hope said.

"Damn right, it is! No wonder Betty was so happy here. If I moved here I'd never leave either," Ava said, momentarily allowing a pleasant little daydream where she did indeed live here – away from the rat race and the main road to Belfast and the weekly shopping ordeal in Tesco. She looked for the key under the third terracotta pot from the left-hand side of the door.

"I'm sure Connor will be dying to see you back – so you may just need to go home at some stage."

"Really?" Ava said with a laugh, turning to waggle the key at her cousin.

"'Fraid so. But let's go in. I take it that is the key to the kingdom, so to speak?"

Ava nodded. "Yeah. Right there, where Jean-Luc said it would be."

"*Ah, oui, Jean-Luc!*" Hope said in a French accent which owed more to *'Allo 'Allo* than her years of French lessons at school. "Isn't that a lovely name? Very masculine and sexy, like that bloke from *Star Trek*?"

"Captain Kirk?"

"No, Picard. Captain Jean-Luc. From the newer ones. Dylan is a bit of trekkie."

"Dylan. The man you came here with before?"

"That's the very one," Hope said, with that familiar nervous feeling rise from her stomach. Coming back here was always going to be difficult. She was just starting to realise how difficult.

"Well, you have all week to tell me," Ava said, pushing open the heavy oak door into an open living space which she could instantly imagine her aunt living in.

Two large, chintzy squashy sofas and a green tweed armchair sat in a semi-circle formation around a large white-washed fireplace with a log burner nestled in the nook. A large, square coffee table – perfect for balancing glasses of wine, or tired feet or bars of chocolate – rested in the centre of the circle and light flooded from the wooden-framed French doors which, Ava could see, led out to a sun terrace which made her want to weep with joy. A small dining table, covered in a fresh white linen tablecloth with four mismatched chairs sat in the corner of the room. A motley bunch of wildflowers was displayed in an old jug in the centre of the table and the smell from the stunning yellow, purple and white flowers scented the room.

"This must be the kitchen," Ava said, walking through an archway to her right and Hope followed.

An old-fashioned Aga stood at the back wall while a freestanding butcher's block made for an impressive kitchen island. Scores of wooden cupboards, painted cream with oodles of glass panels stood at every wall while under the window was a large copper sink. It was clear this had been the hub of Betty's home.

On the butcher's block rested a wicker basket, a bottle of deep-red wine, two glasses and a crisp, white envelope. "It's another letter from Betty," Ava said, picking it up and noticing a small note scrawled on the front.

Take the wine, it said, *and the glasses and some of the lovely chocolate and croissants from the basket and go to the terrace. Pour the wine, sit down, and read this together.*

"What a woman!" Ava said. "Was there nothing she didn't have organised?"

"Apart from sorting out her knicker drawers?" Hope winked.

"Well, apart from that. But then again, if she had done that we wouldn't be here – about to sit out on the gorgeous terrace. So it's not all bad, is it?"

"You have a very good point indeed. I'll lead the way, shall I?"

Ava nodded and picked up the wine while Hope lifted the glasses and the basket. Hope led the way and Ava went to follow her but stopped for just one second first to feel a sense of something she just couldn't quite put her finger on wash over her. *Peace*, she whispered, there was definitely a sense of peace about this house and she allowed it to seep into her very bones.

The terrace exceeded all expectations. The flagstones, bathed in early evening sunlight, were scattered with mismatched pots of all sizes filled with deliciously fragrant flowers and herbs, jasmine and lavender, mint and rosemary. Ava looked to see a wooden swing-seat looking out over the gardens – gardens which looked like they belonged in a lifestyle magazine. It was a far cry from the patch of grass at the rear of her house, the small decking she adored but which housed little more than a small garden table and chairs and Maisie's much-loved sandpit.

A small pathway wound down a slight hill to where the calm waters of a rectangular-shaped pool – complete with a terrace all of its own – glinted back at Ava. However she played it in her mind, it was definitely more impressive than the three, ringed, inflatable paddling pools currently filled with rainwater in her back garden.

"Look at this," Hope said, breaking into her thoughts.

Ava turned to where a large wooden table stood surrounded by chairs, a fire pit smouldering beside them.

"I'm assuming she arranged the welcome fire too," Hope said. "Betty sat here most evenings, when the weather was good enough. Come to think of it, even when the weather wasn't good enough she'd be out here, a blanket wrapped around her shoulders, fire blazing, glass of wine in one hand."

"I can't say I blame her," Ava said. This really was a piece of heaven. Instantly she chided herself. She must stop thinking about heaven when she was, after all, in a dead woman's house. It seemed a little weird. Or wrong. Or both.

"Sit down," Hope said, sitting and patting a chair beside her.

Ava sat down, putting the wine on the table while Hope fished in the basket for a corkscrew. "No screw-top bottles in this house," Hope laughed. "Betty was death on screw-tops. Cheap and nasty, she called them."

"I'm kind of jealous," Ava said, watching her cousin deftly uncork the bottle and pour the ruby-red liquid into the glasses. "That you were here before. That you spent time with her. All I had was a couple of hours at a funeral. I'm surprised she even remembered me."

"You must be unforgettable, toots," Hope smiled, lifting her glass and clinking it against Ava's. "Look, I spent a month here when I was twenty-two and a stupid, young irresponsible girl who didn't know her arse from her elbow nor had a notion what she wanted to do with her life. I didn't appreciate Betty – or what she did for us – half enough. You've probably more right to be here than I do."

Ava laughed but she sensed a certain something in Hope which made her feel that she would be hearing details of the Long Sad Story sooner rather than later.

"Let's just say we both have a right to be here," she said. "I'm sure Betty wouldn't have us here if she didn't want us both here. She didn't strike me as the wishy-washy type."

"No, she was very much the say-it-like-it-is type, which I loved."

Ava lifted the envelope which she had placed on the table and opened it. "I think it might be time to see what else she has to say for herself."

My dearest girls,

Welcome home. Of course I know it's not your home . . . but that seemed like the right thing to write. I remember the first time I walked over the threshold of this place – I thought all my Christmases had come at once. We'd been married a couple of years, Claude and I, and he told me he had found the perfect bijou residence just outside the village. Bijou!! Ha – this was bigger than most of the houses in Derry. And a pool in the garden? It's a far cry from the City Baths, I can tell you! And it was a far cry from the pokey apartment we had lived in before we made our escape from Derry in 1979.

We knew once we found this place that we would never leave. And we never did. We were here seventeen years together before Claude died and, well, it took a pretty bad dose of cancer to get me out of the place. It seems strange that now, as you read this, neither of us is there. We used to say it was our forever home – seems forever doesn't last that long.

I'm sounding maudlin, aren't I? That's not the best welcome, is it? Well, anyway, I suppose maybe that's why I didn't put everything in order – not when it came to the house anyway. I can be a stubborn oul goat at times and this was one loose end – one goodbye I didn't want to say. I suppose I was a coward too. There were some things I so wanted to face while I was still here but I couldn't. You won't be cross at me for that, will you? I so wanted to . . .

But I know you two – you might not think I do but I'm good with people. Shocking with everything else – but good with people. I can trust you with this.

I know I have a bit of a cheek asking you do to this. To go through all our things, to delve through our personal information. All the memories of me and Claude, my old clothes, the cupboards of mismatched china I never could throw away and the loft filled to the brim with a lifetime of my stuff, and Claude's stuff.

I trust you to look after this for me. Please. Protect my memories. Clear out the crap (excuse the language). Keep a couple of pictures, will you? I know that I probably shouldn't really care about all this now. After all by the time you read this I'll be long gone – but well, just the thought of 'just anyone' sorting through it all – it doesn't sit well with me.

Jean-Luc has arranged for a skip to arrive tomorrow (late morning – sleep off the wine). Throw out what you will. Keep what you want. And when you are done, I just need you to sign some paperwork.

I'll be with you. I've left letters – just notes which explain a few things I never could in life which you can read together or on your own. I've left a schedule – attached. If you follow it, you should find the letters in the right order. They should explain a lot. A lot that I so wish I could have explained person to person.

Tonight though . . . relax. Enjoy the wine. And the fire. And the view. Raise a glass for me – for everything I did and everything I didn't do. My intentions were always good.

Much love, my girls,
Betty
xxx

Ava felt the lump that had been sitting in her throat threaten to explode as tears ran down her face. She looked at Hope who was equally gone in a flurry of tears and then she raised her glass, the sun catching on it and sparkling brightly. "To Betty, Claude, her home and her memories!"

"And to us! And to doing her proud."

They drank and then Hope flicked through the schedule, the lists of rooms which were to be tackled and the order in which they were to be faced.

"It's an impressive list," she said, sipping her wine. "I think we'd better make the most of tonight. It'll be pretty full-on from here."

"Cheers then!" Ava said, clinking her glass against her cousin's and looking out over the terrace to the gardens and fields below.

The wine bottle was empty and it was gone seven. Ava found herself yawning. God, she was really bloody going to make a good impression on Hope, wasn't she? A lightweight who fell asleep after half a glass of wine! Christ, her cousin would have her pinned down as the most boring creature on the planet. She hadn't stayed on in Belfast for a drink on the day of the will reading. She had burst into tears after reading Betty's letter and now she was yawning and feeling her eyelids droop. And she still felt sick. She hadn't even had much of the wine – and had tried to settle her stomach with one of the flaky croissants Jean-Luc had left – but, as she listened to Hope speak of her round-the-world trip and how it had brought her to Saint Jeannet, she realised she was going to have to make a complete eejit of herself and make her excuses and go to bed. Wherever bed was. Her case was still in the hall. They hadn't investigated further than the kitchen and the terrace and the downstairs loo – which was bigger than her own master bathroom and twice as nice.

She yawned again as Hope recalled a bout of dodgy tummy-itis in Bali. She felt herself blush. Not only would Hope think she was boring, she would think she was a rude cow as well. That, she realised, could make for a very awkward week indeed.

"I'm sorry," she said when a lull in the conversation was reached. "I must be getting old. I feel wrecked. I don't know whether it was the flight or what, but I think I need to go for a sleep."

She watched Hope's face carefully for any sign that she was annoyed or disgusted with her. If Karen had been there she would have been rolling her eyes with gusto just then and shouting *"Fader!"* from the rooftops – and then she would huff for a week – or ten days as it was now. The bitch.

Hope smiled and put her wineglass down. "Oh God, I've been wittering on – it's just this place. It brings back memories. I'm sorry."

"Nothing to be sorry for. I've been feeling a little out of sorts the last day or so. I probably just need a good sleep and then you can tell me more. I'm very much enjoying listening to your stories. I never did anything exciting like that. I went to university. Got a job. Got married. Had a baby. Stepford has nothing on me."

"Hey, don't knock being settled down," Hope said.

"I know," Ava said, because she hated when she complained about it. It didn't mean she didn't think she was lucky. She knew she was lucky and exceptionally blessed but that didn't mean that sometimes she didn't get the urge to run down the street naked, get a tattoo on the back of her of neck or book a holiday they really couldn't afford just to show she could do something completely unexpected which might just shock the shite out of those who saw her as the sensible, boring woman she was. She would have said that to Hope but she feared she would scare her off altogether. After all, they barely knew each other. Now was definitely not the time for the "look at everything which is so horribly boring and mundane about my life" speech. That could wait till at least day three . . .

Hope showed Ava to a room on the bottom floor of the house. It was where she had slept when she had stayed there all those years ago and she said it would be weird to sleep there again. There were memories in that room, she said, saying she would take the attic bedroom instead. Neither of them said it, but it went without saying that neither would sleep in Betty's room. It would be weird, Ava thought. And while she knew this made her sound mildly like a bad person, she also thought it might just be a little creepy.

The room Hope showed her to was at the opposite end of the house to the kitchen. It was sparsely furnished – a large oak-framed bed, a simple dressing table and chair. A mirror hung on the wall and long voile curtains shielded the room from the worst of the sun. A tall wardrobe stood at the back of the room and Ava set about unpacking her clothes into it, and the two drawers beneath it. She never had been the kind of person who could live out of a suitcase. She had to make each room she stayed in, even if it were only a hotel room for a night, her own. As she was going to be sleeping here for a week she might as well make herself really comfy. Pulling out the picture of Connor and Maisie she had in her case, she looked at it and smiled. Hope was right, of course. She was lucky. Kissing it, she sat it on the dressing table before emptying her case of her make-up and perfume and stacking them neatly. Lastly she pulled her washbag out and walked through to the ensuite where she felt another wave of nausea sweep over her.

Sitting on the toilet, she put her hand to her forehead. She was definitely clammy. She needed a lie-down. It would be okay, if she just had a sleep and a glass of water. As soon as she put everything away. Toothpaste and toothbrush. Facial wash and shower gel. Shampoo and Tampax. Tampax. Shite. Tampax. She had packed them, of course she had . . . but there in the bathroom she had her very own light-bulb, period-is-late, pregnancy-scare, fuck-this-for-a-game-of-morning-sickness moment. Oh. Sweet. Jesus.

She sat back on the toilet and felt even clammier. Then she scrambled to the bedroom and hauled her phone from her bag. She had one of the Apps – those silly little Apps which charted when your last period was and when your next one was due. She tried to work it out in her head. Had she had a period since she received Betty's first letter? She tried to remember. No, she didn't think so, so it must have been just before. But she couldn't remember that either. *Oh pish sticks*, she swore as she swiped through the Apps on her phone to find the right one. Clicking it open, she felt her tummy cramp just a little. She was panicking for nothing. No doubt her period was absolutely and totally just going to arrive. She wasn't pregnant. She couldn't be pregnant. It wasn't like she had been hyper-emotional like she had been with Maisie . . . except she had. She hadn't felt sick . . . except she had. She hadn't boobs which resembled torpedoes . . . except (pause for quick glance down) she did. *Oh bastard*, she swore to herself again. And there it was. Last period. Five weeks ago. Five weeks and three days to be precise. And she was a steady twenty-eight-days girl. *Oh bollocks. Oh bastarding, stupiding, fecking bollocks.* Had she taken a risk? She thought back. The night of the will reading. The champagne. The sex. She had let her guard (and her knickers) down and thinking back they had thrown caution to the wind. She figured just one time wouldn't hurt. One night of leaving the condoms in the drawer would be just grand. Sure people tried for months to get pregnant. She should have listened to the nuns. It did only take the once after all. And feck it . . . now she was pregnant. She didn't even need to test. She knew it, as sure as she knew that she would never, ever drink champagne again.

Christ, they would never be able to *afford* to drink champagne again. Or ordinary wine. She wondered did Tesco do a value range of Pinot Grigio? With an extra mouth to feed and an extra childcare place to pay for, she wondered if Tesco did a value range in everything?

She knew she should have lifted the phone and called Connor but she knew he was probably sitting in his parents' front room in Blackrock, making polite conversation about how they were all doing and the last thing he needed was a semi-hysterical woman screeching down to the phone to him that she was up the duff and what the holy fuck were they going to do about it?

She could call her mother, she supposed, but she didn't want to annoy Cora, who had been in bad form anyway and would more than likely do one of those deep-sigh things. Christ, she was thirty-four and having a stroke about telling her mother. Cora would come round, of course, but she would give her a lecture first about whether or not she had thought this whole thing through, given how hard she found it to balance work, home and Maisie. And much as she loved her mother and was close to her she couldn't face telling her that no, actually, she hadn't thought it through at all and she had simply been half cut on a couple of glasses of champagne and had let go of her inhibitions. She would have to admit to her mother that she'd had sex, which of course was a bit of 'stating the obvious' but not a conversation she relished.

If things weren't so frosty with Karen she would probably call her. Karen, she realised with a thump, would understand her panic more than anyone. She loved her family, she did, but she was barely keeping it together as it was.

There was Hope, she realised. There was nothing stopping her from marching right out onto terrace right there and then and telling her cousin but of course there was the complete fecking fear of coming across as a nutcase in front of a relative stranger stopping her. Oh this was not good. This was the start of her very own Long Sad Story. Oh crap.

She lay back on the bed and looked at the App on her phone again. She reached her hand instinctively to her stomach and cursed herself for not catching on before now. This was not like her. She knew everything. She planned everything. On Ava Campbell's big list of birthdays and anniversaries there was also a small letter P written in blue pen on the day of each month when her period started. How could she have missed that this month?

Not that catching on would have made much difference, she supposed. Pregnant would still mean pregnant. Fecked would still mean fecked.

Trying to steady her breathing while repeating a steady mantra of "It will be okay", she vowed to herself to try and get to a supermarket of some description to buy a pregnancy test just to be sure. She could, she supposed, go to the local chemist but her knowledge of French was shockingly bad and she didn't fancy either having to speak very loudly and slowly to a random stranger that she thought she might be with the child or, worse still, attempt some primitive form of sign language to that effect . . . (standing with a bloated face, gesturing her hands to make a rounded tummy and then play-acting a birth . . . lovely). Then, when she knew, categorically and without a shadow of a doubt, she would decide what to do next.

She would worry about it tomorrow. Closing her eyes and trying to block out the thoughts that were swirling through her mind, she did her best to fall asleep. Thankfully the first trimester came with the added bonus of bone-crushing exhaustion and despite her overactive imagination she was able to fall off into a sleep where none of it mattered any more.

Chapter 13

Hope stoked the dying embers of the fire and pulled the throw rug she had found on the bed she would sleep in around her. She had been tempted to open a second bottle of wine but feared that a second bottle combined with the memories crashing at her relentlessly would have ended in a rather messy fashion. Possibly involving tears, hysterical wailing and Ava running screaming from the villa mentally scarred forever.

She had been expecting the trip to bring back some memories – of course she had – but not this. Not these extremes. Everything about the house reminded her of an interaction she had shared with Dylan or a whispered conversation with Betty or that night . . . that infamous night.

It had been a long, hot day and she had been feeling homesick despite all the comforts Betty had afforded them. They had spent the day picking grapes at a local vineyard and her back ached and her skin felt dry from the summer sun. She was sweaty, and sticky and feeling decidedly unfeminine. In fact she could barely remember the last time she had felt feminine at all. The last few months had been spent in cargo trousers and string tops and a choice of either sensible walking shoes, or vaguely fashionable but still, by necessity, comfortable sandals. Her underwear had turned a delightful grey colour from frequent hand-washes in tiny basins in youth hostels which could not ever be described as luxurious. Her legs needed to be shaved. Her bikini-line was shocking and her hair was matted to her head in a ratty ponytail. When they had walked through the village on their way home from the vineyard, stopping at a small taverna for a cold drink, she had looked around at the effortlessly chic and glam Frenchwomen and felt subhuman. Their hair glistened in the sun. The only thing glistening on her body was her own sweat. They wore loose, crisp white linens and she was pretty sure their underwear was neither grey nor saggy. The feckers probably wore matching sets, with no fear of an unkempt bikini line escaping from their thongs to ruin the look. She had downed half a beer, direct from the bottle, before she had noticed they were all sipping theirs from glasses while giggling delicately and speaking in cute French accents which sounded much less harsh than her Northern Irish drawl. She couldn't have felt less ladylike without the aid of a moustache and perhaps a very loud and pungent fart.

She had looked at Dylan, who was clearly as intrigued with the Frenchwomen as she was but for clearly different reasons, and said she was going back to the villa to freshen up.

It was luxury – to have her own bathroom with a shower they didn't have to queue for, with enough hot water to allow her to luxuriate for as long as she wanted. Hope had stood under the powerful streams of scorching hot water for a full twenty-three minutes – lathering herself time and again with fancy shower gel until she felt she could not get any cleaner. She shaved her legs and other areas and washed her hair four times before leaving on an intensive conditioning treatment to soften it to within an inch of its life.

When she finally stepped out of the shower, and wrapped herself in one of the fluffy towels Betty had left out, she had wandered to the terrace where she smothered her tanned legs and arms with rich body butter before painting her toenails a fresh pale pink. She had brushed her blonde curls, allowing the sun to dry her hair and, instead of slipping into her cotton pyjamas (built for modesty in the crammed dorms of the hostel), she put on a pair of fancy pink knickers with a matching lace bra. She was not doing that to seduce Dylan. Far from it. She just wanted to feel like a woman again. Slipping on a summer dress, she scanned the list of recommended restaurants Betty had left out for them and decided they would absolutely push the boat out that night. Hope's stomach rumbled at the thought of a proper meal in a proper restaurant – one that was not a roadside stall or a basic café serving anything you wanted as long as it was pizza. She had already vowed that she would never, ever eat pizza again.

Dylan was almost delirious at the thought of a proper restaurant meal and Hope laughed as he almost ran to the restaurant doors.

"Can I really have anything I want?" he asked, with a twinkle in his eyes and Hope had smiled and nodded that, yes, of course he could.

She didn't realise that would mean her, at the pool, afterwards.

Even now, many years after the fact, she couldn't quite figure out what had happened. There had been a fair bit of wine consumed, she knew that much, and they had decided to walk home from the restaurant afterwards. It was a glorious night – the sky was so clear that she felt that if she had wanted she could just have reached up and pulled a star right down. The roads had been almost deserted – just a few cars tootled past them – no one in France seeming to be in any rush to get anywhere.

Dylan had looped his arm around her shoulders as they walked through the garden on the way home. She had kicked her shoes off and was enjoying the feeling of the warm grass between her toes. They weren't really talking – just walking, enjoying the silence of the night sky. Moments like these made it all worthwhile – all the sitting on tiny planes beside obese and sweaty people. All the rushing in the heat to a crowded train or bus with no suspension which rattled your bones until you felt like your brain might fall out of your ears. All the nights trying to sleep while someone or other had a sing-song, or an argument or a water fight in your dorm. All the wishing for air-conditioning. All the sore feet and sunburn and dodgy tummies. This, on a beach in Provence, was what made their round-the-world trip astounding.

They had walked back to the villa and down to the terrace beside the pool – attracted to the glint of the moon on the water like magpies to silver – and as Hope dipped her feet into the cool water, she had let out a very undignified squeal which prompted Dylan to break into a belly laugh which echoed through the night sky. He had laughed until he was holding his tummy, begging for the pain of the laughing-fit to pass while Hope had told him it just served him right and put on a mock huff as she sat down on a sun-lounger.

When he followed her, and sat down beside her, she had allowed her head to rest on his shoulder – just as she had done so many times in the past. He had kissed the top of her head, just like he had done so many times in the past and she had looked up to smile at him. And then he kissed her – not at all like he had done in the past. And this time instead of feeling like she was kissing her brother, or Matt Goss on a Bros poster from *Smash Hits* she felt as if she was being kissed properly for the first time.

She closed her eyes and gave into the feelings which were coursing through her body. The wine made her shameless and before she knew it her hand had slipped from his neck, to the small of his back while his hand slipped from the small of her back to the curve of her breast. She gasped – shocked and amazed that she felt her body responding to his touch. With a boldness only brought on by the aforementioned wine she moved her hand to his crotch and when he groaned at her touch – a heavy groan from the very pit of his stomach – she wanted him more than she had ever wanted anything in her life. So, they went, silently, back to her room and then things changed forever.

The sex was great. Mind-blowingly great. Hope might have actually passed out at one stage, it was that great.

But when they woke in the morning it was as if it had never happened. Indeed, if it had not been for the naked man in the bed beside her, she would have questioned whether or not anything had happened at all. He just got up, went to the kitchen, made her some toast and then suggested a trip to one of the local markets. She wanted to ask him what it all meant but it just seemed like one of those things – one of those mad, drink-induced moments of craziness never, ever to be spoken of again. Every now and again Hope had liked to replay it all in her head but she was happy to relive the memory and leave it at that. She hadn't wanted more. She valued Dylan too much as a friend to want to complicate or risk it or any of that old nonsense. Or at least that is how she felt right up until that point, several months ago, when she had realised she was crazy in love with him.

Back at the terrace, the memory of a more recent tryst fresh in her mind, she slipped the blanket from her shoulders and padded down to the pool – still glistening majestically in the moonlight. She dipped her toes in. Funny, the water didn't seem so cold this time round and soon she was sitting on the edge contemplating diving right in. Sure, why not? She slipped in, still wearing her cotton sundress, and immersed herself in the moment. She definitely wanted to be there right in that very moment and not in any moment which involved Dylan, Cyndi and the horrible triangle she had found herself in.

Hope hadn't closed the shutters in her room before going to sleep so when the sun rose it shone right in, waking her from her peaceful slumber. Still, she thought, it was better to be woken by a ray of sunshine glinting in the window than the noise of naked flesh slapping together in the adjoining room. There were definitely no ear-splitting orgasms happening anywhere in their gorgeous villa that morning and Hope was deeply grateful for that. She realised just how well she had slept – obviously wrecked from a day's travelling, an afternoon sipping fine French wine and an evening bobbing around in the pool trying to push her memories as far away from her as possible.

Stretching, she sat up and slipped her feet into the slippers that were by her bed. She decided to make her way downstairs to put on some breakfast. The old habit of having a bacon sandwich ready for everyone in the house was steadfastly refusing to slide and she thought it would be a nice treat for Ava to have something fresh and delicious ready which they could maybe eat on the sun terrace before getting to work.

The skip would be delivered later. She supposed they would have to go shopping as well – find a supermarket or wander through the local village. She had, at best, hazy memories of it and she wondered would it all come back to her as she wandered down the winding streets. She hoped they would find some time for some Grade A lounging around the pool or perhaps some more sightseeing, but she was under no illusions as to why she was here and she was quite happy to keep busy. Busy gave her less time for thinking – and that day she didn't want to think. Although she knew she had so much to sort out in her own head, it could wait until she was in better form for it and until Betty's house had been taken apart and put together again all ready for the new owners.

Pulling her dressing-gown round her, Hope was just about to leave the room to go downstairs when her phone beeped. Lifting it, she saw a text message from Dylan.

"We're just in from work. Wanted to check you had arrived safely? D x"

"*We're*," Hope muttered in a childlike voice. Everything was 'we' these days. 'No, thanks, *we've* eaten.' '*We're* just going to bed' (most often said with a wink and a giggle), 'No, *we have* plans'.

Hope grimaced at the phone and threw it on the bed. She would answer it later, she thought – they'd probably be off bonking by now anyway. Letting herself have the smallest and quietest of screams, she walked out of the room and padded downstairs where the smell of cooking bacon and fresh coffee assaulted her nostrils.

Clearly she was not the only early bird in France.

"Morning!" Ava called cheerily from the kitchen. "Did you sleep well?"

"The best. Must have been the fresh air. And the wine. Definitely the wine helped. How about you?"

"Like a baby," Ava said, her back to Hope as she finished grilling the bacon. "But I'm so used to getting up early with Maisie, I couldn't lie in even if I wanted to. Anyway, I thought we would get a good breakfast into us and get stuck in."

"I was just thinking the same thing," Hope said. "We should really keep to Betty's schedule or we'll never get through it all. She was quite the planner."

"Nothing wrong with that," Ava said with a smile, sitting down across the large wooden kitchen island from Hope. "Planning is one of my favourite things too. Sad but true."

Hope laughed. She didn't want to say to her cousin that she had kind of got that impression anyway. The manila folders were a giveaway. As was the way Ava's eyes had lit up at the mention of extra baggage allowance, the arrival of a skip and the way in which she had got up early, cooked breakfast and cleared up the detritus from the previous night.

It was refreshing actually, Hope thought, to share with a girl. Her holidays with Dylan had always been so much more chaotic. He left all the planning down to her – and she was notoriously scatty. Each holiday had been peppered with a lost passport incident, or lost tickets, or lost traveller's cheques. On one particularly memorable trip to Barcelona, they had even managed to lose their luggage – leaving it in the back of a taxi as they skipped into their hostel of choice while singing the Freddie Mercury and Montserrat Caballe duet loudly, and out of tune, together.

He never cooked her breakfast – unless you counted presenting her with a McDonald's breakfast – and he certainly never suggested making concrete plans. "We'll just follow our noses," he would say, knowing that more times than enough his nose would lead him direct to the beach. And it wasn't that Hope hated beaches, it was just that she *hated* beaches. They were relatively boring – especially to someone like her who was completely fish-phobic and wouldn't dream of swimming in the sea if her life depended on it. And then, of course, there was the sand-everywhere issue. No – she preferred to sight-see, to drink in the local culture. Dylan just preferred to drink in the local drink.

She took a deep breath and sipped from the coffee cup Ava had put in front of her. Yes, she would follow Ava's plans and distract herself from the mess her life was becoming and she would not think about Dylan at all. Not even a wee bit. Well, maybe just a little bit. A tiny bit. Such a small bit she would hardly even notice.

Chapter 14

Breakfast was done, the dishes were washed (of course Ava couldn't leave dishes sitting). She had showered and dressed in a pair of loose trousers, a T-shirt and comfy sneakers. She had tied her hair back and sat down at the small table in the living room with Betty's letters and schedule to make plans. Today was to be 'bedroom' day. The next letter would be somewhere – undisclosed – in the bedroom. Bohemian to the last, Betty was making things interesting.

But there were things Ava wanted to do first. The first thing, of course, was that she absolutely wanted to go to the supermarket and preferably on her own so that she wouldn't have to explain slipping that pregnancy testing kit into the trolley. She would have to fob Hope off – tell her she would be best fixed staying at home and waiting for the skip to be delivered in case it needed signing for.

It wouldn't be easy. Hope knew the area better than she did – she would be able to find the supermarket easily and her knowledge of French was definitely better than Ava's. All Ava could do was look on with admiration when her cousin had eloquently sorted out the car hire the day before while she herself had only been able to hand over the printout of her booking form and her driving licence. Ah! Driving licence. Hope didn't have one and wasn't on the insurance for the hire car – that would be the way of ensuring it was she who went to the supermarket and she was sure Hope wouldn't mind waiting for the skip. Sure wasn't that as glam as it got, she thought with a cringe as she set about planning the rest of the day.

She would pick up some storage boxes, some bin bags, and some more manila folders if she could find them for storing photos and paperwork. And then they would get stuck in.

"You don't mind, do you?" she asked as she picked up her shopping list and the car keys.

Hope shrugged her shoulders. "Honestly? No. I don't mind one bit. Choice of a supermarket and lounging by the pool until you get back? I can live with that."

Ava felt a little bit of a bitch for not telling her the real reason she wanted to go but she simply wasn't ready to say the words out loud just yet – in fact certainly not before she absolutely had to say them out loud.

When she woke that morning she had thought, once again, about phoning Connor but something had stopped her. He was the kind of person who liked definites – who would have asked had she tested and when she replied that nope, not yet, he would have told her come back when she had something more concrete.

Besides, she didn't really want to tell him over the phone from France. A part of her – the very small tiny almost miniscule part which was not freaking out at the very notion of having another baby to look after – wanted to tell him in a nice way. She had always wanted to be one of those women who bought a pair of bootees and handed them to their husband on a silver platter to announce her pregnancy, or who wrote a "To Daddy" card and handed to him, watching for the change in his facial expression as he read those life-altering words. She had missed the boat on that one with Maisie. She had done the test when her period had been precisely twenty-three seconds late (or some other such absurdity) and had burst into tears when the second pink line had come up. Hearing her wailing, Connor had walked into the bathroom to see her sitting, still on the toilet, knickers at half-mast, thrusting the testing stick right at him. That was not a story they would be retelling any time. Phoning, slightly hysterically, from France would be right up there.

Grabbing the car keys and gearing herself up for driving on the wrong side of the road to a hypermarket on the other side of the village, she took a deep breath. It was time to pull herself together. Focus on the task ahead. Get what she needed and quit overanalysing everything.

Hope had wandered from room to room. It was hard to think the house hadn't been lived in for a few months. Betty had gone into the hospice nursing home in January but the house still had the feel of her in every room. Standing in front of the wood-burner, she could almost see her aunt holding court from her favourite green tweed armchair – her Irish chair as she called it – and urging Hope and Dylan to join her in a sing-song. They would, even though they didn't know the words, nor the tunes, to many of the old Irish songs Betty sang. They would all give it a bit of gusto on *Danny Boy* though and, without fail, Hope would notice her aunt wipe a tear from her eye when she reached those famous high notes of *"But come thee back, when summer's in the meadow!"*. If she closed her eyes, she could almost hear her voice echo around the room.

She moved on to Betty's room, where they were due to start their de-cluttering task – pristine, tidy and as if her aunt had left it just that morning while she went for a walk to the village. A small silver-handled brush still sat on the dressing table, kept company by a host of coloured glass bottles into which Betty had decanted her favourite perfumes. The bed was still made. The picture of a grinning Betty and a proud Claude on their wedding day still hung above the bed. All that Hope noticed missing was the framed picture of Claude which used to rest on the bedside table. She imagined Betty had taken that to the hospice with her. She sat for a moment on the edge of the bed and thought how sad it was that she was about to pack up someone's life for good.

Needing some air, Hope grabbed a bottle of water and walked down by the pool where she suddenly became aware of someone watching her from the top of the steps by the villa. Stopping and shielding her eyes against the sun, she looked up, assuming whoever was watching had come to deliver the skip in which they would toss the unwanted parts of their beloved aunt's life.

"Hello?" a man's voice called, his accent soft.

"Hello?" she called back.

"Are you Ava?" he called, "*Je suis* – I am – Jean-Luc."

Ah, Jean-Luc – he who left wine and chocolate and who Ava surmised was perhaps a lover of their feisty aunt and who was definitely not the rotund French pensioner she had imagined him to be. In fact, he was kind of sexy in a George Clooney meets Dr McSteamy from *Grey's Anatomy* kind of a way. She guessed he was in his mid to late 40s, and he clearly looked after himself and was no stranger to the gym.

"No," she replied as he started to walk towards her. "I'm not Ava, I'm Hope. Ava has gone to the supermarket. She shouldn't be long."

"I was passing and I wanted to check if everything was okay? Betty wanted me to keep an eye on you." He said it in such a way, with such a gleam in his eye, that Hope wondered what exactly Betty had been telling her neighbour.

"Yes," she said. "We're fine. It's lovely here. We're just making plans to do what she wished."

He smiled. "Yes. It is lovely here. Your aunt, she loved it very much. It made her happy."

Hope fought the urge ask him what else made her aunt happy. Indeed, had he made her aunt happy? Was he her lover? The thought made her smile – and also made her just the teeniest bit jealous. Hmm, she thought, I was definitely not expecting that.

"And you have no problems with the house? It has been empty for a while. I did pop in every now and again but –"

"No, not that I know of. Everything seems just fine."

"*Trés bien*," he muttered, pushing his sunglasses off his face and onto the top of his head.

She wondered should she be inviting him in for coffee. He was about the only living link she had to her aunt right there and then.

It seemed likely that he, more than anyone, knew exactly what her intentions for the house were.

It would be polite, she reasoned, so she offered and he graciously accepted and she found herself standing in the kitchen making fresh coffee for a man who only had to look at her for her to feel the minute hairs of the back of her neck stand on edge. In a good way.

"I don't remember you," she said and he looked puzzled. "From when I stayed here with Betty, twelve years ago. I thought she had introduced me to absolutely everyone she knew, but I don't remember you."

"Ah," he said with a smile, "twelve years ago I was living and working in Spain. You may have met my father, Pierre? He was a dear friend to Betty and Claude. I moved back to Saint Jeannet nine years ago when he took ill and needed to me to take care of the family business."

Hope scanned her memory and an image of an older short, rotund man with a comedy moustache entered her head. He was a lovely man – a friendly, smiling kind-hearted soul who told her that if she were thirty years younger he would have married her and taken her from the young man she was currently with.

Nodding fondly at the memory, she smiled. "Oh yes, I remember your father. He was a nice man."

"With an eye for the ladies," Jean-Luc laughed – a deep throaty French laugh which made her feel a little funny.

She turned to see him leaning against the worktop, looking around the kitchen. She watched the coffee bubble and brew, making small talk easily with him before she picked up the cups of coffee and gestured that they should move to the terrace where he asked her more about her trip and she asked him about his travelling experiences. They had been to some of the places, it seemed, weeks or months apart. They smiled at that coincidence and moved on to talk more about Betty.

Hope was able to ascertain, without having to come right out and ask, that no, he had not been her aunt's lover but had simply helped around the house when he could. He would call in one or two nights a week and she would make him dinner and in return he would make sure all the little odd jobs around the house were done and he would take her shopping each Saturday morning. There couldn't have been that much between them age-wise but he did not talk of her like she was his great lost love. He talked of her as if she were a friend, or a dear aunt.

From his chat she was also able to ascertain he must not have a significant other making demands on his time. Although – how he was single was simply beyond her.

They chatted for a little more before he looked at his watch and announced that he really must be leaving.

"I have an appointment to attend," he said, standing up.

She stood too.

"Feel free to call me any time," he said. "I'm sorry I did not meet Ava. I wanted to talk to you both about the local markets and see what plans you have. Perhaps I will call in tomorrow? Or we could meet for coffee?"

He smiled and Hope could not help but notice how warm and honest his smile seemed. She noticed that more than his crisp white T-shirt with a slight V-neck and his faded jeans. She noticed it more than the downy hair on his tanned arms, or the dark hair sprinkled with the grey on his head or his three-day-old stubble. She noticed it more – but just a little bit more – than the crinkle around his eyes and then she realised she had force herself to break her stare or risk seeming like a complete and utter psycho muppet.

"Betty has much of our week mapped out for us but that would be nice," she said, extending her hand to his.

"Good," he said. "I will be in touch soon."

"You saw him?" Ava squealed, sitting down on one of the squashy sofas, tired from the exertion of mastering the art of left-hand driving and surviving the madness of a supermarket where everything was in French and where she had received dirty looks for speaking English. "Do tell? Was he a hunk? Was he a bit of an Olivier Martinez or more a Gerard Depardieu? I hope the former and not the latter. I don't get people who find that Gerard Depardieu handsome.

He looks like the kind of man who would have nose hair. Did Jean-Luc have nose hair?"

"I can't say I looked up his nose to check for hair issues, but he didn't look the type. He was quite well-groomed. And quite handsome. Like that doctor from *Grey's Anatomy*? You know, McSteamy? And his accent was divine – better than Belfast or Derry anyway."

"Ooooh," Ava sighed while Hope poured some fresh lemonade into two glasses. "McSteamy . . . sure beats the Derry version, McItYourself," Ava said with a giggle as Hope sat down. "Like the song said, tell me more!"

"Well, there isn't much to tell," said Hope. "He asked if everything was okay. I told him it was. He told me he used to do odd jobs for Betty but, you know, not in that way. I knew his father, as it happens, from when we visited before. He wanted to talk to us both about what happens next and said maybe we could meet for coffee tomorrow? He said we were to get in touch if we needed anything."

"Anything?" Ava asked, raising her eyebrow. "You seem quite animated, Ms Scott."

"Ah," Hope said, putting on a solemn tone so as to remind herself as much as anything else, "you forget I am currently the lead character in my own Very Long Sad Story. It would do me no good to get animated about anything, let alone strange Frenchmen with adorable crinkles around their eyes."

"You never mentioned the crinkles before."

"Did I not?" Hope said, an image of his smile flashing into her mind again – an image which she tried to push out as soon as it arrived. An image which had, at least, replaced her never-ending brain wallpaper of Dylan and Cyndi going at it on the kitchen table.

Chapter 15

It was time to start with Betty's room.

"This will be tough," Hope said, opening the door and allowing Ava to walk in before her. "Ah well, it wouldn't be like Betty not to dive right in. Feels a bit weird though, starting to dig through her stuff."

"It's a gorgeous room," Ava said, struck by how peaceful and uncluttering it was.

There was no overflowing basket of clothes which needed ironing. There were no half-read books scattered there or abandoned teddy bears lying on the floor. It was what she wished her own bedroom was like at home – a haven. Plain walls. Simple curtains. A wooden floor with no mushed-in make-up here and there. No noise but the whisper of the wind in the trees outside the window.

"It still feels wrong," Ava said as she laid out her storage boxes and folders on the bed. There were bags for the stuff which would be dumped. Bags for that which would be recycled. Boxes for the must-keep items and boxes for the items they would sell on.

"I've never cleaned out the house of a dead relative before," Hope said, "but I don't imagine it ever feels right. We just have to keep reminding ourselves that this is what Betty wanted. And specifically she wanted *us* to do it, so we'd better keep that in mind too."

Hope was right, of course and Ava realised that she really needed to detach herself emotionally as much as possible and do what she had to do. There was no good getting maudlin over it – it would still need to be done and this was just the kind of thing that normally sent her into a near-orgasmic frenzy of excitement. Organising things was her thing. She would just have to focus – and focus damn hard.

What she was not expecting, however, was the explosion of emotion which burst through her when Hope opened the wardrobe at the end of the room and she saw not only all of Betty's clothes neatly hung together but all of Claude's too – side by side. Her aunt clearly could not bear to be parted from them. A guttural sob – one which brought forward a river of snot along with it – escaped from her throat and all her previous *just focus* affirmations disappeared as she ran to the lovely ensuite in her own bedroom and locked the door.

Oh God, this was tough. It was going to be tough anyway but, combined with pregnancy hormones crashing through her veins, it was even fecking tougher. She tried to compose herself but each time she thought she had caught her breath another wave of grief and anxiety hit her slap up the face.

"Ava?" she heard Hope say gently, as she rapped on the door.

She shook her head.

"Ava? Are you okay?"

She shook her head again, forgetting that her cousin couldn't of course see her.

"Ava, it's only some old things and it's only natural we're going to find it emotional."

Still shaking her head, Ava stood up and opened the door to face her cousin who seemed genuinely concerned for her wellbeing.

"I'm pregnant," she said. "I'm sorry. I'm pregnant – well, I think I'm pregnant anyway and it's hormones," she managed before she disintegrated again.

"Oh sweetheart, I'm sensing pregnant is not a good thing right now?"

Ava shook her head again as she allowed Hope to guide her to the edge of the bed to sit down. "That makes me sound like a bitch, doesn't it? To think it's not a good thing?"

"Things don't always work out the way we want them to. What does Connor think? Is he okay with it? He is supportive, isn't he?"

"He doesn't know," Ava said, feeling a little embarrassed even though Hope was being perfectly lovely and holding her hand as if she knew just how horrible this was.

"Oh," Hope said. "Can I ask a really, really personal question and you can feel free to tell me to feck right off . . . but . . . the baby? It is his, isn't it?"

Ava laughed at that because she had a hard enough time finding the energy to sleep with her husband never mind carry on a clandestine affair behind his back. "Yes . . . yes, it's his."

"And he's a good husband?" Hope probed gently.

"He is. But this is going to sound awful. It's just – it's hard work. It's fecking hard work." She wanted to say more – like she was terrified on an almost daily basis that she wasn't a good enough mother – that she was in some way damaging her child. The papers were filled with reports of how working mothers were leading their children down a one-way path to delinquency and she was afraid Maisie would grow up feeling unloved and unwanted. She already felt as if she was splitting herself into too many parts – how on earth would she split herself into any more?

They sat in silence for a while before Hope spoke again. "You say, you *think* you are pregnant? Have you tested?"

Ava shook her head before adding that she had bought a test earlier that day and had been fully intending on using it just as soon as she needed to pee.

"Well, do you need to pee now?"

Ava shook her head. It was as if her bladder had gone on strike. It, like the rest of her, didn't want to confirm what she was most afraid of.

"Right, well then, will we go back to Betty's room? And we'll sort some clothes and look for her latest letter and when you are ready we can come back here and you can test, okay?"

Ava nodded as Hope walked into the bathroom and retrieved a tissue for her to blow her nose on.

"That's a girl," Hope said with a smile. "And if it makes you feel any better at all – and until you want to talk about things more – I can start telling you my sad story. Trust me, it will make you feel better."

Hope winked and Ava smiled gratefully as they walked back into Betty and Claude's room and started folding and sorting their clothes.

"Do you think she ever threw anything out?" Ava asked, feeling more composed now as she unhooked each garment from its hanger and showed it to Hope.

"I'm glad she didn't. Some of this stuff is gorgeous." Hope held a long oyster-coloured evening gown in soft satin against her and twirled in front of a mirror. "She had some style – and she knew which pieces to keep and which to throw away. This dress is vintage for sure. She must have trawled the markets like a good 'un. I couldn't imagine my mum getting away with wearing anything like this and there's not that much of an age difference. Betty had style."

"You should keep it. It would look fabulous on you – with some Victory rolls in your hair?"

"I feel like I'm digging in my mother's dressing-up box," Hope giggled. "Only, you know, sans the sensible M&S slacks and Dunnes Stores cardigans."

Ava unhooked a floral tea dress from a hanger and handed it over. "You should try this on too. It's very now."

Hope smiled and took it to look at the delicate floral pattern. "God, she was stunning, wasn't she?" she said, looking from the dress to the wedding picture on the wall and noticing, for the first time, the slightest resemblance between her and Ava who was unhooking a rather less flattering pink velvet jumpsuit which was clearly a wardrobe mistake from the 70s or 80s. Ava held it up and Hope grimaced.

"You don't want to try this one on?" Ava said with a snort.

"Christ no, I'd look like George from *Rainbow*!" She laughed as Ava discarded it in the rubbish pile.

Hope was pleased to see Ava look calmer than when she had run from the room like everyone belonging to her had just kicked the bucket. She felt sorry for her. From what she knew of Ava, she always seemed like the kind of person who had it all together. She admitted it. Even though you weren't really supposed to be jealous of people, she had been heart-jealous of Ava and her marriage and her cute daughter who looked like she walked straight out of an ad for fecking Fairy powder or something. But Ava wasn't happy. And she was scared and that made Hope wonder what it really was all about.

Ava handed her a silver-coloured shawl, with delicate tassels, and she wrapped it around her shoulders and spun around in it. For a second she imagined she was wearing the oyster-coloured dress at her vintage-style wedding to Dylan. They would travel to Saint Jeannet for their honeymoon and she would remind him that, really, this was kind of where it all started. He would laugh and then admit he didn't have a baldy notion what she was talking about and she would remind him of the night by the pool and they would laugh uproariously at the very memory.

Then she remembered that there was a Cyndi in the picture now and her fantasy disappeared before her very eyes and she started to work her way through Betty's drawers. Soft, comfy jumpers, with tailored twin sets and blouses – more functional and less fashionable than the clothes she had worn in her heyday – filled the drawers. All were folded neatly – pressed to perfection. Even her underwear drawer had been neatly arranged – sensible bras and comfortable knickers were folded in piles, together with delicate stockings rolled into balls beside them. Claude's shirts were pressed and folded together in one drawer. His socks were still bundled together as if they were waiting for the feet to come and fill them. It was quite sweet. Hope wondered who would look after her belongings when she was gone. In a moment of fleeting panic she wondered if Cyndi would riffle through the mess that was her underwear drawer and laugh outrageously at the belly-warming big knickers she kept for the days when she had her period. At least, she thought, Ava had Connor even if she was (possibly) pregnant with a baby she wasn't sure she wanted.

She filled a bag with underwear, tied it and put it to one side while wondering how exactly she should start telling the Very Long Sad Story. It could of course start with that kiss in her room in the Halls of Residence at university, or their trip together or their sleeping together in the very house they were sleeping in right now. She sighed, opened another drawer and started to fill another bag until she heard a squeal of delight from Ava who had lifted down a dusty box from the top of the wardrobe and opened it.

In her hand she had a pair of purple shoes, with a rounded toe, a flared heel and the most delicate of brocade detailing at the ankle. Decorated with a sequinned rose, big and bold at the front, they were, simply, stunning.

"Ooooooh!" Hope said.

"I know," Ava answered, hugging them to her. "This was where it all started, you know, with Betty and me . . . and these shoes."

She had been busting for a pee for a full forty-five minutes before she left the pile of clothes and shoes and made for her ensuite.

"I can come with you," Hope said. "You know, I'll sit outside. I won't actually go in there with you. But I'll wait in the bedroom. I'll even put my fingers in my ears so I don't hear you pee if that helps."

Ava laughed and she was grateful that her cousin was with her. It made it easier somehow to have someone who had no real vested interest whatsoever in whether or not she actually was pregnant.

"Okay," she said, walking through the bedroom, taking the test from where she had hidden it in the bottom of her bag and locking herself in the ensuite while she heard Hope sing outside. Her bladder developed a sudden case of shyness again and she shouted to Hope that she couldn't do it.

"Run some water," Hope shouted. "That always makes me want to pee and I'll sing something . . . erm . . . watery!" she shouted before bursting into a verse of 'Raindrops Keep Falling on my Head'.

Ava laughed, unwrapped the stick, did what she had to do and waited for the lines to confirm what she already knew.

As the line appeared, just as she knew it would, she started to laugh – just a little hysterically – and then she cried. She had never been so scared, or so exhilarated, in her life.

"Even a little one for the shock?" Hope asked, pouring herself a glass of wine.

"I'm pretty sure even little ones for the shock are frowned upon these days," Ava said wryly, as she filled the kettle to make a cup of tea.

"Well, you don't mind if I have one for the shock? I've never been with anyone who just found out they were pregnant before."

Ava smiled. Hope had been brilliant. When she had walked out of the bathroom, stick in hand, emotions veering from one extreme to another in a matter of seconds, Hope had simply given her a big hug and told her she would get through this.

"I don't know you that well," she had said, "but I'm pretty sure you have been through worse than this and, while this is as shocking and scary as bedamned, I'm pretty sure that it will all work itself out."

"Are you always so optimistic about things?"

"Me? Fuck no. But I've a feeling about this one and my gut is normally right. Except when it comes to falling in love with the wrong person."

"Ah, the Long Sad Story at last? I had a feeling it might be about Mr Wrong."

"If I'm going to tell you this I am going to need more than one stiff drink and you are going to need more than one cup of tea and both of us are going to need very comfortable seats."

Glad of the distraction and grateful that she wasn't the only person in the room who felt like her life was spinning out of control, Ava followed Hope to the kitchen and then through to the living room where her cousin proceeded to tell her all about her best friend – the man she loved but who loved someone else.

Chapter 16

As it happened Ava was a very good listener. She nodded in the right places, made the appropriate shocked noises in the right places, and didn't mind when Hope kept returning to the topic as they returned to Betty's room and sorted through the rest of her clothes and what was left of her make-up and toiletries.

The conversation had flowed easily, effortlessly even, between the two of them. Hope shared her fears that Dylan would perhaps never love her back – at least not in the way she wanted him to and Ava had spoken about her fears about having another child – fears she was trying desperately to rationalise in her head. And they had spoken, a lot, about Betty and what her life must have been like.

At teatime, the famous letter still not found and the bedroom almost cleared out, Ava had given in to exhaustion and excused herself, saying she absolutely needed to lie down before she fell down.

Hope had retired to her room to think about what had been yet another exceptionally strange day when she noticed her phone still lying on the bed from where she had thrown it earlier.

She realised she still hadn't responded to Dylan's text message which she knew was pretty childish. Dylan wouldn't pick up on it, of course not. He, like most men, wasn't renowned for sensitivity to her ignoring his text messages. She would have to spell out that she was annoyed with him and she wasn't prepared to do that. It would do no good whatsoever to declare loudly that his completely ignoring the fact that they'd had sex annoyed her almost as much as his falling in love with someone else had really, really pissed her off.

Falling in love with each other had never been part of the deal. But he could have acknowledged that night . . . even just a little bit. She sighed and blew her fringe from her face. She tried to remind herself she was a responsible adult, in her mid-thirties, and that she should act her age and not her shoe size.

As she stared out over the luscious green rolling hills, she thought about just how sophisticated and grown-up Ava seemed, even if she was having a panic about being pregnant. She had a serene quality about her which Hope envied. She seemed like the kind of person who always made sensible decisions. Instead of splurging on designer shoes and bags, she would put the money towards a new sofa or getting her bathrooms refitted. Hope was pretty sure Ava didn't have a credit card – or that if she did she was the kind of person who actually did pay off the full balance at the end of every month. Needless to say, Hope was not that kind of person and, even if she had wanted to be, there was no way she could have afforded to pay off the rocketing balances of her plastic with just one month's wages. One year's would be a struggle.

Logging onto to her laptop to check her email she saw that the internet seemed to be working just fine without her being attached to it 24/7. She had a few emails including a few referrals for freelance work which she would follow up when she got back to Belfast and a credit card statement that made her want to weep. She vowed not to use that particular flexible friend for the rest of her holiday as refusal could cause embarrassment.

She clicked onto Facebook to see that Dylan had changed his profile picture – he wasn't there with his trademark toothy grin and slightly foppish hair any more. His picture was two pairs of feet, which at first kind of turned Hope's stomach. She couldn't stand the look of feet – especially not big man feet – but when she saw the dainty pair beside the big man feet, with the toenails French-manicured and a very small floral tattoo twirling its way towards the big toe, she felt even more sick.

There were certain things which signalled a couple were 'very much in love'. Moving in together was not necessarily one of them. Moving in together could just be an act of convenience and a cheaper way to live. Shagging morning, noon and night was not necessarily an act of love either. Lust, yes. Love . . . meh . . . maybe not. But taking a photograph of your feet, naked and side by side, and posting them as your profile picture on Facebook could only mean one thing.

Cyndi with a Y and an I and Dylan with ugly, albeit impressively big, feet were 'very much in love'. Indeed, she gasped when she saw his status update which confirmed, as she had guessed, that "Dylan McKenzie is very much in love". She gave the laptop a bad look, wished a bad dose of Athlete's Foot on the pair of them and closed the screen in a fit of pique. It might just be time to pour another glass of wine.

The sun was starting to set – bold pink streaks were colouring the sky – when Ava woke from her nap. The first thought which entered her head was that, yes, she was pregnant. The second thought was that she had told someone and the world hadn't ended. The third thought was that, sadly, that person hadn't been Connor and she still had that hurdle to jump over.

He wouldn't be annoyed. She knew that. Connor Campbell didn't have a bad-tempered bone in his entire body – but he would be worried. He had been feeling the pressure lately – with his lengthy commute and increased pressure on the accountancy firm. He often brought work home with him and would sit up until the wee small hours working to keep up to speed before getting up for his drive up the road. By the weekend he was exhausted and had complained that he was seeing less and less of Maisie. How they would fit a new baby into that routine was beyond her but then again before they had Maisie they didn't see how they could ever fit a child into their free and easy lifestyle either. And they had.

She lifted her phone and dialled Connor's number – just to hear his voice. Telling herself that the tone of his voice would indicate just whether or not everything would be okay, she listened to it ring before he answered with a whisper.

"I'm just settling Maisie down," he said, "I'll call you back."

She went to answer but he had already hung up so she sat back and stared at her phone and wondered how she would open this conversation. "Hi, babe, I'm pregnant" or "You'll never guess what I've just found out" and then she remembered her dreams of telling him a nice way – in a way that belied her underlying panic and fear. So when the phone did ring and he said hello, sounding delighted to be hearing from her, she decided to keep quiet for another little while.

"Hello, pet," he said, his voice smooth and warm and just gorgeous and she wanted to reach down the phone line and hug him.

"It's lovely here," she answered, "Betty's house is lovely, the weather is gorgeous. She was thankfully quite tidy so the clearing out is not as scary as we thought it might be."

"And the wine?" he asked.

She thought back to the one glass she'd had the previous night before the penny dropped. It had been perfect but she wouldn't be repeating that experience again for the rest of the week. Of course, if she didn't want him to know, just yet, that she wouldn't be drinking for the foreseeable she would need to lie through her teeth.

"The wine is lovely. And the cheese. Oh, and the pâté is divine." She thought she might as well go for overkill and list as many pregnancy-forbidden foods as possible.

"Sounds perfect."

"And Dublin and Maisie?" she asked, not trusting herself to say much more in case she gave anything away.

"Dublin is the usual madhouse. My sister has been over today with the kids. What a handful! And Maisie didn't know what do with herself, surrounded by all her cousins all talking in strong accents. I was worried for a bit, but you know Maisie, ten minutes in and she was bossing them all about. She was wrecked going to bed – tears and everything. She misses you," he said softly, before adding, "I miss you."

She melted. He sounded lonely and she wished she was there to take his hand and give him a hug. "I miss you too, more than you know," she said.

Wide awake now and knowing there was no chance whatsoever of her getting back to sleep, she decided to go for a quick dip in the pool before doing some more sorting in Betty's room. When she met this Jean-Luc the following day she wanted to be able to tell him they had made great inroads and hadn't, instead, spent a great deal of the time gossiping about whatever crises they were going through in their own lives.

The wardrobe was mostly cleared, as was the chest of the drawers and the bedside tables. Most of what they had uncovered would be going to the local charity shop, they decided – with Hope holding onto a few items and Ava, of course, holding onto the purple shoes. She didn't care that she didn't have a single thing that would match them. She would buy something. Or keep them just to try on when she was on her own in her bedroom wanting to feel glamorous and not like a big old mammy machine.

Delving into the back of the cupboard, Ava pulled out a dark wooden box with four drawers at the front – each with a tarnished brass handle. Gently pulling the first drawer open, she saw it contained a range of bangles and bracelets – gold and silver mixed together. She would definitely have to wait for Hope, to delve any further. Except she was nosey, and she wanted to see what else was in the box. And, as it happened, as she pulled open the second drawer an envelope, folded in two, unfurled and she lifted it – once again seeing Betty's handwriting. Aha! She had found the letter. She had to stop herself from giving a girly scream. Feck you, Charlie Bucket and your Golden-Ticket finding, I've found the letter! It was sad, but it gave her a thrill. Carefully tearing it open, she pulled out the single sheet of handwritten paper along with three rings and looked at them. Two solid gold bands, one large, one small and a gold engagement ring with three sapphire stones surrounded by diamonds.

She started to read:

My dear girls,

I hope this letter finds you well and happy. And enjoying the house. I hope I haven't given you too much work. I should have done more myself, but well, things got a little tough.

Ava, my pet, can you do me a favour? Please take care of these rings. Keep them safe. I know I said you could sell on anything at all you wanted but I'm trusting you to keep these for me. They are my most prized possessions. These are the symbols of our marriage – mine and Claude's.

He was very much insistent that he didn't want to be buried wearing his ring. He wanted to pass it on. We had thought, at one stage, we would pass our rings on to children of our own but well, we never did have children, the two of us. Don't feel sad about that – we were blessed in a million other ways.

Ava, I'm asking you to keep the rings and maybe you would pass them on to your darling Maisie when she is old enough, and if she finds a young man of her own? I trust, Hope, you won't feel put out by this but you will both understand, in due course.

Can I tell you, Ava and Hope, about my engagement ring? About how he gave it to me? I remember it all so well. Claude had been working in Derry – so strange for a Frenchman. Dear Lord, Derrymen found it tough enough to find work in Derry in the 70s but there he was – working in a very good job. He had twenty men under him and I, well, I was his secretary. That sounds really cheesy, doesn't it? A secretary falling for the boss, but that was how it happened. I was young and flighty and he would sit and talk to me for hours about his travels. Claude had seen the world and, God, I wanted to see the world but I couldn't see myself ever leaving Derry so I listened and lived my life vicariously through him. God, the world sounded amazing. Anything outside of checkpoints and bombs and riots on the streets sounded amazing. Not that we let it get us down. It's true, you know, what that Phil Coulter yoke sang about – how people in Derry just got on with things.

But, anyway, as we chatted – as we talked – I found myself falling for him. It probably wasn't sensible. I had other commitments which should have come first . . . but love . . . love can come when you least expect it. We just fell so very madly in love with each other.

But things started to go wrong. You know Derry was tough. The history books are filled with how Derry was tough. And Claude, he knew stuff. He had a background in the French army and some boys, well, they started to get heavy. They wanted him to, you know, help them with stuff. Bad stuff. They were not the kind of men you could say no to. If you did . . . well . . . So Claude knew he had no choice but to leave. He didn't want to put his life, my life, or my family's life, at risk – never mind that he felt Derry was his home now. I was heartbroken – devastated to the core. I had just started to feel my life coming together and now everything I knew was being torn from me – for what? Because he wouldn't get involved. Because he didn't want to be a part of someone else's fight.

The very thought of him leaving was horrible. I cried myself to sleep for a full week before he was due to leave and, the night before, he arranged to take me for dinner. I couldn't eat a bite. I could barely talk I was so distraught about it all.

All night I kept thinking, this is the last meal we will share together. This is the last conversation we will have. This is the last time he will kiss me. Does that sound very melodramatic? I had nothing to compare it to. I'd never been truly in love before, not with someone who loved me back anyway, and it just felt like my life was ending. He was quiet too and I was sure he was feeling the same as I was – as it turned out he was nervous.

Because as we walked home, hugging each other, me unable to speak, he stopped, right there as we walked along the quay and he turned to me and took my face in his hands. I can still now, if I close my eyes, feel the warmth of his breath on my face and the heat of his hands. He kissed me – a proper, deep kiss. (Is that too much information, as you young people would say?) And he whispered that he simply could not live without me. He would understand if I said no, he said as he presented me with the ring – it was his grandmother's. He'd had his mother send it over from France especially and even though I knew it would be horrible – unbelievably horrible – to leave my family, I knew I had found the person I was meant to be with. I would have to leave with him. I knew that. There was no way we could stay. I knew that I risked a lifetime of upset with my family – walking away from here and all that I had here. The family would say I was being selfish but I was making the least selfish decision of my life.

Claude and I – we would be okay. We would be better than okay. We would be happy. And my family? They would be okay. They would be better than okay and they would be happy. It might have been tough for them to see that but they would be fine. I knew it.

It's gorgeous, isn't it? The ring? All the same it doesn't mean as much to me as that plain gold band which I wore along with it. Almost nothing in the world is as precious to me as that ring and all it symbolised. If Claude didn't want to be buried with his ring, I wouldn't be buried with mine either so I'm leaving it here for you. Keep them safe. Use them. Pass them on to Maisie. Tell her I wanted her to have them. I know she is only a baby – but it's nice to think they will be around for a long time to come. That people will think of me, and Claude, and our love.

I want these rings to have a happy ending.

Love always,
Betty
xxx

Chapter 17

As Ava slept earlier that afternoon, Hope had spent the time in the farthest reach of the garden, amid the clematis and the wisteria with a bottle of wine for company, still trying to come to terms with the fact that he, Dylan, the man she was supposed to be with was very much in love with someone who most definitely was not her.

She sat on the wooden bench in the shade sipping her glass of Merlot and thought how strange everything was. Ava was pregnant. Ordinarily when such a juicy piece of gossip came her way, Hope would have been on the phone within a matter of seconds to Dylan and they would have started to dissect the details over a cup of coffee.

But things were different now. Weird and strange, even if he was acting like they were just the same – that they were still best friends – and that they hadn't had sex just over a week before. And he had enjoyed it. She knew he had enjoyed it. Men aren't so great at the whole faking-it thing. But yet he was toe-curlingly in love with Cyndi. The very thought made her feel dizzy – and not necessarily with lust or anything remotely exciting like that. She was dizzy with confusion and that strange unsettled feeling that she did not know what was coming next.

She couldn't imagine that Dylan and Cyndi with a Y and an I would want her tagging along for much longer, not if they really, truly were very madly in love indeed. Who wants a third wheel clogging up your living room and spare bedroom when you want to fornicate in those rooms in the manner most newly together and very much in love couples want to do? And what if Cyndi found out what had gone on the night before she had moved in? Not that Hope had any intention of telling her. Sweet Baby Jesus, she wasn't that mad! She was under no illusions that Cyndi could be feisty when she wanted to be and would pound her into smithereens given half the chance.

No, it was pretty inevitable that a lot had to change and that just wouldn't be so easy. She didn't earn enough to rent her own place in Belfast. Staff jobs in the media were like the Holy Grail just now and she didn't want to move back to her parents because, much as they were very proud of her, living back home at the age of thirty-four was verging on the shameful side of things.

Suddenly, and more than likely buoyed by the half bottle of Merlot she had necked at breakneck speed, she felt an urge to phone Dylan, regardless of how things were. He was her friend, even if she could feel that friendship slipping through her fingers.

"Feck it," she decided, lifting her phone from her pocket and walking back to the pool where she could pick up a signal. She slipped off her mules, sat down and dipped her feet in the water – the shock of the cold sending a shiver up her back.

"'Allo 'Allo," Dylan answered in a very dodgy accent straight out of the cult BBC show. "'Ow are yeeeuu?"

"Quit the accent, big lad," Hope teased. "It doesn't suit you. But since you asked anyway, I'm fine thanks. The weather here is amazing. I'm sitting with my feet in the pool right now."

"Aye, rub it in," he teased back and she could sense the smile on his face.

See, she had nothing to worry about after all. He was still Dylan. He was still her friend. There was no tension. Even him being very much in love with someone else didn't change that. Even him sleeping with her and never mentioning it again didn't change it, she tried to convince herself while trying to block the whole horrible, embarrassing messy episode out of her mind. *Think happy thoughts*, she told herself.

"Ach, you're not missing much – just sunshine, fine wine, delicious food and scenery to die for."

"I'm not a woman!" he protested. "I'd be just as happy with a pint of Bulmers down at Cutter's Wharf on a hot day and well you know it. Actually I'd be happy with a pint of Bulmers at Cutter's on a rainy day – no need to be fussy."

"Who are you kidding, McKenzie? You'd give your eye teeth to be lounging by the pool with me right now." She blushed as soon as the sentence was out – thinking of the last time he lounged by the pool with her.

"Don't take this the wrong way but I have my gorgeous girl here with me and that's enough. No pool in the world would entice me away from her."

She felt his words cut through her and she had to fight the urge to tell him to stop being such an insensitive twat. She then had to fight the urge to tell him to go away and cop himself on. Her next thought was to make fake sick noises down the phone at him. Instead she opted for option four – sighing and saying the very last thing she wanted to.

"Sure, aren't you the old romantic? I'm glad to see you're getting on so well."

"I know," he said, his voice taking on a softer tone. "I feel very lucky. She's great."

"Yeah," Hope said half-heartedly, wondering how she could change the subject from reasons why Cyndi was amazing to something less likely to make her want to throw herself into the pool with some rocks in her pocket.

"Can I ask you something?" Dylan said.

"You can always ask . . ."

"Are you okay?"

"Me?" she said, her cheeks flushing. Were they actually going to have that conversation now? Was he actually going to bring up the great unmentionable? Surely not?

"You just seem a little distant, that's all," he said as she gulped.

"Well, my dear Mr McKenzie, that will be the several hundred miles and several bodies of water between us, I would think."

"Ha ha, very funny," he said, the tone of his voice indicating that he did not find it funny at all.

She knew then that she could have launched into it all there and then but part of her didn't want to – didn't feel strong enough to and didn't really know what it would achieve anyway. No, not now, she reasoned. She wouldn't talk about it just now.

"I'm fine, Dylan, honestly. It's a bit strange here – going through Betty's things. The old doll had taste. But there is something sad about it. Sad but lovely. I think she had a very happy life."

"And how are you and Ava getting on? Is it awkward?"

Hope thought of the afternoon they had shared and laughed. No, they had definitely hit the ground running in terms of forging a friendship. Two days in and they'd had a pregnancy-test issue, a declaration of an unrequited love affair and bonding over vintage clothes.

"Not a bit. Surprisingly. We've been getting on really well."

There was a brief silence. "I miss you," Dylan said and she knew that he wasn't just talking about the physical distance which separated them.

"I've got to go," she muttered, knowing that staying on the phone would not end well and she pressed the end-call button on her phone. She was almost tempted to throw the damn thing into the pool but it had cost a lot of money and she needed it for work. So instead she sighed, pushed her hair back from her face and stared straight at the sun until her eyes watered.

Once suitably composed, she walked back to the house, back to Betty's green tweed chair where she sat down, poured the last drop of Merlot from the bottle into her glass and slugged it back, launching into perhaps the single worst ever rendition of *Danny Boy* – complete with closed eyes and the waving of her glass in a slightly out-of-time fashion.

She was just reaching lamenting the valley being hushed and white with snow when she opened her eyes and saw Ava in front of her, looking at her quizzically.

"I would very much like to keep this chair," Hope said, lounging back into it and singing "*Oh yes, oh yes, I'll take it home with me!*" in tune with the song.

She noticed a half smile on Ava's face, a curious mix of concern and amusement.

"*I've had a drink*," she crooned on and Ava sat down opposite her.

"I noticed. But yes, you should have the chair. Of course you should have the chair."

"I phoned Dylan."

She watched Ava pull a face which she couldn't help but feel was hysterically funny. So she laughed – a big belly-laugh.

"I know. It was a bad idea. I shouldn't have done it . . . but you see . . . there was this picture . . . of his feet. And her feet. Their feet. Together. I fucking hate feet. Especially feet together. Especially their feet together. There's no need, no need at all."

She knew she was rambling and she knew she sounded like a madwoman but she didn't care – because his feet were out there for the whole world to see and it was only a matter of time before she got emails and texts from well-meaning associates asking about the big love affair and wondering how she wasn't a part of it.

Ava shook her head. "To be honest, I'm not a big fan of feet either. And they took a picture, of their feet?"

"And put it on fecking Facebook. With a status update. What's on his mind? Well, what's on his mind is that he is very much in love."

"That's . . . erm . . . nice?" Ava offered half-heartedly.

"Yes. Nice. It's fecking nice – not. And he misses me. He told me that. He told me he misses me. And it was more than a 'I miss you' in a platonic kind of way. There was a tone."

"A tone?"

"Oh God, Ava, it's a mess, isn't it? Wasn't it supposed to be simple? Didn't all the books and all the movies just tell us we would fall in love? Isn't the male best friend supposed to fall in love with the female best friend? You know all that 'men and women can't get along 'cos all they want to do is shag' shit or whatever Harry told Sally?"

Ava shrugged her shoulders. "I don't know about the best friend thing but I'll tell you that, yes, I kind of thought by now I'd have it together. I'm a grown woman. I'm thirty-four. And I'm terrified of telling my husband I'm pregnant and I'm even more terrified of telling my mother who will wonder what on earth we've been at, since we've been finding things so hard."

Hope tried to focus on Ava's face but that last sip of wine had tipped her over the edge into full-on drunkenness. "Do you think Betty had it all together when she was our age?"

Ava sat back in her chair, or at least Hope thought she sat back in her chair – everything was a bit swimmy at that stage.

"I think she did," Ava said, showing her the letter she knew she had no chance whatsoever of being able to read. "And she believed in happy endings."

And Hope finally gave into a flurry of tears as Ava read aloud how Claude had been forced to leave Derry and how Betty had followed and even though it had been unbelievably tough she had left her family and found her happiness here in France.

"Happy endings do happen then?"

"I guess so."

"I'd love to have one."

"You might," Ava offered, reaching out to take the glass of wine from her cousin. "How about we get you a coffee? And maybe something to eat? I'm hungry. I could eat something."

"I've made a tit of myself, haven't I?"

"Look," Ava said calmly. "Earlier I had a mini-fit, then peed on a stick and then cried when I found out I was pregnant – so if you have made a tit of yourself, which I'm not at all saying you have, then so have I."

"And I thought you had it all together."

"Fuck!" Ava laughed and Hope felt herself choke.

Ava was a primary schoolteacher – and a very proper-looking responsible adult type and she didn't really expect her to swear –

not proper bad swear words. She felt a giggle rise up in her throat and she laughed as Ava started to laugh too.

"I don't think anyone really has it together," Ava laughed when she composed herself. "No one has it together at all."

Chapter 18

Hope woke to the light streaming in the small window. She was lying on the bed, with a throw over her, still fully clothed apart from her shoes which she surmised Ava had removed, or helped her remove. Christ, she should have drunk the coffee Ava had offered her instead of saying she was perfectly okay to open a third bottle of wine.

The rings had done it. The letter and the rings Ava had handed to her. She had realised with a thumping great thud that she wasn't married or even in a relationship. More than that – no one loved her. Not in that way. No one had ever offered her their grandmother's engagement ring and vowed to move heaven and earth so that they could stay together. The man she was hopelessly in love with didn't love her back – and didn't even seem to acknowledge the fact they had slept together or that she clearly had feelings for him.

She hadn't gone mad. She had drunk one (large) glass of wine while hugging into the tweed chair for dear life and telling Ava how very, incredibly lucky she was.

That was what she remembered clearly with a deep sense of embarrassment. She had hazier memories of Ava very gently taking the wineglass from her hand, and softly urging her to go to bed. She had been handed a glass of water to drink. Or at least she thought she had been handed a glass to drink.

Carefully, slowly and a little bit painfully, she opened her eyes – one a time. Too bright. She closed them again and took a deep breath. Opening them again, and feeling the room swim past her eyes, she glanced at the bedside table where indeed the tall glass of water still sat. Untouched. Oh no, this was not a good way to start the day. She lifted her arm to try and focus on the watch on her wrist. It was gone nine thirty and she was pretty sure they were supposed to be meeting Jean-Luc at some stage – not to mention getting on with clearing out Betty's things. Heavy lifting was not a good idea when your stomach was doing its best washing-machine impression. She should sit up. She knew that she needed to sit up – if for no other reason than her bladder was starting to wake up and she really needed to go for a pee.

Slowly, carefully, she pulled herself to a sitting position and looked out the window at the day in front of her while feeling for the glass on the bedside table. Sipping the tepid water her mind turned again to the rings and to Betty.

Betty hadn't been afraid to take risks – to move her life miles away from home for something she wanted. She didn't fall apart in a crisis or drink herself silly. No, she thought of Betty's kind face and warm smile and how she had brought her out to France and something – a little, tiny something shifted.

Hope realised she couldn't keep doing this. Well, she could, but she would quickly end up a pickled old prune and she would still be on her own and still miserable. Getting drunk and singing Bros' back catalogue loudly wouldn't make Dylan love her. (If that was all it would take he would have been madly in love with her years ago.) Phoning him and letting him torture her with details of his great big love affair wouldn't help either. She felt her stomach sink – a combination of her hangover, embarrassment at what she had got up to the night before, and the realisation that she would have to start letting go – and she sipped from the glass again and set about wondering just exactly what she would wear on the first day of the rest of her life. And, come to think of it, she would really have to start thinking about what exactly she wanted to do with the rest of her life.

The three rings were sitting together on the small table in the corner of the living room and Ava sat staring at them. She had woken early and wasted no time in getting up and going for a swim in the pool. She was filled with determination that she would get as much as possible done and she decided to form her plan while swimming lengths in the pool. It was glorious – to swim, properly swim. She couldn't remember the last time she'd had a proper swim. For the last years any trip to the pool had involved arm-bands, or swim nappies, fun pools and water slides and the inevitable tantrum at the end as she attempted to extract her waterbaby daughter from the pool and tackle her out of her swimming suit and into her clothes before she herself contracted hypothermia in the cold changing rooms. It was never an entirely pleasant experience and it certainly did nothing for her cardiovascular workout hopes. The only time she came close to breaking out in a sweat was when Maisie would dive-bomb under the waves with not a hint of fear about her.

Before she was a mum, swimming was one of the things she did to de-stress and she missed it. Gliding through the water, staring up at the sun, she smiled. Yes, this was perfect. This was the perfect way to clear your mind. Maybe she should recommend that Karen take up some swimming – although she could already hear Karen's retort echoing her in her head. "Swim? Are you mad? The only kind of swimming I want to do is in a big vat of vodka." Karen would laugh and Ava would smile and nod even though what she would really want to do is snap back that really Karen shouldn't be so bloody rude all of the time. And she would seethe with anger at her own spinelessness all the way home. Or, in a worse scenario, she would snap back and then Karen wouldn't speak to her and she would find herself crippled with guilt for the next fortnight. Which, she thought as she pulled herself up at the edge of the pool to catch her breath, was exactly what was happening now.

She wondered how Betty would deal with Karen. She would

probably know exactly what to say to her and how to say it. And she wouldn't feel horribly guilty afterwards. Jesus, Ava realised, Karen would have a canary when she heard Ava was pregnant again. She would no doubt give her chapter and verse on how she was mad as a box of frogs and throwing her life completely down the toilet.

On a previous night out she had already waxed lyrical on why Sophie would be her one and only child. "Oh God, do that again? Are you mad? You know what they say, I'll try anything once . . . well, I tried it and, honestly, I don't get the appeal. All that getting fat and getting stretch-marks and getting the lining kicked out of you for nine months before having to give birth. Oh my God, they can send a man to the moon but they can't come up with a single dignified way of getting a frigging baby out of you? My body was wrecked – you know what I'm talking about, Ava," she had said, giving Ava a full body scan with her eyes as if she had X-ray vision and could see exactly how Ava's tummy still sagged over her C-section scar and how her breasts were only pointing in the right direction thanks to the wonders of M&S underwiring. "And then what? The total loss of freedom for the next eighteen years!"

"You do love her though," Ava had said.

"Oh yes," Karen had said, half-heartedly. "But I'm not doing it again. My life has been turned upside down enough. You'd have to be off your trolley to go there again."

Diving back into the cool water for another length Ava considered whether or not she was off her trolley and whether or not it mattered anyway. She was pregnant. That ship had sailed. The decision was well and truly out of her hands. Karen would have to just lump it and keep her opinions to herself – which even as she thought it, Ava knew was never going to happen. It was up to Ava to learn not to give a damn.

Wrapped in a dressing-gown at the table in the living room, having called Jean-Luc and arranged to meet him in the village, Ava looked up to see Hope, looking slightly worse for wear, walk into the living room and pull a face which wordlessly said: 'I am sorry I got so drunk I passed out and you had to take my shoes off.'

Ava smiled and shrugged her shoulders reassuringly. From her exceptionally distant memory of proper gut-busting hangovers, Hope would be feeling delicate in every way and wouldn't need Ava making any jokes about the state she had got herself in.

"Sleep okay?" she offered.

"Not so much sleep as a coma," Hope answered, walking past her to the kitchen and pouring herself a very tall glass of water.

"Feeling okay now, or a bit delicate?"

"Delicate for definite, but don't worry. I'll get some water in me and I'll be right as rain. I'll get stuck into the cleaning – it's the study today, isn't it? There are so many books in there – we need to sort them – decide whether to leave them, or sell them or just dump them."

"Maybe we could donate some of them somewhere?" Ava offered, thinking there was no way on God's green earth she was going to dump any book of any description.

"Good idea. Sure we'll ask Jean-Luc what he thinks. When should we see him?"

Ava felt herself blush. This was where she had to admit she was an organisation freak and had already made arrangements to meet with Jean-Luc, in about an hour's time, in a small café in the village.

"I spoke to him this morning," she said with a nervous smile. "I hope you don't mind, since you have actually met him. But I was up early and feeling a little antsy so I just got on with a few things."

She watched as Hope sat down opposite her and waited for her to tell her, in the way Karen would have, that she needed to take a chill pill.

"Oh, that's great," Hope said with a genuine warmth that more than took her by surprise. "You're a star. We'll be flying ahead at this stage. And I know I was a bit of a wet blanket yesterday evening and I'm sorry for getting drunk when it was probably you who needed to sound off."

"I was glad of the distraction," Ava said honestly, "but I've had some time to think this morning and I think I'll be okay with my . . . situation."

"That's brilliant," Hope said, reaching across the table and holding her hand. "Babies are good things and I'm sure you're a wonderful mother."

Ava shrugged again. She loved her daughter and she did her best most of the time. She did lose the head from time to time – especially when she was tired which was pretty much around the clock these days – and she did have very limited patience with Barbie dolls and jigsaws. But Maisie seemed, mostly, happy and contented. Was she a wonderful mother? Maybe not. But maybe she was good enough.

"I've been thinking too," Hope said, sitting back. "Now it is entirely possible that I am still a little drunk and that I may have taken leave of my senses but I feel inspired here. The letters – the note last night and the rings . . . and how Betty wasn't afraid to go for what she wanted . . . I'm going to go for what I want."

"Which is?" Ava asked, her mind filled with images of Hope confronting this Dylan friend of hers or slipping arsenic into his girlfriend's tea.

"I'm not entirely sure," Hope replied. "But I tell you this, something is going to change. I'm thinking of maybe, I don't know, travelling again. Staying with Dylan and Cyndi is bound to get uncomfortable and they won't want me there under their feet indefinitely. Can you imagine it? Me? The permanent third wheel? Having my nose rubbed in it every day? Did I tell you about the feet? For the love of God, they have their fecking feet on Facebook!" She pulled a face as if she might vomit and it took Ava a split second to realise, for sure, that this was to express her disgust at the feet picture and not as a direct result of her banging hangover.

"Yes," Ava nodded. "You told me about the feet. You made up a song about the feet. To the tune of 'Mysterious Girl' by Peter Andre. It was around that time I slipped the bottle out of your hand." Smiling at the memory and enjoying the blush on Hope's face, Ava laughed.

"You see! There you have it, the very reason why I need to make a big difference and change my life. Otherwise I will become the madwoman who sits alone rocking in corners singing bad 90s pop songs and crying about the one who got away. I could be a pretty fecking twisted Miss Havisham for the new millennium. And nobody wants to be that."

"I don't know," Ava answered. "It has a certain ring to it."

"It might do," Hope said. "But long term, will it make me happy? Travelling might, or at least it might give me a little more time to think about what it is I do really want. I did use to write a travel column – that year Dylan and I travelled around the world – I thought maybe I could give that a go again."

It sounded brilliant and Ava felt a tiny surge of jealousy rise up in her. Hope could do that, she had that freedom. She could just decide to go travelling. She could just up sticks and change her life whenever she wanted. The world was her oyster. She wasn't answerable to anyone but herself and she didn't have a mortgage over her head to worry about. That must feel good.

"Good for you," she said. "It sounds brilliant."

Hope grinned back at her. "It does, doesn't it?"

Chapter 19

The smell of the freshly percolating coffee normally would have sent Ava into a caffeine-craving frenzy. Without even tasting the dark, rich, hot liquid Ava would imagine it sliding down her throat, warming her to her very core before giving her that little kick of energy that got her through many a morning in front of a very hyper classroom. Her coffee break had long been the highlight of her morning and nothing was quite as enjoyable as a freshly brewed coffee to wash down a pastry in a quaint little coffee shop.

Except things were a little different that morning. Standing at the door of the patisserie in the village the smell assaulted her nostrils as if someone had just left a dirty nappy right at her feet. Which was mildly ironic given that the reason for her sickness was going to end up in a dirty nappy.

"Smells divine, doesn't it?" Hope said from behind her oversized sunglasses which she wore even though it wasn't all that sunny. "If they could wire me up to that damn percolator and infuse the stuff through a drip in my arm I would die a happy woman."

"Hmmm," Ava muttered. "Can we sit outside? Downwind perhaps? Or around the corner?" She grimaced and reached to a chair to steady herself. Oh, she had forgotten the special joy that was morning sickness – and she cursed it for stealing away that joy which came with her morning coffee. What was the advice these days anyway? Could she even drink coffee? Or was it now on the big fat no-way-José list?

Sitting down, she asked Hope to bring her a glass of water, with ice in it. Nothing more, nothing less.

"You look about as bad as I feel," Hope said sympathetically, "but at least I got to enjoy a rake of Betty's finest wine first."

"Believe me," Ava said wryly, thinking of how she let her guard down with Connor after a few drinks, "alcohol played a strong enough role in how I got into this mess. Trust me."

"I'm still ashamed," Hope said.

"Oh please. We've all done it. Got a little pissed. And it had been a strange day."

"Maybe today will be calmer?"

"Oh God, I hope so," Ava said, thinking that calm would be lovely. She just wanted to get on with doing what she needed to do with Betty's belongings.

There was a lot she wanted to ask Jean-Luc and she wasn't entirely sure what to do next. When everything was packed up – sorted and stored in boxes – what would happen next? How would they sell it? Would they even want to sell it? This was not a situation she had dealt with before and they sure as hell didn't make a handbook for how to deal with an eccentric aunt's last wishes. She was starting to feel as if she knew Betty – really knew her – and she was starting to feel attached to her, fond of her and reluctant to let go. Silly really, considering they had only met that one time . . .

She watched as Hope returned with a glass of iced water and a coffee in a white cup on a tray with two croissants. "I thought we could use something to eat."

Ava looked at the croissant and her appetite soared back with a vengeance – another joy of the first trimester she had forgotten and she cut into the crumbly pastry before her, slathered it with butter and took a bite as if she hadn't been fed in a month. It was only when she was two bites in and Hope was taking the first sip from her coffee cup that she realised she was in all likelihood making a complete gulpen of herself. Putting the croissant down, she forced herself to sit back, sip from her glass and count to ten, slowly, before taking a deep breath and going in for another bite. She tried to stop herself eyeing the food like a vulture eyes its prey and reminded herself that while she was here to get a bite to eat she was also here to conduct business and come face to face for the first time with Jean-Luc – who Hope had described that morning as a "quare bit of stuff".

Ava wasn't entirely sure she wanted to think of him as a 'quare bit of stuff' – she preferred to keep her senses about her and remind herself that he was the man tasked with making sure they did everything they needed to do with Betty's belongings and who would oversee them clearing out her house for the last time.

Manners, she reminded herself. At all times, manners. She watched Hope take a small bite of her own croissant and she swore to God she felt herself start to drool. She should have eaten a bigger breakfast. Come to think of it, she had eaten a bigger breakfast – bacon and eggs (runny ones even though she knew she shouldn't) and three rounds of toast dripping with butter. She would be the size of a house before the week was out – but at least that would give her an opening gambit for telling Connor. "Hey, pet, see how I've put on a pile of weight? Well, there will be more to follow . . ." She shoved those thoughts to the back of her head as she figured a respectable enough break in her eating had taken place to allow her to resume.

She was only interrupted again when Hope kicked her under the table and looked across to where a man was approaching. Mid-forties, beige cargo pants, white shirt opened just that little bit to reveal the most delicious tuft of chest hair, salt and pepper hair, a fine stubble and that wrinkle around his eyes that Hope had waxed lyrical about the previous night while under the influence of the wine. This had to be Jean-Luc and the way in which Hope stood up, brushed the crumbs off her trousers quickly and extended her hand, confirmed that this was indeed the person Ava had been speaking to via email for the last two weeks. She watched as he leaned toward Hope, kissing her on each cheek before turning to direct his attention at her – which made her feel a little bit silly and definitely more than a little coquettish. Once again she had to remind herself she was a respectable married, grown-up woman who had shared a number of sensible conversations with this man and who was there to do very sensible things and not to be all flirty. And besides she was pregnant. And in love with her husband. And she feared Hope might, despite her love for her best friend, stab her square in the forehead if she turned into a mega-flirt with the very handsome man in front of her.

"Ava!" he said in a deep strong French accent. "You . . . you look so like her. I was not expecting that." He looked to all intents and purposes as if he had just seen a ghost and she was momentarily floored.

Finding her voice, she said, "I'm sorry I wasn't there to meet you yesterday."

"It is okay," he said. "I was only calling in for a moment and we can talk today. Can I bring you ladies a coffee or something to eat?"

Ava's stomach grumbled and she was tempted to order another croissant, or a jambon or three jambons, but she decided against it.

"I'm fine, thank you," she said as Hope said the same.

Then they watched, a wicked glint on each of their faces as he walked away to get his own coffee.

"I told you," Hope said, with a wink. "I told you he was a quare bit of stuff!"

"And definitely not at all like Gerard Depardieu," Ava said, craning her neck to see him again.

"Not a bit."

"And you're sure him and Betty? They never . . .?"

"Oh God no," Hope laughed. "He was very clear that they were friends. I wonder why she didn't just get him to sort through her things."

"Would you want him sorting through your smalls?" Ava asked, then paused, thought about it, and said, "On second thoughts, don't answer that."

Jean-Luc returned with his coffee and sat down. He sipped from his cup and looked at both of them for a second before he spoke. "This is all a little strange, *non?*"

"Yes, well, it certainly was unexpected. I'm almost ashamed to say I didn't know my aunt very well," Ava said. "I only recall meeting her once."

"Betty was always quick to form an opinion of someone," Jean-Luc replied. "She considered herself a very good judge of character. So if you had Betty's respect then that is enough of a recommendation for me."

"Hope says you saw her shortly before she died?" Ava asked, nodding in the direction of her cousin who seemed to be staring intently at Jean-Luc's, forearms, which admittedly were exceptionally strong, muscular and tanned.

"I saw her the day before. I was not there when she died – that was how she was. She never made a fuss. I think maybe she waited on purpose until she was all alone to slip away. I sat with her at the hospice the day before and we talked. She was very fond of you. She said she wished she had told you to your face. It was one of her regrets. Not speaking to you again face to face. She was so fond of you."

"That's nice to hear," Ava said, blushing. She watched as he sipped from his cup again. There was a feeling of expectation in the air – and she felt herself wait for him to speak as if he held the key to this entire strange scenario.

"It is true," he said eventually. "How are you finding the house? Is it too much work?"

"No," Ava said truthfully. "It has been fine so far. She ran a tight ship. We just want to make sure her most prized possessions are looked after. We hope to bring some items back with us to Ireland. And we wondered about her study. There are many books. Do you know if the new owners would like them or if there is somewhere we could donate them?"

"I'm sure the new owner would be happy with whatever you choose to leave behind but there are a number of nursing homes which would be only too happy to take them off your hands. Perhaps I could take them for you? Or we could visit the hospice where Betty passed away? As for whatever you wish to take home with you, Betty left provisions for anything you need or want to be shipped back."

"She was very good," Ava said, touched by her aunt's kindness.

"Yes, she was. One of a kind, as you say." He smiled as he spoke, a warm smile that seemed to start in his eyes before moving to his mouth.

Ava could definitely see why Hope had been so smitten.

"It feels strange to divide her stuff and decide its fate," said Ava. "And to sell it? Are you sure that is what she wanted?"

He nodded. "She was adamant. She wanted you both to have something for your efforts, be it some money made from her belongings. And she wanted you to experience the markets. It could make a good day out?"

Ava looked at Hope who was still enraptured with Jean-Luc's arms. "I don't know," she said. "Hope? It feels strange to sell her things on."

"It is what Betty wanted," Jean-Luc soothed her.

"But it's a bit soon," Hope piped up, breaking her silence. "It feels disrespectful."

"Please, ladies, don't think of it that way."

Ava sat back and thought of what he was saying and couldn't help but feel Hope was right. It was one thing to go through Betty's prized possessions and put away items which meant a lot to her, but to sell them on, in the hope of making some sort of profit, that made her feel strange. And guilty. And a little sick. Although, in fairness, the sickness could have been a resurgence of the morning sickness.

"The market is on Saturday," Jean-Luc said. "I know someone who sells such old furniture, pictures, antiques. I will leave it with you and you can let me know if you want to go."

"Could we go anyway?" Hope piped up. "I remember the market from my previous stay. I'd love to go again."

"*Mais oui*," Jean-Luc said with a smile. "Please, ladies, let me know if there is anything I can do at all."

Ava very determindedly looked away from Hope, afraid if their eyes met for even one second she would combust into schoolgirl giggles.

"We will," she heard her cousin say coyly.

It was at that moment that the little devil on her shoulder squeaked that this would be the perfect time to interfere that little bit.

"Actually," she said, glancing at Hope, "my cousin here is a travel writer. She is considering writing a piece about Provence but, as you know, it has been a long time since she was here and she doesn't know the area all that well. I'd take her around but, well, I'm pregnant and need my rest and I'm worried she will have a lot of time on her own while I'm napping. Maybe, if you're not terribly busy, you could show her around?" She glanced at Hope who looked as if she could combust at any moment.

"Of course," he said softly. "I could be free tomorrow afternoon."

"But we have so much to do!" Hope said, looking at Ava who did a good job of ignoring her pointed stare.

"We'll get loads done today and then you can see the sights tomorrow," Ava said. "You'll want to get this whole new you off to a flying start, won't you? The first article in your return to form? What better place to start!"

Hope smiled, although her eyes indicated she might just kill Ava later. Ava was used to that look – it was the look Karen would give her when she volunteered them to take a spin around the ball pool with the kids. She had become adept at ignoring the look from Karen and she sure as hell was going to ignore it from Hope right now.

Chapter 20

The study at the back of the villa was perhaps Hope's favourite room in the house. It was, perhaps, her favourite room in the entire world. As she sat, legs crossed on the warm wooden floor, sorting through a pile of books she had liberated from the tall whitewashed bookcase beside the large sash window which faced onto Betty's prized herb garden, she felt a sense of calm envelop her. The room was blissfully peaceful, and light and airy.

"If I had a room like this I'd be the most successful writer in the universe," she said to Ava, who was sitting, feet curled under her, on the large floral sofa which faced a desk and chair, neatly stacked with books, letters and sheaves of paper. "I might also be a fecking big recluse though," she continued. "Because I would never leave and, in fairness, I know it would be a poor show for a journalist never to leave her office. But God, this room is lovely."

"It is, isn't it?" Ava said, looking up over her glasses and away from the paperwork she was sorting through.

"Beats my home office anyway. Well, I say home office. I have a desk in the box room at the front of the smallest terraced house in Belfast. There is woodchip on the walls and my storage system is more of the 'big pile of crap in the corner' than chic whitewashed bookcases against pale blue walls. I have a rattley radiator and the hum of the traffic outside to keep me company and little else. The view is definitely less appealing and less fragrant than a herb garden. Once – and this is a joy – I looked out and saw a man throw up in the street. It put me right off my vegetable soup, I can tell you."

Ava laughed and Hope thought of how, really, she hated that little boxed space where she worked at home. It was a direct reflection of her state of mind – messy, unloved and a bit rough around the edges. She felt trapped in it – day after day, sitting there and trying to generate work before escaping downstairs for an hour to watch *Jeremy Kyle* or *Judge Judy*.

"Perfect reason to get on with doing something different then," Ava offered.

Hope looked at her. She had, just about, forgiven her for landing her in it with Jean-Luc earlier. Admittedly the fact that Jean-Luc was one of the most gorgeous creatures she had ever set eyes on had helped take the sting out of Ava putting her on the spot like that. Still, in her hungover fug, she had felt her cheeks blaze all the way home.

"He'll think I'm a sad case," she had said.

"How do you figure that? As cover stories go, this one is pretty good. And you did say you were thinking of going back into travel writing."

"Yes," Hope had admitted, "but that was in a kind of vague, possibly still a little drunk way."

"So you don't want to do it?"

Hope had looked at Ava who was staring straight ahead at the road in front and smiling to herself. Fecker. She had Hope pegged well and truly.

"No, I'm not saying that . . . I . . . I . . ."

"Are you just trying to make excuses?"

"No!" she replied forcefully. "It's just a bit mad. I went to bed last night sobbing about the state of my life."

"You weren't sobbing. You were singing, loudly."

"In my head, I was sobbing," Hope said with a smile.

"Thanks to your singing I wasn't so far off sobbing either," Ava laughed.

Hope pulled a face. "Very funny!"

"Yes. Yes, it was," Ava said, still laughing.

Hope laughed too and felt the sun shine on her face. This was nice. Okay, so technically she had been railroaded into a day out on the arm of Jean-Luc visiting the must-see sights of Provence and part of her still wanted to kill Ava over that, but this was nice – the way they were talking and laughing. Hope couldn't remember the last time she'd spent any time with a female friend laughing and joking and talking about how sexy the man opposite had been. In fact the only conversations she seemed to have these days were with A) grumpy-arsed editors who weren't keen to give anyone any freelance work at all, B) the faceless people in call centres employed by her bank who she called frequently to beg for an increase to her overdraft or credit-card limit, or C) Dylan who refused, with decent grounds she supposed, to comment on the sexiness of any men in the vicinity.

"I'm a metrosexual, not a homosexual," he would say.

So by the time Ava and Hope had taken to Betty's study and started working through her paperwork and books she was actually mildly excited about her day out with Jean-Luc and definitely okay with Ava and her meddling ways. Those meddling ways were good. They made things happen.

Flicking through the books on the floor, she smiled. There were books of every genre among Betty's collection from well-thumbed classics in both English and French to yellowing copies of modern Irish classics.

"I loved this book when I was a teenager," she said, flicking through a copy of *City Girl* by Patricia Scanlan. "I wanted to be Devlin so much!" She recalled how engrossed she had been in the down-on-her-luck Dublin girl who went on to set up her own successful franchise and meet the man of her dreams. "Sadly I even had my hair cut like her but the frizzy curls in my hair meant I never quite got the sleek bobbed look I had been after. I looked more Coco the Clown."

"I wanted to be Cathy from *Wuthering Heights*, for some

bizarre reason," Ava laughed. "I mean her life didn't end well, and when she was alive she was a complete bitch, but somehow that didn't penetrate when I was seventeen and obsessed with Heathcliff."

"I think everyone went through an obsessed-with-Heathcliff phase," Hope said, looking through the books in front of her, finding Betty's copy of the Emily Brontë classic and showing it to Ava. "She had all the best ones. *Les Misérables*, *Jane Eyre*, *The Great Gatsby*, *Light a Penny Candle*. Someone will get a lot of joy out of these books. Here, keep *Wuthering Heights* for yourself and relive the madness. I read it last year when I was going through a particularly 'My life has been crap since I was eighteen' phase and wanted to relive my angsty years."

Ava reached out and Hope passed it over.

"Anything much in that stuff you're going through?" Hope asked.

"Mostly old letters. Mostly in French. Not sure any of it is important. I think maybe we should just shred it all. Unless either of us want to try and decipher what it's all about. But, from what I can see, it is mostly utility bills and the like. Not exactly the stuff of family heirlooms."

"Fair enough," Hope said. "Search and destroy."

When the books were packed Hope moved on to the desk which mostly contained stationery, neatly sorted into piles, pens and pencils, paperclips and thumbtacks and a neat pile of Post-Its beside a bundle of crisp white envelopes.

"I wonder did she write the letters here," Hope said, lifting a pen and poising it over a sheaf of white paper on the desk. "This would be a lovely place to write letters – looking out over that garden."

"She had a way with words," Ava said. "She probably could have been a writer herself. Maybe that's where you get it from."

"Ah no, I get it from a combination of being exceptionally nosy, the inability to live my own life therefore having an obsession with other people's lives, and also from an obsession with Lois Lane when I was a teenager. I always thought if I got a job as a journalist there would be some Clark Kent hunk of burning love waiting for me in a newsroom. I was never under any illusions that he would turn into Superman at a moment's notice, but I thought, at least, he wouldn't be a complete dick. But as it turns out, the newsrooms of Northern Ireland aren't exactly heaving with romantic male leads. And in terms of freelancing – working on your own definitely decreases the chance of meeting Mr Right."

She watched Ava smile and sit forward, pushing her glasses to the top of her head. "I always thought you had the most glamorous life. My mum was always telling me how my cousin Hope was living it up in Belfast, writing for all the big papers and always out at some launch or another."

Hope shrugged. "Don't get me wrong. It does have its high points and I've definitely had some good times. But it isn't all that glam and I can tell you that in recent years the number of launches has taken a dive with the recession and those that have happened have been seriously short of the glam factor. These days you're lucky if you get a cup of tea and a wilting sandwich never mind a glass of fizz and the chance to wear a posh frock."

She thought back to the last launch she had been at. There hadn't even been a cup of tea, or a wilted sandwich, and the assembled journalists had left in very bad form indeed. Hope had walked away scunnered that she had wasted an afternoon – and a taxi fare in and out of Belfast – to attend it in the hope of getting some exclusive for one of the glossies only to find every other freelance in the greater Belfast area there vying for the story.

"It's a crowded market," she said, sitting back and looking out the window. "And not exactly fulfilling. Unless you are selling something a little different, people just don't want to know."

"Well, travel stories would be different?"

Hope nodded. The initial outlay would be tough but she had lived off the beaten track before. She had blagged her away around the world with Dylan and she had worked where necessary to fund their next adventure. She wasn't afraid of hard work. She was, admittedly, mildly terrified at the prospect of doing it on her own but this could well be one of those cases where she would have to just feel the fear and do it anyway.

"They would," she said, the cogs in her mind whirring into gear and thinking about the practicalities of it all. "I'll have to give it some thought but you know what, I think it could work."

"Good woman," Ava said. "And don't forget to send some postcards."

"Oh, I promise," Hope said. "Actually Betty here has inspired me a little. The way she wrote these letters – proper old-fashioned letters and not emails or text messages. I'm going to start doing that."

"Good woman."

Hope sat upright, lifted the pen and started to doodle on the paper in front of her. She would definitely start writing properly again, ink and paper. She might even write something a little creative. Maybe about a woman who falls in love with her best friend just that little bit too late. She could write that on the long lonely nights as she circumnavigated the world alone. "You're never alone with a book," her old school friend Tina used to say. So technically that counted for writing one too, didn't it?

Smiling, she put the pen down and continued sorting through Betty's desk while Ava finished dealing with the paperwork. Before they knew it, it had hit six o'clock and Hope's stomach was rumbling. It had been a long time since her mid-morning croissant. They had just been so caught up in sorting through the study they hadn't thought to stop for food, and the lack of something to eat was making her hangover threaten to resurface.

"Shall we get something to eat?" she said, breaking the silence.

"Oh yes, please," Ava said. "I've been sitting here starving for the last hour but didn't want to speak up."

"Well, then, let's definitely get something to eat. Should we make something or head out to the village? I promise not to drink and end up singing any 90s pop songs, or any pop songs at all for that matter."

"It would be a shame not to get out and see some more of the village."

"Then the village it is. How about we freshen up? I'll look at that guide Jean-Luc left and get us booked in somewhere."

"Brilliant," Ava said. "I'll go and get ready and we can be off."

Hope closed the second drawer on the desk, put the lid on her latest box for the nursing home and vowed to come back to the room later to finish things off. They had got through a lot today. The room looked a little less homely but she was confident that everything was going where it should be. Lifting the copy of *City Girl* from the floor and carrying it through to her room, she slipped it into her bag and smiled as her mind turned to how she was going to change her life and indeed to her own circle of friends back home. Not that her group of friends was much of a circle. Not, in fact, that her group of friends was much of a group. It was pretty much Dylan. And that was that. Nonetheless she thought he would be happy for her and her new ideas about where her life might go.

She didn't know why the idea of going back to travel writing hadn't come to her before, but now that it had, it seemed like the most natural thing in the world. And now was the perfect time. Freshening her make-up and adding a spritz of perfume, she lifted her bag and with a spring in her step she walked back to the living room and set about making reservations for dinner in perfect French.

Chapter 21

Ava brushed her hair, pulled it back in a neat chignon, took a bright maxi dress from the wardrobe and started to get changed. Glancing in the full-length mirror as she stood in her underwear, her eye was drawn to her stomach. Nope. She didn't look pregnant yet. Yes, she had a slightly protruding tummy but if the truth was known she'd never quite got rid of that stomach paunch since she'd had Maisie, despite her best attempts. Her boobs looked bigger – her bra definitely felt tighter and, looking down, the veins in her breasts resembled a map of the underground. She looked in the mirror again and stuck her stomach out, rubbing her hand over her belly.

It wouldn't be that long until she was belly-big and drinking Gaviscon by the litre. Oh God . . . why did pregnancy have to be so undignified and unpleasant? Maybe Karen had a point. Okay, Karen had taken that point and exaggerated it wildly, making it into more of a horror story than a point, but it was a point nonetheless.

Blinking, she looked again at her outline in the mirror and willed herself to focus on the positives.

She would get a cute, teeny tiny baby whose teeny tiny bum would fit in the palm of her hand and make her heart swell with love.

Babies smell nice. Most of the time. When they haven't pooed. Or been sick. Focus on the nice times – on the sweet smell of their soft skin.

Yes, babies have soft skin.

Maisie would love having a baby brother or sister. Sure hadn't she Ava's heart tortured about wanting a baby all of her own while Ava had wanted to scream at her "But you *are* a baby!".

Shopping. She would get to wander, guilt-free, around the pretty baby section in Next and legitimately have a feel of the tiny Babygros without coming across as a potential baby-snatching mentalist.

Oooh, a new pram. Much as she tried to deny it, Ava was a pram-a-holic. She had gone through three with Maisie, all of which were probably still in a usable condition for baby number two but she would ignore that fact.

People would stop saying "Oooh, isn't time you had another child?" every three seconds or looking at Maisie then back to Ava and saying with a laboured sigh: "You won't leave her on her own, will you? Such a sin. To be an only child."

She might make new mammy friends who weren't Karen.

She would have a legitimate reason to eat as much chocolate as she wanted over the next eight months.

Connor would be delighted.

She smiled again, positive affirmations floating around her head, and slipped her feet into her sandals before sitting on the bed and phoning Maisie. She would be going to sleep soon, Ava thought. She could almost see her daughter now, a little bit sleepy and possibly a little bit cranky, rubbing her eyes and looking for a cuddle. Her heart ached with longing – suddenly Dublin felt too far away – much too far away and she wished she was there to hold Maisie's chubby little hand and kiss her button nose. The phone rang three times before her mother-in-law Brigid answered.

"Hello? Hello?"

"Hello, Brigid."

"Hang on a minute. Maisie, no. Not now. No, the other one. Clodagh, could you help your cousin?" Clearly flustered, Brigid's usually clipped phone voice had slipped a little into her full-blown

Northside Dublin drawl. "No, no, I don't know where your daddy is. He'll be back in a while. He's just away on a message. Hello? Hello?"

Unsure as to whether Brigid actually was talking to her or still to one of her many grandchildren, Ava paused until her mother-in-law spoke again.

"Look, if this is one of those sell-you-insurance or begging calls then I'm very busy and not at all interested so I'm going to hang up now."

"No! Brigid! Wait! It's me – Ava! I was just phoning to speak to Maisie and Connor. But I'm guessing he has left you in charge."

"Oh, Ava pet," Brigid said, softening, "how are you? Wait a minute – I'll just escape into the kitchen. Clodagh! Mind your cousin. And Niamh, share those toys."

Ava listened to a clatter of children's voices, her daughter's soft Northern accent amongst them and smiled. She would, she supposed, have to go through the niceties of talking to Brigid first before she spoke to her daughter.

"Connor and his dad have gone for a swift one," Brigid said. "About an hour ago, so I'm hoping they'll be back soon. I said one but you know men, they always push their luck."

Ava could hear the hiss of a kettle as Brigid rattled around her kitchen.

"Well, my dear, are you having a lovely time? I bet France is lovely. Never been myself. Not so great with foreign travel. A week in Salthill does me just fine. But still, France, it must be lovely. Is it lovely?"

Ava smiled. Connor was so unlike his mother – he was quiet and relatively reserved. Chances are it was because he was never able to get a word in growing up. But Brigid was a great woman – with a house which filled and emptied constantly with a host of grandchildren, all of whom she spoiled rotten. Brigid would be delighted to hear there was another little Campbell on the way.

"France is great. I'm missing Maisie and Connor like mad though."

"Of course you are, pet, but they are fine. Maisie is ruling the roost. All her cousins are delighted to see her. They were putting on a show for us just now. She has a great little voice on her."

"Yes," Ava said, her heart swelling with pride and her eyes filling with tears. Fecking hormones. "She's a darling. Do you think I could maybe have a wee word with her? What do you think?"

"Oh silly me," Brigid said. "Of course. You should have said. I'll get her for you now."

Ava listened as her mother-in-law put the phone down and went to retrieve her daughter. She was almost breathless with excitement and longing when Maisie's voice came on the line.

"Mammy! I did a show. I was singing. And dancing. And singing. And Clodagh was singing and dancing. And Niamh too. And Nana Brigid said I was brilliant!" Maisie was almost stratospheric with excitement. "And Clodagh's going to sleep in my bed tonight and I am going to sleep in it too and Nana Brigid said we better be good girls and go to sleep and not be tortures."

"That's great, baby," Ava said, thinking that her daughter loved to talk almost as much as her beloved granny. "So you're being a good girl?"

"The bestest."

"And is daddy being a good boy?"

"Yes!" her daughter replied earnestly. "Mammy?"

"Yes, pet?"

"Are you being a good girl?"

"Yes, darling, I am, and I'll be home soon."

"When?"

"Soon, pet."

"Are you coming to Nana Brigid's too? We could do our show for you?"

"Maybe, pet," Ava said, lying back on the bed and revelling in her daughter's voice. God, she sounded so cute on the phone. Her voice was softer, higher, lighter. "I would love it if you did your show for me."

"I'm Cinderella," Maisie said. "I dressed up."

"You're always a princess to me, Toots McDoots. I love you very much."

"I love you too, Mammy, but I have to go now. I have to go play. Bye. Bye. Love you, bye."

With that the line went dead and Ava was left feeling the most-in-love mother in the entire universe ever. It wasn't lost on her that it was so much easier to feel completely and utterly in love with your child when you were several hundred miles away from them. From a distance all the early mornings, tantrums and food fads were forgotten. There was never a child like Maisie. She was perfection in every way and Ava missed her terribly. Brushing a hormonal tear away, she got up, finished getting dressed and slicked some lip gloss on before setting out for dinner in a French restaurant.

"You'll be okay if Jean-Luc takes me out for a few hours?" Hope asked, spearing a sautéed mushroom with her fork.

Ava nodded. "Of course. I'll get on with organising here and I might even go for a swim in that pool and perhaps have a lazy afternoon nap. Don't underestimate the joys of a sly nap. I don't often get them with Maisie around. She hasn't taken an afternoon snooze since she was eighteen months old. It will be bliss. And if I don't sleep I'll sit on that terrace and read *Wuthering Heights*. Or try and find the missing letter from today. I mean, we pretty much turned that room upside down and *nada*."

"Yeah," Hope said, pulling a face. "She could have left them somewhere a little more obvious. She obviously wanted to make sure we did a good job on her house. No half efforts allowed. For all her quirkiness she was a proper clean freak."

"Nothing wrong with being a clean freak," Ava laughed. "All the best people are anally retentive."

"Not *all* the best people," Hope laughed, thinking of the mess she had left at home in her office.

"Okay, some of the best people," Ava said. "But, seriously, don't worry about me. I will be fine. It's really not a hardship."

"As long as you're sure?"

"I couldn't be more sure. The clean freak in me will also get started on the kitchen. I'll be happy as a pig in the exact opposite of shite."

"We'll get the study finished before I go. Jean-Luc said he would pick me up at twelve so we have plenty of time."

"Grand job!" Ava said, sipping from her coffee.

It had just gone nine and the girls had enjoyed a nice lie-in – anything after six thirty was considered absolutely luxury by Ava these days. She couldn't quite believe it when she had woken, lifted her phone and looked at the time. She had smiled and snuggled back under the covers for a few minutes, just enjoying the blissful silence. There was no Peppa Pig blasting from the living room or danger of being cannon-balled by an overenthusiastic Maisie ready to greet the morning with her usual enthusiasm. Yes, of course she still missed her but there were some things she was absolutely okay with missing.

Finishing her coffee and lifting the plates to take them to the sink, she turned to Hope and said: "Do you ever wonder why Betty chose us? I mean really? There are so many in our family – she could have chosen any one of them."

"I don't really know," Hope said, adding with a wink, "apart from the fact that we are clearly the best ones. But I'm glad she did. I'm enjoying myself – which, if you knew me, you would be surprised at. I mean, obviously the house is gorgeous and the South of France beats the suburbs of Belfast any day of the week, but being here – sorting through things, making arrangements. It's not exactly me, but I'm enjoying it."

"Me too," Ava said, already looking forward to the day ahead. "Me too."

Still in her pyjamas and dressing-gown, Hope was going through the last of the drawers in Betty's study. The room was looking a little bare now – books stacked in piles and stored in boxes. Ava had taken down the sketch drawings of Derry which had hung on the walls and stored them away, leaving a fine trace of where they once were.

Opening the bottom drawer, Hope pulled out a cardboard box which was a bit battered around the edges. Opening it, she saw it was filled with old snapshots. Faded in colour, a plethora of interesting fashions and haircuts sat before her. Various faces she vaguely recognised as her relatives, only much younger. Babies. Toddlers. Brooke Park in the heart of Derry with Gwyn's Institute looming large. France. Paris. A faded Eiffel Tower. She lifted one, a younger Betty, her hair swept back off her face, her smile broad, grinning at the camera amidst the flowers of her garden. Turning the picture over she saw Betty's handwriting, spidery and fading. *"Taken by my love, April 1983."* She turned it over again and looked at her aunt's broad smile. It said everything. Her eyes were warm, her smile glowing, her entire demeanour relaxed. She was clearly at ease with this man in front of her taking her picture. She was clearly madly, passionately in love with Claude and Hope felt her heart lurch. She wanted to look at someone like that and know that they loved her back and that she could trust them to never, ever hurt her. She slipped the picture into the pocket of her dressing-gown and continued looking.

Among the photos was one of a family group – Hope gasped as she recognised her mother and father, holding a bonny baby with a head topped with tight blonde curls which looked not unlike a busted bag of Quavers and an expression on her face midway between extreme joy and a grimace. Hope recognised the baby at once as her smaller self – with the smile wide across her face, the trademark Scott grin taught to her by her doting daddy.

"Ava!" she called, waving the photo as if shaking it would make it develop more and bring the faded colours back to light.

Looking at it again, she focused on the second, fluffy-headed baby beside her, a solemn expression on her face as she sucked her thumb. And she was pretty sure that was her Auntie Cora grinning with the serious baby on her knee. Oh, this had to be Ava! Oh, this was spooky. She called again before re-examining the photo. Betty, her hair tied up in a ponytail, her faded flared jeans scraping the floor, stood at the side staring at the camera intently – a look of almost defiance on her face. Oh this was precious – all of them together!

"Ava," she called again, jumping to her feet as her cousin walked into the room. "Is this you? And your mammy? Is this all of us together?"

Ava looked at the photo and gasped, pulling it closer to examine.

"Jesus H Christ and the Wee Donkey, so it is! Oh my God! I was a sour-looking wee shite, wasn't I?"

"Ah, sure we were beautiful!" Hope said, examining the picture yet again. "There's me like a mentalist with my gummy grin, you looking like you are about to tell us all to sit down and behave ourselves and Betty looking like an ad for Top Shop circa 1977. Gorgeous, the very lot of us!"

"We should get copies," Ava said, smiling and sitting down. "That's just priceless."

"I better make sure not to lose it," Hope said, resting it on the desk, glancing back at it and sitting down on the floor again to tip out the remaining photographs.

It was the crisp whiteness of the envelope against the yellowing photographic paper which caught her attention. "Ooooh! Ooooh! I think . . ." She delved in and turned the envelope over and sure as anything there it was, Betty's handwriting. "We've got it! Oh, I feel all like Anneka Rice when she won one of her challenges. Surely a prize should come with these letters!"

"Ah, the letter is prize enough," Ava said.

"Easy for you to say, you got diamonds in yours," Hope said with a laugh. No, she wasn't really jealous that Betty thought it more likely that a two-year-old would get married than she ever would.

"What does it say?" Ava said, pulling her feet onto the footstool in front of her.

Hope tore open the letter, hauling out two sheets of paper. Scanning them, she saw mention of a wedding and midnight flit and it all seemed terribly exciting.

"Oooooh, more on her and Claude and the big romance!"

My dear girls,

So Claude and I decided we would marry and we would move together to France. We didn't have much time to get things organised – we didn't want to wait around Derry any longer than we absolutely had to. Claude had been able to put the boys off a few times but they were starting to get impatient. The threats were less implied and more obvious.

My parents didn't react well to the news. You're not to feel disappointed in them or annoyed with them. That was just how things were and, well, I had given them enough trouble in my time. I don't know how I had expected them to react. I suppose I wanted them to be happy for me – and for us. I was settling down and they had long since wanted me to settle down.

Then again, I wasn't settling down in quite the way they wanted me to. But I hadn't done anything the way they wanted me to. I was in their eyes a handful. I can't deny I made some wrong choices in my life. But Claude, well, he made me want to be a better person. He made me want to make things okay. I wished my parents could see that. But they couldn't see past the upset that my leaving would cause.

Daddy didn't come with me to the church. Your parents did, girls. They came and they stood beside me. But there was a gaping hole where Mammy and Daddy should have been. We didn't even get married in Derry. We didn't want any fuss. We didn't want people talking – surmising that a shotgun wedding meant I had got into trouble.

So we went over the border to Donegal. And I wore a dress I picked out of a charity shop the week before. Cora told me it was "dootsy" but I loved it. I'm sure it was about twenty years old, with little lace-covered buttons and the daintiest of detailing around the neckline. Cora made me a bouquet – I swear the flowers looked like they had been picked out of someone's garden but I felt like a million dollars all the same. There was none of that going to a salon to have your hair done in those days, or your make-up, or false tans. I did my own hair, dressing it with some silk flowers, and slipped my feet into a pair of cream shoes which were the only new items I wore on that day. None of that mattered, though.

Standing at the top of the aisle, before the priest spoke, Claude asked me was I sure. He knew he was asking a lot. I think for that one millisecond the thought crossed my mind that this might be the wrong thing – that this was going to make things tough.

I looked at Cora, and she smiled at me. Ava, you know your mam's smile. It makes everything okay and I knew I was doing the exact right thing and that everything would be as well as it could be at home.

I took a deep breath and we did it – we got married.

God, I remember the glint of the sun off my wedding ring when we stepped out into the sunshine. My hand felt heavy. I felt a bit like a child playing dress-up but it felt right. Hope, your daddy doused us in confetti. I was still finding it the next day. That stuff gets everywhere. I tried my best to ignore the fact our parents weren't there and Claude kissed me.

There was no fancy reception. Just a plate of chips in a nearby café. Sure they looked at us like we were cracked in the head when we walked in. Me in my old wedding dress. Claude in his best suit. Clattering our chips in red sauce and vinegar and laughing as we ate them.

You girls would have been so proud of your parents. They paid for us to have a honeymoon of sorts – a night in a hotel in Moville which had a squeaky bed. We didn't even have to do anything bar sit on it and it would squeak as if we were having an orgy. Which would have been okay, had the two matronly ladies staying in the room next door not started saying the Rosary loudly if we so much as breathed on the damn thing. Still, we always laughed about it. We dined out on that story for a long time afterwards.

When we came back to Derry we visited my parents. I suppose I was still looking for their blessing. Our flights were booked – from Dublin to Paris. All my worldly possessions had been packed up. I suppose I wanted them to say they understood. And that they loved me. And they wanted me to be happy.

My mother, she wouldn't talk to me at first. Daddy, he just sat, waiting for her lead I suppose. When she spoke she said she would never understand how I could walk away without looking back.

She didn't know that I was always looking back. Always. But I can't say I regretted it – not in that way. I often wondered what would have happened if things had been different. God, I thought about it. Claude and I, we talked about it. But we knew we had done the only thing we could.

I told her I loved her, and then, Hope, I went to see your parents. I told your daddy how I loved him and how he was so very lucky to have you and that he bloody well better keep in touch because I wanted to hear all about you.

Then, Ava, I went to see your mam and you and say goodbye and I'll always remember this . . . always . . . you climbed up on my knee just before I left and gave me the biggest, sloppiest kiss and told me you loved me in your baby babble. After that, I cuddled your mam. Sure you know what sisters are like . . . and we cried. I cried like I thought my heart would split in two right there and then until Claude told me it was absolutely time to go.

So we went and we came here . . . and we were happy. God, I know this is all sounding like a very sad story but we were happy. So happy. And I kept that dress and I'm sure there is probably still confetti caught up in the lace somewhere.

It wasn't the fanciest of weddings but it was perfect for us. And I wouldn't change it for the world.

I suppose, that is enough for now. Until the next time . . .

With all my love,
Betty
xxx

When Hope finished reading, they sat for a few minutes. Each lost in her own thoughts. Each thinking of the lace wedding dress, and the emotional goodbye, and thinking Betty did the absolute right thing and thinking they just wished she was there so they could tell her, face to face, that they would have been right behind her.

Standing in her room surveying the clothes she had packed and wondering what would be a suitable outfit to wear for the first day of the rest of her life, Hope selected a pair of dark-grey jersey harem pants, a white string vest, some chunky beads and bangles and a pair of gold gladiator sandals.

She dressed, letting her hair dry naturally and settle into soft curls. With her sunglasses perched on her head and a wee dash of perfume between her breasts she felt empowered and even able to push all negative 'I'm going to die alone' feelings to the back of her mind. This was it – a new her. Betty had balls and so would she. She did a little happy dance as she slicked some Urban Decay Sin across her eyelids, then she skipped down the stairs and waited for Jean-Luc to arrive and the rest of her life to start.

Chapter 22

The house was blissfully quiet as Ava worked her way through Betty's large kitchen. *I would kill for a kitchen like this*, she thought to herself, all big and homely with a dresser filled with mismatched and colourful crockery which screamed that this room had been the centre of the house.

Ava wasn't much of a cook. It wasn't that she couldn't. She just didn't often get the time. She tried – about once a month – to throw herself into whatever recipes Jamie or Nigella were spouting at the time but, after an hour and a half making a soup or stew that Maisie would turn her nose up at in favour of potato waffles or plain mashed potato and gravy, she would give up. At last count she had seventeen cookbooks gathering dust in the cupboard beside her cooker which she rarely looked at. Toast though. She did good toast and sure everyone loves toast.

Maybe, she thought, if she had more time she would have one of those kitchens she always dreamed of. One that smelled of freshly baked bread and percolating coffee and was the kind of place where people gathered over a kitchen island to laugh, share secrets and oooh and aah at her culinary skills.

If the study was Hope's favourite room, this was without a doubt

Ava's and she was kind of glad that she had it all to herself. She was loving opening every cupboard and drawer and seeing what she could find. It seemed Betty didn't have a cookbook, or seventeen of them for that matter. She did have a notebook, scrawled on in French and English with occasional doodles and splashes of whatever sauce she had been working on. Ava flicked through it and her mouth started to water. She would keep that book and she would, she vowed, use it to inspire her to be more adventurous in her kitchen and Maisie would just have to widen her tastes too. Smiling, she sat the book on the worktop and started working through the drawers, the second of which contained nothing but two letters – eureka! – another letter! Although after the emotional rollercoaster of the last letter she could have done with a little reprieve.

Seeing Betty's trademark handwriting, she smiled and looked upwards. "I could do with a day off! I'm pregnant, Betty. And emotional. And you have a way with words."

But she was intrigued. This time, instead of being addressed to 'My dear girls', each letter bore a name. Ava felt a swell of emotion as she saw her own name because she knew, just absolutely knew, that this was going to be something special and personal and a link to the aunt she didn't really feel she deserved.

Her second instinct, after begging for a day off, was to tear open the letter and devour it as quickly as she could but then she thought, no, stop, wait, savour it. She boiled the kettle, standing staring out the window as it rattled and hissed to its climax. Dropping a tea bag into a delicate china cup from the dresser, she poured in the milk and hot water and waited for the liquid to turn the required murky shade of beige.

She lifted both it and the letter and walked to the terrace where she sat for a moment, allowing the sun to warm her face. Then slowly she opened the letter and pulled out the latest find from Betty. This one was different. It was special.

My darling Ava,
I'm glad you have found this. I know it was kind of a bit silly of me to leave so many letters around the house and

hope you would find them. Jean-Luc said I should have left them all out – or in fact just written one big long letter which said it all. But I didn't want to do that. Writing these letters has become a little hobby for me lately. They are my way of writing it all down – my life, what happened, my regrets, my joys. And I know I can share all of that with you and Hope and you won't think I'm just a mad old woman.

You don't think I'm just a mad old woman, do you?

Well, presuming you don't, I wanted to say some things. Some things which are just for you. Some things I wish I had said to your face – that we had talked over. But I suppose I didn't think it was my place. You get brave in death. You say things that you never would have in life because no one can answer back, or tell you to feck off. And it's easier. And we've already established I could be a bit of a coward at times.

I wanted to say thank you, my darling. I believe you came into my life for a special reason and now I'm hoping you can let me into yours and you won't mind me having my say.

Where to begin? When I came home for Mammy's funeral I was in pieces. It had been a long time since I was home – not that I considered Derry to be home any more. I'd only come back a handful of times – to see my parents, to attend their funerals. Coming back was too painful. I didn't feel welcome – the air of disappointment hung thick in the air and the guilt crushed me. In France I could put that aside– and I did. Please don't think for even one second I had a lifetime of misery. I didn't. But when I came home to Derry I had to face up to it. For a long time Derry held only sad memories for me and feelings that I didn't really belong. Things were different in the 70s. We didn't have the internet or email, of course, so when I moved away my connection back home came through the odd letter and the odder phone call. (My parents had a pathological fear of the phone and an even bigger one of phone bills. No call was ever longer than five minutes. I swear I could hear Daddy counting down in the background each time they called.)

We couldn't afford to come home very often and it was hard to come home anyway. The tension which was there when I left, well, it eased but it never went away and it seemed every time I came home that wound was torn open again. Needless to say, my family back home couldn't afford to come and see us either. They all had families and commitments or were struggling to find work. Times were tough.

When I first moved away, Ava, I pined for home. And I think I kind of built a rose-tinted image of it. France was, and is, stunningly beautiful but a part of me hankered for the hills of Donegal and the steep streets of Derry. I would love the few times I would come home – it would feel so special and I would cry as I drove over the Glenshane Pass or up the road from Dublin when I would get that first glimpse of the Foyle meandering towards the city.

But after a while, this became my home. My true home. And my memories became a little bit hazy. They didn't go away – understand they didn't go away – but they were memories. They weren't my life.

And when I arrived back for Mammy's funeral and everything had changed . . . oh, I felt like an outsider. I was an outsider. The room was filled with family members I didn't know and had never met and who didn't really know me. I hadn't expected a big welcome. I was hardly the prodigal daughter and in fairness you all had so much else to be concerning yourselves with, burying your granny and all.

So I sat, in the corner of the room, and felt alone. And, Ava, I mean I felt utterly alone. There was no Mammy and Daddy there. I know I was in my fifties and perhaps should expect such things but I still felt like an orphan. And Claude was gone too. The last time I had been home he had been at my side and that made it all – everything – much more bearable.

I was missing him that day. And missing my parents. And missing an old Derry and the life I used to have when I was younger. Mad, isn't it? The Derry I left was being torn apart by bombs and bullets and wasn't pretty to look at. But I was missing it all the same, and I thought that if and when I died, no one from home would probably even notice or care. Not really. I mean they would tut and shake their heads and say it was fierce sad but then it would pass and they would get on with their lives. Which is the way it should be.

I felt that if I got up and walked out of that room in that moment no one would really notice. I know that's awfully selfish. Everyone was grieving. Everyone was dealing with their own issues but, you know, sometimes you can't help how you feel.

So I was about to get up and walk out. I'd paid my respects and I thought I really don't fit here any more and then you sat down beside me and you smiled and you said you loved my shoes.

Do you know how that comment saved me that day? I don't mean I was about to go for a long walk off a short precipice or anything but I was feeling utterly lost. You loving my shoes hauled me right back up and out of my grump. And your smile . . . Ava, my darling, you have such a lovely smile.

I could tell you were preoccupied that day, concerned about your baby who hadn't been sleeping and Cora who was taking Mam's death particularly hard. You looked tired. And when I say tired, I mean to-the-bone tired – the kind of tired which comes from the inside out and makes you want to walk out of rooms filled with your family and keep walking until you find some sort of peace.

I'm not being presumptuous, am I? I'm not off the mark? You probably think I've no right to pass comment.

It's just that I saw in you a little of what I felt in myself that day. Like someone who didn't really know what they wanted any more and didn't really feel they belonged anywhere?

That's a hard feeling to live with, Ava. It wears you and leaves you feeling even more tired.

Ava stopped reading and put the letter down. It wasn't that she was done but she just couldn't read any more for now. Was it that obvious? Even then? Even when Maisie was tiny and she'd only just met Betty? Sweet Jesus. She had thought she looked normal – happy even. She shook her head. It wasn't that she was unhappy or depressed. She just wasn't right. Standing up and leaving the letter on the table, she walked down to the pool, trying to quiet the voices in her head. Betty saw it. Betty saw it as soon as she met her so who else saw it? Jesus, was she wandering around all this time looking like the fecking Mother of Sorrows?

She wasn't fed up all the time. Yes, she was tired. Yes, she was stressed out. Yes, motherhood had been the hardest thing she had ever done in her entire life and, yes, she felt like she was stuck in some sort of hamster wheel running constantly and never getting anywhere. She felt like she was some sort of a failure because all around her mums were getting on with it and taking to it like a duck to water and she wasn't. She was struggling. Struggling with making sure she did any of it right and didn't mess up Maisie's life. And struggling with trying to hold on to any shred of her old pre-baby life she could because that was the only her she had ever known.

She couldn't admit it to anyone. Connor just didn't understand it. He didn't understand a mother's inbuilt perfectionist streak – her desire to get it all just right. No, not a desire, more of a need. He would kiss her on the top of her head and tell her to relax and that she was doing a great job – but she didn't want to do a great job.

She wanted to do the best job – at parenting and at work and at being a wife.

She couldn't tell Cora. Cora would give her the "maybe you should give up work" speech followed by the "you young women want it all" speech which made her feel like she had somehow done something terribly wrong and bold by going and getting herself an education. For a woman who grew up in the bra-burning era, Cora was a traditionalist at heart. Ava had tried to argue the bit with her many a time when she was younger – telling her that everyone said a modern woman could have it all. Her mother had tutted and turned her head a little to the side and said "We'll see" in a patronising manner which made Ava actually want to smack her in the face. (Which she would never do, because you know, it's a very bad thing indeed to smack your mammy in the face.) Now, she could hardly sit down and say, "Actually, mother, you know all those beliefs I argued the toss with you about? You were right and I was wrong." No, there were some things which no good could come of, and admitting to her mother that she had in fact been right all along was one of them.

As for Karen, Karen would just tell her to get drunk and to stop taking it all so seriously. Which, appealing as it was, wouldn't make things better overnight. She would just wake up the next day with a hangover and a nagging sense of guilt that she just wasn't getting it right at all. Any of it.

She wished, not for the first time, that Betty was there. That she could sit and talk to her and share her thoughts about the letter with her and perhaps, more than anything, thank her for noticing that things weren't perfect and she wasn't coping.

She felt herself inhale and suddenly she struggled to breathe out again. Sitting there by the pool she felt her chest constrict with the weight of the realisation that, despite her very best attempts at trying to look and be as perfect as possible, she was as transparent as a shard of glass. Karen thought she was a martyr. Connor was always telling her to relax. Her mum would give her a look which told her to slow down and now, even from beyond the grave, Betty was telling her that she wasn't quite as in control as she thought. She put her hand to the lounger to steady herself even though she was already sitting down and she willed her body to just breathe. A simple action. A simple in and out – a slow inhalation followed by a slow exhalation. Tears sprang to her eyes as she breathed and she wished she hadn't been so blasé about Hope going out for the afternoon with Jean-Luc. She could have done with some company there and then – for Hope to smile and tell her she was lovely and friendly and seemed like a great mammy.

Slowly her breathing returned to normal. Slowly she told herself she was okay. It was okay. Then she stood up and walked back to the letter and decided to keep reading, realising that even if Betty had seen she was miserable she had clearly also seen something else in her – something she liked.

She breathed in, easier this time, and lifted the letter to continue, picking up where she left off.

But even though you felt that way, Ava, even though you had your own grief to deal with and your own worries in your life, you sat and you talked to me. And we had fun, didn't we?

I never thought I would laugh at my own mother's funeral, but we laughed and chatted like old friends. I felt like I belonged again. You made me feel anchored to something again – something I had pushed to the side.

I've often thought about you since and wondered do you feel as if you belong? At the funeral you didn't sit with the rest of your family – the family you see all the time. You sat with me. Do you feel like an outsider sometimes? I often wondered about that.

Did you know that every year your mother would send me a Christmas card with a long letter – filling me in on all the family news? So I heard about you – how you did well in your job, how your wee girl was growing. And I thought of that girl who sat beside me and looked tired and I just thought . . . well . . . I don't know . . . I wanted to make things easier for you.

You deserve to have things a little easier. So I've brought you to France – for a break, for a chance to stop and look around and think about what you really want.

I know what you modern women are like – a bit like the rest of us really. Sometimes it takes someone holding a great big mirror up to your face to make you stop and reassess. Sometimes we take the scenic route to get there, but we do get there, darling. We do. That sounds like I read a lot of self-help books, but I don't really. I only bought the one and read it halfway before Claude told me that I didn't need a book to let me know what I wanted in life.

He was always right. So you know, anyway, yourself, what you want, don't you?

With lots of love,
Betty
xxx

Chapter 23

Hope stood on the terrace overlooking the village of Saint Jeannet. Her feet ached, as did her calves from walking up and up and through the village's winding streets to reach the rustic, yet majestic church of Saint-Jean-Baptiste.

"It's beautiful," she had breathed as soon as she had breath enough to speak.

"I think so," Jean-Luc had replied and she glanced at him.

She wondered what he must have made of her – this slightly sweaty and rather wheezy girl from Ireland – while he stood there not a drop of perspiration to be seen, in his loose cotton shirt with his sunglasses nestled on the top of his head. She must have looked a sight, and yet he had a smile on his face. If she reeked of body odour there was no wrinkling of his nose to betray the fact.

Mercifully the chapel was cool and Hope sat on one of the wooden benches and took it all in. She had enjoyed her day with Jean-Luc – the drive along the hairpin bends of the Riviera, the lunch at a small café close to the coast and the walk to the top of the village which, in fairness, had almost killed her. But the views had been worth it. And she didn't just mean the scenery. They had chatted almost effortlessly – and Hope had been delighted altogether with herself that she hadn't fallen into her old habit of adopting other people's accents within seconds of talking to them. She was pretty sure a faux French accent would not have gone down all that well on this occasion.

When she had recovered and cooled down, Jean-Luc had taken her hand and led her to the Fontaine du Boeuf where she had splashed cool water on her wrists and the back of her neck. She wasn't sure she wasn't suffering from some form of sunstroke but when she looked over at Jean-Luc he seemed to be entranced by her actions. This was impressive, she thought. Dylan rarely even noticed when she did her make-up or washed her hair, never mind when she just splashed herself with some water.

"Come and see the terrace," he had said, reaching for her hand again and she had smiled and followed. "It will be worth it," he grinned and she knew it already was.

Having traipsed over, he pulled her in front of him and faced her towards the view – his mouth was deliciously close to her ear and she didn't flinch. She could feel the warmth from his body and the heat in his hands as he held onto her arms.

"This is France," he said. "This is what you should write about. This is what kept Betty here. It kept her young and gave her a sense of purpose. This is what life is all about."

She felt herself melt and realised that if she did not get a hold of her faculties very soon, what she would be writing about might well bear more of a resemblance to erotic fiction than travel journalism.

I must not go to strange countries and sleep with hunky men with whom there is no future, she told herself before stepping away from Jean-Luc's grasp and gazing at the village below.

"This certainly has its own charm," she said unsure of what she was talking about any more. She felt dizzy with it all – and not just because of the height of the hill. Just two days before she had been breaking her heart over Dylan and now here she was, desperate to kiss a man who for all she knew was a complete and utter gigolo anyway. He had that look about him – that look like he would jump in the sack with anyone he took a fancy to and that all he would have to do to have them bend to his will was speak in his accent and flash that winning smile.

And she was tempted. Not only because they had shared a deliciously gorgeous day together but because it had been a Very Long Time Indeed since she had jumped in the sack with anyone who truly wanted to be in bed with her and there was a part of her which just longed to remember what it felt like to have a man do whatever the heck he wanted to her and to just allow herself to enjoy it without thinking about what it might all mean. Looking at Jean-Luc she knew, absolutely and without reservation, that she would enjoy it without all that complicated unrequited-love crap getting in the way. With some men you just know it would be good, she thought. It's all in the swagger.

No, she must distract herself because she was not in France to fall into bed with anyone. She was there to fulfil her aunt's last wishes and act with a certain level of respect and decorum. Betty clearly had been very fond of the man standing beside her and it would do no good at all to muddy the waters of their relationship. Even though she kind of really wanted to.

"It has been a lovely day," she said. "You've given me a lot to think about." And she wasn't, of course, just talking about the sights, sounds and smells of Provence.

"I'm glad, but don't tell me you want our day to end already?"

"It's gone five," she said, looking at her watch.

"Perfect time for a glass of wine then. Let me take you to a little restaurant in the village? We can have something to eat before I take you home. I'm sure Ava won't mind. She is probably still napping."

Frig it, she thought. One glass wouldn't hurt. Nor could one more hour in his company.

As they sat, a bottle of Merlot on the table, Hope spoke. "You have told me a lot about Saint Jeannet, and a lot about France. You have told me everything I could ever have wanted to know about the history of the lovely chapel on the hill. But why don't you tell me a little about yourself?"

She was aware that sounded like a cheesy pick-up line. She couldn't help it. It seemed that everything she did or said or thought that day seemed better suited to the pages of a Danielle Steele novel than to real life. Then again, this was hardly real life. This time next week she would be back in Belfast, cooking bacon baps and listening to Cyndi orgasm. Not to mention she would be back to the reality of trying to pitch articles and deal with her overdraft. No, she quite liked her pretend life here in France. She could most absolutely definitely get used to this sort of thing, cheesy lines and all.

"There is not a lot to know," Jean-Luc replied. "You know why I am helping Betty out and you know why I moved back to Saint Jeannet. That is all there is to say."

"Well, I'm a journalist and I say different. We have to know the who, what, why, where and when. There must be something else you can tell me? How old are you?"

Jean-Luc laughed. "Older than you!"

"Yes, but five minutes older, or five years?"

"You are, what, twenty-eight?" he said, with a twinkle in his eye.

Even though she knew it was probably just a line he had doled out on more than one occasion, she smiled.

"Near enough," she said with a wink.

"Well, then, I am twenty years older than you. Old enough to know better." The glint was unmistakable. The man was a born flirt and she loved it.

"Ah, forty-eight. That's not so old."

"You say the nicest things," he said. "Now is there anything else you absolutely have to know?"

Oh God yes, there were many things she had to know. None of them particularly appropriate for the setting they were in. In fact, as they sat there she felt her brain turning to absolute mush until all she could think about was kissing him and knowing what that felt like – what he felt like. The realisation shocked her to the core.

Another hour couldn't do any harm?

How wrong she was.

She had two glasses of wine, and Jean-Luc had barely touched a drop when he drove her home. She wanted to speak and to ask him so much more about himself but her verbal skills had now moved beyond cheesy romance novels and on to utter gibberish. The wine was more potent than she had realised and, combined with the sultry evening air, she didn't actually trust herself to even try and talk any more.

The house seemed empty when they arrived.

"Maybe Ava is on the terrace," Jean-Luc said.

She nodded. "It's lovely there," she said.

"It's lovely here too," he said softly and she looked into his piercing blue eyes.

Now or never, she realised, so she closed her eyes to steady herself and before she took a breath she felt his lips very gently touch her cheek.

"Mademoiselle, it has been a pleasure," he said, kissing her hand and getting out of the car to open the door for her.

Surely he would kiss her at the door of the house? Surely this was not it? Not after the mammoth flirting all day and all evening? She wanted to stamp her feet and shout "Not fair!" but she realised this was probably not the sexiest thing she could do at that moment.

At the door he said, "I will see you again before you leave. The market?"

"Maybe," she muttered, her disappointment seeping from her pores.

"I would like that," he said, kissing her only on the cheek again before turning and walking back to his car.

Walking dejectedly through the living room, Hope saw Ava curled on the sofa, a blanket across her knees, lost in her book. She looked up and smiled.

"How did it go?"

"Crap. Well, not crap. It was lovely actually. But it ended crap. I thought at least I would have got a snog, or a quick grope or a snog *and* a quick grope. All I got was a friendly kiss on the cheek and a big old see-you-later." She sighed as she sat down dramatically on one of the loungers, clutching her bag to her. "What's wrong with me?" she said in an overly dramatic manner to no one in particular. "Am I boot-ugly? Because you can tell me if

I'm boot-ugly. Am I so singularly unattractive that after a day of witty banter, romantic views and enough sunshine to make anyone a little soft in the head, all I can score from a very sexy man is a kiss on the cheek?"

"I wouldn't knock a kiss on the cheek," Ava said. "And, no, you are not boot-ugly. But let's just stop one minute and rewind. You wanted a snog? You wanted a grope? When did this all change from being a day out to see if you wanted to go back to the world of travel journalism to wanting a snog?"

Hope grimaced before laughing. "Ava Campbell, don't try and tell me it wasn't your intention to get me to fall madly in lust with Jean-Luc! It was you who set today up after all."

"It's a fair cop," Ava said, with a wink. "But still . . . how, why, what? Details, woman, details!"

"Yes, miss," Hope answered with mock petulance although she felt herself relax as she curled up into the tweed chair and kicked off her sandals. "We had a lovely day," she began. "He took me all round the village, and through the countryside. The coastal drives are amazing. With the top down on his car I felt like a million dollars – like something out of a 50s movie. We had lunch, which he insisted on paying for, and we talked some more. He's forty-eight, you know, but still swoonsome. And then he left me back, and he kissed my cheek, said he would like to see me again, and then kissed my cheek again."

"So he wants to see you again?"

Hope nodded, then shook her head. "Well, yes, and no. I mean we have to see him when we go to the market so he's kind of obliged to see me and not necessarily longing to see me."

"But he kissed your cheek?"

She nodded again. "Two times."

"And you had a lovely day?"

"Blissful," she said with a weak smile.

"And through all of this how many times did you think of Dylan and his Ballymena Babe?"

"None," Hope said with a start. She'd only realised then that Dylan hadn't come into her mind all afternoon. It was rather

Claire Allan

disturbing because Dylan tended to live in her mind a lot which she knew was a bit nutso but she couldn't help how she felt.

"Well, that has to be good in itself?" Ava asked, eyebrow raised.

"I suppose so."

"You suppose so? Maybe there is hope for you after all. I mean yesterday you would never have dreamed of wanting to snog another man, never mind being disappointed when he didn't lunge back at you. This can only be good. This can only mean your passion for the handsome Dylan is not as strong as you first thought."

Hope wasn't so sure. She wished she could be. But now that they had mentioned his name she felt a little ashamed. How could she not have thought about him for six full hours? She sipped from her glass again before muttering "Maybe."

Ava sat forward. "There is no *maybe* about it, miss. Jean-Luc could be the best thing that ever happened to you even if you never get a snog from him because at least you know there is life outside the four walls of Glenville Street and you don't have to pin all your affections on someone who is clearly besotted with someone else!"

Hope thought of the picture of Dylan and Cyndi – their naked feet – together on Facebook and nodded. "A snog would have been nice though. I bet he is a good kisser. He looks like he could make a girl swoon with a brush of his lips on hers. It would have been nice. Apart from Dylan and our ill-fated *Brigadoon* nights of passion, it's been a long time since I've been kissed. Embarrassingly long, if the truth be told. Like *really* embarrassingly long. Months long. Actually thinking about it, it might not be too far from being years long. Christ, I need a drink!"

Hope sat back and rubbed her temples. Her last pre-Dylan-drunken-fumble kiss – well, her last snog to be precise – had been a good twenty-two months ago. She had been out at an event in Belfast – a press launch which turned into drinks after with a group of hacks from the local newspaper. Six glasses of chardonnay (which was five more than her usual limit) and she found herself snogging someone with kebab breath and wandering hands at a taxi queue at Botanic. It was not an altogether pleasant experience and not one she ever wanted to repeat. The subsequent slump in the freelance market in Belfast had put paid to her social life and the majority of her days were spent in their house, lusting after fictional TV doctors (House, McSteamy, McDreamy and Adam from *Casualty*) and, latterly, Dylan. It struck her that maybe her feelings for him were as based in fiction as her feelings for Dr House. Once the end credits rolled, he would turn back into the friend she had always known. Maybe she wasn't such a lost cause after all.

Chapter 24

Ava listened to Hope speak animatedly about her day with Jean-Luc and she wondered when would be the appropriate time to hand over the letter she had sitting beside her which was clearly marked for Hope. She knew her letter had left her feeling emotionally raw and she imagined that Betty, the crafty wee devil, had probably written something equally personal for Hope.

After she had finished the letter, and dried her tears and said some choice bad words, she had climbed into bed and slept for a solid two hours before waking to the ringing of her phone. Unable to rouse herself from her sleep, she let the phone ring onto answer service and had listened later to a message from Connor saying he missed her and loved her. She should have phoned him back but she knew that if she did she would have blurted the news that she was pregnant out there and then, and that was not what she wanted. Betty was right – she needed to get everything right in her own head and this was the perfect chance to think things through properly. Reading the letter had made her realise things needed to change – something needed to give and there was no reason it couldn't. Maybe she could go part-time at work? Maybe Connor could look for work closer to home again, or even set up on his own? There were options. There had to be options. It didn't have to be this hard. Other families made it work. She had smiled as she thought of the possibilities, buoyed up by Betty's assurances that things can get better even when you find them all completely overwhelming.

She had got up, made herself something to eat and sat on the terrace watching the sun move across the sky. Looking at her watch she waited, impatiently, for Hope to come home eager to tell her that everything would be fine and to share with her the letter Betty had left with her name on it.

And now as she listened to her talk about the turn of events with Jean-Luc, she wasn't sure when to drop the 'And I found another letter' bombshell.

"I'm sorry I left you all day," Hope said. "I didn't expect to be away so long. Time kind of ran away with us. I do feel guilty. Were you okay? Did you get much done? Oh God, that sounds awful like I'm expecting you to have done loads and you pregnant and all. Jeez, what's wrong with me?"

Ava looked at her cousin who was working herself into a complete tizzy and she knew that now was the right time to hand over the letter.

"Actually," she said, smiling at Hope and reaching out to hold her hand, "I had a strange and interesting day myself. I went through a lot in the kitchen. Sorted through the paperwork and put aside a few things you might want to look at or which we might want to try and sell on or whatever. But the most interesting thing is that I found more letters from Betty."

"Letters? Plural?"

"Yes, two of them. One each. These are different, Hope. Mine was a long one – a tough read in places but a lovely read. There's one for you too."

Ava reached behind her and took the letter from the table and handed it over. She watched as Hope picked it up and started to open the envelope and she decided it would be the perfect time to go back to the kitchen and finish packing away the colourful china and heavy-leaded crystal and let Hope get on with reading the letter herself. She might even re-read her own letter again, for the fifth time, and try to digest the information. Yes, that is what she would do while she made another cup of tea and sat in the kitchen which she wished was her own.

Hope curled up on the tweed chair and pulled a soft woollen blanket around her as she pulled the paper from the envelope. She was surprised to find a second letter inside, in an envelope folded in half, marked with the words "*Do Not Read*" in bold letters, scrawled in red ink. One eyebrow raised, she set the mystery envelope to the side and unfolded the pages she was allowed to read in front of her.

My dear Hope,

Maybe you were expecting this at some stage? That I would write to you both individually. You must have known there were things that we would share, just us. Things that I wanted to say to just you. I wish I had stayed in touch more after your stay here – perhaps we were both a little lax there. Jean-Luc told me I should get a computer – you know, with the World Wide Web on it so that we could email. He even said I should join that Facebook thing. Can you think of anything more silly? Me on Facebook? I looked at it once in the internet café and it was all poking here and there and silly games and the like. No, I prefer good old pen and paper.

You probably think me an old fart for thinking that way. I imagine you and your lovely journalism career means you have a fancy laptop and that you are au fait with modern technology. I struggle with the DVD player, to be honest. I'd probably break a laptop if anyone was foolish enough to give one to me.

Anyway . . . I'm sorry I didn't get in touch more. I did so enjoy your Christmas cards and birthday cards with the snippets of your news. I know I didn't always reply but, believe me, I appreciated them. I have them in a box, you know, in the attic. I never throw things like that away. It would have been like throwing away someone's secrets.

Oh Hope, you meant the world to me. I know to you I was probably just a mad aunt who occasionally sent a card and who drove you mad during your stay here in Saint Jeannet – but I loved you so much. Is that too much? Does that make me sound mad?

I have been thinking a lot recently about my life. That happens when you know the Banshee is on her way for you.

I've been thinking a lot about that summer when you and your friend came to stay. As you know, I hadn't got over Claude's death. I was pottering around here on my own, not sure of what to do any more. That's the problem when you devote your life to someone else entirely. When they are gone you find yourself not sure of what to do next or where to go. I thought it was time for me to just lie down and wait to croak it myself. I wanted to die, I suppose, and to be with him. I know that sounds awful. Believe me, especially now when I know what it is like to look death square in the face, I know how pathetic is sounds to even think about wanting to die before your time. But that was how I felt.

Do you know what my first reaction was when I got your phone call asking if you could stay for a bit? Now excuse me, because I'm going to use some choice language here, Hope, but I thought about telling you to feck away off. The thought of anyone being under my roof that wasn't Claude was not appealing. I mean, how could I get on with my Grade A moping and grieving with people in the house who needed to be cared for?

Pierre talked me round. He told me it would do me good and, much as I wanted to tell him to feck away off with himself too, I soon realised that no amount of grieving and weeping was going to bring Claude back and no amount of me just lying around and feeling sorry for myself was going to hasten the arrival of the Grim Reaper either. Oh, I was foolish to wish my life away.

So you arrived. Sun-kissed. Slightly smelly. Sounding like home. Full of life. I realised within an hour of you and Dylan being here that rather than fixating on death as I had done, I had to start fixating on life.

That meal I prepared the first night, the chicken hotpot with the fresh baked bread and the wine? That was the first proper meal I had eaten in weeks. I realised that night how hungry I was – not just for proper food but for life.

Oh Hope, didn't we have fun? Chatting by the pool? Walking into the village together? Singing in the living room into the wee small hours?

You forced me to get out and about – to take you to see places and do things that I never thought I would do – and I realised I still had a life to lead. And it was a beautiful life. Sure the colour had faded a bit with Claude's passing but how dare I want to throw the rest of it away?

You brought me back to life, my darling girl, and showed me that there was so much still out there. When you left I didn't lie back down on the sofa and cry from morning till night. I picked myself up. I joined a few night-classes. I even joined a choir! Singing in French! Now there's an experience! I took to volunteering at the nursing home two days a week and I lived my life.

Hope, you gave me hope. Don't ever underestimate your ability to bring joy and comfort to people. You're here for a reason.

But now that we' have the mushy stuff out of the way, can I talk to you, woman to woman, about that Dylan character?

Don't spend your life waiting for things to happen. In my

case I was waiting to join Claude again but, in your case, are you waiting for him? I can't explain why, but I think you are and I know this might make you want to tell me to feck away off with myself but it's not going to happen, sweetie. If a man wants a woman he wants her. He falls in love with her. He doesn't wait fifteen years to see if there is a better option and then fall in love with her. And you are amazing – and you deserve for someone to fall in love with you the moment they see you and to love you forever. You don't want to be anyone's consolation prize and you don't want to be with anyone who plays games with who they love and why they love them.

Are you cross with me now, petal? Am I off the mark? I don't mean to offend. I just want you to be happy. Dylan seems like a nice man. We got on very well when he was here but I don't want you to be stuck in a rut. A rut is not a nice place to be. A rut makes you live on toast and cry all day and pray for an early death.

I've brought you here to give you a little time to think – to have some space. Maybe to remember how vibrant you were when you were here those years ago and think about who you want to be. I didn't get round to doing it when I was still alive, but I can now.

I'm just sorry I'm not here to see you again and give you a big hug and tell you face to face how you made my life special.

Now you may wonder what the second envelope is all about. It's an envelope only for you. I hope to God you've found it and this letter. But, on your last day, Jean-Luc will give you one final envelope. Can you do me a big favour and give him this letter then? He has been so good to me, this is just a little something for him and I would love it if you would hand it over.

I know I've asked a lot, Hope, bringing you here. Getting you to sort out the house and now asking you to pass on this letter. But it will all make sense soon. It will all come out in the wash, as they say.

I love you, Hope. You deserve to be happy.

Lots of love,
Betty
xxx

A big fat tear plopped onto the page, which Hope quickly tried to brush away before it soaked into the paper and caused the ink to run. Every single emotion on the planet ran through her mind. Guilt at not coming to see Betty more. Love – so much love – and how Betty made her feel. Sadness at the loss her aunt had experienced. Embarrassment that Betty had picked up on the whole completely-unrequited-love thing going on with Dylan.

And anger at him too – for using her and playing with her emotions. She thought of Betty's words – how if a man is going to fall in love he just falls in love and he doesn't wait to see what is out there first. Fuck. Betty had just nailed it. Dylan was keeping her as his in-case-of-emergency girl. She was his fall-back when he needed his breakfast cooked, or his clothes washed or just needed a random shag. He was a shit. A total shit. A big shitty sleep-with-you-the-night-before-his-girlfriend-moves-in kind of a shit. He was exactly the kind of shit she wrote about when she wrote all-men-are-shit articles for glossy magazines. He was exactly the kind of shit her mother warned her about, and her friends warned her about and the whole world warned her about. Grabbing her phone, she stomped to the terrace and dialled his number, anger coursing through her veins. She would tell him. She would rage and tell him just how angry she was – and how she had spent the day with someone who didn't make her angry and how Betty believed she deserved better.

The phone rang twice when Cyndi answered, her broad accent bellowing down the phone. "Hiya, Hope!" she said cheerily. "How's it going?"

Hope didn't want to answer how it was going. She didn't want to explain everything that was going through her mind. She didn't want to talk to Cyndi at all. Or even think about her. But there she was, part of her life, part of the joint life she had been building with Dylan – reminding her that he wasn't hers, not even a little bit. He belonged to someone else.

She felt herself sag – her anger sink from her.

"Grand," she replied. "It's going grand. Is Dylan there?" Though she knew when he came on the phone she wouldn't say anything. She wouldn't do that to him in front of Cyndi. She wanted him to know how much she was hurting and how she wouldn't let him hurt her again but she wasn't a complete bitch. She didn't want his life to implode. Even if he was a shit.

"He's in the shower," Cyndi giggled.

Hope took this as code for 'just had sex, needs shower, is all dirty sexy dirty' and she felt herself blush with shame at the memory of their most recent night of passion.

"Oh, okay . . . maybe I'll get him later . . ." Now that her anger was being replaced by a certain sense of shame, she wanted to get off the phone – and quickly.

"Nothing important?"

"No, nothing at all," Hope replied, saying her quick goodbyes and putting the phone down. She stood for a second on the terrace feeling the evening air wash over her and then she dried her eyes. "If only it were as easy as just moving on, Betty," she whispered, feeling a little bit like a failure because she couldn't.

Chapter 25

Ava had a fear of attics. She couldn't quite explain why but they gave her the major heebie-jeebies. There was something about the closed-in space at the top of a house which made her feel uncomfortable. Perhaps she had read *Flowers in the Attic* one too many times as a teen or maybe it was just that they were horrible places with hidey holes for spiders and creaky ladders acting as your only means of escape should a giant Daddy Long Legs decide to get you in his sights. She shuddered as she climbed steep staircase to join Hope in Betty's attic. This had been the part of the entire trip she had been dreading most but, by all accounts, this was where the majority of the work was to be carried out. Looking around her to catch her bearings she was grateful see several small skylights casting a glow of natural light in the room. She hated attics with no windows more than anything. All that wood and darkness and stale air. You might as well just stick her in a coffin and close the lid.

"Are you okay?" Hope asked, reaching her hand down to help Ava up.

"Not a fan of attics," she whispered, clambering up to look around.

"Oh, I love them!" Hope said, opening the skylight and letting some fresh air in. "They are so romantic."

Ava raised her eyebrow. If there was one word she could choose out of all the words in the planet to describe an attic it would not be *romantic*. "Are you mad? Jeez, they're old and musty and rotten."

"And filled with a lifetime of memories!" Hope sighed, looking at a large wardrobe in the corner of the room. "And obviously I'm a nosey fecker and places like this allow me to indulge the very best of my nosiness."

"They freak me out," Ava said, shivering even though it was exceptionally warm.

"Come on," Hope said, reaching out her hand, "get stuck in and you'll not even have time to think about how they freak you. You never know what we might encounter."

"That's what I'm afraid of," Ava said, having a sudden stomach-churning vision of a mouse running across her feet or a spider spinning down on its web and landing square on her head. "So we should just get this over and done with. Before we call Jean-Luc about the spa and the market," Hope said determinedly.

"And maybe about another date with you before we go home?" Ava smiled and watched as Hope shrugged her shoulders.

Things had been a little awkward the previous evening after Hope had read her letter. She had walked into the kitchen and poured her glass of wine down the sink, saying she wasn't really in the mood for a drink after all. Ava noticed she had been crying which hadn't really surprised her. After all, Ava had done a fair bit of weeping after reading her own letter earlier that day. It was unlikely that Hope's letter had been any less emotion-ridden than hers.

"Do you need to talk about your letter?" Ava had asked.

"Not really," Hope had said. "I hope you don't mind. I just want to process the information for a bit. You know, work out how I feel about it."

"I know what you mean," Ava said. "I had to take to my bed after mine. My emotions were all over the place."

"Hmm," Hope had said, signalling she really wasn't quite ready to be drawn into a conversation yet.

Ava knew it was time to stop probing and, while it smarted a little bit, she realised that maybe she wasn't ready to talk herself either. I mean it would be a hard call to tell anyone "By the way, Betty thinks I'm a miserable cow so she brought me here to try and sort my head out."

Maybe Hope was feeling the same. So they sat in a kind of awkward silence over two cups of tea before Hope had yawned in a slightly melodramatic fashion and declared that she was really sorry but she wanted to go to bed and she knew she was being really awful company anyway.

Ava had nodded. She was tired herself, despite her afternoon siesta, and could do with more time to think and plot and get excited about the possible changes she would make to her life.

"Don't worry, darling," Ava soothed her. "Go and get a rest."

"I promise not to be a grumpy hole tomorrow. I'll be on my best behaviour. We'll power through that attic and then we'll treat ourselves to something really girlie. Jean-Luc was telling me about a spa up at the village – at a castle no less. It looks lovely. He said if we wanted to book in just to get in touch. Apparently there are strings he can pull."

"Is there no end to his talents?" Ava said with a soft smile.

"I've yet to find out," Hope said with a sigh which came directly from the soles of her feet, and she hugged Ava goodnight.

"Tomorrow is another day," Ava soothed.

"I hope you're right, Miss Scarlett," Hope had drawled in a fake Southern accent. "I hope you are right."

She had certainly looked brighter when she padded into the kitchen the following morning. Ava had been sitting nestling a glass of orange juice as if her life depended on it – feeling very much hungover but knowing the kind of nausea she was feeling was not going to be swept away by a couple of Paracetamol, a fizzy drink and a cooked breakfast. She had woken that morning, overwhelmed by a flash of nausea which had forced her to run to the bathroom where she had retched even though there was nothing left in her stomach to bring up and then she had looked in the mirror at her pale face, bloodshot eyes and straggling hair. "Pregnancy glow, my arse," she sniped before brushing her teeth (gently so as not to induce gagging), pulling her hair back in a ponytail and dressing in soft cotton cut-off trousers which were loose around the waist and not likely to put any pressure on her digestive system. A glass of orange juice would help, it would bring her blood sugars up and settle the wishy-washy feeling in the pit of her stomach. As she watched Hope bound in, perfectly glowing, her hair glossy and her make-up bright, she felt herself turn a little green again but this time with jealousy. She knew she looked like a dog's dinner and she felt every inch of it.

"Are you okay?" Hope had asked, brewing a pot of coffee, the smell of which was not helping the continuing waves of nausea.

"Morning sickness," she mouthed. "One of the lesser joys of pregnancy. It feels like a hangover without the pleasant memory of the night before and without the comforting knowledge it will lift in a few hours."

Hope grimaced. "You poor thing. Can I make you anything to eat? Anything at all?"

Ava nodded. "Some dry toast maybe. I'll be fine in a bit."

"Did you have morning sickness when you were pregnant with Maisie?" Hope asked as she busied herself in the kitchen.

"Just a little. They do say it's a good sign though – that it means Baby is nice and healthy in there but, Jesus, it's rotten. I think I had blanked out just how rotten."

"Will you be up for the attic?"

Ava knew this could have been her get-out clause. Sure, she could avoid the attic and all her fears all together by saying that of course she wouldn't be up for it, but she knew it was the biggest part of the job so she nodded. "In half an hour I'll be right as rain," she said, and she was. The nausea had lifted as soon as she'd eaten a slice of toast and then when it lifted the fierce appetite she had been nursing for the last few days returned until she made herself a bacon sandwich and munched her way through a bowl of grapes.

"Let's go," she had said enthusiastically, the thought of a spa treatment later giving her a new lease of life.

It was only now, standing in the attic, willing herself to open the wardrobe at the end of it, that she felt nervous. And it wasn't just in case a mouse popped out or a spider fell down. She had a sneaking suspicion somewhere she would uncover another letter which might just unsettle her all over again.

Hope appeared at her elbow. "Shall we look inside?" she said, her eyes wide.

Ava laughed. "You're half expecting to be able to walk right through that thing and smack-bang into Narnia, aren't you?"

"Very funny," Hope mocked, sticking her tongue out. "I'm just curious. That's all."

Ava watched as Hope opened the wardrobe, revealing several suit-carriers neatly hanging on the rail, beside a stack of boxes where old clothes and mementoes had been mothballed and stored away for safe keeping.

Hope handed Ava a carrier and took one herself. Sitting down on a wooden chair propped against one of the attic walls, Ava unzipped the bag to find a gorgeous ruby-red dress in a soft, shiny satin staring back at her. Strapless and nipped in at the waist before pooling to the floor it looked exactly like the kind of dress a Hollywood starlet would wear. She made an involuntary "Oooh!" sound, before lifting the dress and showing it to Hope whose jaw dropped at the sheer gorgeousness of the frock.

"Betty had style," Hope said.

"And class."

"And the good sense to store it all properly, even if it is in a scary attic," Hope mocked.

"Very bloody funny. Shall I try it on? Or should you try it on? It might just fit you better?"

"Stick it there in the try on pile and we'll take it downstairs later and have our very own, really quite sad, trying-on party."

Ava laughed and felt the fug which had engulfed her from

yesterday lift. She folded the dress, feeling the softness of the fabric between her fingers and imagined a life where she got to wear fabulous dresses like that one and not just wear clothes which were both stain-repellent and able to withstand the worst a group of over-enthusiastic four and five-year-olds could throw at them. Then she thought of Betty's words – of her gentle reassurance that life doesn't have to be so hard and she thought, feck it, she might just get wear out of that dress and she bloody well would try it on just as soon as she could.

Her thoughts were interrupted by another loud gasp from Hope who was holding up a pale pink chiffon dress, with a high lace collar. Ava could imagine it would look amazing on her cousin with her wavy hair pulled up on her head.

"Fancy!" she said.

"Retro," Hope replied, holding it up against herself. "I love it! A cross between Barbie and Dolly Parton and in my size. One for the trying-on party!" She folded it and sat it on top of the red gown and reached for another carrier which contained perhaps the most offensive banana-yellow all-in-one-suit Ava had ever laid eyes on.

"So she didn't get it right all the time . . ." she said, running her hand over the polyester and hoping not to create enough static to shock herself stupid.

"I'll give you fifty euro if you try it on!" Hope laughed.

Grimacing, Ava laughed. "It would take more than fifty euro – it would take more than five hundred euro. But that has given me a laugh."

The jumpsuit was folded and placed with the 'must get rid' pile and they went on with their search through Betty's haul which yielded a quite impressive mix of gorgeous and offensive items. When the rail was cleared and the boxes searched through, they were left with just one item – a large rectangular box at the bottom of the wardrobe.

"This looks interesting," Hope said, lifting it out and putting it down on a nearby table. "Let's have a look."

Ava lifted the lid to find several layers of yellowing tissue paper which she carefully peeled back to uncover a delicate ivory lace gown. With an emotional thud, she realised this had to be Betty's wedding dress, recalling the photograph from the bedroom of a smiling bride and groom.

"Oh Hope!" she sighed. "Oh, look at it!"

Delicately she unfolded the material, satin sheathed in lace, and thought of all the hopes and dreams which had come with it. Slim and simple, pooling to a small train, with satin-covered buttons and lace-trimmed detailing at the delicate neck-line. It was the perfect wedding gown, elegant and understated. Stunning.

"You should try it on," Hope said, softly this time.

"Have you seen the waist on it? She was so thin then. I wouldn't dare even try. It would get stuck on my thighs."

"We should still keep it," Hope said, sitting down beside her. "We should definitely keep it."

Ava nodded, a lump forming in her throat. "Definitely. It's beautiful."

Hope lifted it and held it to the light. "It absolutely is."

Betty had labelled most things in the attic. Each box was marked 'Bric-a-brac', 'Pictures', 'Books' and so on. They were able to sort through most things quite quickly and had gathered together a collection of pictures and ornaments they were only too happy to pass on to Jean-Luc to pass on to the market, having already decided that any profit they made could go to the nursing home which had cared for Betty in her last days.

What neither woman was expecting to find was the small wooden crib in the corner of the room or the box marked 'Baby Things'.

Ava was the first to spot it and her heart lurched a little. Betty had no children. They both knew that. This box of things was not expected. Of everything they had uncovered this was not anywhere on the radar. Ava stood looking at the one, medium-sized cardboard box sellotaped up and placed in the crib before she noticed the small white letter on top of the box.

"I don't want to read this one," she said aloud, as much to herself as anyone else.

"What?" Hope asked, looking up.

"Betty didn't have any children? Did she?"

Hope shook her head. "She never really talked about it. Just said they had never been blessed. I never asked for any more details than that. Why?"

Ava, feeling a lump form in her throat, pointed to the crib and the box and the letter.

"Oh," Hope said, putting the pictures she had been sorting through back into their box and walking over. "Oh. Poor Betty."

"I can't read it," Ava said, pointing to the letter. She didn't even want to touch it. She didn't want to think about what it might say even though her mind was racing with all the possibilities.

"You don't have to read it," Hope said. "We don't have to read it. We don't have to read everything she left. We can just pretend we never found it. Sure, she would hardly expect us to find everything, would she? I mean, they're so scattered we couldn't find every letter?"

Ava sat down, and pulled her fingers through her hair, caught in the crux of the dilemma.

"But we should read it," she said eventually. "Betty obviously had something she wanted to say."

"But we don't have to now," Hope said gently. "It's been a long morning. I'm tired and dusty and more than a bit sweaty and we should be good to ourselves. We'll take it down, and just leave it on the side for now and come back to it when we're ready. Come on, let's go down."

Ava picked up the letter and reminded herself once again that she hated bloody attics. No good could ever come of them and there were scarier things than spiders and mice and banana-yellow jumpsuits to be found in them.

Chapter 26

Two hours later Ava was laid out like the starter dish in a fancy tapas bar. Cucumbers covered her eyes, some sort of green avocado-based mush was smeared onto her face and her hands and feet were swathed in soft towels enriched with divine tropical-smelling creams. The rest of her was wrapped in the softest, fluffiest bathrobe imaginable and she could hear the soft silence of the heat of the day buzz around her.

She was lying on a sun-bed on the terrace of the spa at the chateau, while Hope lay beside her – the fruity creams being applied to her feet and the avocado mixture already baking on her face in the glorious sunshine. So far the experience had been exceptional. The therapists had made one godawful fuss of her when they found out she was pregnant and had been kind enough not to mention her existing stretch-marks when she stripped off to her swimsuit before taking a swim in the gentle waters of the chateau's pool.

Jean-Luc had been able to get them booked in quickly and had directed them to travel to the chateau where they were greeted like royalty or minor celebs. Trying to push any thoughts relating to what might or might not be contained in the envelope from the attic to the back of her mind, Ava had tried to throw herself into the spa experience. They were set up for half an hour's sheer relaxation before they'd decide whether or not to brave the full body massages, the hot-stone treatments or the seaweed bath. Although Ava was already pretty confident that the seaweed bath would be the least of her notions. Now, if they had one of those chocolate-bath thingies she would have been up for that. And she would have asked for an extra big bath.

"Will we have a drink?" Hope asked, smiling over from where she lay in a rather skimpy and tummy-flashing bikini.

"You know," Ava said, "I think we should. I'll go the whole hog and have a glass of sparkling water but you should have a little fizz."

Hope sighed. "If you're sure it won't make you feel as if you're missing out in some way then I will, if that's okay."

"Trust me, I don't feel as if I'm missing out. It was champagne which got me into this predicament in the first instance."

Ava nodded to an impossibly petite therapist who scuttled over in her pristine white uniform and asked if she could help. Having ordered the drinks, Ava lay back and closed her eyes and let the sun seep her worries out of her. She felt her eyes droop while she allowed herself just the smallest of siestas under the French sunshine.

Hope had wanted to tell Jean-Luc as soon as she spoke to him that she had a letter for him from Betty but he had seemed a little cold – businesslike even – and she wondered had she imagined the easy way in which they chatted just the day before.

"The spa? Oh yes. I will book that. And, of course, the market. I will come by later and pick up some things and take them to my friend? Then we can go together tomorrow."

"I would like that," Hope had said and he had replied that he would come while they were out at the spa so as not to get under their feet.

She wanted to say "Please, get under my feet. My feet need someone under them and you seem like a nice option" but she didn't. Crestfallen, she had said yes, that would be fine, and she thanked him for his help before putting the phone down and cursing at it.

"It's official. I'm cursed," she said to Ava. "I am a one-woman man-repeller. There is something about me which makes men get all smoochy and then forget it ever happened the following day."

"You're not cursed. Men are just strange," Ava said. "And I mean all men. Connor even has his moments. I swear he gets male PMT – once a month he goes a bit funny, sits up all night drinking beer and watching *Men Behaving Badly* reruns and eating Indian food. You dare not go near him when he's in one of those moods – that's his alone time. I just leave him to it . . . and open the windows for the beer/ Indian fart carnage."

Hope laughed, and packed her bikini into her case and threw in some hair-clips and her best, most bejewelled flip-flops. Ava sat on the edge of her bed as they chatted. Hope was trying her very best to keep things upbeat. Ava had been quiet since they had left the attic and while Hope could completely understand why her friend would be nervous at the contents of the ominous letter on top of the crib, the nosy journalist in her was dying to find out what it said. She could have been easily distracted by Jean-Luc coming across as all flirty with her, but given his apparent disinterest in flirting she would have to get her kicks elsewhere and that would be at the spa. She closed her beach bag and hooked her arm around Ava's.

"Come on, missus. Let's forget arsey men, their stinky farts, secrets in the attic and everything that isn't lying under the sun getting pampered by lovely French ladies with oodles of expensive products."

"Oh," Ava said, "do you think it will be very expensive?"

"You can count on it," Hope said, "But it's my treat. A way to say sorry for leaving you all on your own yesterday and then coming back and being a complete grumpy-hole and clearing off to bed early."

"I can't let you do that!"

Hope shook her head. "Enough, woman! I have spoken. Now

let's go and get pampered and remember that we are technically on holiday and as such should at least do some vaguely holiday-type things and not just spend our time going through an old woman's things or being messed about by strange Frenchmen."

"Or obsessing about being pregnant and wondering how your overworked husband will respond to the news?"

"You've not told him yet?"

Ava shook her head. "Not yet. I will. When I get home. I want to pitch it just right. I want to get it right in my own head first."

"And is it . . . right? In your own head?"

"Getting there. It's still a bit of a shock and I'm still trying to figure out how we'll manage but we'll get there."

"You will, sweetheart," Hope said. "To be honest, I'm in awe of anyone who manages with a baby at all. I struggle to get *myself* ready and out of the house in the mornings, never mind another human being who needs everything doing for them." God love any child who came under her care, she thought, thinking of how she lumbered around the house most days in her jammies and lay eating toast while watching Jeremy Kyle when she should be working and wondering how to pay her credit-card bills. It didn't scream responsible parenthood.

"They're worth it, you know. I mean, obviously there are times when I want to hit the pause button, or even the mute button, but Maisie is great. I miss her loads," Ava sniffed.

"I'm sorry. I didn't mean to make you cry."

"It doesn't take much. Fecking hormones. I'm really selling this whole pregnancy thing to you, aren't I? All tears and snotters and morning sickness."

"You look radiant!" Hope said, figuring that was exactly the kind of thing you said to a pregnant woman even if Ava didn't look an ounce radiant.

"You lying baggage!" Ava laughed. "Okay, let's go!"

Lying under the sun and listening to the gentle snores of her cousin beside her, Hope wondered just exactly where her life was going.

She sipped from her champagne flute and lay back, unable to concentrate on the book she had brought with her, and mulled over the words in Betty's letter again.

She would have to let go. Wouldn't she? If there really was no hope with Dylan. She would have to move on. Sure hadn't her day out with Jean-Luc, who was admittedly acting like a big old weirdo at the moment, showed her that there was more to life?

All she had to do, she realised with a thud, was to actually figure out if in fact there was no hope with Dylan. Given that he was living with someone else and declaring his 'very much in love' status all over Facebook, the signs were not good. And she knew that Betty was probably right and that it was highly unlikely he was about to fall madly in love with her. But then again . . . there was a time not too long ago when she wouldn't have thought it even a remote possibility that she would ever, ever fall in love with him. Betty could be wrong. Just because she was old and wise and dead, all mysterious and all, didn't mean that she was necessarily right about everything.

Lifting the cucumber from her eyes and rummaging in her bag for her phone she stood up – which prompted a sudden flurry of activity from the very petite therapist.

"Are you okay, madame?"

"I just need to make a phone call," Hope said.

"I'm afraid you cannot use your phone in this area, but if you want to go to the courtyard . . ."

"I'd love to go the courtyard," Hope whispered, hoping not wake Ava from her doze. She would only ask questions and probably tell her it was a very bad idea indeed to be calling Dylan. Which was kind of right . . . but still. She just needed to talk to him – to hear the sound of his voice, to see how he was feeling and to try and gauge in her own way if there was even half a chance of anything even remotely romantic ever happening between them.

"How are you, *mademoiselle*?" he answered, his voice bright and cheery.

She felt herself smile and her mind fled back for just a moment to when they were in France together. If he was here he would be in raptures about the trip to the market.

"I am doing the absolute best in the world," she fibbed. "I'm standing here in a bikini covered in salad, drinking champagne and am about to be pampered to within an inch of my life."

He laughed – a really rather dirty laugh. "Bikini? The Frenchwomen better lock up their sons. Hopeless is on the prowl!"

She bristled at him calling her Hopeless. It wasn't nice, she thought. Not one bit. Okay, maybe this phone call would be easier than she thought. Maybe it would be obvious really quickly that her obsession with him was most definitely a very wrong thing.

"I'll not be prowling anywhere, if you don't mind," she said. "How are things back home anyway?" She decided not to ask the questions she really wanted to ask, such as did he miss her? Had he maybe fallen out of love with Cyndi? Had he realised he was actually madly in love with her instead?

"All quiet. Actually too quiet. I miss you being around," he said. "This house isn't the same without you leaving empty biscuit packets everywhere or drying your underwear on the bathroom radiator."

"Ah, does the bold Cyndi not use the bathroom radiator for her undergarments then?" Hope said, trying to steady her voice and stop the constant round of 'I miss you, I miss you, I miss you' running around her head.

"She doesn't wear any," Dylan said and Hope felt herself blush and feel slightly nauseated. "No, she bought a clothes horse, a fancy one too. She is transforming us from our slatternly ways."

"Ooooh, clothes horse indeed! She'll have one of those fancy tumble-drier machines fitted next."

"There's talk of a dishwasher," he said.

"We'll not know ourselves," she said, thinking that she definitely wouldn't know herself. She would have to move out, really. She was getting too old and too bitter to play the gooseberry.

"I do really miss you though," he said, interrupting her train of thought. "All joking aside. As that song says, I've become accustomed to your face."

"You old charmer," she teased but she felt the breath catch in her chest.

"There is something so odd about you being off on your travels alone. Surely we should do such things together."

"The bold Cyndi would have something to say about that, I'm sure."

"You're right, she probably would," he said, "but that doesn't mean I miss you any less. You are my best friend, H."

"Ha!" she blurted in a kind of half-laugh and half-cry which sounded strangely twisted. "Away with yourself, young man! Sure don't you have Cyndi?"

Now was his time – his time when he could say yes, that indeed he had Cyndi but that he would always need her. She would always be that extra special someone that he would turn to when he needed someone special to hold.

"I sure do," he replied and she could sense the grin all over his face. "She's amazing. I never thought I would meet a woman who took care of me better than you did, Hope, but there you have it. Life has a way of surprising us at times."

"It sure does," she said, feeling her heart sink and her head hurt with the realisation that he was never going to love her back. Not in that way. What he felt for her was never going to be enough. Betty was right. The bitch.

Lying on heated towels, her eyes closed, Ava felt the therapist knead her muscles into submission. She hadn't realised just how much tension she had been holding in her body until that very moment. Every part of her had been tensed up – so much so that she had become aware she was making vaguely orgasmic noises as the small blonde Frenchwoman unknotted the muscles in her shoulders.

"You are very tense," her therapist had said in soothing tones. "You must relax for your baby."

"I know," Ava said.

"We women, we worry too much, we do too much," the little

blonde woman said in her soft French accent. "We all need to learn to relax. The world still turns. The sun still comes up. As long as we have our health . . ."

"I know," Ava said.

"And you have your baby. Your baby is a blessing. A very beautiful blessing."

"I know," Ava said.

Chapter 27

The house was strangely empty when they returned to it. The boxes they had been stacking by the front door for the last few days were gone, including all those going to the charity shop and the nursing home. It felt a little impersonal – and strangely quiet. As if part of Betty was gone too, which Ava supposed was the case. So many trinkets and pictures and personal items were cleared out. It was a little disconcerting. She felt herself shiver a little.

"Strange, isn't it?" Hope said.

"It definitely is," Ava said, walking through the living room and looking at the bare surfaces of the sideboards and the vague outlines on the walls where some of the pictures used to hang. "Can you imagine that your entire life could be packed away in a matter of days? Everything that mattered to you?"

Hope gave a half laugh. "My entire life could be packed up in about thirty-four minutes. A laptop, a suitcase crammed with clothes and a bag for all my make-up. There's not much more to me than that."

"I'm sure you'd be surprised if you looked at it closely enough."

"Nope. That's pretty much it. Apart from a *Sex and the City* mug and a favourite cushion I like to cuddle when I'm on the sofa. The rest just came with the house – that's the joy of renting. It's shocking really how easily I could walk away from it all and not look back."

She said it with a smile on her face but Ava could see she was hurting. She had been quiet all afternoon at the spa, having confessed she had spoken to Dylan on the phone.

"Why does he have such a hold over you?" Ava had asked as they sat together in the pool.

"He's my best friend," Hope had said simply. "Or at least I thought he was. We have been through so much together, Ava. So much. I've grown up with him. I mean, we have lived in each other's pockets for so long it is hard to imagine a time when we won't be together."

"It must be hard."

"It is," Hope said. "After that last time – that time we had sex, I was convinced it would all change. It just seemed different. Different to that time before when we did it, you know, here in France. Yes, we were both drunk and it is a bit hazy but it felt like something more. I hate to sound like a complete drip but it felt like we were making love . . ."

Ava looked at her cousin's sad eyes and felt heart-sorry for her. At least she had been lucky with Connor – very lucky. They had met and fallen in love and it had all been fairly simple and traditional and as things should be. They had dated for a time and gone through that stage where they wanted to spend each and every moment with each other which was about the time they had rented a small flat together while they, very sensibly, saved for a deposit for a house of their own. After a while Connor had proposed. He had whisked her away on a romantic break to London and had proposed on the London Eye which was as romantic as it sounds and made for a great story to tell back home. Marriage followed – a lovely big wedding, a white dress, three bridesmaids and a turkey dinner everyone tucked into and declared it to have been a great day out. Then they had settled down – slowly furnishing their house and building their careers until they had decided it was time to have a baby and everything had gone perfectly well with that as well.

Occasionally Ava thought it was all, well, just a little too predictable and a little too boring. That's not to say she didn't love

Connor with every part of her being and that she wasn't grateful for their lives – not to mention their daughter – but there were times when she had wanted to do something wild. Now, though, looking at Hope, she realised she was foolish to feel trapped by it all. Hope would give everything to have what she had. To have someone who loved her back and who she knew would always be there for her. With the wave of pity she felt for her cousin, came a wave of love for her husband and she thanked her lucky stars there were only a few days to go until she could see him again.

"Do you think it felt different because you felt different?" she asked her cousin gently. "You said the first time you slept together it was all very out of the blue and this time it was different. The difference might have been your feelings."

Hope shrugged her shoulders. "I just don't know. Was it? I mean, I felt something . . . I was sure he felt it too."

Ava was acutely aware that even though, in the space of just a few days, she had shared an awful lot with Hope she also didn't really know her. Not enough to say: "Perhaps he was only after a shag?"

She hadn't met Dylan and there was something about him that made Ava feel uneasy. But she couldn't say that – not without fear of offending Hope completely. And being stuck in France with someone who had right royal hump with you would not be a pleasant experience – especially when you were stuck in a house together with nowhere to run and fewer places to hide.

She had changed the subject subtly shortly after and now, listening to Hope talk about how she could pack up all her life, she decided to try and put a positive spin on things. "It would make it easier for you to go on your travels then, wouldn't it? Without having to worry about where to store everything?"

"I suppose. Every cloud," Hope said with a smile before announcing she was going for a shower.

Alone, Ava found her mind turn back to the letter they had found in the attic. She knew they should read it, that it obviously contained something which Betty wanted to share, and while she would have very much liked to continue to put it off for as long as possible, her nosiness was getting the better of her.

Maybe, however, she should get Hope to read it. Hope could edit it, after all, if there were any parts which she would deem too possibly upsetting for a hormonal pregnant woman. She picked up the envelope nonetheless and held it, wondering what it could possibly contain.

When Hope padded back in her dressing-gown, a towel turbaned on her head, Ava nodded. "I think I'm ready to read this bad boy now."

"Are you sure?" Hope asked.

"Well, not really. But we should, shouldn't we?"

Hope nodded. "Look, we'll read it together. Safety in numbers and all that."

"I like the sound of that," Ava said softly, tearing open the envelope and pulling out several sheets of paper.

They sat close together, Ava holding the letter, her eyes fixed on the first page as Hope began to read aloud: *"My dear girls, please be together when you read this. I need you to be there for one another. Hope, I know how strong you can be and, Ava, I have every faith in you."*

The girls glanced at each other and back to the letter. They both felt scared to read on.

Then Hope continued: *"I have thought long and hard about writing this letter. Some things, they say, are best left in the past. But some things – some things have a habit of coming out in the wash. I sort of thought this would come out before now. That I would have had a call or a letter to tell me that the truth was out. I waited for it. I hoped for it, I longed for it and I feared it. I promised myself that I wouldn't be the one to drop the bomb – that I would wait patiently for someone else to do that for me. As the years passed I started to realise that might never happen – but then I wondered what if it did – what if all this came out sometime in the future and I wasn't there to explain it? I wasn't there to answer your questions. I could forgive myself for a lot, but I couldn't forgive myself for that."*

Ava and Hope looked at each other again, alarmed. Ava felt her heartbeat quicken. The paleness creeping over her cousin's face made her realise she was not alone in feeling as if the carpet was just about to be pulled square out from under their feet, sending them both heading, arse first, to the floor with a thump.

Hope read on, her voice shaking as she formed the words: *"Ava, my darling, please forgive me . . ."*

There was a part of Ava that wanted to put her fingers in her ears and shout *"La la la, not listening! Can't hear you!"* as loud as she could while walking out of the room. The sound of her heartbeat thudding in her ears threatened to drown out Hope's voice. Focus, she whispered under her breath as she felt Hope's hand on hers – a steadying force when everything felt as if it was falling apart.

"Claude was my real love. I have told you that. But three years before there was someone else. It was wrong. I knew it was wrong, but I was young and stupid and thought I knew all there was to know about the world. My friends tried to warn me. Derry girls, especially Creggan girls, didn't go out with soldiers from the British army. But, when I saw Tim, I thought we could rise above it all. He was a hopeless flirt – with his broad London accent and his buzz cut, he looked and sounded more exciting than the Derrymen with their big mops of hair and their anger at the world. So we went out – a couple of times. And he told me I was special and that we would get away from it all. And I believed him. I believed him so much that when he said he wanted to take me to bed, I let him. And I got pregnant."

Don't throw up. Don't throw up. Ava felt a layer of her life slip away. Hope's grip on her hand grew tighter. She dared not look up.

"You can imagine how that went down at home. Perhaps you can't. You've grown into adulthood in a changed world. My parents weren't bad people. They were scared people. I'll never forget the look on your grandfather's face. This was an age when girls who went out with the Brits were tarred and feathered – tied to lampposts, paint poured on them, signs tied round their necks declaring them to be whores. And those were the lucky ones.

My parents wanted to make things better. They wanted to sort it out. They didn't want to have the double shame of a daughter with a baby and no wedding ring whose father was some soldier who had done a runner. But the fact that it was a Britsh soldier was beyond all endurance. So there was a family meeting. Everyone came. Ava, your mam came."

Cora's my mum. She's still my mum.

"Cora had been trying for a baby for the longest time, but it hadn't happened. She was devastated. Of course in those days you didn't go running to the doctor. You just accepted your lot. God, she wanted a baby. She really wanted a baby and it wasn't that I didn't want you, Ava . . ."

The guttural sound which came from Ava's mouth rang around the room. Her stomach contracted, her hands turned clammy and she pulled them away from Hope which was a mistake. Hope had been her anchor. With her anchor gone she was free-floating, floating away, the room swimming.

She rushed to the terrace to drink in what air she could, deep into her lungs. No amount of breathing – fast, heavy, hurried, would calm her down. The air whooshed in and out of her lungs at a speed she could barely control. Was Betty really telling her she was her mother? She couldn't be her mother. That was ridiculous. Sure, she had seen her birth certificate. *Mother's name: Cora Mullen.* Not Betty Scott. *Father's name: William Mullen.* Not Tim the soldier. She had seen it. Christ, she had dug it out not two months ago when she was reorganising her filing system. It was a birth certificate. She was sure of it. Wasn't she? Her mind flashed back over the thirty-four years of her life. Images of Cora cuddling her. Her granny holding her extra tight. Faded images of Christmas trees and Sindy houses and dolls and prams. "You're my girl," her mammy would say, kissing her head. Her mum crying on her wedding day. Holding her hand as she pushed Maisie into the world. She was her mum.

Then Betty's smile. They had felt connected. How Betty had held her extra tight when she left. She thought it had been through drink . . .

Feeling her head start to swim, stars dancing in front of her eyes she felt Hope behind her, holding her up.

"It's not true," she said, as Hope led her to a chair. "It's not true."

Hope didn't reply except to shush her tears. Ava supposed there wasn't much she could say. Should she phone Cora, and ask her straight out? Did she even want to phone Cora? Should she still call her 'mum'? Was her whole life a big fat lie? Who was she? Her head hurt as much as her heart.

"Give me the letter," she said, steeling herself, and Hope handed it over then sat beside her. She scanned it again, re-reading the words – the confession – as she rushed to read what else Betty would or could say to try and make this make any kind of sense.

It wasn't that I didn't want you, Ava. I didn't know what I wanted really. I thought I was all grown up but faced with a baby and all that entailed and the fear that if people found out . . . Needless to say, Tim didn't want to know. I told him and he didn't even respond. He just walked away. What a big brave soldier he was.

It was Mammy who came up with the idea that Cora and I would go away to look after an 'elderly aunt' and when the time was right we would come back and Cora would present 'her' baby to the world. We went to Dublin, to a distant family member who thankfully was a bit more liberal about such matters and didn't spend five and half months making me feel like a fallen woman. As far as the doctors were concerned, my name was Cora Mullen. I was twenty-six years old and married and this baby belonged to me and my husband William. It was easy really."

My whole life has been built on a lie.

"We could get away with it, because no one knew us. No one questioned the medical files. If they had their suspicions they said nothing. So I had you. Cora was by my side, with me calling her Betty and she calling me Cora and she was the first person to hold you. You were beautiful. A part of me ached for you. But seeing my sister – the joy on her face – the love for you. Knowing that I wanted to go home. That I

had to be able to show my face. That I was young and stupid and had no security to offer you. I let her hold you. I let her welcome you into the world, all the time knowing that you had changed my life completely and utterly. That you had turned my life upside down.

Cora wasn't selfish. Cora wasn't cruel. She asked me so many times if I was sure. She held me as I cried and she apologised a million times. She offered to let me hold you so many times but, as much as I could chatter and smile and goo and gaa at you, it hurt too much to hold you in my arms.

The image of the photo they had found danced into her head. Betty standing at the side looking on. Cora grinning. How could she say Cora hadn't been cruel? Nothing about this wasn't insanely, horrifyingly cruel. Her grandparents? Had they been that scared? Images of wrinkly, cuddly old people who smelled of cinnamon lozenges and slipped fifty-pence pieces into her hand while smiling at her flooded her mind. They weren't stupid people. They weren't cruel people. Could they not have just stopped it all?

She pushed the images of her parents out of her head. She didn't want to think about that. She could hear their voices in her head: "Never tell a lie" – "Your children are the most important things in your life" – "You mean so much to us . . ."

Her mother had never discussed her labour and delivery, Ava realised. She had said it had been eight hours but she had never said "God, it was tough!" It was always distant. This was why?

"Can I do anything?" she heard Hope say. "Get a drink of water? Sweet tea?"

"Jesus . . . tea with sugar in it makes me sick. No. No. Vodka? Have we vodka? Oh fuck, I'm pregnant!"

Cora had never been pregnant. But Betty – her poor barren aunt – well, she had most certainly been pregnant.

"Are you sorry we read it?" Hope asked.

"Of course not," Ava said, steadying herself. "Wouldn't you

want to know? You know, preferably not when you are thirty-four and think you have it all sussed. Jesus. A letter? She tells me in a letter and she's not even here for me to shout at? The bitch!"

Ava wasn't really angry with Betty. Or maybe she was. She didn't know who the fuck she was angry with. Or sad about. Or what her name was any more. She was named after Ava Gardner, her mother had told her. Who had chosen that name? Oh Christ. She dropped her head to her hands, while Hope rubbed her back.

"Did you know?" Ava asked, sitting bolt upright. "Is that why you are here? Do you know? Did she tell you when you were here? When you had one of your midnight chats?"

"No," Hope said. "No. She didn't tell me much. She was still grieving for Claude. All of this is new. Jesus – I would have told you. I would have."

Ava shook her head, which felt weird. All of her felt weird. Lifting the letter again, she read on:

I fell into a routine. And you must understand when I met Claude he was my escape. In many ways it was a blessed relief that he had to leave the city. It gave me a get-out clause. It gave me permission to move on. I don't understand why Mammy and Daddy were so against it. They said I was selfish and walking away – but you weren't mine, Ava. You never had been.

Was I supposed to stay and have my nose rubbed in it? To watch you growing up from a step away?

Maybe I was being selfish but I had a chance at a new start – away from it all. And I loved Claude. He knew about you. I couldn't have kept it from him and even as he proposed he said he would understand if I couldn't go. But you had your life and I knew you couldn't want more love than you were surrounded with. You may not feel it now, Ava, but you were lucky.

I almost told you. When I was back for Mammy's funeral. I wanted to. For the first time really. Cora had always said that if I wanted to tell you, someday, she would try and understand, and I came so very close. But it would have been wrong.

It's wrong now.

I know you are probably thinking it is wrong now. But as I said – just in case it came out. Just in case you wondered.

Don't consider me your mammy."

As if.

"Cora always was and always will be. I just had to tell you. Don't you understand that I had to tell you?

Claude and I never had children. We did try. It didn't happen. The irony wasn't lost on either of us. We had been so sure it would happen. Claude had made a crib and I bought some things. This time I would be allowed to get excited about it. But it just never happened and we tried as best we could to put it behind us. Claude was wonderful. One day, after we had been trying for a few years, I came home to find the crib in the attic. The box of clothes in the attic too. "We'll take them down when we need them," he said softly and I nodded. What else was there to say? What I didn't tell him was that in that box was a small, delicate, white, knitted cardigan. The first you wore. Which I knitted myself while in Dublin. Every now and again I would climb into the attic (and I bloody hate attics!) and take it out and look at it. Just hold it and smell it. And remember you.

Please forgive me. Is that asking too much? Maybe now it is, but maybe in time. And go easy on your mam. And know that I love you for the person you have become – the person you always were.

God bless you always.

All my love,
Betty
xxxx

That's it, Ava thought, my life in a few pages. Or what is my life. What could have been my life.

"I need to phone Connor," she said.

Hope nodded. "I understand."

She didn't want to speak to Cora. What would she say? In her mind there were 101 kneejerk reactions – veering from "Feck you anyway" to "I love you and I understand" and everything in between. Connor would make sense of it. Connor would know. He would say the right things in the way he always did and make her feel better. If not better, he would make her feel less shite. Right now, less shite would be good.

Lifting the phone, trying to find the right number and finding herself with the worst case of fat fingers ever, misdialling, skipping past his number and back again, she ended up throwing the phone at the corner of one of Betty's squashiest cushions in frustration and screaming out a swear word. She looked to where Hope was sitting, staring at the ground. She felt sorry for her, ironically. It was Ava's life which had been blown apart but Hope looked like she could run for the door and not stop.

"I didn't know," she muttered again.

"I know."

Ava sat down, the swearing out of her – too numb to cry, shaking too much to dial Connor's number. "I'm pregnant," she said, feeling it was the only cohesive thought in her brain. "He doesn't know that either. This will be some phone call. 'Hi, honey. My family have been lying all my life. Yes, they broke the law and, technically, I think I don't even exist. Oh and I'm pregnant."

She looked at Hope, who continued to look so utterly forlorn that she felt a burst of hysterical laughter rise up from her until she was almost bent double with the complete absurdity of it all.

Even as she laughed she knew it was a sign that the tears would follow. They always did and when she felt that something in her shift she was glad Hope was once again there to hold her until she stopped shaking. But God, she wished it had been Connor.

"I'll phone Connor for you if you want," Hope offered.

"No," Ava said, her tears subsided and the numbness returned. "I'll phone him. Can you dial the number though?"

Retrieving the phone from the recesses of the sofa, Hope scrolled through the numbers until she found Connor's listing. Pressing call, she handed it to Ava who took a deep breath and waited to hear his voice. She was not expecting him to answer amidst the hustle and bustle of Brannigan's Bar.

"Hello?" he roared over a particularly raucous cheer.

"Connor?"

"Ava? Sorry, I'm in the pub. The match is on. Hang on. Hang on."

The cheers became muffled as she heard him mutter and excuse his way through the throngs.

"Hang on!" he shouted again and she sat back on the bed, wondering just how many jars he had sunk already. Chances are he was out with his dad, and his brothers and maybe a cousin or two and things were probably getting messy. She chewed at her fingernail, her determination to tell him fading. Not this way at least.

His voice came on the line again. Cheery, beer-fuelled. "Hello, my pet, how are you? We're in the pub – me and the boys. Mum has Maisie."

She drank in his voice, even though he was obviously well oiled and high on testosterone. Tears pricked in her eyes as she realised it would be unfair to tell him any of it, not here and not now.

"I'm fine, Connor. I just wanted to talk to you . . ."

There was a pause before she heard another cheer go up and Connor roared, leaving her half deaf before apologising profusely. Rubbing her ear, she heard him mutter, "I'm sorry, I'm sorry, pet. They scored! They only bloody scored! Sorry, what were you saying?"

"Just that I missed you," she lied.

"Aw," he said, his voice softening. "I miss you too, darling. Look, it's crazy here. Can I call you later? Or in the morning? Not long now till you're home."

"Okay," she said dejectedly.

"Are you okay?"

"I'm fine," she lied for a second time.

Reluctantly he said his goodbyes and she hung up. Putting her phone down, she padded back to the terrace where Hope was leaning over the chiminea, setting a fire.

"That was quick," she said.

"He was in the pub. It wasn't right. But he's going to call me back. In the morning maybe. I'll tell him then. I'll definitely tell him it all then."

Chapter 28

Hope wanted to sleep. She was desperately tired, from the inside out, but she couldn't. Ava had gone to bed, numb and pale, and Hope had gone to her own room trying to make sense of it all. Big fat use she was to anyone! She hadn't been able to find her voice, never mind be the comfort Betty had obviously hoped her to be. If nodding had been an Olympic sport, however, she would have been a shoo-in for the gold. Truth was, what on earth did you say to someone in those circumstances? "Two mammies"? "Ah well, at least we're still cousins"? "Worse things happen at sea"?

She thought of her daddy – how he had never mentioned anything at all to her all these years. Her mother – who was as nosey and in love with gossip as Hope herself was – how did she not let it slip? Not even after a few gin and tonics at Christmas when she would talk about everything.

Hope wanted to phone her. Truth be told, she wanted to phone Cora and shout at her. And she had half a notion to go to the cemetery and shout at Betty too, for the sake of it all. This wasn't the carefree trip she had hoped for. This wasn't a simple riffle through someone's knicker drawer. This was big – fecking huge. Instinctively she lifted her phone to call Dylan, but glancing at the clock she could see he would be at work. And if he wasn't at work, he'd be humping Cyndi. Christ, she thought, even her best gossip-buddy was a no-go to her.

"Oh Betty," she sighed, as she tried to plump the pillow under her head in a vain attempt to make the bed more comfortable. "Why did you have to do it this way?"

She didn't know who she felt worse for. The young Betty who found herself in a godawful mess, or her new friend who was no doubt trying to sleep just as hard in the room downstairs, having had her world torn apart.

She was tempted to get up and pull the rest of the house asunder, to try and find whatever other secrets might be lurking in Betty's letters. Jesus, there couldn't be anything else, could there? She threw off the covers – overheated and overstressed – and padded to the kitchen where she sank a glass of wine and cried until her throat was raw.

And she thought *her* life was complicated.

Ava wasn't sure what woke her. It was dawn, a half-light fighting to stream in the windows. She blinked her eyes open, a feeling that something was wrong swamping her while she lay waiting for her body to catch up with her mind. Everything was silent – she was sure it hadn't been a noise which had woken her. Oh Christ. Yesterday. The letter. But that wasn't it. That wasn't all. Slowly she became aware of a stabbing pain in her stomach and as she roused herself she wondered how she hadn't registered it sooner. She tried to speak but all she could do was gasp as her hand reached down and she felt the bed wet beneath her. Inwardly she screamed as she realised her hand was covered in blood but still she couldn't find the words. *I've lost you!* she screamed inwardly. *I didn't even know you but I've lost you!* And she was talking to her baby, and to Betty.

When the breath returned to her body she steadied herself. Slowly she sat up, almost afraid to move, not sure what to expect, terrified of what she might see. She had never had a miscarriage before. There were no manuals on how to deal with this – this physical process – this pain. It wasn't like this in the movies. She didn't know whether or not she should move. She was terrified of what she might feel, or see. She wished Connor was there and she felt herself whisper his name while grasping at the bed sheets as she sat on the bed. She wished her mammy was there. Oh God. Her mammy.

Was she safe to stand up? She didn't know. She was afraid there might be a gush, like when her waters broke. She looked behind her at the stained sheets, suddenly, irrationally consumed with embarrassment. She felt a scream rise up in her chest – a guttural expression of physical and emotional pain which screeched forth from her body with a force of its own. "Hope!" she called when she could form a coherent word. "Hope! Please! Hope!"

Bleary-eyed and pale with worry, Hope walked into the room and much as she tried Ava could not find the words to explain what was happening. If she said it, it would be real and she didn't want it to be real. Instead she just stared at her cousin, her eyes pleading with her to do something – anything.

"I don't know," Hope stuttered. "I don't know what to do."

"The baby," Ava muttered.

"I know," Hope said, running to her and kneeling down in front of her. Feeling the warmth of her cousin's hand as she took hers, Ava realised she was shaking violently. It wasn't cold – she realised she must be in shock.

"I've lost the baby," she heard herself say but the voice she heard didn't sound like her own, just a strangulated version of her voice. It sounded funny, like she was drunk.

"We'll get help," Hope said.

Ava looked her straight in the face. Poor Hope, she thought, she looks terrified.

"Oh God, I'm so sorry," Ava said, knowing that she was saying sorry to everyone – not just Hope. She was saying sorry to Connor, and Maisie, and herself and Betty for fucking up her life and more than that to her baby. The pain was back and she wasn't sure if it was physical or emotional or both but it pulled the air from her lungs and doubled her in two and she tried to find the breath to let out a sob. "I don't want this to happen," she said. "I don't want this to happen."

"Jean-Luc – I'll call him. I'll call him and he'll know what to do. He'll get help. Don't worry, I'll get help."

Running from the room to get her mobile Hope felt her stomach threaten to turn over. No, she couldn't be sick now. Ava needed her. Oh God, poor Ava! She looked so distraught and terrified. Everything paled in comparison to this moment. Running to her room, she scrabbled in the drawer of her bedside table to find her Blackberry. Her hands were shaking so violently she could barely grip anything, never mind lift the sleek phone and try and scroll through her contacts to find Jean-Luc's number. Swearing as she scrolled past his number and managed to miss it as she scrolled back up again. She stopped, stood still and tried to remind herself to breathe. She'd be no good to Ava in this state and Ava needed her right now.

"Okay," she said out loud. "Jean-Luc." Finding the number, she pressed the call button and held the phone to her ear as she rushed to the kitchen to pour a glass of water for Ava. She didn't know why she was getting the water but at least she felt as if she was doing something. The phone began to ring and Hope tried to keep her patience as she inwardly prayed he would answer – and quickly. She wondered whether to go back to Ava – hating the thought of her being in her room alone – but she didn't want to panic her by letting her overhear her conversation with Jean-Luc.

"Come on," she said, impatiently as she turned the tap off and waited for him to answer. When the phone went to answer service, she swore and kicked the kitchen cupboard, sending a shock of pain right through her body. Now, she really did feel as if she would be sick. Feeling tears spring to her eyes, she hit the redial button. She would call and call and call again and again until he answered. Christ, she didn't know what to do. Did you call 999 in France? Should she call an ambulance? There was a lot of blood. She had to get back to Ava, she knew that.

"Come on!" she said, louder this time and she felt her body sag with relief as Jean-Luc answered, his voice heavy with sleep.

"Good morning?" he said. "Is everything okay?"

"Jean-Luc, I'm sorry. We need you. It's Ava. She's bleeding and it looks bad. She's losing the baby. I didn't know what to do but I thought you would know – that you would know know a doctor or someone. I'm sorry, I'm really sorry."

There was a sharp intake of breath as Jean-Luc digested what he had just heard and then he spoke, in a soft reassuring voice.

"I'm going to call the doctor right now," he said. "Ava – how is she?"

"I'm going to check now. I came away to get my phone."

"Stay with her. Don't leave her. I'll call you back."

It was only when he hung up that Hope let a big, fat tear slide down her cheek which she roughly pushed aside before sipping from the glass she had poured for Ava and walking back to the room.

Ava was sitting, her eyes gaunt, staring at the window.

"I need to phone Connor," she said, calmly.

"Best wait to find out what is happening," Hope replied softly.

"He needs to know."

"Jean-Luc is phoning the doctor. He will call back in a minute. We'll know more then."

"I'm losing the baby," she said, turning to look at her cousin, the pain in her eyes making Hope wince. "I have to be. You can't lose this much blood and still have a baby. I'm losing the baby, Hope – and he needs to know. Oh God, how do I tell him? He doesn't even know I'm pregnant. Oh, Jesus Christ help me!"

"Oh, sweetheart," Hope soothed. "Try to stay calm. It might be okay. People bleed in pregnancy and it's not always bad. Try to stay positive, my darling."

Hope closed her eyes and tried to focus on the positive herself. It was true people did bleed in pregnancy. She had written about it during a stint on a health magazine. They bled and it was just one of those things and they went on to have happy, chubby, perfectly healthy little babies. It happened all the time. In fact, in her mind's eye she could see one of the features she had written, in print, with a perfectly happy baby girl in a gingham Babygro, looking like she never caused her mother a moment's worry in her life. She wasn't sure if they bled this much though . . . there was a lot of blood. A scary amount of blood.

In that moment, if she could have, Hope would have swapped places with Ava. She would have taken the hurt on herself if she could. She would have done anything in her power to stop the pain her cousin was in and it hurt her that she couldn't. She couldn't do anything but sit down beside her, and wait for Jean-Luc to call back. She took Ava's hand and they stared wordlessly at the early morning sky. It had to be okay. It had to be.

Hope jumped when the phone rang and she answered swiftly.

"The doctor said to tell her to lie on her left side, and do not move. I am on my way, we'll go to the hospital, but for now just tell her to lie down."

"Did he say anything else?" Hope asked, hoping that the doctor would have said something very reassuring – telling them this was perfectly normal and it would be fine and the baby was okay but looking at the blood on the bed she knew this was not normal. Not at all.

But Jean-Luc was gone.

Hanging up, she looked at Ava and gently stroked her cheek. "You need to lie down on your left side, sweetheart. Jean-Luc is coming and we will go to the hospital, but you need to lie down."

"I can't lie down here. I can't go like this," Ava said, nodding towards her blood-soaked bed and blood-soaked nightie.

Hope knew she had to take control, so she did. Standing up, she pulled the duvet over so that Ava could lie down on a fresh bed, then she gently helped her lie down. "I'll get you some fresh clothes. Just stay still. He'll be here soon."

Kissing her softly on the forehead, Hope went and found some tracksuit bottoms and a T-shirt for her friend to wear and set about finding some towels for her to sit on in the car. She wasn't sure if that was the right thing to do but, as she gathered a few bits and pieces together, and listened to her friend crying, she just wanted to do what she could.

"The doctors here, they are very good. They will help as much as they can," Jean-Luc said as Hope answered the door to him.

"I know," she said, allowing him to give her a gentle friendly hug.

Jean-Luc nodded and smiled – a sad smile which made her feel like crying – and she steadied herself to go back into the bedroom.

Ava had calmed down. She seemed to have morphed into typical Ava mode, talking very matter of factly about when she would call Connor and what she should take with her. A nighty and a flannel. She needed a flannel. And a toothbrush.

Hope was almost grateful to see her cousin calm and in control. It helped her feel calm herself. It helped her believe that everything would indeed be okay. The baby would be fine. Ava would be fine. "We should go," she said gently, folding over Ava's case and zipping it.

Ava nodded, staring ahead, seemingly lost in her own world. "They won't be able to save the baby, will they? Not at this stage in the pregnancy."

"You need to let the doctor see you, darling," Hope answered.

She didn't know what else to say. She simply didn't know how to react. She didn't want to say that it would be okay as she didn't know if it would be okay. Hastily she brushed a tear from her eye and walked out to where Jean-Luc stood leaning against the car in the cool morning air.

She would have given anything to just climb into the car with him, drive off to the horizon and pretend none of this was happening.

"I don't speak much French," Ava said from the back of the car. She was rabbiting on, nine to the dozen. Shock, probably. She told them that, just then. "Excuse me rabbiting, it's probably the shock. I talk a lot when I'm nervous. Of course not in French, obviously. That would be a skill, wouldn't it, to talk in a different language every time you were stressed? You would get on the TV with that. Or in one of those magazines that you write for, Hope. Would you do a story on me? If that happened?"

Ava looked at Hope who was nodding gently, a look of 'Poor

Ava has lost her marbles' written square across her face. "You think I'm mad," she said, without adding that if she didn't talk she would think about what was happening and she didn't want to think about what was happening. "I'm scared," she said, with a little sob, which she gulped back as quickly as she could.

Hope squeezed her hand.

"The doctors, they speak good English. I'll be around, if you need me," Jean-Luc said.

Ava felt comforted by this. "You're very good. Isn't he very good?" she asked her cousin, before shivering. "I'm cold. That's probably the shock too." She was trying to gauge whether or not her tummy was more sore or less sore than it was twenty minutes before. She didn't want to look down. Never look down. So she looked at Hope who was trying her best to wrap a blanket around her shoulders while she sat stock still, staring ahead. Don't look down.

"I didn't ask . . ." she said, trying to block out the thoughts racing through her mind, "but the market – will we be okay missing the market?"

She wanted them to answer – she wanted the conversation to be normal. Hope just looked at her, the same nodding-dog sympathy-look gawping back at her. She felt a bubble of anger rise up in her. Could they not just be normal? Could this not just be normal? Oh Christ, she felt sick.

"I feel sick," she said, "I feel sick. I'm scared. I'm really scared."

Chapter 29

The doctors were very nice – they spoke good English and pulled appropriately sympathetic faces.

"Let's have a little look at you," the tall, blonde and shockingly young female doctor said to her in the cubicle of the Accident and Emergency department.

Ava had nodded – her high-speed nervous chatter from earlier had gone and she was almost afraid to move or speak. Hope sat holding her hand. Hope's hand had been her almost constant companion since all this started. Her vicelike grip had kept her grounded in reality – the whole way in the car and as they walked through the sliding doors to the crisp, clean corridor of the hospital. She was still holding her hand as she lay on the hospital bed and waited for the doctor to come and assess her. In fairness she had at least let go, briefly, after a softly spoken nurse wearing impossibly squeaky shoes had come in and offered her a hospital gown to change into.

Now she was lying there, aware that there was little between her unfolding tragedy and the rest of the world apart from a thin curtain and a language barrier.

The doctor sat on a stool beside the bed and asked a few questions. Ava willed her not to ask about her mother. There was no reason she would, but wouldn't that just be the icing on the horrible, big fecking cake if she did? She asked her when she had tested positive, if she had bled before, if she'd had a miscarriage before, how long she'd been bleeding and how much had she bled. She said they would do a blood test to check for her hormone levels and then she would do an internal examination and maybe a scan, depending on what she found.

Ava continued to nod and answer as concisely as she could. She cringed at the thought of an internal – funny how even now, when she felt as vulnerable as she had ever done in her entire life, there were still some things which could move her even further out of her comfort zone than she already was. She knew it had to be done but she felt a tear slide down her cheek at the very thought.

The doctor gave her a trademark sympathetic smile again and squeezed her hand gently. "I know this is very tough, but we need to know what is happening."

Any comfort Ava felt at the gesture soon dissipated at the sight of the very large needle which would have to be inserted in her arm.

"I'd like to get a cannula inserted too, just in case," the doctor said and Ava winced. Two needles. Still, if it would help . . . if there was a chance the baby would be okay. She chided herself. She was being ridiculous trying to build her hopes up. She lived in the real world and she knew what the chances were of things being okay.

She would have to phone Connor and tell him. The thought made her sick to her stomach. He would be devastated. God, how could she even start? How could she tell him in one breath that she was pregnant and in the next take away all that hope and excitement. He'd be destroyed. A couple of needles were the least of her worries.

Extending her arm, she winced as the doctor inserted the first of the needles, all the while maintaining her perfect French bedside manner.

"Connor will be devastated," Ava said to Hope who clearly didn't know what to say. Ava felt sorry for her. What could she possibly say to make a difference? She was trying her best, making soothing sounds and of course holding her hand as if her life depended on it, but she couldn't perform miracles. She couldn't make the baby be okay and she couldn't take away Ava's pain – or Connor's for that matter.

"He loves you. He'll just want to know you're okay. Try to focus on that now. As long as you're okay . . ."

"He doesn't even know about this baby and now . . ." Ava stared into space again.

"Can we just have a little look?" the doctor asked as Ava wiped a tear away and Hope squeezed her hand a little tighter.

"I'd like to do a scan," the doctor said.

Ava covered herself up. Her legs were trembling. "The baby is gone, isn't it?"

"I'd like to do a scan," the doctor repeated. "There is no doubt you have lost some blood – quite a lot – but I can't find the source of the bleeding and your cervix appears to be closed."

Ava looked at her, confused, and then at Hope.

"What does that mean?" Hope asked.

"I'm not sure," the doctor replied. "If we do the ultrasound, we will know more. I will go and get the scanner. Try to relax, Ava. I know this is hard, but try to just breathe and relax as much as you can."

The doctor left and Ava lay back in a sort of limbo – waiting for the arrival of the great scanner – and all she could think was that she didn't want to look at the screen. She remembered the joy she had felt the first time she had been scanned when she was pregnant with Maisie. She had been blissfully naïve and it hadn't crossed her mind for a second that anything would be wrong. She had practically skipped into the sonographer's room with excitement and had grinned maniacally at Connor as a black-and-white fuzzy image of a very active little jellybean popped up on the screen. The sonographer had switched the speaker on the ultrasound on and they had listened to the rhythmic fast beat of their baby's heart.

Ava pushed all thoughts of how Betty must have felt, a baby growing inside her that she would have to give away. No, she could only focus on one catastrophe at a time.

"Will you look? When she comes back? I don't think I can."

"Of course," Hope said. "Ava, I'm so sorry you're having to go through this. So very sorry."

"I know," Ava said, feeling as if someone else was speaking.

When the doctor pulled the curtain back and pushed in the ultrasound machine, she thought she might throw up. She tightened her grip on the overly starched bed-sheets below her and took a deep breath, biting back the panic in the pit of her stomach and staring straight at the ceiling. She would just keep doing that, she thought, stare at the ceiling and count the tiles and do anything that would distract her from what the doctor could or couldn't see.

She could feel the cold jelly on her stomach and the pressure of the scanning wand as the doctor moved it across her stomach – a slow pull to the left, and a few taps on a keyboard, before a slow pull to the right and a dig into the very top of her pubic bone which made her gasp. There was another pull of the wand and the doctor sighed and pressed another few buttons. Ava closed her eyes. She couldn't even bring herself to look at Hope – she just wanted to shut the whole experience out. If she could just switch herself off she would have done so. As the wand was dragged against her stomach again she couldn't stop the tears from falling. Frig this. She was tired now of trying to keep it together and she let the pain and grief course through her body.

"It's okay," Hope soothed.

"No, no. It's not okay. Would people please stop saying everything is okay or is going to be okay. It's not okay."

"Ava," the doctor said, "there is your baby. There is a strong heartbeat."

Ava stared at the doctor, still afraid to look at the screen, not quite able to believe what she had just been told.

"I think there is a clot behind the placenta. This could be causing the bleeding. I want to get an obstetrician to look at you. I must stress to you that I am not a specialist in this area of medicine, but for now your baby is still there. Will you look?"

Slowly, Ava turned her head to the screen and straight at a fuzzy image of a wriggling baby. There in the centre of his or her chest was a little heart, fluttering furiously as if to say "Hi, Mammy! I'm here. I'm still here. Stay with me now."

"Oh God," she said, "it's a baby."

"It's your baby," Hope said. "And it's still there. That's a good thing. Where there is life, there is hope. Sure didn't Granny use to say that all the time, and it's true."

"Phone Connor," Ava said. "Please, can you phone Connor? I need him. I need him to see our baby."

"I'll do it now," Hope said, kissing her cousin on the top of the head. "Will you be okay here on your own?"

"I'm not on my own," Ava said, entranced by the image on the screen of the baby doing somersaults.

Hope wished she smoked, but she didn't. She tried it once, after a lengthy boozing session when she first turned eighteen and it made her want to puke. Actually it had made her properly puke, and look like an eejit as she coughed and spluttered her way to a fetching shade of green. But there were times when she wished she smoked – that she had a crutch she could turn to when she needed. Times such as that occasion when the bank machine had chewed her beloved gold credit card, leaving her broke and red-faced on a night out with friends when she had run up an impressive bar bill and had offered to pay for the tapas too. Times such as just after Dylan had brought her to the most intense orgasm of her entire life, and times such as when Dylan pretended nothing had ever happened the following morning. And of course, times such as now when a great big family secret had just been cracked open followed by a very real fear that she had been about to nurse her cousin – a woman she'd come to consider a friend in just a matter of days – through a miscarriage. She couldn't believe it, she thought as she stood and gulped in huge, life-affirming gasps of fresh air. The baby was there. She didn't know much about babies or pregnancies but she had been convinced, utterly convinced, that things were about to go horribly wrong and she hadn't had a notion how she would deal with it all.

"A coffee," she heard a gentle voice say behind her and she turned, tears pricking her eyes, to see Jean-Luc with two cups of coffee in his hands, proffering one to her.

He had waited. She hadn't expected that. She didn't know exactly what she had expected – perhaps that as soon as he had dropped them off he would have turned on his heel and gone back to his life, away from the drama of the two madwomen from Northern Ireland. She was touched but equally determined not to burst into tears all over him, even though she had the strongest urge in the world to fall into his arms and have him tell her it would all be okay.

"It's not the best coffee in the world, but I thought you could use it," he said softly.

Hope nodded gratefully and took the cup, sipping from it, wincing at the bitter taste.

"You're right," she smiled. "Not the best, but thank you."

"And Ava? Is she okay?" He looked awkward, his usual suave exterior wavering. Clearly women's troubles were not in his usual conversation repertoire.

Hope felt sorry for him. Whatever he had promised Betty – however deeply he was involved in all this – he had clearly not bargained for this whole medical-emergency scenario. His vulnerability and awkwardness was endearing – so endearing that Hope had to remind herself of his cool demeanour just the day before on the phone.

"We don't know yet – not really – but it looks much more positive than it did earlier. The baby is there and there is a heartbeat. That's a good sign. They just want to find the source of the bleeding. I'm just going to phone her husband now. When I get my breath."

Jean-Luc smiled, the wrinkles around his eyes creasing, his shoulders visibly sagging with relief. "That is good news," he said. "That is very good news."

"Yes," Hope said, looking deep into his eyes. "It is."

She wanted to understand Jean-Luc. She wanted to make sense of why this all mattered so much to him where yesterday he had been professional – cold even. And today he had waited, for two hours, in a waiting room on his own just to make sure Ava was okay. Had he known the full story? Had Betty confided in him when she couldn't confide in anyone else? She looked at him, trying to size him up and, if she hadn't been so concerned about just what she was going to say to Connor, a man she vaguely remembered having met once before, when she phoned him to blow his world clean apart, she would have challenged him. But she figured she had enough challenges to be dealing with just now.

"I have to phone him," she said. "Connor. I have to tell him. What do I say?"

"I'm sure you will find the right words," Jean-Luc said softly before reaching out and pushing back a loose curl from her face. The touch of his hand made her want to weep – and not just because he was an exceptionally attractive man but because it was just nice to feel the warmth of his hand, the gentleness of his touch and the softness of his skin. It was all too brief a moment, however, before he stepped away and left her to the phonecall she had been dreading.

She lifted Ava's phone, took as deep a breath as she could and scrawled through the address book until she came to Connor's name. Pressing the call button she waited for the call to connect, secretly hoping it would go to answerphone and she could leave some garbled message and at least not have to answer questions outright when she wasn't sure what to say or how he would react. He seemed like a nice man, from what Ava had said. She was clearly very much in love with him and even though they were under a certain amount of stress they seemed solid. Biting her lip as the call connected, she thought how she'd always dreamt that one day she would tell a man he was going to be a father – she just always thought she would be the pregnant one. Then again, having seen just how stressful pregnancy could be, she wasn't sure she ever wanted to go there. Ever. She could think of less scary things. Like swimming with sharks. Or being charged by a stampede of elephants.

"Hey, pet, sorry, I was to ring you back. You wouldn't believe the state I got home in. Then again, you probably would. I was out with Pearse and you know what's he like after a couple of pints of the black stuff. Ma nearly had a stroke when we got home!"

He sounded so cheerful, his voice so warm that Hope was almost tempted to hang up there and then and say nothing or try and do her best Ava impression and just tell him everything was grand. Even though it wasn't.

"Connor," she started, realising he had never heard her voice before. "It's Hope. Please don't panic. It's okay." Instantly she hated that she had told him not to panic. Her own reaction to anyone uttering those words to her would be to go into a Grade 8, full-blown, screaming and hyperventilating panic. She heard his intake of breath.

"Ava? What's wrong with Ava?"

"Ava is fine. It's . . . well. Oh crap. Connor, hang on." She lifted the phone from her ear and took another deep breath. "Right," she said, steadying herself. "Ava is pregnant. She found out a few days ago. She was waiting till she got home to tell you. Actually she was going to tell you last night."

"But instead she got you to tell me?" Connor sounded bemused.

"No. Well, yes. Look, I'm sorry. She started to bleed this morning and we've taken her to hospital."

"Oh my God," his voice was slow and laden with emotion. Hope could tell he was trying to take it in and she didn't know whether to allow him a moment to grasp what she was saying. "The baby? Ava? Are they okay? Is she okay? Jesus . . . a baby . . ."

"She is, she's okay, Connor. And so is the baby up to now. There's a heartbeat. She's had a scan."

She heard him sob.

"But they can't find the source of the bleeding. They are doing more tests. Specialists are being called to see her."

"She must be so scared."

"She's better than she was," Hope said, honestly. She felt no need to tell how she had crumpled that morning. "Connor, there's more," she said, figuring she might as well get it all out in the open. Glancing around to make sure Jean-Luc was still out of earshot, she continued: "She got a letter – from Betty. There is no easy way to say this, but Betty is her mother. Betty was unmarried then, of course, and there was a whole identity-swap thing. The father was a British soldier. We only found out last night. She's so mixed up, as you can imagine."

There was silence.

Hope stood there, waiting for a response. It was a lot to take in, she knew. She had to give him time.

"Christ," he said, eventually. "Jesus. And she knew this last night? When she called me? And I was down at the pub like a drunken eejit. Oh God. I can't . . . I can't believe it . . ."

"I'm sorry to break it to you so suddenly. It's been a huge shock. For everyone. Not least Ava."

"Has she spoken to her mum . . . to Cora?"

Hope shook her head before speaking. "She was too upset."

"Tell her I'll be there as soon as I can," he said, determinedly. "Tell her I'll be on the next flight. Tell her it will be okay. Everything will be okay. And tell her I love her."

"I will," Hope soothed, wondering if someone was there to offer him a hug, or a cup of hot sweet tea, or a brandy or whatever he needed in that situation. "Text your flight details when you have them. We'll get you picked up from the airport. Try not to worry."

She heard him steady his breath, just as she was trying to steady her own.

"Just look after her, please. She means the world to me."

"I know," Hope said, ringing off and staring at the phone for a few moments. She looked down the courtyard to where Jean-Luc was standing.

Noticing that she had finished her call, he walked back to her.

Her head was spinning "Do you mean the world to anyone?" she asked him.

The bemused look on his face didn't leave. "What do you mean?"

"Do you mean the world to anyone? If something were to happen to you would there be someone who would jump on the next plane to be by your side before you could catch your next breath?"

Looking at her, his head cocked a little to one side, he gestured to her to sit down, proferring the bitter coffee once again. "No, Hope. I'm not sure there would be anyone. But I've not given up on the notion that one day there might be. And I'm a lot older, and more wrinkled than you."

She didn't dare look up at him because if she did she would kiss him, whether or not he wanted to be kissed. Which could make her look like a bit of a bunny-boiling psycho. But she wanted to kiss him. She wanted to tell him not to give up hope. Despite everything, she still believed that everyone had their other half, their missing link, the Cyndi to their Dylan.

Dropping her head to her hands, she took several deep breaths before sitting up and looking square at him. Nope. No. Definitely not. The deep breaths had not worked. They had not brought her to her senses. She was still going to kiss him and by the darkness in his eyes and the tilt of his head she could tell he was going to kiss her too. Slowly, shaking with emotion and trepidation and probably a fair dose of lust, she tilted her head towards his and allowed herself to be kissed – more deeply and more passionately than Dylan had ever kissed her.

Chapter 30

The room on the ward was peaceful – shades of cream and lilac on the wall, the window slightly ajar allowing the warm breeze to sweep through the room. She was alone, on a bed more comfortable than the one she had lain on in A&E. The doctor had given her pictures from the ultrasound and she couldn't help but look at them over and over again, tracing her fingers around the outline of the very tiny, shrimp-looking baby which was clinging on for dear life in her womb.

"Try to get some sleep," the nurse with the squeaky shoes had told her as she accompanied her to the ward but even though she was absolutely exhausted she knew there was no chance of her drifting off.

Ava still couldn't quite believe there had been a baby on the screen after all. She couldn't quite believe anything about the last twenty-four hours. None of it made sense. None of it fitted in with her nice and in control plan for the rest of her life. She looked at the picture again and tried to focus on that. That was all she had the strength to focus on for now.

The doctor had warned her to be cautious still and she didn't know if seeing that little heart beat had made her feel better or worse. It was reassuring in a way – of course it was – but, God, now this little baby was all the more real and she didn't know just how she would cope if she did go on to miscarry. She shook her head and stared at the wall, trying not to think that Karma was teaching a very painful lesson indeed. There she had been freaking out for the first few days of her pregnancy – terrified of the pressure a new baby would put on her life, and on their finances – and it was only when she had actually dared to become excited about becoming a mother again that fate had decided it might just have another ending in mind for her. She wasn't a bad person – and she knew, rationally, that miscarriages were not down to how good a person you were – but now she wanted this baby she couldn't imagine letting it go. It wasn't lost on her either that while she had worried the pregnancy would put pressure on her and Connor, the loss of their precious baby could do so much more damage.

"How was he? Was he annoyed I hadn't told him?" she asked Hope who has resumed her handholding, brow-wiping position beside her friend.

"No," Hope had said, shaking her head vigorously. "How could he be? He sounded a bit shell-shocked. I think it was a lot to take in all at the one go and I'm not even sure I said all the right things but he said he would get here as soon as he could."

Ava wished with all her might that Connor could be there right there and then and that she had told him as soon as she had even suspected she might have been pregnant, or as soon as the test had come up positive. She had wasted several days getting it right in her head without worrying about what it might feel like in his head. She wished she had spoken to him the night before and had insisted he listened to her and not just gone back into the pub to watch the end of the match. She wished, just wished, everything was different. Everything, that is, apart from the baby in her tummy.

"I know," Hope said, cutting through her thoughts, "I know this is hard. But you stay strong. Try and rest. As much as you can. He'll be here soon and the doctor will be here soon and hopefully it will all be fine."

Ava was absolutely, knee-clenchingly, tummy-achingly desperate to go for a pee. She was also absolutely, knee-clenchingly, tummy-achingly terrified to move from the bed on which she lay. She didn't know if she had stopped bleeding yet. She didn't know if moving would somehow unstick the little baby in her womb. And she was sure that as soon as she disappeared, the consultant she had been waiting on for the last hour and a half would appear, see her bed was empty and put her to the back of the list.

"I have to go to the toilet," she whispered to Hope, who was at this stage slouched back in her chair, her eyelids drooping.

"Go then. Do you want me to help you?"

"But what if the doctor comes?"

"She'll wait, surely?"

"I don't know," Ava said, tapping her fingers on the bed. "Shouldn't she be here by now? This doctor? Shouldn't she be right here telling me what is going on?"

She hated living in this kind of twilight state. Of course it was lovely that for now she was still pregnant, but would she stay pregnant? The thought that she wouldn't was almost too much to take and yet she wanted an answer. Knowing had to be easier – well, preferable anyway – to not knowing.

"Do you want me to enquire what is happening?" Hope asked and Ava nodded meekly.

She watched as Hope stood up and walked towards the door of the very lovely, serene little room in which she was resting and she thought about Connor. He should be on his way to the airport now, maybe even boarding his plane. She wondered what was going through his mind. Wishing that she had spoken to him, but knowing that she wouldn't have had a notion what to say, she rested her head back on her pillow and closed her eyes. This baby would be beautiful. It would have Connor's fair hair and remarkably long eyelashes. It would have her nose – Connor loved her nose. She could almost see the baby now, crinkled, newborn, perfect, and she felt her heart sink at the thought that she hadn't cherished every brief second of morning sickness, every fatigued moment of her pregnancy.

Brushing a tear away from her cheek hastily, she steadied herself and took a deep breath. "If ifs and ands were pots and pans . . ."

she told herself before looking at the door and wishing Hope would hurry back and bring the doctor with her.

"You have a subchorionic haematoma," the consultant said matter of factly. "What this means is that there a large area of bleeding behind your placenta. This may go away on its own, in the best case, or it may get worse."

Ava stared at the screen in front of her, at the dark spot the consultant was pointing to. "If it gets worse?"

"Then you may miscarry. Many, many women with this condition go on to deliver perfectly healthy babies – perhaps a little early."

"But some don't?" Ava felt her voice shake. "Can you treat it? What can you do? What can I do?"

"For now, you rest," the doctor said. "We will see if the bleeding stops but I'm afraid there is nothing we can do to stop it. It must stop of its own accord. I will get you some aspirin, sometimes this helps, but the most important thing for now is to rest and try as much as you can not to worry. I know this is hard to understand, but given the amount of bleeding you have had, this is the best possible diagnosis. Baby is still there."

"Thank you," Ava said, her head buzzing as she tried to take in all the information.

The doctor patted her on the knee and with a whoosh she was gone.

"It's good news, isn't it?" Hope asked. "It sounds very positive. It sounds like you are in with a good chance."

A good chance. Ava hadn't wanted the doctor to let her know there would be a good chance. She had wanted her to say, in her very lovely French accent, that there was a no-doubt-about-it, 100%, without a doubt, absolute and total 'chance' that things would be okay and that this was just a silly little blip on the road. She didn't want her say that it would possibly be okay, but it might not and in the meantime, all this way from home, she had to lie there and take a fecking aspirin.

"I want to go home," she said, petulantly.

"You need to rest. This isn't quite Betty's pad, but it's not bad either," Hope offered.

"I don't mean Betty's house. I want to go home, home – to my own house and my own doctors and my own fecking aspirin. I've had enough of Betty's fecking house," she said, equally petulantly.

She knew how she sounded but she didn't care. Was it the stress of last night's revelations that had brought all this on in the first place? At that moment she was pretty sure that if she could she would walk away from France and never look back. If she could turn back time and never see the damned letter, or never agree to go to France in the first instance she would. Jesus, she thought she was getting into this for a pair of shoes – not a birth mother, a baby and a stay in hospital. Biting her lip she knew she was verging on mildly hysterical and there was a part of her which knew she should be sitting there relieved and that the doctor was right – this was the best possible outcome, given the bleeding, but her head was spinning. This talk of a subcorri-doodah wotsit meant nothing to her other than the fact that she felt completely out of control – and Ava Campbell did not like feeling even a little bit out of control.

"When will Connor be here?" she asked Hope. "I need Connor."

"Soon," Hope soothed. "Soon."

When Ava had dozed off Hope left again to crave another imaginary cigarette and get a breath of fresh air. Jean-Luc was still there, sitting on a green plastic bench, examining the hairs on the back of his arms. As she approached he looked up and smiled awkwardly. Smiling awkwardly back she wasn't sure where they went from here. The last time she had seen him, an hour before, he had kissed her and she had kissed him and it had been one big, mad, delirious snog fest which had left her feeling weak at the knees. They had broken apart and she had mumbled that she had to return to Ava and he had mumbled that he understood and she had stumbled off.

She couldn't talk to Ava about it. Ava had more than enough on her mind and she was pretty sure that she wouldn't have appreciated

Hope wailing in, lumping herself down on the chair beside her hospital bed and telling her she had kissed a Frenchman and liked it. So she had sat, with this secret – and this sense of confusion bubbling through her about what had happened. She would have asked Jean-Luc what on earth it was all about but she was too shell-shocked. From his interest on their day out, to his coldness on the phone the day before to this passionate clinch as her cousin lay in a hospital bed, she couldn't quite work him out.

Staring at him again now as he looked at her with the awkward smile which made him look twenty years younger, she still wasn't sure what to think.

"Connor sent a message," she said. "He's at Dublin airport now. His flight leaves in an hour."

"I can pick him up from the airport and bring him here."

Shaking her head but smiling, Hope told him there was no need and that they had imposed on his time enough.

"No, it is not a problem," he said, "I want to do something. And you have to stay here, I imagine, with Ava? She will need you."

"Yes," Hope nodded. "But the news is good. They think she might be okay. That the baby might be okay."

He sighed, running his fingers through his hair. "Oh thank God," he said. "I was worried."

He looked, Hope thought, with slight alarm, as though he might actually cry. Looking at him, sitting down across from him and trying to make sense of it all, she heard herself blurt out, "I just don't get you."

"Get me?" he asked, confused. "What do you mean, get me?"

"Understand you. I don't understand you. Here you are devoting yourself to two ladies you barely know. Looking for all intents and purposes as if you genuinely care about Ava and her baby. Did you know? Do you know?"

"You are speaking in riddles," he said, looking more than a little perplexed.

"About Ava and Betty?"

"What about Ava and Betty? And you, as you say, don't 'get me'? I don't get you."

"That Ava is Betty's daughter? You must have known."

The look on his face told her that he absolutely did not know. He glanced around him, quickly, as if waiting for someone to jump out declaring he was on candid camera.

"No," he said, solemnly. "No . . . I did not know."

"I thought that was why you were so worried. That you were in on it all – this whole big story. We didn't know until we found a letter last night."

"I'm not a monster," he said, "I'm not only worried because of some big secret which I knew nothing about. I'm worried because she was scared and in pain."

"And you kissed me?" she asked, wanting him to tell her that he hadn't kissed her out of some sort of sense of guilt either and that he wanted to. She knew she was verging on psycho status but she couldn't stop herself.

"You kissed me back," he said.

"I did, but I know my motives."

"Motives?" he said, looking pissed off. "There were no motives. No, I did not know Betty was anyone's mother. I am waiting here because I thought you might need me. By you, I mean you and Ava. And I care about Ava and her baby because she looked so . . . distraught. And the kiss? I kissed you because I wanted to kiss you."

"But yesterday . . ." She knew she was annoying him with her questions but she was tired and sweaty and, she realised, scruffy. She hadn't even had time to brush her hair that morning, simply hauling it back in a scrunchie. She had no make-up on. She was wearing a pair of loose tracksuit bottoms and a T-shirt. She wasn't even sure she had put any deodorant on that morning. She wondered why today – when she looked like she had been dragged through a hedge backwards – he had kissed her when the day before he had treated her like a business colleague and she needed to know.

"Yesterday?"

"You were cold. You were cold and distant and I didn't know what to think. And I've been messed around, Jean-Luc, by men who don't know what they want. So if you want something, if you want to kiss me, just kiss me. If you want to care, just care. If you want to spend time with me, just spend time with me. But don't," and she felt her voice shake as she said this, knowing that she was about to make a complete tit of herself but somehow being unable to stop, "don't fuck me and leave me on the carpet."

She heard the words come out of her mouth and she saw the look of confusion flash across his face and she was instantly embarrassed for swearing and for being crude and for talking utter shite and she dropped her head to her hands and shook her head.

"I'm sorry," she said, "I'm sorry."

"I never left you on the carpet," he said, his voice thick with frustration. "And I never meant to mess you around. It's complicated."

"It's always complicated," she said, peeking through her fingers and feeling the heat from her face blaze against the palm of her hands. "I'm sorry. It's been a strange few hours. I'm so sorry. I don't know what to think any more." She felt sick. God, she should have just shut up. Christ, the carpet? Had she really said that? She was mortified. There she was shouting at him as if he was Dylan and losing the run of herself altogether. "Connor is landing at six thirty-five," she said matter of factly.

"I'll pick him up," he said softly. "And I will bring him here. And maybe we can talk. When you are a little calmer."

And a little less mental, she chided herself. This was definitely a conversation to finish when she was a little less mental.

Chapter 31

Ava brushed her hair and scrubbed her face clean before rubbing some moisturiser into her skin, feeling it sting. She hadn't cried in an hour. She actually felt strangely calm. The bleeding had eased. It was still there and she was still afraid to move, but it had definitely eased. A nurse who spoke no English whatsoever had just been in to take her temperature, check her blood pressure and fuss about something she didn't understand. She had just nodded and that had seemed to appease the nurse and she had scurried off again, returning with a jug of iced water and an extra pillow.

Thanking the nurse and straightening her dressing-gown, she blew her fringe from her face and sat back and glanced at the clock on the wall. Surely he would be here soon? With every new set of footsteps she heard walking down the corridor she felt her heart quicken. She just wanted to see him, and for him to hug her and tell her it was all okay, and part of her was scared shitless. What if he was hurt? What if he was upset that she hadn't told him? He would be hurt that Hope knew first. And random French medical people. And a hunky Frenchman. Telling her husband should have been the first thing she did. Taking a deep breath, she exhaled slowly to steady herself. She should phone Cora too. Cora didn't know. Cora didn't know she was pregnant or, probably, that her big old secret had been blown apart. No, she shouldn't phone Cora after all. She couldn't bring herself to call her. Not now. She would focus on her baby and nothing else. If she thought about Cora too much she would get upset and angry and Lord only knows if getting upset and angry had landed her in hospital. *No,* she chided herself, *calm thoughts. Don't think about the lie your life has been. Don't think about the hurt and pain you caused just through being born. Don't think that you'll never get to tell Betty you understand . . .*

The nurse appeared again, more animated this time, babbling nineteen to the dozen.

Ava shook her head and shrugged her shoulders. "I don't understand," she muttered.

"Visitor," the nurse said. "There is a visitor."

Hope stood up. "I'll go and see. It's probably him. I'll check and tell them to let him in if it is."

"Okay."

"He loves you so much," Hope said softly. "I don't know him very well, but I know that much for sure."

Ava nodded, feeling slightly sick. "Okay. I know. Okay, thank you."

And with that Hope was gone, just about at the time when Ava really needed her to hold her hand most of all.

When Connor walked into the room Ava found herself speechless – which was almost unheard of for her. She always had something to say. She was famous for saying the right thing at the right time in almost every situation. No one was able to shock her into silence. Even when one of her charges in school brought in his dead hamster for show and tell she had responded with a warm smile and the appropriate kind words about little hammy having shuffled off his mortal coil. But when Connor walked in and she saw him – looking as though he had aged ten years in the five days since she had last seen him – she was speechless and she felt the tears she had been sure had run dry fill her eyes. In that second she reminded herself of one of her charges who had taken a fall in the playground. They would come round, and stay calm, but as soon as their mum arrived to pick them up all the hurt and the pain would rush out and they would dissolve into hysterics. Every part of her wanted to dissolve into hysterics. She wanted to tell him she was sorry for not telling him as soon as she knew and for not wanting this baby more. She wanted to tell him it was okay, or maybe okay, or at least she thought it would be okay. She wanted to tell him that she wanted her mum, but she wasn't sure who her mum was any more. She wanted to tell him that she wished Maisie was there because she had just learned how precious children could be and she wanted her little girl as close to her as could be.

Most of all, however, she wanted him to hold her and to soothe her and to tell her it was fine and that he loved her and their baby.

Ava looked up, blinking back tears, and the hysterics came and he, just as she knew he would, held her and soothed her and told her she would be fine and everything would be fine and he loved her more than anything in the world.

Wrapping his arms around her and pulling her even closer, he said, "Ava, I'm so sorry. So, so sorry about everything. But we're here. You, me and this baby. And please God we'll have this little one safe and sound. We'll focus on that. Just focus on our baby and it will be okay. We will be okay."

"You don't worry it will change anything? You're not worried that we're under enough pressure?" She felt stupid saying the words because she already knew that she didn't care what pressure they were under, this baby was the most important thing of all.

"Of course it will change everything," he said with a laugh. "But in a good way. Another little Maisie running around? What could be better? Or madder?"

"Cora's not my mum," she sniffed.

"Yes, she is," Connor said. "She'll always be your mum – the person you run too. Biology doesn't change that."

"Doesn't it?" she asked, because she didn't know the answers at all any more.

He shook his head. "I know your mum. I've seen her cry on your wedding day. I've seen her fuss over you when you were pregnant with Maisie. I've seen the two of you together, lost in your own world. I've seen how she does your head in. Only a mother can do your head in that much."

Ava laughed, despite herself. "She should have told me."

"She was probably scared shitless she would lose you."

In that moment, Ava knew that Cora hadn't lost her. And never would.

A half hour had passed before Connor emerged from the room, looking less gaunt and drained than when he had gone in. "Thank you," he said, extending first of all his hand to Jean-Luc and then pulling Hope into a hug. "Thanks for looking after her."

"It was nothing," Hope said, embarrassed and exhausted and happy to accept a hug from a man who had no intentions towards her whatsoever other than simply to hug her.

"Ava said you should go home and get some rest. It's been a long day and I'm here now. They said they'll get me a fold-up bed to sleep beside her – and I've no intention of leaving any time soon anyway. So go home. And rest up. And I'm truly grateful. We both are."

Hope nodded, feeling emotion swell up inside her. She was almost afraid to speak.

"I will take you home," Jean-Luc said softly and she wasn't sure if she dared get into a car with him.

The drive home wasn't as much awkward as it was excruciatingly painfully awkward. Hope did as much staring out of the window as possible, playing over the whole 'carpet' and 'fucking' statement in her mind and cringing at the very memory of it. Part of her wanted to say 'Oops, made a bit of a tit of myself there, didn't I?' and beg him to kiss her again but part of her just didn't trust herself to open her mouth – at all – except to breathe and perhaps to sip from her water bottle and maybe to thank him, quietly and politely when he left her off.

He remained as quiet, staring ahead at the road in front. Occasionally Hope found herself glancing at him, trying to figure him out but trying to be covert about the whole thing. He already, most likely, thought she was a nutjob – cottoning on to the fact that she had taken to staring at him out of the corner of her eye would do nothing to make him think otherwise.

When they pulled up at Betty's cottage, she realised her chances to say anything were becoming limited. She imagined she would see him again. She still had to give him the letter Betty had left and they still had to deal with all the odds and sods which were supposed to be at the market today. It felt odd to talk to him in a businesslike manner after the day they had spent together but she didn't trust herself to say anything else.

"Where do we go from here?" she blurted out before realising that sounded a bit *Fatal Attraction*. "About the house and the items we were taking to market, I mean? What do we do now?"

"I can take the items to market tomorrow, if you want to be here for Ava. And we can meet on Monday to tie up any loose ends."

He sounded formal – back to the business like the Jean-Luc she had spoken to on the phone the day before. Her shoulders sagged but she didn't have the energy to say anything other than to tell him that would be fine and to thank him for his assistance. Just like her romp with Dylan, her kiss with Jean-Luc was apparently one of those things which was never to be mentioned again.

"Take care," he said, softly, as she turned to walk into the house.

"Fuck it," she swore as she closed the door behind her and stared at the bare room in front of her – devoid of personality bar the green tweed chair in the corner. "Fuck you and the horse you rode in on!" And she kicked the leg of the chair in her temper and marched into the kitchen, pulling the largest wineglass she could find from the cupboard and opening a bottle of Merlot and pouring it almost to the brim, watching the deep-red, blissfully intoxicating liquid swirl around the bowl of the glass. She imagined the oblivion she longed for coming when the deep-red, blissfully intoxicating liquid swirled around her stomach. She could forget about everything that happened that day. Connor was there to mind Ava. Jean-Luc was off doing his strange and mysterious thing and she could sit there in her tracksuit bottoms and T-shirt and drink herself stupid. She gulped from the glass, choking as the wine hit the back of her throat. It was the choking that brought the tears to her eyes in the end but that was only the start of it. As she recalled the day she had just spent with Jean-Luc, her cheeks burned as deep red as the wine she was drinking. And that brought more tears. Why could she not just get through a single interaction with a man of the opposite sex without coming across as some needy, desperate, slightly mental woman?

This, she figured, as she choked again on her second gulp of wine, was all Dylan fecking big-footed-master-shagger McKenzie's fault and in that instant she hated him. Hated him for shagging her. Hated him for *only* being her friend. Hated him for his Facebook status updates. Hated him for telling her he missed her and that he had become accustomed to her face. Hated him, most of all, for messing up any chance she ever had with any other man by giving her mixed signals and confusing her entirely.

Hating him, she picked up her phone and dialled, waited for the phone to ring. He would be up now. He would be getting ready for work. He would be fawning over fecking Cyndi with her blonde hair and big tits and her perfectly manicured feet. The rage bubbled as the phone rang – the slow ring of an international call. He answered and the rage, built of exhaustion and humiliation, sprang forth.

"Dylan McKenzie, you are feckwit of the highest order and a very bad person and you should *not*, repeat, should *not*, be telling me you like my face, or you miss me or saying anything for that matter which would lead me to believe that you could conceivably have feelings for me when you are in love with someone else and not one bit interested in ever being in love with me. You know I'm vulnerable. You know that more than anyone and there you are shagging people, okay a person, in our house and still expecting me to make your breakfast and cuddle you after she goes home and sleep with you when you get drunk and all sorts of other things which are clearly across the line from a purely platonic relationship. And you give me hope that this could be some kind of '*When Harry Met Sally*' type of situation and that you might tell me you love me one day and that she was your rebound person, but the truth is,

Dylan fecking McKenzie, you just want it all. Well, let me tell you, you can't have it all. You can't have me and you can just stop fecking me about. I'm moving out. I'm sure that will make you happy – you can hump wherever the fuck you want, no pun intended – and me and my sad-sack ways won't be there as your second prize any longer!"

She put the phone down without waiting to hear a response and when he called her back she hit ignore as quick as she could and found that, contrary to her original opinion, she did have more cursing steam left in her and she rounded that whole thing off with a big "And so there, you with your big fat fucking face!" before breathing out and gulping from her wineglass.

When he called back a second time she saw his name flash on the screen and she lifted it, almost tempted to drop it with flare into her wineglass but instead she simply hit ignore and then tried to steady her pulse.

When her phone rang a third time, Dylan's name once again flashing across the screen, she gave her phone a bad look and sat it across the room on the dresser. When it rang a fourth time and the glass of wine was no longer choking her, she decided he was clearly going to be persistent and she would need to talk to him.

"Frig it," she said, and answered. "Hello?" she said, her cheeks warming with the after-effects of the wine and her growing sense of humiliation at her prior behaviour.

"What – the – fuck was that all about?" Dylan asked.

She couldn't quite work out whether or not he was angry or very amused. A part of her knew, just knew, he would have been secretly delighted that she was working herself up into a lather about him. He was that kind of man – loved attention from the ladies no matter where it came from. He would make a great politician, or footballer.

"You have to ask?" she snapped. "You really have to ask?"

"Clearly I'm a flawed human being, but yes, I need to ask."

She sighed – one of those deep from her gladiator sandals sighs. "It was about you. And us. And whatever is going on, or isn't going on. And it was about Cyndi. And her feet for that matter. Really,

Dylan, the foot picture is a bit much!" She knew she was sounding childish, bitter and perhaps once again, slightly insane.

"What *about* me and us and all those other things?" he asked.

She took a deep breath. "You're flirting with me, Dylan. It's not right and it's not fair – not just on me, but on Cyndi too. She deserves better and I deserve better."

"I didn't mean to flirt," he said. "When did I flirt?" He sounded as if the very notion of him flirting with her was alien to him and that he was trying to humour her.

"Well, you did. Yesterday with that 'miss your face' shite. And you slept with me, or did you not realise you were doing that either? Did you just think I would forget it? I'm not like you, Dylan. I can't just forget and move back to so-called harmless flirting and being friends. I don't work that way. Not any more." She breathed in and exhaled again. "I think we need a break."

"Erm, you are in France. I think that pretty much constitutes a break, doesn't it? Not that we were ever together to 'break' anything in the first instance, were we?" He sounded like a smug bastard – who must have felt as if he was just humouring her and not taking her seriously at all. Silly little Hope-less, off on one again.

"Oh stop being so fecking smug!" she snapped.

"I don't know what you mean."

"You know exactly what I mean, Dylan McKenzie."

She heard him sigh – a deep frustrated sigh from the depth of his stomach. It rankled with her. Not that she needed much help getting wound up just now.

"Seriously, Hope, I don't. You phone me up out of the blue giving me dog's abuse about flirting with you when I don't think I have been and then you talk about taking a break when we've never been together in the first place."

"But we have been. It might have been just a shag to you but it was more to me. Both times."

"What?" He sounded genuinely confused.

"Here," she muttered, her face colouring further. "Betty's house. You do remember, don't you?"

There was a pause. She imagined he was mentally flicking through the rolodex of his conquests to find the one filed under 'Big Mistake' before he replied.

"Oh then! Hope, that was a long time ago. Have you had feelings for me since then?"

"No!" she said sharply and loudly. "But lately, you must have known? I'm not the kind of person to jump into bed with someone on a whim. You knew, Dylan. I know you knew."

"I didn't . . ." he said, his voice trailing off.

She wanted to shout back, louder, that he did. Of course he did. He had to, didn't he? He wasn't stupid. He must have been aware of her growing neediness. He must have noticed the look of shock in her eyes when he told her he was shacking up with Cyndi. He must, she thought, have realised how when he hugged her lately she hugged him back a little bit tighter and maybe for a little bit longer? But then things with them had always just evolved. She couldn't pinpoint a defining moment so why would he?

"I'm sorry," she said. "I'll talk to you when I get back. Maybe we just need a little time to think about where we go from here."

"I'm sorry too," he said, and he sounded contrite – as if she had pulled the carpet out from under him and left him sitting on his bare arse on the cold floor, not sure of what to do next.

She hung up and sank to the floor, where she finished her glass of wine and pondered just what a shitey mess her entire life had become.

Chapter 32

Ava was surprised at just how well she slept. As soon as Connor came, and held her hand, and told her he loved her, she was overwhelmed with tiredness and had drifted off. When she woke she looked across the room to where he was sleeping, on a very uncomfortable-looking fold-up bed covered by a completely insufficient cellular blanket. She smiled and took a deep breath. She had to admit she was a little afraid. For a minute or two as she lay there, watching him, she tried to assess whether or not she was in pain.

No pain was good, the doctor had said. The doctor had explained things further as best as she could in her heavy thick accent. She had seemed more hopeful and had offered them printouts of information in English which she said they could read at their leisure. She was recommending rest and regular scans but now that the bleeding had eased off things were looking better.

Connor had squeezed Ava's hand tightly and, when the doctor left, he had leaned over and kissed her before placing his hand once again, very softly, on her tummy.

"I wish I had known straight away, Ava," he'd said sadly.

"I know, but I wanted it to be special. I mean, after I stopped freaking out I wanted it to be special. Not over the phone. That wasn't right."

"If we had lost this baby . . ." he'd started and she didn't need him to finish the sentence.

She'd known what he was feeling. If she had lost the baby she would have at least known it – had a chance to dream for it, look forward to holding him or her, thought of all the songs she would sing and books she would read and imagine all the adventures that Maisie and her baby brother or sister would share.

"We didn't," she'd said. "We nearly lost it all, but we didn't. And I've realised how much I want this. How we would be okay. How we could make this work and how maybe we needed something big to make us sit up and make our lives easier. Well, this is about as big as it gets."

"Maisie is going to be delighted," he'd smiled. "She'll be like a proper wee mammy – we should let her help choose the cot and the pram. Maybe we could let her choose the name?"

"Not unless we want the wee pet named after Mr Fecking Tumble or Peppa shagging Pig."

Connor had laughed and she'd breathed out. "The mental image of Peppa shagging Pig has scarred me for life," he'd said.

"We'll get through this, honey," she'd offered, getting off the bed, walking to him and taking him in her arms.

"Not if she names the baby," he'd said, kissing her on the head and laughing gently.

She knew as she lay now and put her hand to her still flat stomach that they were not out of the woods yet. The baby was still small. It didn't even really look like a baby yet. It kind of looked like a shrimp. But it was her shrimp with a little, beautiful flutter of a heartbeat. And she knew, from how Maisie was, that a little tiny shrimp with a fluttering heartbeat would turn into a funny, cute and loveable (if tiring and occasionally brattish) little child with her daddy's smile and her mammy's eyes.

It was after ten when she finally felt ready to talk to Cora. She knew her mum would hate it that she was calling so late. She would probably give her the whole "I thought someone was dead" and

"No one calls anyone at this time of the night" speech. Well, there were times, Ava thought, when it was okay to break the rules.

True to form, Cora answered with a slight hint of panic in her voice. "Hello? What's wrong?"

It would have been churlish to ask "What is right?" so she bit her lip. She had been surprised by just how emotional she felt hearing Cora's voice. Suddenly she was reduced to five years old, lost in the supermarket and panicking because she wasn't sure she would ever see her mum again.

"Oh Mum!" she said, feeling her voice break.

There was a silence on the other end of the phone. A silence which was just broken by Cora's voice, less confident than Ava had ever heard it.

"You know, don't you?"

Four words confirmed everything. Feeling them like a body blow, she replied: "I know."

"We thought we were doing the right thing. We did do the right thing," Cora replied, her voice shaking.

"You should have told me."

"I know. I wanted to. But, oh, Ava, don't you know that you were so a part of me that I thnk I convinced myself you really were mine. That I had carried you."

She could hear the pain in her mother's voice.

"I'm pregnant," she stuttered.

"Oh Ava!"

"I'm in hospital. I've been bleeding, but there's a heartbeat. They think it will be okay. But it's been scary."

"You've been bleeding? Oh Ava! Is it bad? How pregnant are you?"

"I'm only a few weeks, very early. Maybe five or six weeks." She felt tears well in her eyes. "It was bad." She wanted her mammy. She wanted to cuddle into her and have her stroke her hair and call her a poor pet and assure her that it would be okay in the way only a mother could.

The emotion was thick in Cora's voice. "I can book a flight. Let me book a flight. I can be with you."

Ava took a deep breath, so tempted to beg Cora to fly out right there and then but needing time to come to terms with everything without her mother's fussing.

"Connor is here. It's okay."

There was a pause.

"I should have told you," Cora said, a world of pain in her voice.

"Yes, you should have. If you thought there was a chance I could find out, you should have told me."

"I wasn't sure if you would. Betty had kept quiet all these years. I'd always said it was down to her to make that call. I didn't know she had. Part of me wanted to tell you as soon as I knew you were in her will, but I couldn't find the words. So I'm a coward and I thought maybe you would go and not find out."

"I needed to know."

Cora was silent. Ava was silent too. There was so much she wanted to say, but she just couldn't find the words. She was tired and she knew Cora was too.

"I do love you. More than anything in the world. You mean the world to me, Ava. You have to know we did it all for you. I did everything in my life just for you."

"I know, Mum," she said, feeling the word *mum* heavy on her heart.

"I love you."

"I know," she said, hanging up and turning in her bed to look to where Connor was snoozing. She should have said 'I love you too' but she just couldn't. Not that she didn't, just that she couldn't say it. Not yet.

After two glasses of Merlot. Hope decided to re-read the letters Betty had sent to her and Ava. She kind of wished she could find another letter from Betty – or that Betty could be there to tell her what to do. But in the absence of both of those distractions she read over the words she had already seen, reminding herself of Betty's distrust of Dylan, her own bravery at moving across Europe for someone she loved, her determination to get on with her life after

Claude had died. And she realised that she could stay, there on the floor reading old letters, or she could face, head on, the mess she had made of her life and start putting it back together.

She'd had enough of making half plans. Of threatening to move out of her house. Of thinking maybe she would go back to travel writing. Of wondering whether or not she fancied Jean-Luc and whether or not he fancied her back. But the thing she was most of all fed up with was her Dylan obsession.

Get over yourself and get over him, she chided herself as she stood up and poured the remainder of the bottle of wine down the sink. Walking through to the bathroom she glanced at herself in the mirror. Her lips had that dodgy red-wine staining thingy going on and her complexion was more than washed out. It was almost corpse-like. Her hair stuck lankly to her head and her eyes looked sad. Not just tired but sad. What would Betty do, she asked herself as she pulled her hair back off her face and examined the wrinkles and blemishes and tiredness staring back at her.

"She sure as feck wouldn't be drinking herself stupid," she said aloud.

She switched on the shower and watched as the curls of hot, reviving steam rose and filled the small ensuite. Stepping under the steam she lathered herself with her favourite Jo Malone Lime Basil and Mandarin body wash and stood for ten minutes just letting the fragrance infuse into her spirit before washing her hair and stepping out of the steam. Drying off, she wrapped herself in her fluffy dressing-gown and brushed her hair out into loose curls. She made a cup of tea and walked through to Betty's study where she sat at the desk, pulled out of a clean sheet of paper and a pen and started to write.

> *Dear Me,*
>
> *I'm sorry for treating you the way I have done. I'm sorry that I've not given you the life you always dreamed of so far. That doesn't mean we won't get there. Believe me, I want to get there as*

much as you. To be honest, I'm not entirely sure where 'there' is any more. I thought it was with Dylan - I know you felt the same. But you know, I don't really think it is.

I thought it was working in Belfast but, you know, we've become a bit boring in our old age, haven't we? Remember how you loved adventure? Remember how you would be the first person to want to stick a pin in that map and go wherever that blind faith took you? I know you ended up in some pretty dodgy places but you ended up in some pretty cool places too. I miss them. I miss that following my nose and hunting a story and walking down dust tracks and over mountains and on crowded buses filled with chickens and mad people. I know I used to say I would give anything for an air-conditioned room and a soft bed, but you know if you get air-conditioning and comfortable beds all the time it becomes a bit frigging boring.

Do you think you settled down because it was the right thing to do? Do you think that you just thought "Oops, thirty now, time to get a job and a house and a man in my life"? I think maybe I made that mistake. And I'm sorry for being so focused on doing what I thought I was supposed to that I forgot to think about what I really, really wanted.

I'm going to change though. Yes, I know that is scary. I'm scared. And I'm not even 100% sure how I'm going to do it. I mean, the settled years have not been kind for my bank balance but I'm not going to wait any more.

So much of my life, our life, your life, has been on hold waiting for something to happen. We waited for university to finish. We waited to travel the world. We waited till we got home. We waited, and waited, and waited for Dylan to love us back. And yes, I know you still love him. I know a part of you will always love him but he can't be the love of your life if he doesn't love you back. Love doesn't work that way. It might feel like your heart will break into a million pieces because he isn't drawing little heart bubbles with your name in the middle but if he really was the one, the universe would have fixed it for him to know that.

Betty knew. She knew with Claude. Even when it was tough and even when she couldn't have another baby. She knew that there was one man she could always turn to - and who would always turn to her. Dylan isn't your Claude. I hate to say this but you may never meet your Claude - but we will be okay with that. I don't know how I know but I do. Being here, being through this, well, that has taught me that.

I'm done with waiting. I'm going to get on with living. Are you with me?

Much love,

Me

X

Hope folded the piece of paper and took it through to slip it in the corner of her suitcase and promised herself she would write another letter, and another, and another and she would keep writing them until she had convinced herself that she really had made the changes she wanted to in her life.

Smiling, she picked up her phone and called Jean-Luc. As he answered she steadied herself and said with a confidence she most certainly did not feel, "Hi Jean-Luc. I'm sorry for my behaviour earlier today. Truly I am. I would love to go to the market at Marseille with you tomorrow if you don't mind and I promise to behave myself."

There was a pause, during which time she wondered had she made the entire situation worse and not better, before he spoke.

"I will pick you up at ten. I look forward to seeing you."

Slipping off her dressing gown and under the covers of her bed, Hope drifted off to sleep thinking that Scarlett O'Hara and Annie were both right. There was a lot to look forward to about tomorrow.

Chapter 33

Hope felt a rush of excitement flood through her veins as they drove into the bustling port of Marseille. Jean-Luc had arrived bang on ten o'clock, smiling warmly as she opened the door to him.

"We will say no more about yesterday," he said. "We will just talk about France and the markets. Have you been to *Les Puces de Marseille* before? When you were here before, perhaps?"

Hope shook her head. She had heard of the market – but she had never been. After their round-the-world adventure they'd had about their fill of markets with over-the-top salespeople trying to con them out of their money, so when they had hit France they had stuck with the small village shops and the occasional trip to the hypermarket.

"It can be very busy, but stick with me," said Jean-Luc. "My friend he owns a small shop – antiques and oddities – he was delighted with what he was sent from Betty. He thinks he can get a good price."

"I'm not worried about the price," Hope said. "It feels wrong to profit from Betty's death – to sell off her possessions."

"Your aunt, she was not a terribly materialistic person. She will be happy that the items have found new homes and you should treat yourself with the proceeds."

Shrugging her shoulders, Hope thought it would be a good start to her travel-the-world fund. Some would still go to charity, of course, but some would help her fulfil the promises she had made to herself the night before.

"Do you miss her?" Hope asked.

"Betty. Of course. She was a dear friend. She, how do you say it, kept me on my toes. She didn't miss anything."

No, Hope thought, there wasn't much that got past Betty and her eagle eyes.

"Did she seem unhappy to you? She says she was happy, and she seemed it when I visited, but do you think she really was, carrying around this big secret?"

"I think she was," Jean-Luc said, simply. "She maybe realised just how precious life really was."

"I suppose."

The salty smell of the sea assaulting her nostrils, Hope stepped out into the baking heat and allowed the sun to wash over her. If she never set foot inside the market and never sold a single thing, a part of her would still believe she was somehow in paradise.

"It's wonderful," she said.

"It's noisy and busy," Jean-Luc replied with a laugh.

"You are just used to it," she said, "You never appreciate what you are used to."

"Sounds to me like you are missing home," Jean-Luc replied, closing the car door after her and guiding her towards the gateway of the marketplace.

"It's not home I'm missing," she said with a wink. "It's something more than that."

"You are an intriguing character, Mademoiselle Scott," Jean-Luc replied and she smiled, her heart light as she walked into the hustle and bustle of the market.

Stalls stood beside small stone shops, with enticing window displays. The shouts of the market traders, selling their wares – everything from fresh fruit and vegetables to vintage clothes – rang in Hope's ears as she tried to get her bearings. People brushed past, lost in their own world – getting what they needed for their families and themselves. This was their life. Just as in Belfast when people milled around Victoria Square, grumpy faces drawn as they ran in from the rain, concerned with their shopping trips and what they might do that night for dinner. But Hope stood there, feeling alive.

"Please come this way," Jean-Luc said, weaving his way to a small shop cluttered with pictures and tasselled lamps and 101 things which Hope could not decide whether she loved or despised.

Jean-Luc introduced Hope to a stocky man called Louis, with penny glasses who looked a little like a short, fat Poirot, only that he wore jeans and a T-shirt which was at least two sizes too small. He smiled widely and held out his hand for her to shake, looking her up and down as if perhaps she too were on sale. She felt uneasy, and a little bit queasy if the truth be told.

"The items are selling well," he said. "They are not worth much, just bric-a-brac really but I will do my best. You are welcome – most welcome – to stay as long as you want."

Standing there, in the dark room, with a man who gave her the creeps while the whole world was waking up around her, Hope realised no. She didn't want to live in the past any more. She wanted to move on. She couldn't wait to move on.

"No, thank you," she said. "I'd love to see some of Marseille, though, Jean-Luc, if you have no business here. Or when you are done. I am happy to wander the streets on my own. More than happy."

"I have a few items I wish to discuss with Louis, but we can meet in a while. I'll bring you back to Saint Jeannet or to the hospital, whichever suits."

"Great," she said, eager to get out and see the world. "How about we meet at the museum when you are free?"

"It's a date," he said and she turned and left the past behind, in more ways than one.

The verdict was in. The bleeding had eased but the doctor had warned Ava that the clot was still there and it could grow, or it could be reabsorbed by her body. She would definitely have to take it easy – but the chances were good. Lots of people bled in pregnancy and went on to have absolutely healthy babies.

"We'd like to keep you in for another 24 to 48 hours just to monitor you and perhaps run a few more tests but you should be okay to fly home."

"Thank God," Ava had said, turning to smile at Connor and then back at the doctor. "We have a little girl at home and we would love to get back to her soon."

The doctor smiled. "Ah, what age is she?"

"Just two."

"Well, two can be a tough age," she said, "so no lifting her up when you get back. You will have to slow down and take things easy and you will have to see your doctor on a regular basis, but please stay positive. This little baby obviously wants to be here so let us try and get him or her here safely."

When the doctor left, Connor got on the bed beside Ava and hugged her. "Now, Ava Campbell, I know you very well and there will be a part of you which didn't hear all the positive stuff and only heard the bad stuff."

He knew her so well. She didn't consider herself a pessimist, more a realist, and for the last five minutes her stomach had been swirling like a washing machine, stopping each time the doctor said something positive (the bleeding has stopped, many women bleed in pregnancy and it works out okay, you are fine to go home) and launched into a reverse spin every time she hinted at caution (the clot may grow, you have to take it easy, no lifting the two-year-old).

"The bad stuff is scarier," she said, sniffing and wondering how on earth she would ever manage not to lift Maisie. The first thing she wanted to do when she got home was to lift her as high as possible and cuddle her for at least half an hour.

"The bad stuff is just a possibility," said Connor. "Look, pet, remember when you were pregnant with Maisie and watched all those birthing programmes on Sky and terrified yourself stupid that something would go wrong in the delivery? Well, all those things could have gone wrong but they didn't. Worrying didn't change that or make it okay, it just made you feel wound up and, to be honest, act quite the grumpy cow for the last few months."

She elbowed him gently in the ribs but she knew he was right.

"I'm scared," she said.

"So am I. But we'll just take things as they come."

She allowed herself to fall back into his arms and lie there, just the two of them in the room, listening to the French chatter of the staff and the sound of the birds just outside the window.

"Betty couldn't have any more children," Ava said, softly. It had been playing on her mind – that crib in the attic – since all this happened. "She was okay with it in the end, but it was hard. She had a crib in the attic that Claude made for the baby they never had. There's a cardigan there too – she said she knit it for me."

"We could take it home with us?" Connor said softly.

Ava turned to look at him. She wasn't sure. "I don't know."

"It could be nice to have something from her – something she intended for you."

Ava closed her eyes and breathed in again. This was all still so surreal. The thought that someone other than her 'mum' had given birth to her. The thought that she had been thirty-four years old before she found out.

"I don't know."

"We don't need to make any decisions now. I know this must be strange for you."

"You have no idea."

"Well, maybe not. But you should take the little cardigan – and maybe the crib too. Some day, you might like to have them around you. Some day you might be grateful for them. Some day it might make sense."

"I don't know who I am any more."

"You are you. Ava Campbell. Wife. Mother. Teacher. Obsessive compulsive. With a big heart and a dimple right there on your right cheek. You wear Size 6 shoes. You like to colour-code your life. You like *EastEnders* and you hate *Emmerdale*. After three glasses of wine you get a little giddy. After champagne, you get a little frisky. You take two sugars in your coffee, but none in your tea. Your favourite perfume is Chanel No. 5 and you know all the words to *The Sound of Music*, even the dialogue. If any of that has changed in the last few days then let me know. Otherwise, you are still you."

"We'll see about the crib," Ava said, kissing him lightly.

They lay together for a while longer, drifting in and out of a doze, until Ava's phone sprang to life. Lifting it, she saw she had a text message from Karen.

"Just saw your mum. You're pregnant? WTF? You've some explaining to do, girl!"

Ava rolled her eyes. First of all she figured she would kill Cora for passing on her news, especially when she knew how touch-and-go things were and second of all she just felt angry and hurt at Karen.

"Why does Karen think I need to explain anything to her?" she asked Connor, handing him the phone. "I'm pretty sure she is a big girl and, given that she is a mother herself, she knows where babies come from. I'm pretty sure she would, therefore, have an idea of how I'm pregnant. And I'm pretty sure my mother – who I will kill – would have told her that I'm in hospital so why the hell would anyone send a fecking WTF message to someone in hospital? Whatever issues Karen has about me, or motherhood, or pregnancy, or whatever, you do not send a WTF message to someone in hospital who may or may not be losing her baby. And you do not demand explanations from a thirty-four-year-old. I'm not a child. I'm a sensible married woman with already one child and if I happen to get up the stick again – admittedly after one too many glasses of champagne – then it is none of her fecking business. I've relied on her for too long, Connor. I've let her talk down to me for too long. I've felt hideously guilty because the last time we spoke we had a row. I felt sorry for feck sake and now this – *this*," she said pointing to her phone, "is how she responds! Well, she can stick her WTF up her WTF-ing hole!"

She stopped to take a breath and saw Connor looking at her in wonder.

He put her phone down and started to clap, slowly at first. "About bloody time," he said. "She has been bringing you down for too long. You don't need her."

"No," she said. "All I need is right here in this room, apart from that wee bit that I need that is in her Granny Brigid's house."

"Are you going to reply?"

"I sure am," Ava said, lifting the phone and battering out a text message in response.

"Nothing to explain. Am pregnant. We are very happy. Hopefully baby will be fine. And by the way, life lesson to remember, if you can't say anything nice then keep your mouth shut. And no, I won't be apologising this time."

She pressed send and switched her phone off. She had more important things on her mind, like quietly snoozing with her husband and their teeny tiny baby and making sure everything stayed put.

"I think it is a perfect example of post-modernism combined with a hint of the realists," Jean-Luc said, standing back and staring at the frame on the wall with a cheeky grin on his face.

"Indeed," Hope said, grinning back at him before falling into a fit of the giggles. If they weren't careful they were going to be kicked out. Already a very surly-looking man in a museum uniform had shushed them loudly as they erupted in giggles in front of a rather risqué image.

Stepping back from the glass-framed fire evacuation sign they had been staring at, they walked towards the exit.

"I told you I wasn't much of a museum person," Hope laughed as they stepped out into the open air. Her ribs hurt from laughing and she was sure her make-up was streaked across her face from rubbing the tears from her cheeks.

"I don't think I have ever enjoyed a museum as much," Jean-Luc replied, directing her to towards a small café.

She sat down and smiled as he nodded towards a waiter and ordered two coffees in an accent which made Hope feel all tingly.

"We were a little childish, no?" he said, a smile still drawn across his face.

He was exceptionally handsome when he smiled. When he

wasn't smiling he of course had that dark and brooding look down to a tee – which was attractive in its own right. But when he smiled, and the crow's feet crinkled, she felt a little flutter of something more. To top this, the way he said "leetle" made her feel a little weak at the knees. It was a damn good thing she was sitting down.

"Maybe a little," she said, trying not to mimic his accent in case he thought she was taking the mick, "but it was fun. We should really do it again some time? Although in fairness I understand that the Ulster Museum in Belfast might be a bit of a trek for you."

He smiled that gorgeous smile again. "Just a leetle bit," he responded and Hope was grateful in that moment that a waiter arrived, bearing two cups of coffee, because she might just have been tempted to haul him over the table, snog him senseless and demand he let her take a picture of his naked feet to put on her Facebook profile.

They had met just over an hour before. After she had left Louis' shop, she had wandered round the market stalls buying souvenirs. She had stood, with a ring on each finger at a gaudy costume jeweller's and had smiled as she paid for each and every one of them. They would come with her on her travels, she decided. She would ask Dylan if he wouldn't mind storing her stuff until she thought of what to do with it but there were certain items which absolutely were not going to be left behind – such as her collection of jewelled flip-flops, her rings and her bangles. She would look stylish at every turn and, she decided, she would even invest in one of those dinky little netbooks so she could file copy back to whoever wanted to buy travel columns and keep updated with her life back at home. The world didn't have to be a lonely place even if she was travelling on her own. Walking around the market, she felt completely at ease as she also had done as she wandered the streets of Marseille to get to the museum. She knew she was positively beaming by the time she was joined by Jean-Luc.

"Have we time to go in?" she had asked him, batting her eyelids and not actually caring if he flirted back.

He looked at his watch. "*Mais oui*," he replied before guiding her inside. "You seem happier today, Hope."

She cringed a little as she knew what he really meant was that she seemed less volatile. She was definitely less of a crazy woman and more confident in herself. It was amazing what a good talking-to via the letters of a dead aunt and a good half hour under the shower with Jo Malone could do for a girl.

They had walked around slowly, chatting and smiling, their conversation becoming easier as they went, until they were holding their sides laughing by the emergency exit. Now sitting by the port with a latte in her hand, Hope felt herself relax completely.

"Oh I needed this," she said, sipping from her coffee and of course by 'this' she didn't mean the coffee. More the chance to relax and have a laugh and not think about doomed crushes on housemates or the feet of their girlfriends. It was okay to think of Jean-Luc's feet. She imagined them to be a rare breed – non-scary-looking man feet. His would have no curling toes, no jutting bones and no masses of hair. There would be not one trace of a manky yellow toenail. He probably had pedicures. He struck her as the metrosexual type.

"If I may be so bold, you seemed a leetle down yesterday," he said, his eyebrow raised just slightly."

"By 'down' you mean 'mad'?" She laughed, feeling her face redden. "I am so sorry about that. It wasn't you."

"Well, I certainly know it wasn't me on the carpet if that is what you mean. You confuse me, Hope. You let your guard down sometimes. I know there is something else troubling you though. Someone troubling. The man from the carpet?"

He was perceptive. Perceptive and handsome. With nice feet. She liked him.

Biting her lip, she looked straight into his eyes. "I'm so sorry for dragging you into my sad story. Let's just say you bore the brunt of my frustration. To tell you it all would take a long time and would involve me making an eejit of myself."

"Eejit?" he asked, puzzled.

She liked how the word sounded in his accent, how it rolled off his tongue. She very much enjoyed the look of bafflement.

"Oh, 'idiot'," she said. "I have made an idiot of myself."

"We all make mistakes," he offered.

"You've not heard my story yet."

"But I have, how did you say it, borne the brunt of it?"

"Do you really want to know?" she asked, figuring that, at least, he deserved an explanation.

"I have time."

So she began to talk. She told him about her first day at university. She told him how she had been made to feel a part of Dylan's family. She told him about the unsuccessful Christmas snog and the holiday hump that was never to be spoken about again. She told him about them moving in together, and her growing sense of loneliness, and of course her growing dependence on Dylan for any form of contact. She told him about Cyndi, and about the feet, and about her earlier phone call and the flirtation and the sleeping together. He listened intently, interrupting only every now and again to ask a question or to ask her to repeat herself when he had trouble deciphering her accent. On more than one occasion he had reached over and rubbed her arm reassuringly. He had not even one bit minded when she had found herself choked with emotion and had let a tear or two fall.

When Hope had finished talking she was spent – wrecked, if the truth be told – and longing for a glass of wine.

"You deserve happiness," he had said, simply. "And you will get it."

There was a sadness in his eyes which made her think he had a similar sad story, but she was almost afraid to ask him. Still, she felt they had bonded. Sure hadn't she just told him how she had spent the last few years falling in love with someone who was never, ever going to love her back?

"And you, are you not happy?"

"What makes you ask that?"

"Just a hunch that maybe there is more to you than meets the eye. Just, well, you say I run hot and cold but you seem guarded too, sometimes. And then sometimes you are lovely."

"Which am I now?" he asked, reaching for his coffee cup and sipping from it.

"Lovely. But, you know, yesterday we kissed and then we were back to business again. And today you are lovely again."

"You like that word, 'lovely'," he said with a smile and set his coffee cup back on the table.

He said no more and she knew she was maybe pushing him. She didn't want to come across all demanding and needy again so she just smiled and said yes, sure wasn't lovely a lovely word anyway and there was no harm in using it.

"I like the way you say it," he said before draining his cup and offering to take her home.

"Thanks – that would be great."

"Or if you like you can go to the hospital?"

"Ava has texted and she is resting. I'll go and see her tomorrow. Home is fine," she said, feeling slightly frustrated that she couldn't draw anything out of him after she had bared her soul.

"I'm not him," he said as she got up to walk to the car. "And I'm not always lovely."

"Him?"

"The kind of man who would lead someone on. A man like Dylan. I don't work like that. But I am not perfect."

She wanted to kiss him there and then, to put her hand to his face, to feel his skin on her skin but she just wasn't sure how he would take it. Instead she said what was in her heart.

"Perfect is overrated and I know that you are nothing like him."

Hope had known all along that there was going to be a 'moment' when they reached the villa. It wasn't, she had known with absolute clarity, going to be like it was the last time he had dropped her back to the house. He wasn't going to drive off. He was going to kiss her and she was going to let him. While he had been a great friend to her all afternoon, she had also been aware of the growing fizz of attraction between them. It was strange, she thought as she stared out of the car at the winding road on the way to the villa, how she knew it. It wasn't like with Dylan when she had played 101 guessing games with herself. If he had phoned her within an hour of going to work she had convinced herself he was mad for her. If he had kissed her on the top of the head as he walked to put his mug and plate in the sink she had told herself it was obvious he was fighting the urge to throw her onto the kitchen floor and have his wicked way with her. When he went away with friends for the weekend and texted her at two in the morning with some garbled message she couldn't even decipher she had kidded herself it was a declaration of never ending love.

Of course that had been bullshit. But with Jean-Luc she knew there was something. Okay, so he was still being guarded but she knew where he was coming from and she knew that he was interested in some way. She knew that he wouldn't hurt her but she wasn't under any illusions either. She wasn't mad enough to convince herself he was madly in love with her but she knew, as sure as eggs are eggs, that he was going to kiss her.

She was so sure, in fact, that when he stopped the car a few hundred yards from the house and looked over at her she silently thanked Jesus, Mary and the Wee Donkey that she was already sitting down because if she had not been sat firmly on her seat she was sure her legs would give out from under her.

"I have had a lovely afternoon." he said. "I don't want to be presumptuous but . . ."

"You're not." She looked him deep in the eyes and then her eyes were drawn to his lips.

"Good," he said, gently cupping her face in his hands and kissing her so softly that she felt as if she were floating.

"Will you come in for coffee?" she asked, knowing that she was being a bit forward and knowing that it was not really coffee she was offering.

"Yes," he said, without hesitation. "I would like that very much."

They were no sooner through the door than the pretence that they were going to have coffee was gone entirely. She closed the front door and turned to find him so close to her that she could feel his breath on her face. She closed her eyes and felt his hands on her waist, pulling her close to him. Her eyes still closed, Hope tilted her head to his and felt the first soft brush of his lips on hers. It was then she realised just how fast her heart was thumping and just how much she wanted this. Nothing else mattered as his kiss deepened. Nothing else even crossed her mind as his hands slid up from her waist until they were caressing her – her hair, her face, her breasts. She felt herself gasp with pleasure – sheer unadulterated pleasure with no ulterior motives and no grand plan – and she gave in to exactly what she was feeling right there and then on the living room floor but this time, when they were both sated, he didn't get up and walk away. He just kissed her, gently on the nose, and told her she was amazing.

Chapter 34

"You can go home," the doctor said, putting the scanner away. "Baby seems to be happy. The clot has not got any bigger and, if you continue to take aspirin, it may well disperse. I am happy to discharge you if you are happy to go."

Ava felt herself smile. Another twenty-four hours with no bleeding had been such a relief. Admittedly she had barely moved from her hospital bed bar a short walk around the grounds and the occasional shuffle to the ensuite bathroom. Every time she had made to move, Connor had jumped to attention and offered to fetch whatever it was she wanted.

On one occasion she'd had to tell him that much as she appreciated his attention there were some things which he absolutely could not do for her, such as pee or brush her teeth.

"I'm only trying to look after you," he said in a mock huff before settling back down into his chair and letting her get on with her ablutions.

As she stood in the bathroom she smiled – in a strange way it had been nice to spend some time with Connor. Okay, so when it came to second honeymoons a couple of days in a French hospital had not been top of her list but now that they were there – just the two of them – it had been quite nice.

They had talked about it the night before as they lay side by side in their twin beds chatting. "I don't remember the last time we did this," Connor had said.

Ava had pulled a face. She was pretty sure they had never done this before. "What do you mean?" she asked.

"Talked into the wee small hours. Don't you remember when we were first together and we would sit up all night talking?"

"I'm pretty sure talking was not the only thing we did," Ava said with a smile, remembering the nights when it felt as if they just couldn't get enough of each other.

"Yes, well, that was good too and, you know, if ever there is a time when you feel like repeating that particular kind of behaviour and you are medically able to do the same then I'm your man," he said with a laugh. "But don't you remember, those nights where we just couldn't sleep until we knew as much about each other as we could and how it didn't seem like any time had passed before we were watching the sunrise and wondering where the night went?"

Ava nodded. Those were memories she looked back on time and time again – memories which reminded her why and how much she loved him. "When did we stop that?" she said softly. "I remember thinking we would never stop that and that we would always be just like that – the couple who talked all night and couldn't get enough of each other and would never want to stop holding hands."

"God, I don't know," he said softly, turning over in his bed and reaching out his hand to hers. "I suppose life gets in the way. If we stayed up all night now we would be pulverised the next day with our exceptionally enthusiastic daughter and I would never survive the drive to Belfast and back. And you know those kids who rely on you to teach them the very basics? They would sense your weakness and they would bring you down!" He said the last sentence in a deep American accent as if he were doing a voiceover for a movie trailer.

It made her laugh so loud that she snorted. Jesus, she realised, even though it was one of the most unattractive sounds in the world she couldn't remember the last time she had laughed until she snorted. But she was pretty sure that had been with Connor too. That's why they had worked. That's why they had fallen in love, because they could always, always, make each other laugh but somewhere along the line that faded, or got broken or got put on the back burner.

"I love you," she said softly when she had stopped laughing.

"And I love you too. You know that, don't you? And all the stopping talking all night and being grumpy and stressed has never ever meant I love you any less."

"I know," she said. "And I'm sorry too, for being grumpy and boring."

He laughed. "I hadn't noticed."

"You're a terrible liar, Mr Campbell," she said, squeezing his hand gently.

"But I'm not lying about this. I do love you and I'm just sorry it took something like this to get us talking again."

"This isn't so bad," Ava said, feeling buoyed with a new-found confidence. "This could still end well. We can make this work and at least we have had the chance to finally sit down and be together."

"We'll do it more often," Connor said. "Not necessarily in a hospital setting. I can think of better places, but we will do it. And we'll even bring Maisie and we'll get out of our boring, stick-in-the-mud routines."

"That sounds like a very good plan indeed," Ava said, turning to kiss him softly.

Most of the night was spent talking, talking and making plans. Ava was relieved that Connor felt much the same way that she did – that things just absolutely had to change.

"But can we afford it? If I cut my hours, or stay at home with the kids? Could we manage?"

"We can cut back – somewhere. We'll move house if we have to – downsize if necessary. Or I'll work more hours."

"No," Ava said, the last thing she wanted was Connor under

any more pressure. It wouldn't help anyone at all if he was even more tired than he already was. "You are under enough stress. Could you get work back nearer home? Get rid of the commute? And I'll get a part-time job. I'm sure my mother would help out. If it was a few hours?"

Connor sighed. "I don't know. There isn't much work around at the moment. But I'll look, or see if I can work from home for a bit? Or just get a different job, flipping burgers or whatever. We'll do what we need to be together and to make this work."

Ordinarily this kind of talk would have sent Ava into a fit of anxiety. The ifs and buts. The talk of moving from her beloved house in the suburbs. The thought of asking her mother for help normally made her want to boke but part of her figured Cora would owe her a favour or two these days. The talk of changing from the career she had trained for and worked hard at usually made her want to run for the hills but now, she thought, lying in the dark, it was different. What had Betty said? That sometimes you take the scenic route to get to where you are meant to be? Maybe the last ten years had been the scenic route and this baby was her way of getting where she actually was meant to be. And where she was meant to be was a happier place where she wasn't constantly second-guessing herself or feeling torn between all the people she thought she was meant to be. Lying in the bed she realised this was the first time she had thought of Betty fondly – not that she had hated her. She just didn't know what to feel, but two days and a near miscarriage and talking to Connor into the wee small hours made her realise that Betty hadn't meant to hurt her. Betty hadn't meant to hurt anyone. No one had. The past was the past and she couldn't change it. She would just have to learn to live with it and accept it. Connor was right. She was still who she always was.

And the person she was wasn't meant to be anything but happy, she realised.

When the doctor had told her she could go home, she felt a little step closer to that happiness. The following day she would be safe to fly home to her daughter. Cora had already gone and picked Maisie up from Dublin so they could fly back into Belfast and be at Cora's within ninety minutes. There they would work out just exactly what they would do but know that at least they could talk to each other again. At least there wasn't this unspoken tension between them.

"Thank you," she said to the doctor, who smiled back. "Thank you so much."

"Now make sure you take it easy, and see your doctor when you get home. I will give you a letter to give to him and enough medication to see you through. You have been lucky, Ava."

"Yes," Ava said, "I know I have."

When the doctor left she turned to Connor who was smiling back at her.

"Let's get back to Betty's house then," she said. "You look like you could do with a hot shower, nice sleep and a swim in the pool and maybe a cold beer once the sun is over the yardarm."

"Are you okay with going back to Betty's?"

She shrugged then nodded. "There might be another letter for me," she said. "We weren't finished. That and we don't have much of an option. The house is amazing though – before all this, well, I felt more at peace there than I did anywhere in a very long time."

He sighed and rubbed his stubbly face. "In that case," he said, "that sounds like heaven on earth. Much as I'll miss this stunning accommodation, complete with slightly creaking fold-up bed, interesting cuisine and frequent visits from lovely nurses who, frankly, could have at least worn something a bit more *Carry On Nursing* – the thought of a hot shower, a warm bed – where I can actually cuddle up to you properly, a swim in a nice pool and . . . seriously, a very, very cold beer is enough to get me into a bit of an excited frenzy."

"Down, boy!" Ava said with a grin, packing her pyjamas into her case and making the bed behind her even though she knew the nurses would be in soon to strip the bed and prepare it for the next patient. It just wasn't in her to leave an unmade bed.

"We'll get a taxi, save Hope coming here. It's not far. We should be there in half an hour or so and then you can get a decent sleep. We can get a decent sleep," she said, resting her head on his shoulder.

"I can't wait."

Hope was dozing, lying in bed with Jean-Luc's arm resting over her. She had been dozing on and off for at least an hour, surprised and delighted each time she opened her eyes that he was still there. They had drifted off somewhere at around six in the morning after spending the night lost in each other. She was amazed at how relaxed she felt in his company. Looking at him, his long eyelashes resting closed on his cheek, she felt a surge of something – some sort of deep happiness and contentment. And some sort of a deep need to go and pee and make a cup of coffee.

Slipping out from under his arm, she padded to the kitchen and put on the kettle before setting about making breakfast. She would wake him soon and he was bound to be hungry. Pulling her hair back from her face and tying it in a loose bun she gazed out the window over the hills – the hazy summer sky glimmered back at her and she felt herself smile back at it. She smiled as her tummy rumbled and she set about digging through the fridge to put together something filling to eat.

Cutting into a crusty loaf and slicing some ham and fresh tomatoes she enjoyed the aroma of the fresh coffee wafting through the kitchen. There was no doubt there was a peacefulness in that room that soothed her. She smiled as she cracked some eggs, scrambled them in a bowl and added a generous dollop of butter, and she was just contemplating bursting into song when she heard Jean-Luc walk into the room. His hair was ruffled, his face crumpled and in his sleepy state he looked younger than his years. For the first time she saw a vulnerability about him which made her want to look after him – even if it was just for a few days.

"Are you hungry?" she asked, gesturing towards the food.

"Yes, very," he said and there was something about how he spoke and how he looked at her which made her tummy do somersaults.

She turned to pour his coffee and found her hands shaking just that little bit and she felt acutely aware of him behind her, watching her.

"You make me very nervous," she said.

He laughed. "But why?"

"I'm not sure," she said, turning to face him and feeling herself blush. "But you do."

"I'm sorry."

"Don't be," she replied, feeling her heartbeat quicken as he walked towards her. Perhaps she wasn't quite as ready for breakfast as she first thought. She looked at him again and chewed her bottom lip. There was no doubt she really, really wanted to and it would be comforting – comforting to be with him, close to him, so very, very close to him. This would be over soon enough and she knew that – she was only too aware of how she would be back to face her very own reality – one in which a very strong-accented blonde-haired woman was currently lying on *her* sofa, eating food from *her* fridge and bonking *her* best friend.

He reached out and slowly rubbed the back of her hand with his thumb. She couldn't help but look at his hand. She had always had a thing for men's hands – more so than for their feet – even the big ones – and Jean-Luc's were without a doubt very fine specimens indeed. She looked from his hand to his arm and moving upwards to his shoulders, his neck – which she longed to nuzzle again – his face and those deliciously full lips. She spent a second or two just there, looking at his mouth before her eyes met his. He moved closer and as she closed her eyes she felt his full lips brushing against hers, his hand sliding up her arm and around to her back, guiding her towards him. They kissed and in that moment she forgot everything – everything except how he felt and how he tasted – how he made her feel.

"I do have a story," he said, as they sat on the terrace an hour later eating breakfast. Wearing a yellow sundress, Hope was sitting with her legs across Jean-Luc's knees, not quite able to bear being apart from him just yet. She looked at him, a little confused. All talk of sad stories seemed to be yesterday's news. They were hours beyond that. Hours and multiple orgasms beyond that, if the truth be told.

She didn't expect him to confide in her. She was happy simply with the what you see is what you get, the way things had gone. Which had been very, very *lovely* indeed.

"You don't need to tell me, Jean-Luc. I didn't ever mean to be pushy. I just wondered. It's my job – a journalist. Forty per cent talent and sixty per cent pure unadulterated nosiness."

Jean-Luc smiled, softly. "No, you deserve to know. Not that it's that interesting really. It's just one of those typical stories where things didn't work out and in the end it turned me into a bitter old man."

"You don't seem bitter and you aren't that old," Hope said with a smile, sipping from her fresh orange juice and luxuriating in the way he stroked his hand up and down her legs as he spoke.

He laughed and looked at her. "You are wonderful, Hope Scott. Do you always see the good in people?"

"Most people have more good to see in them than bad," she said. "But I'm no saint. I didn't see any good in Cyndi for a long time and I'm still not sure we will ever be friends . . . but . . ."

"But, you are still a good person. And I don't mind telling you my story. I want to tell you my story."

"Okay," she said, slowly.

"When I moved back here, when my father was ill, I had a girlfriend in Spain. We had been together for five years. I thought I would marry her. When Papa took ill I knew I had to come home and I asked Luisa to come with me. In fact I asked her to marry me and come with me."

"She said no?" Hope blurted.

"She said she would think about it. I know perhaps that should have been enough. I was asking a lot, after all – to move from her friends and to come with me here to Saint Jeannet. I didn't know how long I would be here, but Papa had no other family. He had friends, yes, like Betty, who did what she could to help. But he needed me. And I needed to be with him. Mama was already dead. I know this sounds silly, but the thought of being an orphan even though I was an adult . . . that was hard. That was sad for me."

Hope nodded. She couldn't really begin to understand what he was feeling. Both her parents were still alive and still very much in good health. Not to mention exceptionally annoying at times – badgering her to settle down and find a proper job and a decent man. Her mother had been at her all these years to move away from Dylan and set up on her own. "He's holding you back, love," she would say. "What man will want to come near you when you've a full-grown man sitting in your own living room hanging around like a bad smell?" They were a constant presence on the end of the phone and she couldn't really imagine them never being there. Poor Jean-Luc, it must have been hard for him.

"Luisa said she loved me and just needed time. Papa, he did not have time, so I came back to care for him and I waited for her response. But I knew she was never going to follow. If she had loved me, the way she had said she loved me, she wouldn't have had to think about it. Not after five years. She would have come, wouldn't she?"

Hope looked at him and nodded slowly, then shrugged her shoulders. "I imagine yes. If it was me . . . it had been me . . ."

He sighed. "She never actually said no. We just drifted apart until I realised we were past saving. She came here for Papa's funeral but it was not pleasant. It was . . . stilted . . . and I could see we had grown apart. So when she went home . . . well, we didn't have to say it. Not really. She told me she was sorry and I said I was too and that was that."

"I'm sorry," Hope said, acutely aware of all the sorrys hanging in the air, weighing the atmosphere down.

"Betty, she picked me up and dusted me off. She stopped me moping. She could be scary when she wanted to be – and very bossy. I think you get that from her," he added with a laugh.

"The scary part or the bossy part?"

"Both," he said, with a wink. "She meant a lot to me. She was a very good friend."

"Which is why you have helped her with all this?" Hope said, gesturing around her.

He nodded. "It was the very least I could do." He paused then took her hand. "You know, Hope, that is why I was cold and distant with you. Because for the first time since Luisa I could see someone who challenged me and made me laugh – and I was a little scared of that. I had to make sure this all went well for Betty's sake – I didn't mean to feel anything for you. I didn't want to mess things up."

She sat for a moment, it all making sense, and realised that far from messing things up he had actually helped fix so many things.

"This was definitely unexpected," she said, "but this whole trip has been unexpected. Everything about it. You were just an added bonus."

"You are kind. Lovely," he said with a wink. "Thank you for not running screaming from the madman with the sad story."

"And thank you for not running away from the madwoman with the sad story," she said in return, clinking her glass on his and reaching over to kiss him.

"You're welcome," he said, kissing her back. "You are very welcome."

Jean-Luc left shortly after eleven. He had some business to attend to, he said, but he promised to come back later. He had promised that he would take her to visit Betty's grave and say her final goodbyes before she left France the following day.

Hope sat by the pool contemplating just how hard it would be to walk away from the house when she heard movement on the terrace. Looking up, she saw Ava, looking definitely less pale than the last time she saw her, waving down.

"I'm back!" Ava called, as Hope watched Connor walk onto the terrace behind her and stop to take in the view.

Hope stood up and clambered up the stairs. "Can I hug you without breaking you?" she asked her cousin but didn't have the chance to wait for a reply before Ava pulled her into a bear hug before grimacing and stepping backwards.

Stricken, Hope stood back. "Oh Jesus, did I hurt you? You are okay, aren't you?"

Ava laughed and covered her chest with her arms. "Oh I'm fine. It's just the pregnancy boobs have kicked in. No one can get within twenty feet without me feeling as if someone has set them on fire."

"I call it one of nature's cruellest tricks," Connor said, smiling and reaching out to hug Hope. Even though she barely knew him, hugging him felt just right. They had all been through so much.

"Let me get you a tea, or a coffee, or a glass of water, and a soft seat?" Hope fussed, wanting to make sure her cousin took things nice and easy.

"I'm fine, honest," Ava said. "I'm enjoying getting moving about a little again."

"But do make it just a little," Connor said softly, kissing his wife on the shoulder. "You have to take it nice and easy, remember."

"I will," she said and turned to kiss her husband gently. "Now don't take this the wrong way but you kind of stink. Shower for you and then why not get a sleep?"

"I'm not going to argue with you," Connor said, rubbing his chin. "Just lead the way."

"I'll be back in a few," Ava mouthed as she turned to show Connor to the bedroom.

Hope watched them walk off, Connor's hand reaching out to hold his wife's and she smiled. Ava looked calmer than Hope had expected. She doubted she would be so calm in the circumstances. She would probably be lying, prone on the floor, letter in hand and an empty bottle of whiskey at her feet. Even though she didn't drink whiskey.

She sighed, stood up and padded back into the house and back into the study, where she sat down at the desk (the desk she would absolutely ask Jean-Luc to ship home for her just as soon as she worked out where home was) and she started to write again.

Dear Betty,

I don't know if there are any other letters hiding in this house. We've not found them and tomorrow we go home. I'm going to see you soon. Jean-Luc is going to bring me to your grave. I know you didn't really want any fuss and weren't bothered about visitors but it's something I want to do.

You've played a real blinder this trip. No one expected it. I didn't. You could have told me, you know. I'd have understood. I might have freaked out a bit, but I would have understood. I might have told you to tell Ava before now, because I think she would have liked to talk to you about it all.

I understand why you did what you did. Well, to be honest, I find it hard to think things were so very different not so long ago. I remember the Troubles, but was it really that bad? I'm embarrassed by how ignorant I am of it all.

All that said, I want to say thank you from the bottom of my heart. Thank you for bringing me here – for letting me see this place again. For taking me away from it all when, believe me, I really needed to get away from it all.

Thank you for letting me find myself. Thank you for trusting me to be there for Ava. I'm not sure anyone had such faith in me before.

Thank you for the amazing clothes and lovely wine and the remarkable sunsets and the chance to breathe again.

I wish you were here so I could say all this to your face. I wish I could hug you. I know so much more about you than before and I love you even more. You were amazing. You were the kind of person I want to be. The kind of person who did what she wanted to do and didn't let the bad times weigh her down and just kept going.

I hope I touch as many lives. I hope I make as many people happy. I won't let things get me down again. Betty. I promise.

Love,

Hope

xxxx

Sitting back, she folded the letter and put it in an envelope and decided she would take it and place it among the flowers on Betty's grave and she just knew her aunt would see and know she had been there.

Chapter 35

While Connor was in the shower Ava sat on the bed and stared out of the window. There was no trace of the trauma which this room had seen just two days before. Hope had clearly sorted out the bed, aired the room and had even put a small display of wildflowers from the garden in a vase on the dressing table. The letter which had blown her world clear apart was sitting on the bedside table, folded and back in its envelope. She put her hand on top of it, not sure if she wanted to read it again.

Closing her eyes and asking for some sort of guidance from someone – anyone – she opened them to notice the sun streaming through the windows.

"Oh Betty, you mad old bat. You should have said!"

She lifted the letter and read it again, poring over the words. She felt less sick to her stomach this time. She did feel desperately sad for Betty. She stopped at the section about the box of baby clothes, the knitted cardigan and she knew that even though she hated attics and even though Connor would kill her for even attempting it she would have to go back there. Putting the letter back on the bedside table she listened to the rush of water from the shower in the ensuite and decided there was no time like the present.

The stairway to the attic was old and rickety. It had got no less rickety in the last few days so Ava moved slowly and carefully.

Even though the sun was streaming through the skylight in the attic, it still felt a little cold and scary.

Ha, she thought to herself, scary my ass. I've seen scary these last few days. I've stared down the barrel at scary. This is just an attic. With a box of clothes. Which I have to look at.

Crouched on a box she pulled the dust-covered sticky tape from the box marked *Baby Things* and opened it. A fine layer of tissue paper protected what lay beneath. There were Babygros, a few vests, a small knitted hat in crisp white. Below another layer of tissue paper was a white, soft, tiny cardigan with pale yellow buttons sewn on carefully. Was this the first thing she had worn? She lifted it and held it to her cheek before sitting it on her knee and marvelling at the smallness of it. She had worn it and Betty had knit it, each stitch an intricate declaration of love. She stroked it, feeling the dedication and longing in every knit one, purl one, every dropped stitch.

Under the cardigan was an envelope, yellowed and battered – its contents had clearly been spilled out many times. Tipping them out, there was a small, equally yellowed, plastic band the circumference of a 50p piece. In spidery handwriting there was a declaration that this baby, born on October 16, 1976, belonged to Cora Mullen and weighed in at 7lbs and 1oz. There was a card, gaudy and glittery, bearing the message *Thank You* which was signed from Cora to Betty. "*There are no words,*" it said. No, there were no words but there were shite cards. A thank you? In glitter with a big fecking bunny on the front? Hardly seemed a fair swap for a baby. Ava choked through her tears – fair play to her mum though. Manners to the end. A thank-you card for every occasion.

Then there was a photo – a faded polaroid in which she could make out someone who looked for all intents and purposes like Ava holding a baby and smiling, not at the camera but at the baby. With a thud, she realised she was looking at Betty, in her hospital bed, holding her. There was such love in Betty's eyes that it took her breath away. Turning the photo over she saw, in Betty's handwriting *Ava Louise and I, October 17, 1976.*

"Oh God love you," Ava said, "it must have been so hard." She thought of her own first few days with Maisie, how she marvelled at every wrinkle, crinkle and crease. How she couldn't get enough of the softness of her cheek against her face. How the very smell of her breath, soft and gentle on her face made her feel more alive than she ever had done.

Wiping the tears from her cheeks, she reached back into the box and pulled out one more envelope – this time crisp white, with her name written alongside two kisses.

My darling girl,

If you have opened this then you can't be angry with me. Not really angry. Thank you. I'm sorry to have done this to you in this way. I'm sorry to have done this to Cora. Please don't be angry with her. She was a lifesaver to me – literally. And you were a lifesaver to her.

I want you to know I never forgot you. I thought of you often. Every year, every event, every birthday and every Christmas. I wrote letters and cards but kept them – which is all a bit much for you now. Mr Semple has them in storage should you need them. It might be a bit much for me to expect you to want them, but they are there all the same. As is a card for Maisie. I bought it but couldn't send it when she was born. You will still pass on my rings to her, won't you? Even if you are very cross with me.

I wanted you to know some things. When we tried for a baby, Claude and I, it was never to replace you. I suppose had we been blessed, all this might have come out sooner. We would have told our child about the sister it had back in Derry.

The day you were born, Ava, was forever etched in my memory. Your mam was the first to hold you, but after she had been shooed away by the nurses I had time with you to cuddle you and tell you all my secrets. I loved you. I loved you from the first moment you were placed in my arms.

Letting go wasn't easy, but it was the right thing to do.
You were always in my heart. Always. You never left.
I hope you can forgive me. I hope that you can think of me fondly.

With much love,
Betty
xxxx

Clutching the cardigan and the letter to her, she climbed back down the rickety stairwell to the bedroom where Connor was sitting on the bed, towel-drying his hair.

"There's another letter," she said. "I went and looked."

He glanced at the cardigan and looked back at her. All she could do was shrug her shoulders. "I'd like to bring this home," she said, handing him the cardigan and sitting down beside him. "And I'd like to take the crib too."

He nodded, wrapped his arms around her and she allowed herself to sink into them. *I'm still me*, she thought, *but a part of me will always be here.*

"So," Ava said, sitting on the swing on the terrace with her feet curled under her. "What have I missed? Has it been terribly boring? Did you go to the market? Tell all."

She watched as her cousin smiled brightly and she had a notion there was good deal of nice gossip to hear.

"I have spent the vast majority of the last two days in the company of Jean-Luc who, as it happens, is a very nice kisser. And who, as it happens, likes me a bit. And who, as it happens, is a very considerate lover."

Ava almost choked on her glass of iced water. Seriously? Hope had gone full circle from pining over her man back in Belfast and complaining that Jean-Luc was messing with her head to having sex with him?

"You had sex with him?" Ava asked, just to be sure.

"Four times," Hope said with a wink. "And he stayed till morning – which is, in fairness, when the fourth time happened. And we talked and he's lovely. He likes that word 'lovely'. We said that word a lot. And not once did he call me Hopeless."

"Who calls you Hopeless?" Ava asked, shifting in her seat.

"Dylan. It's one of his pet names for me."

Shocked at how anyone could think that was an acceptable name to be called by someone purporting to be anyone's best friend, Ava tried to hide her reaction. She was starting to see that not only was Dylan not the right man for her cousin to be in love with but that he really, perhaps, wasn't a very nice person at all. Yes, she was definitely taking against him.

"Well, if you will forgive me, he sounds like an eejit and I can't believe he would speak to you like that."

"Ah, it was all in good fun. Well, when it started it was all in good fun. I suppose I didn't see it so much like that recently, especially when Cyndi moved in and I did feel hopeless . . ." She trailed off and looked a little sad and Ava wanted happy, bubbly, Hope back.

"But Jean-Luc, he never called you Hopeless?"

"Oh no, he was all down with the *ma cherie's* and all that lovely *ooh la la* French stuff. Actually, oh Ava, he's had his heart broken in the past and has been scared to let anyone in again."

"And he has let you in?"

"I think, as we discussed, he let me in four times," Hope said with a laugh. "Look, it's not love in a bucket but we've had a lovely time together. It has been great but I think, maybe we have just been a stepping-stone for each other – proof that we can move on. I don't know if that will turn into anything else because, Ava, I've decided I'm doing it. I'm definitely doing it. I'm packing in my tiny wee home office and I'm leaving my house in Glenville Road, and Dylan and his shagging girlfriend and I'm travelling the world."

"Wow!" Ava was genuinely impressed. She was delighted, however, to realise that she wasn't jealous as she would have been a few days before. She was happy for Hope and happy for herself. "I'm impressed. That sounds amazing. You know, Connor and I were talking and we're going to make some pretty big changes too. We're not entirely sure how we're going to do it, but we talked, and talked, and talked and I think we might just have a little of ourselves back."

"I'm delighted for you, Ava. So happy."

"And I'm happy for you."

"So you should be. I just had sex with a very handsome man. I couldn't be happier for me if I tried!" Hope laughed before her face darkened just that little bit. "He's calling over later. I'm not sure how you feel about this, but we're going to go and visit Betty's grave."

Ava felt herself shiver. The thought of Betty's grave made her feel odd. This was where she would confront her, she supposed.

"Would you mind if I came along?" she asked, thinking that she really needed to go even though part of her dreaded it. "And can you maybe come and hold my hand?"

"Of course, darling, of course," Hope said, coming to sit beside her and take her hand.

"I'm a bit scared," Ava confessed, brushing a tear from her face. "But this is something I need to do, isn't it?"

"Only if you feel ready."

"We're going home tomorrow. I'd need to feel ready. It would only annoy me if I went home without doing it. And I do have things I want to say to her. Even with all that has gone on I want to thank her for giving me a good life. And I want to thank her for bringing me here – more than anything it has given me the chance to realise what I really want and what really matters." She saw Hope sniff and she hugged her close. "I'm grateful that she brought us together. Connor and I both are. And I'm glad I came with you. You know, when we were thrown together I was a bit apprehensive. I didn't know you bar hearing talk about you and your big glam life and I was sure that you would think I was the most godawful boring prude on the planet." Her faced blazed as she spoke.

"Truth was," Hope replied, "I was kind of scared you would be the most godawful boring prude on the planet. All I'd heard from my mum was about my perfect cousin and her gorgeous house and her beautiful child. All perfect, gorgeous, beautiful. I was afraid I would either want to kill myself from feeling completely inferior or kill you for your smuggy ways. But the truth is, you don't have too many smuggy ways."

"And *you* don't think I'm a self-pitying martyr?" Ava asked, figuring that even though she had decided Karen was most definitely not going to factor in her life any time in the future, she would test Karen's theories on someone who had got to know her really quite intimately over the course of the last week.

"You what? Self-pitying? I see none of that. Jesus, Ava, even when . . . when . . . you know . . . the big scary thing happened, and then the second big scary thing happened you didn't feel sorry for yourself. You worried about the baby and about Connor and about Maisie and even about me. You're the least self-pitying, self-absorbed person I know! Who told you that?"

"Just a friend. Well, an ex-friend as it happens," Ava said, wiping away a few more non-hormonal tears from her cheeks.

"Well, what the frig would she know anyway?" Hope said. "Silly old boot!"

A soft warm breeze tousled Ava's hair as she walked through the lines of perfectly manicured plots until they arrived at a simple black granite stone bearing both Betty's and Claude's names and the dates of their births. In fresh gold lettering the words *Do not stand at my grave and cry, I am not there, I did not die* were etched into the stone.

"Betty wanted that," Hope said. "She never really wanted anyone to come here. She didn't want people to think of her like this. As a plot of grass and an imposing stone. She loved that poem. She loved to think that once she was gone she would still be around in some kind of a way."

"Like a not-scary ghost," Ava said, wiping away a tear and laughing.

She knelt down, feeling the need to kneel down before she fell down, and placed a simple posy of flowers from the garden at the headstone. "I know you said she didn't like flowers being left, but I wanted to leave something."

"I have something too," Hope said, reaching into her pocket and taking out the envelope containing the letter she had written earlier. "I figured Betty left us so many letters it was only right to leave her one in return, even if she won't ever read it."

"That's a nice idea," Ava said. "I'm sure she would love it. I can't believe we didn't come here sooner."

"Oh I can," Hope said, crouching down to draw her fingers over the lettering. "This is lovely, but she's right. She's not here. She's back at the house – in the garden, in the attic, in the village, in the air. She's in you, pet. This is nothing, except some remains and she would hate to be remembered like this."

"Do you think she is with him again?" Ava asked.

Instinctively Hope put her arm around Ava. She felt like she could do with a little bit of protecting. Letting Ava lay her head softly on her shoulder, she soothed her. "With Claude? Oh I'd really like to think so. I'd like to think they are kicking up a storm up there – laughing and dancing and having the craic. And singing *Danny Boy* as loudly as she can and deafening all the angels."

Ava laughed and sniffed and Hope felt herself overcome with emotion.

"I can't believe I'm starting to feel so emotional leaving this place," she said. "I didn't expect this. I've been here before and left without looking back, but . . ." She trailed off, unable to find the words to say what she wanted to say.

"I know," Ava said, hugging her back. "You know, we should go back to the house and give it a proper send-off. Of course I can't drink and I'll mostly just be sitting on a comfy chair taking it easy, but we should go back and give it one last big bye-bye and treat it to one last rendition of *Danny Boy*."

"Have you heard me singing?"

"On a drunken occasion yes," Ava smiled.

"Then you will know that my rendition of *Danny Boy* would not be considered to be a treat by anyone. But, with a half a bottle of plonk in me I'd be willing to give it a go." She stood up and helped Ava to stand. "And I promise, absolutely, not to attempt any early 90s hits or in fact anything other than that one verse of *Danny Boy*. Even then, you'll have to help me hit the high notes."

"I'll do my best," Ava said as the pair turned to walk towards where Connor and Jean-Luc were standing in the early evening sunshine.

Hope didn't look back as she walked away from Betty's graveside. She didn't feel the need. She just smiled as she walked back to where Jean-Luc was waiting and allowed him to pull her into a hug just as Connor pulled Ava into a hug.

"Do you want to stay a little longer?" Jean-Luc asked.

"No. No, I'm fine. We're fine. But we want to go back to the house and open a bottle of something and toast Betty for one last time on the terrace and we would love it, and think it only right, if you joined us." She looked at Ava who smiled.

"Yes, please, Jean-Luc."

"I would like that," he said.

"Great," Hope said, shaking off the emotion that was threatening to choke her. "Great. Let's go then. I'll open the first bottle and, tell you what, I might finally try on one of those dresses?"

"Dresses?" Jean-Luc asked, his eyebrow raised and a wicked smile spreading across his face.

"Only the finest," Hope laughed. "And if you're lucky you might even see a very special jumpsuit."

Ava was sitting on the bed watching Hope as she dressed.

"Are you sure I can't tempt you to try a dress on?" she asked as she zipped up the red satin number. She had piled her hair onto the top of her head, letting her curls fall softly, framing her sunkissed face, and she was revelling in her new-found tan – not to mention absolutely delighted that the dress was zipping up and not screaming for mercy.

"If I even tried I would bust the seams and put undue pressure on this little mite – and given that I have spent the last few days building up a lovely pallor I'm not sure I wouldn't just look like a washed-out rag. I do, however, have my very lovely shoes." Ava clicked her heels together and flashed her purple satin shoes.

"Do you know what I think? Dorothy's ruby slippers can kiss your ass. Those shoes are amazing."

"I know!" Ava said enthusiastically. "And she wore them to a funeral! I hope I'm still wearing ridiculously impractical shoes to funerals all the rest of my days, although if the truth be told these are the first pair of ridiculously impractical shoes I have ever owned."

"If you are going to wait thirty-four years for fabulous shoes, then those shoes are definitely the kind of pair worth waiting for."

"I wholeheartedly agree," Ava said, raising her glass of orange juice towards Hope, who was sipping from a glass of fine champagne.

Hope turned to clink her glass against her cousin's. "Whadd'ya think?" she asked, swinging her hips and praying her boobs stayed put where they were meant to.

"I think," Ava said, "that Jessica Rabbit can kiss your mighty fine ass! Oh to think someone very closely biologically related to me wore this! Clearly I did not inherit her ass." She was laughing as she spoke.

"Your ass is fine, my dear," Hope said. "But she was incredibly glam, wasn't she? Wow, she had style – apart from the yellow jump suit, naturally." She turned to look at herself in the mirror and was blown away by how good she looked. She had always avoided satin like the plague, convinced that the material would make her look as though she was due to give birth to a team of baby elephants. But Ava was right on this occasion. On this occasion she looked amazing – like a sultry, sexy 50s movie star with a glint in her eye that she hadn't seen in a long time. Smoothing down the dress and winking at her reflection, she raised her glass to the mirror and smiled. "Here's looking at you, Ms Scott! The world is going to know your name."

It was then, filled with the confidence of several glasses of wine, that she turned to Ava and began to serenade her with a rather impressive (or so she thought) version of the theme from *Fame* complete with dance moves which weren't as easy as they would have been had she not been wearing a full-length gown.

"I'm sure we haven't seen the best of you yet and I'm sure we will all remember your name," Ava said, laughing, standing up to dance (just a little bit) in her purple satin shoes before lying back on the bed as Hope continued her dance routine.

When she was finished and slightly breathless, she manoeuvred herself carefully, so as not to tear the dress, onto the bed beside Ava and clinked her glass on her cousin's again.

"It's been very nice getting to know you," she said.

"Oh, I agree. You've been very lucky," Ava teased. "I am a babe!"

"A complete and utter babe."

"With amazing preggo boobs," Ava said, glancing downwards.

"Yes, they are indeed amazing. But don't take this the wrong way, they are not as fabulous as your shoes."

"Oh I know that," Ava said. "The shoes are truly amazing."

Both descended into giggles and held hands as they lay on the bed before Hope spoke again. "Do you think we should go out there? The men will be expecting us?"

"They seem to be getting on just fine," Hope said, thinking of how they had left Connor and Jean-Luc discussing world politics and the recession.

When they had got back to the house, Jean-Luc had offered to cook dinner and both girls had been only too keen to agree.

"You can spend time outside and I will, as they say, slave over a hot cooker for you?" he said.

"You know, the old Hope would have argued with you and insisted you sit down while I cooked but the new Hope is going to throw caution to the wind."

He took her hand and gently kissed her palm before looking deep into her eyes in a way that made her feel a little weak at the knees. "I like that you are throwing caution to the wind. And with my cooking, that may be needed. It is not true that Frenchmen are great chefs. But I will do my best."

She kissed him lightly on the lips, letting her kiss linger longer than she intended but enjoying the feel of his lips against hers.

"Your best is fine by me. Your best is really very impressive."

"You have not tasted my chicken," he said with a grin and Hope found herself laughing.

"I'm sure it will be fine, but I intend to have a glass or two of champagne first so, I can let you into a little secret, I'm not really going to be bothered about how it tastes anyway."

"You are funny, Hope Scott."

She revelled in his laughter. "I hope funny ha ha and not funny peculiar?" she asked and the blank look on his face let her know that some things were always going to be lost in translation.

"So," she said, "champagne!" Lifting a chilled bottle from the fridge, she popped the cork and poured three glasses, handing one to Jean-Luc and putting the other two, plus a flute of orange juice on a tray to carry out to the terrace where Connor and Ava were sitting.

"I'll come back and keep you company," she said but he shook his head.

"No, go on. Enjoy the view. I cook better on my own."

"You may just be the perfect man," she said with a wink and walked out.

After dinner, when the sun had set and the night air had become a little cooler, Hope sat on the terrace, close enough to Jean-Luc that when she wanted to – which was a lot – she could reach over to touch him. Ava and Connor sat on the swing-seat, wrapped around each other as they chatted. The chiminea gave off a warm glow and the terrace was basking in the light and scent of citronella candles mixed with the delicious aroma of Betty's herb garden.

The wine was flowing and the chat was becoming more animated and it was around the time Hope and Ava were regaling the men with tales from the attic that they decided the fashion show was a must. They hadn't expected to leave the men for quite so long but once they were locked in Hope's room, with the fabulous shoes and dresses, time got away from them until, dressed to impress – Ava in her pyjamas and her gorgeous deep-purple shoes and Hope in her stunning gown – they walked, arms linked, back onto the terrace.

"*Ta-da!*" Hope crooned, twirling around while Ava tip-toed her way back to the swing seat where she sat down and wiggled her toes at Connor.

"I think the fresh air might be getting to you," he said with a grin.

"Not at all," Hope said. Turning to face Jean-Luc, she smiled. "What do you think?"

"I think," he said softly, "that you are just like a vision."

Hope stood for a moment and let his words wash over her. She had never been told she looked like vision before. She had been told she looked 'a right sight' on several occasions but never a vision. Looking at him, focusing on his eyes and the warmth in them, she breathed out and tried not to brush the compliment away or tell him he was off his head, or in need of glasses or similar.

"Thank you," she mouthed and decided there and then was the perfect time to throw caution to the wind and walk over and kiss him square on the lips.

The cheer from the other side of the terrace let her know she was absolutely doing the right thing. Tomorrow she would face her real life once again when she flew back into a no-doubt rainy and dull Belfast but tonight she was enjoying the buzz of feeling as if she was finally back in the driving seat of her own life.

"Did you ever hear Betty sing *Oh Danny Boy?*" she asked.

Jean-Luc shook his head.

"Oh but it was one of her favourites. I remember so vividly her crooning it to me when she had one too many glasses of wine. Ava and I promised that we would sing this one. I would advise you that if you are at all of a sensitive nature you would do well to leave the immediate vicinity or cover your ears. However, if you are willing to accept the following performance, and I use the word 'performance' loosely, in the spirit in which it is intended then please, enjoy."

"I'll take my chances," Jean-Luc said, sipping from his glass of wine before resting it on the table.

"Did you have to say that?" Connor butted in. "I thought you might be with me on this one and run for the hills!"

Ava laughed and nudged her husband square in the ribs before Hope threw him a bad look.

"I could *not* like you, Connor Campbell, no matter how good you are to my lovely cousin."

"Don't worry," he replied with a smirk, "I'll take my punishment like a man. I'll sit here and listen and only complain once and, trust me, I'll will my ears not to bleed at the high notes."

"A real comedian, this husband of yours, isn't he?"

"Why do you think I married him?" Ava said, reaching out to kiss him. "Although if he slags off my singing one more time I may have to divorce him."

Jean-Luc laughed and Hope looked at him, thinking this was the most relaxed she had seen him all week. And he was even more handsome when he looked relaxed. And even more sexy. She could have easily told Danny Boy to stick it and begged him to take her to bed one more time but no, she reminded herself gently, this was about Betty and it wouldn't perhaps be respectful to her late aunt to spend her last few hours lost in a passionate embrace with Jean-Luc, even though she knew Betty had a lot of time for him.

Okay, she thought, focus. Settling herself, she walked to sit beside Ava and Connor on the swing-seat.

"I should warn you," Ava said, "Connor is right. He didn't marry me for my singing skills."

"You should know," said Hope, "that Betty didn't have a note in her head either but what she lacked in talent she made up for in enthusiasm. We'll just give it our best."

So together they launched into a rendition of *Danny Boy*, which no one would ever forget. When they were done she noticed a tear of emotion in Jean-Luc's perfect green eyes – she just wasn't sure if it was a tear of sadness or of mirth. She liked to think the former.

An hour later the haze of the bottle of wine was upon Hope and the flames had gone from the chiminea, the last embers glinting now and then and the smokey smell hanging in the air. Her head was rested on Jean-Luc's shoulder and Ava and Connor were lost in their own conversation.

"I'm going to miss you," he said, softly. "Strange, I know. I have only known you a few days but I know I am going to miss you."

She revelled in his words, and realised she was going to miss him as well. Maybe she would come back some day on her travels and see him. Suddenly the thought of leaving the house the next day was not the only thing which made her feel emotional and teary.

"I'm going to miss you too," she said, deciding that would do. She didn't want to start launching into the where and the why. She was just absolutely astounded that just a week after she had walked out of a house in Belfast convinced she would never, could never, love anyone else other than Dylan she was having such strong feelings for a man she had only just met. "Maybe I'll come back some time for a visit, if you'll have me?"

It was then he started and swore under his breath. "The letter," he said.

"The letter?"

"I have a letter for you both from Betty. I was to give it to you on your last day. It's in the car. It's after midnight – that counts as your last day, doesn't it?" With that he was gone, leaving Hope sitting by herself and Connor and Ava looking on a little confused.

"He can run fast," Ava said.

"I have a letter for him," Hope confided. "I'm supposed to give it to him after he gives us this letter."

"That Betty was a crafty old bat, wasn't she?" Connor said with a grin.

"You have no idea," Ava said, standing up and walking towards the door. "I wonder what it says?"

"Lord only knows what great big declarations she has made in this one. I'll tell you something, when we go home, I'll miss those letters. Do you think we found them all?"

Ava shrugged her shoulders. "Maybe. Probably not. But I think we found the ones we needed to."

"I think you're right," Hope said. "Would have been nice to find a few more though. I'll miss her and her batty ways."

"Every time you look at yourself in that dress you will think of her," Ava said.

"No, every time I look at myself in this dress I will think how amazing I look, and then maybe I'll think of Betty," she said with a laugh.

But the truth was she was nervous. She didn't know what the last letter from Betty would say and she was scared it would feel like a big, formal and final goodbye. She also had no idea what

Jean-Luc's letter said or how he might react to it. It made her feel a little uneasy if the truth be told. Especially with three-quarters of a bottle of finest wine in her.

He walked back in holding one of the white envelopes they had come to know so well and held it out.

"Which of you ladies would like to read the letter first?"

Hope suddenly felt reluctant and shook her head, turning to Ava who was looking at her for some guidance.

"You do it," Hope said.

"How about we read it together?" Ava offered gently. "Sure haven't we found these letters are much less scary read together?"

Hope felt her heart beat a little faster. "I'm not sure," she stuttered, sitting down on the green tweed chair and holding her head in her hands.

"It will be okay," Ava soothed, "I mean there can't be any more big confessions. She's not your mum too," she said with a wink while budging in beside her cousin and putting her arm around her.

Hope watched as Ava took control of the situation, in the way she had always imagined Ava to be able to take control of a situation. She admired that. She felt vaguely jealous of it. She realised that when she was travelling the world on her own she would absolutely have to be like Ava. She must ask her how she did it. Focusing again on the letter and Ava, she noticed a slight tremble in her hand as she tore open the envelope and revealed the sheet of crisp, white paper with their beloved aunt's handwriting.

"Here goes," Ava said.

"Here goes indeed," Hope replied, a deep breath.

Chapter 36

My darling girls,

They say that goodbye is the hardest word to say . . . well, actually, I think they say sorry is the hardest word. Ironic that in these letters I've had to say both.

This is the big goodbye though – the last letter. I almost don't want to write it. I'm not ready to let go. But time isn't on my side – not this time.

So I'll start with the sorry. I'm sorry if this week hasn't been at all what you expected. I'm sorry for the upset I've caused but I trust you understand my reasons.

I'm sorry for bringing you here under false pretences – but you understand why I needed you both to feel close to me.

And now for goodbye . . .

God, they say houses are only bricks and mortar and it is the people inside them which make the memories. I suppose that is true – to a large extent. This house wouldn't have been a home without Claude. But you know, I like to think of it as more than that. I know that all sounds strange. I've asked you girls to come here and pack away my life and my memories. I've asked you to get rid of all those things I don't need any more and I'm okay with that. I'm even okay with handing over the rings I wore on my fingers for all those years. Ava, I'm happy to have handed over those shoes. They deserve someone to wear them until they are ready to fall apart. I have a feeling you may well do that.

But this house. This house is too hard to let go of.

Ava, my darling, this house is yours now. I can't tell you what to do with it, but I'd like to think you will come back here, often. A letting agent is appointed, through Jean-Luc, to let the house out when you are not here. All proceeds will go to you, and to Maisie. Mr Semple has the paperwork and he will be in touch in due course.

You can come here every year. You can, please, bring your family. You can use this house as a base to travel around France or you can stay here and soak up the sunshine on the terrace. All I ask is that when you come here, just once, you stand on the terrace and remember Claude and me. And remember how much I loved you and how much I didn't want to let you go.

That is not all. Hope, this is for you also. What I would love is that if both of you had a little break in life – just something which could make your life easier. I didn't leave this world a multi-millionaire or anything like that but I did have something – something a little more than just this house and something more than a pair of purple satin shoes – even if they are the most fabulous shoes in the world.

I have a life insurance policy and some shares. It will amount to around £100,000 each.

I'm sorry for not telling you before. I'm sorry for not trusting you with the information but I wanted to do whatever I could to make sure you both came here without distractions.

As with everything, my gift comes with a condition. The condition is that you use the money to do something you will always remember. Do something which makes life memorable. Life is too short not to be memorable.

With that, my girls, I bid you au revoir. Please know that I was thinking about you, always and everywhere, in my last weeks.

Live well,

All my love,
Betty
xxx

There was a silence in the room as the girls tried to absorb all that Betty had said. Ava felt her heart thud in her chest and she looked to Hope for some indication of how she should react.

Hope was staring at the letter, her mouth open, her eyes streaming.

"Oh shit," Hope said.

Ava looked at her, puzzled, her mind racing with 101 things. There was such sorrow that this was her parting shot from Betty but so much else to try and process. As she heard Hope repeat the "Oh shit," she thought how inappropriate that was. Her reaction – her internal voice was screaming every swear word and every cheer and every expression of grief she could think of. This would change her life. Her life was changed. Her life was never going to be the same. Everything about this week had changed her. But this, this was something more. This was in basic terms the answer to both her and Connor's prayers. This was everything. This was a holiday. This was not having to say goodbye to this house where she had finally connected with the woman who had given her life. This was money – money which could pay off a mortgage, or help Connor set up his business, or allow her to have time off with her babies. Things which would, undoubtedly, change her life for the absolute better. Things that would lift the pressure. Which would allow her to be her and not just some shadow of who she used to be – some person who was busy being everything to everyone else.

"Oh shit," she said as well, turning to Hope who was shaking her head – her hands shaking as she re-read the letter.

"Oh my God," Hope said, looking up, her face tear-stained while a smile broke broadly across it. "Oh my God. Can you believe it? Can you really believe it? Can you?"

She looked almost comical, there in her ball gown, her hair slightly tousled and her lips stained red from the wine, but she looked stunning, her smile as wide as it could be even though there were tears streaming down her face.

"What are you going to do?" Ava muttered, finding her voice without including swear words.

"See the world. See all of it. Write. And be happy. And be so fecking happy!" Hope said, standing up and punching the air. "Betty!" she called. "I love you. I frigging love you!"

Ava just sat, still feeling the shock wash over her, watching her cousin now dance around the room until she was aware of Connor and Jean-Luc smiling at them.

Ava looked at her husband, trying to find the words to tell him that for now their financial worries were greatly alleviated and that she had a feeling things were going to be just fine.

"Jean-Luc has told me," he said, walking over towards her and pulling her into a hug. Whispering gently in her ear he told her he loved her and that he didn't care what she did with the money as long as it made her happy. She pulled back from him and smiled, drinking in his eyes, his face and the softness of his smile. "We'll be happy," she said. "We'll be very happy."

Hope stopped dancing and looked at her new lover. "You knew? You knew about the house and the inheritance?"

"Not all the details. Just some. But even though she is gone I wouldn't dare cross Betty. She made me vow to keep it to myself. She made me promise. I knew if I broke her promise that she would come back and haunt me."

Hope thought of the letter, the letter she had in her room for Jean-Luc and she laughed again. Yes, Betty definitely always could come back to haunt someone. "You know," she said with a wink, "I think she has. Hang on."

Padding to her room, her heart still thumping and her mind still racing, she delved into the bedside table and pulled out the envelope. Strangely she felt jealous as she looked at the envelope. To the best of her knowledge she had seen her last letter from Betty. Jean-Luc was still to delve into her aunt's world. Holding the letter to her, she breathed in and tried to imagine Betty writing it – trying to imagine the comfort her aunt had felt from putting these words together in her last few months.

The cheering gone from her head and her heart, she sat on the bed and whispered, "I will make you proud, Betty. I'll come back here every year and every year I'll make you proud. Thank you."

Walking back to the living room she found Connor and Ava were alone. "He's gone down to the pool," Ava said, gently. "He seemed a little overwhelmed."

"I think we are all a little overwhelmed," Hope said, suddenly aware she was still wearing a vintage ball gown and that she was a little squiffy, although in fairness the contents of Betty's letter had done a good job in sobering her up.

"I'd better go down there," she said, to herself as much as to anyone else.

"Good luck," Ava said gently and Hope turned and walked into the night air, following the flickering light of the tealights down the steps towards the pool where Jean-Luc was sitting, looking over the water.

He turned to look at her silently, shrugging his shoulders as she gestured towards him with the letter.

"I was not expecting this," he said softly.

"None of us were expecting any of this," Hope said, as she handed him the letter. "Perhaps I'll leave you to it."

"*Non*," he said, "Please stay. Please."

She nodded. "Yes, I'll stay."

"Okay," he said, carefully opening the letter and unfolding it.

He laughed and then breathed in deeply as he read what Betty had written, before handing the letter to Hope.

My darling Jean-Luc,

You know how I love you. You know how you are like the son I never had. Well, you know I would never hurt you and only want good things for you. Please heed my advice on this one – and I hope I'm not way off target (but somehow I think I'm right on this).

She is not Luisa. Trust her. Allow yourself to love again. And please don't hurt her.

With all my love,
Betty
x

Chapter 37

Hope and Ava were sitting on the terrace eating breakfast. Connor had said he would leave them to their girly chatter and had disappeared inside with a book in his hand. Jean-Luc would drive Hope to the airport. Ava and Connor would be taking the hire car. Ava had known there was no point in trying to persuade Hope to come with them. She might have been pretty self-absorbed the last few days but she knew enough to realise that Jean-Luc had changed her friend in a million ways. She didn't look sad any more and when she spoke of Dylan she didn't have a pained expression on her face. That, Ava reckoned, was a good thing. They had wandered back from the pool the night before lost in each other and that morning they had been lost in their own conversation wandering around the pool together, chatting animatedly.

"I take it you will see him again?" Ava asked.

Hope smiled. "One day at a time, sweet Ava. But yes, I think so. He's been longing for a break for a while. He devoted so much of his life to caring for his father and then for Betty. He said there is nothing holding him back now. He's going to join me for some of my travels."

"So you are going to travel then?"

Hope nodded confidently. "Without a doubt. I've nothing stopping me now. And with a companion who actually wants to be with me. Yes, short of a major catastrophe I'll be travelling. But you will stay in touch, won't you? I don't want to sound like a desperate primary three but – you will still be my friend?"

"Of course," Ava laughed, reaching out to hug her cousin. "Of course I will. How could I not? After all we've been through? It's been something!"

"It sure has," Hope said, clinking her mug against Ava's. "It sure has."

Opening her eyes she breathed out just as the taxi pulled up to that little terraced house on the outskirts of Belfast. Hope had been replaying the last moments she had spent with Jean-Luc, how he had kissed her and told her to never, ever feel she didn't deserve the very best ever again. She had felt as if she were floating on air as he had promised to stay in touch and arrange their first trip. That said, as the taxi man barked the fare at her in a broad Belfast accent and she scrambled through her purse for what little sterling she had stashed away and thought of walking through the front door that wasn't really hers any more, she felt grounded back to earth with a bang.

"Keep the change," she smiled at the taxi man who looked down at the notes she had pressed into his hand and grunted.

"I'll be careful not to spend it all in the one shop, will I, love?"

She had half a notion to tell him to shag off but decided not to. Soon enough she would be away from Belfast and grumpy taxi-drivers so instead she just smiled at him and said "I guess so" before hauling her case out of the boot unassisted and walking to her front door.

It was mid-afternoon and she knew Dylan and – by default Cyndi – should be in. Whether or not they would be up would be another matter but nonetheless they would be there. She shivered at the notion she might well walk in on them in the act, but she reminded herself that for now at least this was still her house.

Walking in, she knew things had changed. There were new cushions on the sofa. New tea and coffee canisters sat on the worktops and the fug of a cheap airfreshener swamped her. On the mantelpiece, where it had every right to be, was a picture of Dylan and Cyndi. Thankfully it was of their faces and not their feet. She sat on the sofa, looked around her, sensed how things had changed and smiled. Different didn't need to be bad. Different didn't need to be scary.

She walked through the kitchen and switched on the kettle, instinctively reaching for the cupboard where Dylan kept his not-so-secret stash of chocolate. Reaching in, she pulled out a packet of cream crackers and a Milky Bar. This must be the work of Cyndi, she thought, as the kettle started to whistle. Dylan and she didn't eat plain biscuits, let alone crackers. And as for white chocolate? Fuck that! White chocolate was for wimps, or Ballymena folk. Eyeing the bar with the disgust it deserved before throwing it to the back of cupboard, she dropped a tea bag into a mug and opened the fridge to find a carton of skimmed milk staring back at her – mocking her even. No, she definitely needed to leave. Then again she desperately needed a cup of tea so she poured the watery anaemic-looking liquid into her cup before topping it up with boiling water.

She was just swearing at how "someone" (being Cyndi with a Y and a fecking I) had rearranged the cutlery in the drawer, when she heard his voice behind her.

"Want to make me one?"

She turned to see him smile and in that instant every second of their friendship flashed through her mind.

"For old times' sake?" she said.

He shrugged. "Surely old times' sake requires something stiffer than a cup of tea?"

"It's a bit early for drinking," she said.

"But it isn't too early for chocolate biscuits," he offered, delving into the back of her cupboard. "I hope you don't mind. I used this as a bit of a hiding space. Had to keep Cyndi happy."

She smiled and took two biscuits from the packet.

"You're really going to go, aren't you?" he said.

"I think I already have," she said. Part of her – but just a small part which lived right next to her ego – wanted him to start begging her not to go while declaring his undying love for her, but a bigger part just wanted him to be happy for her.

"I wish you wouldn't," he said, "But I understand. I wish it could have been different."

"I don't," Hope replied confidently. "There was a time I did – about a week ago – but I suppose if you and I were going to work, we would have worked a long time ago. And Cyndi, well, she's not so bad . . . for a countrywoman . . . and she makes you happy."

"She does," he said with a smile.

"That's fine then," she smiled back. "But if you could wait till I'm fully moved out before you 'christen' my bedroom then that would be good."

The smirk on his face told her she should have laid down that particular ground rule before she went away.

"You will be okay, won't you?" he asked as she sat at the table.

"I'll be better than okay. Have you time for me to tell you about someone special? And about my very mad aunt, her lovely house and my new-found inheritance?"

He smiled, sat down opposite her and said, "For you, my only Hope, I always have time."

Ava walked up the path to her mother's house, bone-tired from the flight and feeling more than a little nervous. So nervous in fact that she felt sick to her stomach. Which could, of course, be morning sickness which would be a comfort. Or it could be because she was going to come face to face with her mother for the first time since she learned the truth about her birth.

She had spoken to Cora on the phone earlier – it had all been very matter of fact and typically Ava – filled with making arrangements and plans. Cora had booked her an appointment for the following day and had offered to keep Maisie so that Connor could go with her. She had even offered to keep Maisie overnight to allow Ava to recover from travelling and to ensure she could take it easy, but Ava couldn't wait. She had to see her daughter again – she had to feel her soft little body in her arms and smell the Johnson's baby shampoo from her hair and feel her soft breath on her face. And she had to see Cora again and tell her that she was her mum and always would be.

"Remember you're not to lift her," Connor warned.

"Mum?" Ava asked, jolted from her thoughts

"Maisie, you banana," Connor said softly. "You're not to lift Maisie. But don't lift your mum either."

She smiled, half-heartedly, her heart thudding.

"We'll be okay, won't we?" she asked, looking to him for reassurance.

"You, Cora, Maisie, Me, Shrimp Baby . . . yes, we will all be okay."

She reached up and kissed him, then knocked on the door, knowing that really there was no need as Cora would have been standing in the hall, patiently, or impatiently, waiting for the knock.

Her worry lifted a little as she heard the clatter of her daughter running down the hall screaming, "Mammy! Daddy! Mammy! Daddy!"

Ava felt her heart contract with love. And as her mother opened the door and she saw her, her heart contracted further.

"It's okay," she whispered and Cora fell into her arms crying.

"I'm sorry."

"Enough of sorry," Ava said. "Everyone has said sorry too many times now. We'll just move on."

And now, hearing her daughter run towards her, she offered a silent prayer of thanks to Betty and to her mum, who was always going to be her mum, and looked down at her fabulous deep-purple shoes.

"Love you, Betty," she whispered as she watched her husband scoop Maisie into his arms before ordering Ava herself to the softest chair in the house where he placed her rosy-cheeked girl on her knee and she smothered her in kisses.

"I love you, baby," she said. "I love you so much."

"My love you too," Maisie chirped, covering Ava's face in sticky kisses. "My love you all the way to the moon!"

Chapter 38

One year later

The wisteria had grown a little taller and the lavender seemed to smell a little stronger. Maisie jumped onto the gravel of the driveway and shouted, "We're here, we're here! Look, Mammy! It's our happy holiday home! Look, Mammy, we're here!"

Ava smiled as she climbed out of the car and lifted her daughter.

"We sure are! Isn't it lovely? Look at all the flowers."

"Down, Mammy, down," Maisie wriggled. "I see a butterfly. Look, Mammy. Look at its wings!" She pelted off towards the garden, skipping as she went, the exhaustion from the journey having passed with the excitement of reaching their final destination.

"I'll get her," Connor said, smiling and chasing after their daughter. "You get Toots there out of the car and bring her inside and I'll follow!"

"Yes, boss," Ava smiled, opened the back door of their hire car and reached in to unclip the car seat where baby Beth was sleeping soundly, her rosebud lips closed in a perfect pout and her long eyelashes fluttering softly onto her cheeks. She had been great through the journey – Ava hadn't been sure, having never travelled with an infant before but at four months old Beth was already proving to be a great traveller. She had smiled at the lady at the check-in desk in Belfast, slept throughout the flight apart from waking for a quick feed and had snoozed as they drove through the countryside to Betty's house. Ava stroked her cheek – she looked deliciously cute in her romper suit and sunhat. It was hard to believe all the drama they had been through just one year before, right in this very house.

To think they hadn't even been sure Beth would make it, but here she was, a perfect little bundle of contentment. At least she was content most of the time – and that was good enough for Ava and Connor.

"We found out about you here," Ava whispered to her sleeping baby as she carried the car seat to the big oak door which was slightly ajar. "This feels like your first home," she said, pushing the door open and calling her hellos.

"We're through on the terrace," she heard Hope's voice carry back as she set the car seat down on the new leather sofa, which didn't look a patch on the tweed chair, and unstrapped baby Beth who stayed blissfully asleep and curled up on her mammy's shoulder. Ava could hear the sound of Connor and Maisie chasing each other and giggling in the garden and she thought how nice it was that this house was finally ringing with the sound of a child's laughter. Betty would have been proud, she smiled, carrying her baby through the French doors to be greeted by a smiling Hope and a grinning Jean-Luc.

"*Bonjour et bienvenue*," Hope trilled, running to hug her cousin. "Oh my God. Is this Beth? Well, of course it's Beth! Who else would it be?"

Ava proudly handed her daughter over and Hope gazed at the sleeping baby who decided to have a little fuss before nestling into the crook of her arm.

"She's just even more delightful in real life! Look at those squishy cheeks! Oh my, you make beautiful babies, Ava Campbell! And where's the other one?"

"Still chasing butterflies," Ava said with a sigh. "She'll be in soon." She reached over to kiss her cousin again while Jean-Luc bided his time in the background. "You look well," she said, "Travelling obviously agrees with you."

"And motherhood obviously agrees with you. I've brought a couple of those dresses in case you feel you can try them on this time."

Ava laughed. There was no way she was telling Hope that her looking so well was down to a pair of extra-strength support knickers and good fake tan applied two nights before. "I'm happy with my purple shoes," she said.

"Sit down, ladies," Jean-Luc said. "It is so nice to see you both together again."

Ava noticed he was looking more at Hope than at her as he spoke. Kissing him on the cheek, she smiled. "Sure it's only been a matter of weeks since you saw this one. You can't have missed her too much!"

Jean-Luc smiled and kissed Hope on the top of the head. "I always miss her when I'm not with her and we're not off on one of our adventures."

"Where's next then?" Ava asked, as Jean-Luc poured a glass of champagne.

"America next. New York. Not quite so off the beaten track as Tanzania or Vietnam but we fancy a little luxury," Hope replied.

"Sounds blissful," Ava said.

"If your cousin is true to form we will spend the entire time walking the streets and uncovering hidden treasures."

"It wouldn't be suitable for my readers if we didn't dig a little deeper," Hope said. "Which reminds me. Ava, there's going to be a book! Okay, so it will be a small print run and it's not likely to set the bestsellers list alight – but there is going to be a book!"

Hope looked so excited that Ava felt excited for her too. "Based on your columns?"

"And a little more! It started last year, actually. I took Betty's lead and started to write a few letters to myself. I thought maybe that would be it – that there would just be one or two but I found I quite liked it. I pitched them, along with the travel ideas, to a publisher and well, there you go. A book on the way!"

"That's amazing," Ava said, genuinely proud. "You must be delighted."

"Over the moon. I'm going to dedicate the book to Betty's memory. Wasn't quite ready to go the whole hog and, you know, name a baby after her," she said, nodding towards the sleeping Beth, "but I figured a book dedication would impress her."

"She would have made everyone she knew buy a copy," Jean-Luc said. "There would never be any book like it in her eyes."

"Well, I look forward to reading it," Ava said, genuinely impressed at how relaxed and happy her cousin looked.

"Can we swim in the pool?" Maisie shrieked, running full pelt through the house and throwing herself into her mother's arms.

"Of course, sweetheart. Will we get our swimsuits?"

"Sounds like a plan," Hope said, handing Beth to her daddy and putting her arms out to Maisie. "Hi, Maisie Moo! Do you know me? We've spoken on the phone loads!"

Maisie eyed Hope with a little trepidation before turning to whisper in her mammy's ear. "Is that Auntie Hope?"

Ava nodded.

"She's pretty," Maisie said, wandering over to allow Hope to hug her. "Do you want to come swimming too, Auntie Hope? I won't splash you," she said solemnly.

"Well, I sure would love to go swimming. Let's get our suits, and some towels."

"That sounds like a good idea, indeed," Jean-Luc said, grinning.

"Pool party!" Connor said, placing a still sleeping Beth in the buggy he'd just pushed through the house.

"Well, we are on our holidays," Ava said, smiling. "And this house likes parties."

"It sure does," said Hope, linking arms with Ava and walking back into the shade of the house to get ready for their first party of the week. Smiling she offered a silent thank-you to Betty and promised that before the night was out, and despite whatever protestations from the menfolk around her, she would launch into a chorus of *Danny Boy*. For old times' sake.

If you enjoyed
If Only You Knew by Claire Allan
why not try
It's Got to be Perfect also published by Poolbeg?
Here's a sneak preview of Chapter One

It's got to be
Perfect

Claire
Allan

POOLBEG

1

I wouldn't say I was jealous of Fionn. Just because she was getting her happy ending while I was plodding along waiting for my life to start. She deserved her happy ending – I believed that entirely. But still, as I watched her walk out of the changing room in her stunning shot-silk gown, her eyes misty with emotion, I couldn't help feeling a little green around the gills with envy (and the remnants of last night's vodka).

"She's gorgeous, isn't she?" the over-enthusiastic shop assistant almost squealed, and I nodded.

"Do you really like it?" Fionn asked, her face begging me to say yes.

"I do," I said, and I wasn't lying. It was a stunning dress which accentuated my friend's natural beauty but when I choked back a tear it was because I couldn't ever see myself in her position – no matter how carefully I had planned every aspect of my life. You see, I had this wonderfully crappy habit of messing things up. If there was a degree in being a fuck-up, I would have passed with first-class honours.

"I'm so glad you like it," Fionn said, waving her hands in front of her face to try and stem her tears, "because I really think this is the one. This is my wedding dress, Annie. *My wedding dress*." She emphasised the words while twirling around like some sort of demented overgrown fairy princess and the shop assistant actually did squeal with delight at this stage.

I just sobbed into my hanky. In a most undignified manner.

"Like a princess," I said, sipping my wine. The buzz of the bar had lifted my spirits and Fionn and I were three-quarters way down a very fine bottle of Sauvignon Blanc.

"I was, wasn't I? Like a Disney Princess."

"Hmmm," I answered. "Cinderella."

"Or Ariel. I like her wedding dress best of all. The way it sparkles in the sun when she kisses Eric in the last scene." Fionn sighed dreamily, before sipping from her glass again.

I raised my eyebrow – or at least I think I raised my eyebrow. The wine was combining with the previous night's vodka and it was possible that any facial gesture I tried to make at that moment looked more like I had developed some weird facial tick.

"Okay, okay," Fionn blushed. "I know I sound like an eejit, but Emma is going through a particularly fierce and ferocious Disney Princess phase at the moment and it's about all I can think about. Every moment of every fecking day some cheerful tune is dancing through my head."

I smiled. Fionn was not taking to motherhood all that well. That's not to say she was doing too badly at it, but since she had moved in with Alex in the run-up to the Big Day she was finding it challenging to come to terms with the demands – and viewing habits – of his five-year-old daughter, Emma.

"But I can't just tell her I don't want to watch them, can I? Because if I do, I'll be the Wicked Stepmother and, believe me," she said with emphasis, "I've seen enough of those movies to know that doesn't bode well."

"Emma loves you," I soothed. "And it's just a novelty having a woman about the house to indulge her princess fantasies with."

Fionn nodded. "I know, but promise me this. The next time I come into work with fairy-dust on my cheeks, can you point it out to me before the ops meeting? I don't think it does well to have me looking like an overgrown schoolgirl."

"I don't know about that," I laughed. "I think Bob liked it. You brought a little colour to the office that day."

Ah, Bob. (Or "Bawb" as Fionn and I usually called him, in a faux-American accent.) He was our boss and obsessed with client portfolios and, it seemed, little else. I didn't think he actually had a life outside of the office, which was why he liked to exert as much control over his minions (as he had been known to call us) as possible.

Fionn shuddered. "I don't want to talk, or even think, about Bawb just now. It takes away from the whole wedding-dress, fairy-tale experience. And I don't want anything to take away from that."

Which was precisely the reason I didn't explain to her how the last twenty-four or so hours of my life had been the most spectacularly painful of my existence. If she didn't want Bob to ruin her dream wedding-dress day then she sure as feck didn't want to hear about Chewbacca.

Have you ever made a mistake? You know, a big, huge mistake which makes your heart sink to the pit of your stomach and the contents of your stomach try and escape through your mouth every time you think about it?

It was one of those things which seemed like a good idea at the time. I was wanted. I was fancied. I was irresistible. But that was then.

Lying there, in the stale air of my bedroom, with the exceptionally hairy arm of my mistake draped over my stomach – clammy with sweat – I felt my mind whir and my head thump. Too much vodka on an empty stomach – it was never going to end well.

I glanced at the clock on the chest of drawers and my heart thumped harder. It was 10.29 a.m. On a workday. So not only was I trapped under the weight of a man who was a walking *before* advertisement for a good back, sack and crack wax, I was also approximately eighty-nine minutes late for work.

I glanced at Chewbacca lying beside me. He was out for the count. I moved my head closer to his, wondering if he was actually dead, but the stench of booze-breath wafting out with every exhalation was enough to reassure me that he was very much alive – if comatose.

I lifted his arm, weighed down by the sheer volume of hair on it, and inched my way out of the bed – doing my best to leave him sleeping. I wanted him awake, and out of my apartment – but preferably not while I was still naked. The last thing I wanted was him to wake and get a notion that there was a chance in hell of a repeat of the previous night's performance. Even though my hazy memory told me it had been quite pleasurable.

It was 10.33. I wanted (needed) a shower, but that would only make me even later for work and even further into the bad books of Bob who by now was probably halfway to a stroke. I lifted my phone to call him, but then it dawned on me: I could just get ready and get to work as soon as possible. When he asked where I had been I could say I'd been out meeting a client. It wasn't unheard of, and it might just work. If only I could get Chewbacca out of my flat any time soon.

After a speed-wash with a sponge, I slipped into my suit and dabbed on some foundation – although I doubted even the finest Clarins had to offer was going to make me look anywhere near human. Pulling a comb through my hair and tying it up into a topknot, I slipped my feet into a pair of court shoes and glanced back at the clock: 10.43. And he was still sleeping.

I tried slamming a door. I even set off the alarm clock and had a very loud conversation with myself. Not so much as a flinch. I pulled the duvet off the bed – hoping the cool would shock him awake – but then I wasn't reckoning on his carpet of self-insulation.

It was therefore supremely ironic when it was my phone ringing with a call from my boyfriend that actually woke him.

"Hello," Pearse said, his voice showing his confusion. "Where are you? I tried phoning you at work. They said you weren't in yet. I tried calling last night too – you didn't answer."

Pearse Campbell liked to know where I was and who I was with at every hour of the day and night. Having gone off radar for the last twelve hours would not have gone down well with him. Not at all.

"I'm with a client," I lied, my face blazing. I was sure he would know I was fibbing. He could read me like a book – even over the phone.

And it was at precisely that moment Chewbacca chose to shout, loudly, "Babe, do you know where my boxers are?"

It was 11.23. The underwear had been located and returned to its rightful owner shortly after Pearse had given orders that we would talk later, muttered something about how could *I* do this to *him* and hung up. I had got rid of my mystery man-beast and was now fighting against the traffic to make it into the office at all before lunchtime. Bob would not be happy, client or not. This day was not going well and that sinking feeling in my stomach was back – which did not sit easily with the hung-over feeling which seemed to have taken over my entire body.

I drove on demented, pushing all thoughts of Pearse and the battle that would ensue later to the back of my head. I just didn't have time to think about it now. Okay, this day was a balls-up – but if I didn't get my ass into work pretty damn soon, it would be the most spectacular balls-up day of all time.

I was somewhere between weeping with relief and crying with fear when I pulled into the communal car park and secured the last parking space left. Jumping out of the car, snagging my tights as I went, I dived through the rain to the office, stopping only momentarily to plaster a look of nonchalance on my face before entering.

"Oh Annie, how nice of you to join us!" Bob crowed from across the open-plan room. My colleagues, well aware of the seriousness of my offence, didn't even look up. Apart from Fionn, that is, whose Bambi eyes gazed at me, begging me silently to keep my cool and not ruin her dream day which would, of course, end in the Great Wedding-dress Trying-on Extravaganza.

"Nice of you to notice," I bluffed back, with more confidence than I felt. Perhaps if I pretended that everything was just tickety-boo, Bob would be lulled into a weird sense of security and forget just why he had cause to be angry.

I walked to my desk and sat down, lifting the phone from the cradle and rattling in an imaginary number while my computer booted up. Bob just stood, for a few seconds, open-mouthed, before storming into his office.

An audible sigh of relief rose from everyone outside.

"Where were you?" An email from Fionn pinged into my inbox.

"Long story. Nothing exciting," I lied. I had already made the conscious decision not to tell her about Chewbacca or Pearse – not when we were going on a wedding-dress hunt. What a downer that would be.

"Where were you?" An email from Bob pinged into my inbox.

"With a client," I lied. I had already made a conscious decision that I would not crack under pressure, ever.

"Which client?" he asked.

Fuck. I couldn't cope with this kind of pressure. One false move and it was P45-land for me.

"A new one. I'll tell you when it's a little firmer. Don't want to risk it. It's a big one." I pressed *Send* and crossed my fingers, hoping that would buy me time.

"It better be," he replied and that was that.

Now that my job remained secure, I just had to clean up the other pieces of my life.

It was, I admit, hard to get into the spirit of work – despite the whiteboard behind my desk detailing all our up-and-coming campaigns – several of which I was in charge of. Being an account executive for NorthStar PR was rarely plain sailing, but there were times when I found it nigh on impossible to get excited about the latest branding of the local supermarket or some fancy perfume.

I tried to ignore the fact that one of our major campaigns for the month was to be Manna – Pearse's restaurant – and that my involvement in "keeping the client happy" might have just gone disastrously wrong.

Instead I turned my attention to our campaign for the new "adult" shop, Love, Sex and Magic, which was set to open in town amid a furore from right-wingers everywhere.

It wasn't a sleazy shop, per se – I mean it was all really in good form – no seriously hardcore stuff – but we still knew we would have a killer of a time putting a positive slant on it when the local do-gooders were already planning a protest on opening day – complete with placards and everything.

Bob wanted this to work. He really, really wanted it work. He was even trying to convince myself and Fionn to dress in French Maid costumes while handing out leaflets outside – but I figured that was more to satisfy his own seedy desires than anything else. We had, however, been talked into dressing as magician's assistants and it was my job to source suitable costumes. Did I just say life in PR could be dull?

"FSB?" Fionn emailed.

Ah, Fake Smoke Break. Even though neither of us smoked we still allowed ourselves the periodic traipse out to the smokers' corner of shame for a gossip, away from the glare of our computer screens (and Bob's eagle eye).

"I think he would kill me if I dared move from my desk," I jotted back and she smiled sympathetically.

Truth was, I wanted to avoid her best as I could, in a bid to keep my disastrous morning under wraps. And I genuinely did think Bob might kill me.

Reaching for two paracetamol from my desk drawer, I swallowed them down with some water and started phoning.

I was starting to feel almost jolly, until, that is, the phone rang and Pearse barked a hello at me. From the noise in the background I could tell he was calling me from the restaurant kitchens and this show was one all of his staff were enjoying

"Hi, Pearse," I whispered, careful not to prick Fionn's curiosity. The girl had bat ears – anything in a twenty-foot radius was fair game.

"So, are you going to tell me what happened?"

Oh God. He couldn't really want to have a meaning-of-life-the-universe-and-everything chat just now, could he?

"I'm at work," I replied.

"And what? Your job is more important than me and our relationship? Is that what you're saying?"

In any other circumstance I probably would have gone to him. I would have made my excuses to Bob – on the pretext of the forthcoming campaign for Manna – and cleared off to talk things through. I would have apologised and told him I didn't know what had come over me (except I did, and it was a hairy big fecker from Donegal) and begged his forgiveness.

But sitting there in the office it dawned on me that I wasn't quite sure if I wanted him to forgive me. Surely I wouldn't have done what I'd done – or who I'd done – if things had been perfect? Pulling at a loose thread in my laddered tights and watching the material unravel, I sighed.

"I can't, Pearse – things are mad here. But I am sorry."

"Well, what about after work?"

"I have to go a wedding-dress fitting with Fionn," I said. "I can't get out of it."

"I'm sure you could, if you wanted to."

His assumption that I would be able to stop doing whatever I was doing in order to be at his beck and call was really astounding. It shocked me that I'd once found it alluring and sexy. Once. Perhaps that was the keyword in all of this.

I could imagine him standing proud in his chef whites, his minions running round him, listening to him ordering the little woman around.

"I'm sorry, Pearse. If I could get away, I would," I lied.

He put the phone down, his anger obvious by the slam of it against the receiver. Oh, this was not going to be good.

•◆•

If you enjoyed this chapter from
It's got to be Perfect by Claire Allan,
why not order the full book online
@ www.poolbeg.com

•◆•

POOLBEG WISHES TO
THANK YOU

for buying a Poolbeg book.

If you enjoyed this why not
visit our website:

www.poolbeg.com

and get another book delivered straight
to your home or to a friend's home!

All books despatched within 24 hours.

POOLBEG

WHY NOT JOIN OUR MAILING LIST
@ www.poolbeg.com and get some
fantastic offers on Poolbeg books